BATTLETECH
VOIDBREAKER

BY BRYAN YOUNG

BATTLETECH: VOIDBREAKER
By Bryan Young
Cover art by Tan Ho Sim
Interior art by Alan Blackwell, Jordan Cuffie, Chris Daranouvong, Stephen Huda, Harri Kallio, Duane Loose, Matt Plog, Anthony Scroggins, Franz Vohwinkel
Cover design and layout by David Kerber

Printed in USA.

Published by Catalyst Game Labs,
an imprint of InMediaRes Productions, LLC
5003 Main St. #110 • Tacoma, Washington 98407

This story is dedicated to all those who work to ensure the free exchange of ideas, who fight those who would ban books and make our schools and libraries poorer places.

And to the authors brave enough to tell stories that matter.

THE INNER SPHERE: 3151

A thousand years ago, humanity spread its wings across the Inner Sphere, colonizing planet after planet across the heavens.

Because massive expansions of territory come with massive expansions of power, war was commonplace in this new Inner Sphere. The Great Houses fought with each other across their borders, bickering for influence across the planets of the Inner Sphere. Their primary weapon became BattleMechs, monstrous mechanical marvels with more firepower than most small armies; heavily armored and deadly beyond belief.

Despite the constant war and threat of collapse, communication between stars was easy after Star League scientists led by Professor Cassie DeBurke mastered interstellar communications. Thanks to the hyperpulse generator (HPG) network, messages and information could travel through the stars faster than ships and light. Overseen by ComStar after the fall of the Star League, the techno-religious cultists used their monopoly over communications to ensure the HPG network was sacrosanct among the warring factions across the universe.

But twenty years ago, on Gray Monday—7 August 3132— the communications network went dark. A few HPG stations were attacked, but most were believed to have been infected by some sort of malicious code, traveling from one station to the next, robbing each planet of its ability to communicate with its neighbors. Who would do such a thing?

No one but those responsible knew the answers to such questions.

Many tried to fix the HPG stations, but the method by which they were attacked made their repair mostly impossible, leaving humanity in the chaos of their new Dark Age.

The BattleMech-filled armies of the Great Houses, dozens of minor factions and opportunistic armed groups, and the warmongering Clans, who fought bitterly during this period, each vied for power amidst the chaos of the communications blackout. Bands of professional mercenaries found ample demand for their services.

The Great Houses, each in control of major portions of the Inner Sphere, existed for centuries, and mercenaries are as old as the history of Terra itself. The Clans, however, have only openly been in the Inner Sphere since 3049. They were mistaken for aliens upon their initial arrival and intended conquest of Terra. They were the descendants of the Star League Defense Force, the largest military power in the history of humanity. Under the leadership of SLDF Commanding General Aleksandr Kerensky, this army left the Inner Sphere in 2784, seemingly never to be seen again. After an intense and costly internal civil war broke out among the exiles, Kerensky's son Nicholas formed his loyalists into the twenty Clans, giving rise to a brutal caste system and warrior mentality that characterized Clan society. When they returned, they had developed superior firepower and technology with an aim of liberating Terra and becoming the ultimate defenders of humanity by forging a new Star League.

Thanks to ComStar's military victory at Tukayyid, the Clan Invasion was halted before Terra could be reached and a temporary cease-fire was reluctantly agreed to.

The Clans have remained in the Inner Sphere since, battling each other and the Great Houses until they could make their final bid for Terra. There was no rest for the Inner Sphere during this time. When ComStar's fanatical splinter group, the Word of Blake, launched an all-out war across the Inner Sphere, they were defeated only by an alliance of Great Houses, mercenaries, and Clans. In the aftermath of the so-called "Jihad," the charismatic Devlin Stone established the

Republic of the Sphere with Terra as its center and established a decades-long Pax Republica. When his successors found their efforts to preserve the Republic failing during the Dark Age, they sealed it and a small number of neighboring systems behind the "Fortress Wall", a barrier impenetrable to hyperspace travel.

In 3151, Alaric Ward, Khan of Clan Wolf, discovered a way through the Fortress Wall and made his play for Terra, inviting Malvina Hazen, the Khan of Clan Jade Falcon known for her ruthless brutality, to join him. Together, they competed to conquer the birthplace of humanity. Shattering the Republic Armed Forces together, Clans Wolf and Jade Falcon then battled each other to the bitter end for the right to become ilClan. As the ilClan, they would be the Clan above all Clans and rule the Inner Sphere by creating a brand new Star League.

After Clan Wolf's victory on Terra, Clan Sea Fox's dream of becoming the ilClan was abandoned, with other goals taking priority. Where the other Clans focused on the martial aspects of being the best warriors, Clan Sea Fox had the most cunning minds, gaining a reputation for long-term planning, strategic vision, and innovation. They became the top merchants of the Clans, dealing in 'Mechs and other war materiel. Instead of capturing wide swaths of territory, Clan Sea Fox mostly stayed in the stars as nomads, traveling from planet to planet for trade.

Despite their reputation as shrewd business negotiators, they were also capable warriors—deadly in any form of combat, but especially BattleMechs.

As Clan Sea Fox looks for a way to stand out and make a name for itself among the other Clans, it is faced with two major priorities: the first is to become indispensable to the supply and logistics chains of the other Clans, especially the Clan that eventually becomes the ilClan. The second is to find a way to get the HPG network up and running. Regardless of the political power on paper, or with planets controlled, or knees bent in your direction, they know that whoever controls the flow of communication in the Inner Sphere stands to become the *real* power in an all new era...

PART 1

"Free and neutral communication is the
cornerstone of a peaceful galaxy.
Only by safeguarding that will humanity ever
hope to shine as bright as we once did
before our lives were shattered by the war.
The free exchange of ideas—no matter how
threatening we personally might find them—is
the cornerstone of humanity's ascent to the stars."

—JEROME BLAKE
IN A LETTER TO ARCHON JENNIFER STEINER
DATED 20 MARCH 2787 PUBLISHED IN
The Silver Shield Papers

"Watson, come quick. I need you."

—PROFESSOR CASSIE DEBURKE, UNIVERSITY OF TERRA
FIRST HPG TRANSMISSION
1 JANUARY 2630
FROM ALEXANDER GRAHAM BELL'S
FIRST TELEPHONE MESSAGE
10 MARCH 1876

CHAPTER 1: THE WATCH AGENT

KENTWOOD
IRIAN
FREE WORLDS LEAGUE
21 APRIL 3151

The exhilaration of freefall with nothing more than a parachute on her back made Star Colonel Kenja Rodriguez feel alive. Her heart pounded, and adrenaline raced through her veins. Too often, her job was nothing but tense lies and playacting, but here she was just honest freedom. That falling sensation wasn't unlike the feeling of weightlessness every member of Clan Sea Fox was all too accustomed to, but a high-altitude jump out of a VTOL came with a different set of risks. She had to be precise in getting over her target zone before she jumped, but since it was night, she had to rely on the technology in her goggles that let her know how close she came to death before releasing her tactical parachute.

Nothing like the threat of death to make a person feel even more alive.

Kenja tightened her body into an arrow, as though she herself was a projectile being thrown at the enemy, and counted down the seconds until she was close enough to rip the cord that would ensure her safety.

Freefall military drops were risky—everything in her line of work was—but when the plan had been laid out, it was the best way to get inside without being detected. The complex of ITCC—the Irian Tactical Communications Corporation, a wholly owned subsidiary of IrTech—was its own fortress, and approaching it by land meant inviting disaster. The ITCC BattleMech sentries were *Guillotines*, manufactured by their parent corporation, and they meant business. No, the drop was the only way to bypass security and insert herself into the mission zone with everything she needed to complete the operation without being detected.

At least, that was the plan.

She was to infiltrate, sync up with other assets, download vital information, and destroy ITCC's ability to retain the information. Maybe by the end of it, they would have more clues about how to fix the HPG network.

It sounded simple when she broke it down that way.

Even if Kenja hadn't been a Sea Fox Star Colonel tasked with facilitating the restoration of the HPG network by her superiors in the Tiburon Khanate, she imagined she would still be working toward that goal. There were few things that could bring peace to the Inner Sphere faster than open communication—as well as profit to her Clan.

With the target area—the roof of the main complex building—coming up fast, Kenja somersaulted forward, pointing her feet at the surface, and deployed her small parachute. As the wind caught her on its violent cushion, the straps pulled up on her harness and the weight of Irian's gravity kicked her in the stomach like a mule, but she didn't have time to think about it. By then, her feet were about to reach the rooftop.

She rolled on the roof's slick surface and unlatched her parachute all in one fluid motion. Myomer tethers automatically refurled the chute, packing it into a neat bundle on the rooftop to prevent the drifting fabric from attracting attention.

By the time Kenja popped back up into a crouching position, she had a silent needler raised and aimed. She checked the roof for targets, back and forth, making sure she was truly alone here. With the area clear, she holstered her pistol and shed the rest of her parachuting gear. Stashing it all quickly in a dark corner, she was left dressed in tight fitting tactical gear and heavy boots, the deeper layers of her disguise tight beneath that.

Glancing at her chronometer, she realized she was late. Not by much, but enough to make a difference in a precision operation like this. The pilot must have miscalculated the route, and now she'd have to make up the time.

She raced to the ventilation unit she identified from satellite photos and stolen blueprints, cut it open, and in less than five minutes found herself on the top floor of the twenty-story building.

Lavishly appointed, it was the sort of office building people with more power and wealth than taste built. Thick carpets, gaudy art on the walls, and massive windows in every office looking out over the sprawling megalopolis.

Checking each hallway, leading with the needler and hoping she wouldn't have to use it, she found the right office. Lights low. It was after hours, and no one should have been in there. From her pocket she withdrew the device to cut through the digital lock code and affixed it to the panel next to the door. She glanced at her chronometer once more as the digital lockpick did its work.

If everything was going smoothly—and she had little way of knowing if it was—she would be protected by the closed circuit surveillance with dummy footage of empty hallways. The security detail wasn't clocked to head into that particular hallway for another three minutes.

She should have had six.

The footsteps and indistinct chatter she heard coming from around the corner were a complication she didn't want to deal with.

The device on the door had one digit left to decode.

Kenja glanced at the corner, evaluating what she might have to do if someone rounded it right then.

But then the device did its work.

The door slid open, and she stepped inside the dark, extravagant office. She turned as the door slid shut. Putting an ear to it, she listened for whoever might have been dogging her steps in the hallway. Hearing them pass, a modicum of relief washed over her.

She didn't like killing unnecessarily.

Unfortunately, the rustle of hands on a laser pistol and the telltale sound of it powering up, ready to shoot right behind her, deflated her relief.

"Put your hands up." The voice was gruff. Possibly male. In a thick Irian accent—a mishmash of English and Hindi spoken by the early settlers of the planet, transformed by almost a thousand years of its own evolution into something entirely new.

Kenja did as she was told, raising her hands, but not dropping her own silenced weapon.

"Turn around," they said.

Kenja obliged, her mind racing through possibilities of how to get out of such a predicament.

The person with a gun raised was a black outline in the dark. But she saw enough of the details to know this was part of the plan.

"I'm alone," she said finally.

The figure hesitated for a moment, and then holstered their gun and stepped into the light over the door. "As ever," he said with a grim smile. The Irian accent disappeared entirely, replaced with his native Clan-standard accent.

"Seth," she said with a nod. "We have to get to work."

"I'm not the one who's late."

Star Colonel Seth, a man with no Bloodname, was dressed similarly to her, and had taken a different route into the building. For operational security, they weren't aware of how the other planned to get inside. They had agreed on a rendezvous time, and each worked out their own insertion.

Kenja withdrew another device from a pouch on her belt and went to the desk. "I'll take care of this part. Then we'll head down."

"Aff," he told her, but he said it in that same Irian accent and it sounded more like "oaf." Then he reverted. "It'll be nice to get off Irian. I've been here too long." Still undercover in the Inner Sphere, his speech was littered with contractions.

"It hasn't been that long."

"Long enough to want to be elsewhere."

Working quickly, Kenja attached the device to the massive noteputer base hub sitting beneath the desk. Installing its cables firmly into the back ports, she pressed the button on the top to activate it. A flashing green light told her she'd done it properly.

"We're covered here," she said, ensuring the device couldn't be obviously seen.

"Ready to head to the party?"

"As I'll ever be."

Seth checked the door and out the windows one more time to be sure they were in the clear, then tore away the top of his tactical jacket to reveal a high collared shirt in the local dress fashion and a matching bowtie. Offsetting the white shirt and giving it hard angles were black chevron stripes running up the front. Between two of the stripes was pinned a bright red flower—a local plant, so Kenja couldn't place the name of it.

He hid the rest of his materiel for the job in the discrete pockets of his black pants and in a small bag at the small of his back, hidden beneath the cape he unfurled. His barrel of a chest filled the costume perfectly and he looked as manicured as the executives and hangers-on partying downstairs, blissfully unaware of what was happening under their noses.

Kenja's transformation was slightly more difficult, but she didn't have to carry the explosives, so for that she was grateful.

She shed the tactical gear to reveal a silk dress beneath. It was interwoven with strands of "Clan copper", memory metal that instantly smoothed any creases, patterned in shades of black and red that would mean something to locals on Irian and shout to any onlookers that she was important and wealthy. Like Seth, it boasted a high collar, but was a classical gown with a slit up the sides of her legs, offering a glimpse of her smooth, copper skin and toned legs with every step. Again, it was in the local style, and meant she would blend in at the party, which was all she needed to do.

From the bag at her back, she withdrew a pair of heels and then she turned the bag inside out, transforming it into a fashionable clutch just large enough to hold her needle pistol. It swung smartly off her shoulder. Then, she pulled the band from her small black ponytail, shot with strands of gray, and her bobbed hair fell into place. She smoothed the flyaways with her hand and applied a quick layer of lipstick from the tube supplied in her bag.

"It astonishes me how nicely you clean up," Seth said.

She looked him up and down with a smile. His muscular warrior's body and perfectly coiffed silver hair with streaks of brown leftover from his younger years—with just a touch of product parted to the side—would make anyone believe he was capable of anything. "Likewise."

He checked his own wrist chronometer, then looked back at her. "Our time dwindles, my dear." He held an arm out for her to take.

"You're not that much older than me," she said, taking him by the arm.

"Just playing the part."

Kenja took in a deep breath, steeling herself. "There is no time like the present," she said, bracing herself for the covert work she felt good at, but never good about. They always asked her to do things she couldn't imagine would actually help anyone in the Inner Sphere, let alone Clan Sea Fox. But she followed orders to the best of her ability.

"It'll all be fine," Seth assured her. "If I've told you once, I've told you a thousand times the only thing you need in these situations is confidence and a look that says you know where you're going. You've been doing this almost as long as I have."

"Aff," she said. "But I'm fine. You don't have to play mentor forever."

He smiled. "It's a very old habit by now."

Wiith that, they stepped out into the clear hallway, found the elevator, and stepped inside it.

CHAPTER 2: LATE TO THE PARTY

ITCC HQ BUILDING
KENTWOOD
IRIAN
FREE WORLDS LEAGUE
21 APRIL 3151

The elevator doors slid open, and Kenja's view shifted to that of a grand lobby space converted for the executive party. There were ornate glass staircases in the minimalist ferrocrete building and red carpets full of mingling partygoers, twittering like birds. An elaborate crystal chandelier the size of a light 'Mech hung over the center of the gathering like some pompous relic of a bygone era, scattering shards of light across the gathering. Servers buzzed about like bees with trays, offering drinks and hors d'oeuvres to anyone who glanced in their direction. Music filled the space; the persistent, throbbing backbeat of an old Bengali cybergrind standard.

Kenja took a confident step into the bustling party in full swing and immediately felt eyes on her—eyes were always on her when she dressed like she was—but she paid the leering masses no mind. Seth had told her the last time they had found themselves in such a position, he relished having her on his arm as part of the ruse.

She liked it, too.

It made people underestimate her. They looked at her and thought she was nothing more than "arm candy," which was exactly why she and Seth had utilized this ruse on the occasions they worked together.

It felt good to have an ally at her side. More often than not, she had to work alone.

Such was the life of a warrior serving in the Sea Fox Watch. They did what needed to be done. For the good of the Clan.

And not just for the Clan—for the good of the entire Inner Sphere.

Scanning the crowd, Kenja caught sight of the target for her next phase of the operation. Ashwin Hughes, the CEO of ITCC. According to the dossier and briefing about him, he was of extreme moral flexibility, and was also dangerously in debt, which was why he had not paid back the loans and bonds backed by Clan Sea Fox's Spina Khanate. He was half the reason they were there. But instead of killing him or anything else so base, they were going to hurt his bottom line and remind him and anyone like him what happened when the Sea Foxes came to collect their debts.

The other half—and the reason Tiburon Khanate agents were leading this mission—was the information her device was collecting and transmitting upstairs. They were looking for clues to fix the HPG network. And Irian Tactical Communications Corporation was still in control of a working HPG station, a rarity in the Dark Age. How had they avoided the disaster that befell the others on Gray Monday?

It didn't much matter that they had a working HPG station, though. That was like having a working JumpShip, but no DropShip to get to it. There weren't many operational HPGs left, and only the station on Devil's Rock was close enough to send a signal to the Irian station anyway. Though it was possible for HPGs to send radio bursts in the open, a number of HPG stations that had survived Gray Monday had subsequently burned out their transmitters after doing so. It was now generally accepted that the safest way for surviving HPGs to operate was to send directly to another HPG's shielded receiver chamber.

But it was enough of an oddity that they had to investigate.

It was a top priority for Tiburon Khanate, and Kenja's Alpha Aimag in particular. But with the data being collected upstairs, it was time to execute the next part of their mission.

Ashwin Hughes was dressed much like Seth was, in a high collared shirt and a cape of orange and black that matched the colors of the Irian Technologies logo. He wore the cape like he wore his arrogance—boldly—but everyone around him pretended not to notice either of them. They just made nice because he was a powerful player in the corporate sphere of Irian, which made him a powerful player in the corporate sphere of the Free Worlds League. And that made him a major player in the Inner Sphere.

As they approached, Kenja wondered how many of the sycophants at the party knew what dire straits he'd thrown his portion of the company into.

A passing server stopped in front of the couple, offering thin flutes of Irian sparkling wine brought down from orbital hydroponic facilities. They each took one and stopped for a moment to sip. It wouldn't do to appear like they were locked onto Hughes like an LRM.

"Just a minute and we'll go see him," Seth said, covering his mouth with the glass before sipping. His voice echoed in her ears, transmitting both to her earpiece and close enough to hear him anyway.

"That's Ginevra Zorin he's talking to, isn't it? From MaxiTech?" Kenja lifted her own glass to her lips and took a sip of the sparkling wine. It was tart and bubbly, with a floral hint of citrus, but it paled in comparison to real champagne, something she'd only been able to taste once. Terran spirits were not terribly widespread across the Inner Sphere.

Seth nodded. "And her lovely wife."

Zorin was dressed in a satin red ball gown trimmed with large black chevrons, matching the corporate power shirts the men tended to wear. Her wife was dressed in black pants and a white, high-collared shirt decorated with red chevrons to match the more masculine fashion. They were quite the stunning couple. "I wonder what they're doing here."

Seth shrugged, waving off the irregularity of it. "At this point, it's immaterial. This is a business party. They're probably talking business."

"I didn't mean at the party, I meant on Irian. That seems like something that should have been in the briefing."

Zorin controlled a small company that ran a 'Mech comm system production facility. The bulk of their business came in the form of data encryption and security technology. If there were advanced systems in place to safeguard the information Kenja was taking, it was going to complicate their mission sooner or later.

"We go in with the information we have. You know that." Seth emptied his glass, put it on a tray carried by a passing server, then extended a hand in their intended direction. "Shall we?"

Kenja took Seth's arm again, and they meandered in the direction of Hughes and the Zorins. On the way, they engaged in meaningless small talk as a cover, not loud enough to distract them both from listening in on the conversation between the two corporate magnates as best they could. If they could glean anything about whatever partnership their adversary had forged, if any, it would be valuable information for the Watch.

But the conversation between Hughes and Zorin was nothing but polite small talk about the golfing on nearby Alphard and the price of private DropShips to get there for a game.

Completely banal.

It made Kenja sick to think about the rank excess, but this was why she did what she did. Clan Sea Fox would clean up the excessive profiteering, filter it into their own coffers, and act in the benefit of their Clan and all of humanity.

Kenja and Seth kept their backs to Hughes as another round of drinks came by. At least for Seth. Kenja hadn't finished her first. She didn't like to consume more than one for show at parties like this, because the last thing she wanted was to dull her senses and reflexes. There was no telling when she'd need to beat a hasty exit.

Sensing a lull in the conversation behind her to match their own, Kenja and Seth both turned automatically toward Hughes, and Seth lit up like a *Tiburon*'s command console when it was first fired up.

"Ashwin Hughes?" He edged his way between Hughes and Zorin, cutting the MaxiTech CEO out of the conversation and hemming Hughes in.

"Do I know you?" Hughes asked, his brow furrowed.

"We've met before, but I doubt you'd remember me. Marcus. Seth Marcus. I represent a small concern of buying power from the anti-spinward side of the Free Worlds League."

"Oh, of course," Hughes lied, his expression brightening.

Kenja had seen it a hundred times. People of power like Hughes will pretend to remember you rather than feel like they might be wrong or have forgotten something. But as Seth kept talking up nothing in particular with Hughes, that's when Kenja made her move, like a bishop taking a pawn and stepped up to Seth's side.

"This is my wife, Esme," Seth said, introducing Kenja.

Hughes drank her in, then took her hand and kissed it softly, maintaining intense eye contact. "I'm delighted to meet you."

"Charmed, I'm sure. But I'll leave you two to talk about your business. I'd like to get a stronger drink."

"Of course," Hughes said, letting go of her hand.

She smiled at both of them, then winked at Hughes as she strolled beyond him, brushing against him to cover her lifting his keycard from his pocket and palming it. That was the last piece they needed for the final part of the operation.

And it went off without a hitch.

All she had left to do was pass it back to Seth and they could be on their way. At the bar, listening to them talk through her earpiece about the possibilities of a future partnership and interest in expanding alternate communication technologies across the Free Worlds League, she dropped the sparkling wine and got a drink more suited to her tastes. Whiskey, neat. An 18-year McCracken with a smoky peat taste and smooth texture. Just the way she liked it.

It made the sparkling wine taste like orange Fusion Juice.

She returned to Seth's side and clasped her arm around his, depositing the keycard discreetly into his pocket.

Money in the bank.

"We'll have to meet up sometime more formally," Seth told Hughes.

"Arrange it with my secretary, I'd love to show you what we can offer. You said you're a small buyer, but it sounds like it could turn into a large contract."

"Well, just because we're on the fringe doesn't mean we don't have needs."

"Truer words were never spoken," Hughes said with a sly smile.

Kenja smiled back at Hughes, doing her best to seem uninterested in their conversation. It helped she was actually completely uninterested in the conversation and her adrenaline was pumping at full capacity. The feeling of dangling on the verge of being caught was acute, but she embraced it nonetheless. "It was lovely meeting you, Mr. Hughes."

"The pleasure was all mine," he shot back, reaching out his hand to grab hers. She let him take it and he kissed it.

He looked right at Kenja like she was an object, and instead of letting the creeped-out shiver run down her back, Kenja had to pour on her acting skills. She allowed herself a smirk that told him his advances were welcome, and returned his look of thirst, hoping the chandelier light would sparkle in her eyes from just the right angle and whisper silently that there were possibilities for the two of them.

She hated doing it, but that was the job sometimes.

And they really just needed to get away for the next phase of the operation.

"I hope to see you again," Hughes said.

Kenja didn't break eye contact with him. "Me, too."

Seth smiled again, that gracious, arrogant smile of money. "I'm sure we'll make it happen. But until then, thank you for the invite to the party, Ashwin."

"Any time, Marcus. Any time."

Together, they turned and disappeared into the party, the penultimate phase complete.

On to the hard part.

CHAPTER 3: BREAK OUT

ITCC HQ BUILDING
KENTWOOD
IRIAN
FREE WORLDS LEAGUE
21 APRIL 3151

The basement of the ITCC building housed the computer servers and secrets of the Irian Tactical Communications Corporation. And that was where Kenja and Seth, still dressed for the party, found themselves next.

Kenja wished she could have stayed in her tactical gear, but the ruse at the party had been necessary to gain access. She and Seth split the explosives he carried between them to set. It would be enough to destroy the room, but not the building. Even that would cost the ITCC dearly and set them back significantly, if the other teams' simultaneous strikes on ITCC's offsite backups and lead researchers were on schedule. And, if things were going according to plan, they were still transmitting all the data they could get from the interfacing transmitter she'd planted upstairs, putting the Sea Foxes well ahead.

But if they were caught in the meantime, death was the most likely outcome for both. And Kenja knew neither she nor Seth had any plans to die tonight.

The room was laid out with the server racks, most well over two meters high, tall enough to hide behind, were in long rows on the ground floor. There were no doors in the server pit; a mezzanine level along one side, with stairs at intervals leading down, was the only means of access.

"We've got six minutes left," Seth told her. They'd begun on opposite ends of the room to plant the explosives, so his voice came through her earpiece.

"I'm going as fast as I can." She started at the opposite end of the room, on the far side of the one door. Each of the small bombs were synchronized to go off in that window. They had six minutes to get out. It would require careful timing, but it was also when the VTOL would be heading back to extract them. And if all went well, it wouldn't get shot out of the sky by the Irian *Guillotines* on their way out.

She affixed another explosive device magnetically to the server casing. The entire room, frigid from the air conditioning required to keep the computers cold enough to operate at peak efficiency, made her shiver as she pressed the button, activating one more bomb. "Two left."

But for some reason, Seth had nothing to say in response.

"Seth?"

But still nothing.

She looked down at her chronometer, and then back up to the ticking countdown on the explosive device. Five minutes left. She crossed between racks of servers and looked up at the entrance door to find it wide open. She *knew* they had sealed it when they came in. She'd watched Seth input the lock sequence herself. Was he gone already? Lost his nerve?

No.

Her former mentor would never desert her.

As she scanned across the rest of the mezzanine level, a dozen Irian security personnel in their orange and black uniforms streamed through the door, each one hefting a deadly accurate laser rifle and pointing it at the server room in search of their enemies. Before they spotted her, she pulled back into cover at the end of a server rack, hoping they hadn't seen her.

"They're inside," she said quietly to Seth, hoping their earpieces hadn't been jammed by the Irian security techs.

They hadn't intended for the cavalry to block their escape route.

"Come out now!" a voice shouted. A hint of the Irian accent, but not as thick or as gruff as Seth made it sound when he affected it. "Come out now and he won't be harmed."

Kenja planted the next explosive device and activated the timer. She'd long ago accepted that her life was always going to be at risk. That didn't mean she wasn't going to try to find a way to escape. She absolutely was. But the transmission was what was most important. The Sea Foxes had to be first in the communications race, not a company so corrupt as IrTech, the suspected ringleader of a cabal of major Spheroid corporations that constituted the primary competition for Sea Fox merchants. Communications had to be handled by a neutral party who put the needs of the entire Inner Sphere above their own, and that was exactly what the Clans were supposed to do. It was their sacred charge to safeguard the Inner Sphere and protect it from threats. They were warriors, but they were ushering in peace. That was the mission.

And if she died making that a reality, so be it.

"Seth?" she shouted tentatively, stepping back between the rows of servers to steal another glance at the situation.

And there Seth was at the base of the stairs below the mezzanine, face bloodied and kneeling before Ashwin Hughes, who held a laser pistol held to his head.

Ducking back behind the cover of the server and remaining hidden, Kenja didn't have time to get angry. Her thoughts pulled back into the logical and most important. First, was there a way to escape? Secondly, if there was, was there a way to escape with Seth in tow? She needed to rescue him if she could. There was no telling what information he could leave behind in the hands of an enemy or competitor.

"Don't take their bait!" he shouted. That was his voice. No silly accent. His *real* voice. He meant it.

Kenja took in a deep breath and raised her needler. Looking left and right, she could almost sense it before it happened, but the security stooges stepped forward into the aisle between server racks she'd been hiding in, one on each side of her, getting in a shot. She crouched as they fired. Laser beams flew past right over her head and the guards hit each other, and she fired her pistol at the one on her right, then spun and shot the second one for good measure. Both took a compact spray of flechette rounds to the neck, gurgling and collapsing in puddles of their own blood.

She hoped their bodies would warn the others not to try it, but now they knew where she was.

"There's no way out, madam," Hughes said. "Now tell me who you work for and why you're here, and I might let you live."

"Blow them all to hell, Kenja!" Seth said.

Kenja heard Hughes grunt, and peeked around the server just in time to see him pull the trigger on his laser pistol. Crimson light flashed, and Seth collapsed to the ground.

Ducking behind the server once more, Kenja clutched her needler and took a deep breath. She promised herself that would be the only breath of grief she'd allow herself before making her next move. Anything more and she'd fall to pieces.

Steeling her resolve and tightening her grip on the gun, Kenja snuck glances at the situation from both sides of the server rack, counting enemies and their weapons. She thought of herself as the most powerful computer in the room, going through the odds and escape routes, tagging likely methods of destruction. How much of the escape plan was compromised? Would she still make the pickup? Would the *Guillotine* sentries be on high alert? Could she make it before the server exploded into an inferno?

In a split second, a plan formed. Or at least a stratagem. Perhaps it wasn't fleshed out fully enough to be a plan, but Seth had always told her sometimes the best chess gambits started with nothing more than a distraction.

So that's where she'd start.

Cataloging the assets at her disposal, she felt the weight of the last explosive she had meant to plant in her hand.

"You can't escape!" Hughes shouted. "And your companion is dead. There is no use hiding any longer if you want to survive."

She began by kicking the heels off her shoes. They were cleverly disguised ammunition for the needler, and she fed one into the gun. The other she tucked into the top of her dress in case she needed it. Then she kicked off the ruined shoes and stepped over the body of one of the dead Irian security guards. Exposed, she chose the right aisle because it had fewer guards and fewer oblique angles for her to be shot from by the other column of guards, especially if she stayed close to the server rack itself.

She fired at the guard standing directly in front of her on the mezzanine. The needles hit the woman in the middle and she doubled over the railing, falling to the floor below, losing her rifle in the process. At the sound, other guards began firing, Kenja tossed the explosive, reset to detonate on impact, into the fray, pitching it above the head of Ashwin Hughes. He fired at her, too, but every shot missed. As the explosive arced in the air, she fired at it, hoping at least one volley would hit it.

The *KRACK!* of the explosion and the ensuing smoke and heat, enough to force her to flinch and hold her eyes shut through the worst of it, told her at least one of her shots hit the mark. The smoke caused confusion and sowed just enough chaos that some of the guards must have lost sight of her. She started moving forward as lasers carving into the servers behind her.

"Stop shooting at her!" Hughes shouted through a hacking cough. "You'll destroy the servers!"

He was smart enough to realize what was at stake and where the little value his company had left resided. But he didn't have the advantage of knowing about the explosives that were going to destroy it anyway, so that was a mark in Kenja's favor.

Charging through the smoke and debris, right past the ITCC sentries in the server corridor, Kenja shot two more on her way. One she caught in the face, turning it into a sea of deep red wounds, the other she caught in a glancing blow across their rifle arm, enough to disrupt their aim and prevent them from firing.

Keeping her momentum up, Kenja jerked left and right, running in a zig-zag pattern through the smoke at irregular intervals to confuse the shooters. She fired once more, and tagged another guard before leaping onto the staircase.

"Get her!" Hughes shouted.

Of course he'd want to capture her. He likely had no idea why they were there and definitely had no idea who they were. He'd already disposed of his prisoner. A lump caught in her throat as she thought about it, but she dismissed his name.

Mourning came later.

Now was the time to survive.

Leaping up the stairs four at a time, her bare feet were hardly up to the task. Another drawback of undercover work at ridiculous soirees.

Kenja stayed crouched as she barreled up the staircase, doing her best to make herself a difficult target. When she reached the last steps, she rolled onto the mezzanine, laying down suppressing fire from a kneeling position as soon as she came to a stop.

"Don't let her get away!" Hughes said, pointing up at her from the hazy floor of the server room, Seth's body lying at his feet. "Seal the door!"

Kenja glanced back and forth to either side, tracking the movements of the guards still on the mezzanine level, but then her gaze fixed upon the double-wide door that led out. A guard on the other side saw her and looked almost surprised. Instead of firing at her, he made for the door controls.

It was the last mistake he'd ever make.

Kenja pushed herself forward from her crouch, leaping like a *Grasshopper* through the doorway as it began to slide closed.

Extending her arm out just after crossing the threshold, she stiff-armed the neck of the guard in front of her and, using the momentum from her leap, dragged him to the floor, pounding his neck and back into it.

He groaned, which meant he was still alive, lucky for him. But instead of taking the time to finish the job, Kenja just kept moving.

She didn't have time to tangle with every underling the ITCC folks kept sending after her. Especially when in—she glanced at her wrist—in two minutes, the entire server room would blow sky-high.

She'd live to see it if only she could escape.

CHAPTER 4: ET VOILA

Kenja burst out from an emergency exit into the cold, fresh air of the Irian night. Her skin rippled with gooseflesh with the shift in temperature, and her breath appeared in front of her in foggy bursts.

The cold wasn't the problem.

The problem was the *Guillotine* looming large in the path of her exit, its broad searchlight methodically scanning the area at its massive feet, no doubt looking for her.

She was lucky, but doubted she was lucky enough to survive a hit from anything that 'Mech could shoot her with. Pressing herself up against the building, she narrowly avoided the harsh edge of the spotlight's bright reach and then started advancing against the wall toward the extraction zone.

Over the shrieking alarms, Kenja heard the telltale sounds of an approaching VTOL, that distant thump of motors whirring with all possible speed. She only hoped it was her extraction, and not more reinforcements from IrTech.

Behind her, she felt the faint concussive force of the explosions going off in the server room. No doubt the transmitter up above had sent everything of use, and had now begun its self-destruct sequence as well. Mission: accomplished. Now to get away.

The *Guillotine* stomped forward, and Kenja made a break for the clearing on the dark side while the spotlight scoured the ground on the 'Mech's far side. It wasn't a matter of *if* the MechWarrior spotted her and started shooting, but *when*.

Barefoot, Kenja sprinted across the ferrocrete expanse to the next spot of cover. There was a watchtower and pallets of supplies and ammunition near its support legs. She ran hard, hoping she could duck behind it before the *Guillotine* swept its penetrating gaze back around and before the guards in the watchtower spotted her.

Every second that ticked by was another second closer to discovery and death.

Reaching the watchtower, she crouched close against the pallets and barrels, Kenja looked down at her needler and checked the ammunition. After everything it had taken to make it out of the server room, through the maze of corridors, and to this point, she had just enough for one more shot. The needler would be useless against the *Guillotine* and definitely not against the guards at the top of the watchtower. Needle pistols had a short range, but since they were powered with compressed gas, they were as quiet a firearm as someone could ask for when embarking on delicate missions like this one was supposed to be.

If she wanted to make her last shot count, she would have to get in close.

She doubted she could find her way into the *Guillotine*'s cockpit, but the watchtower, high, and with a meter and a half of open air between the rail and the roof, was a possibility. Especially since they wouldn't suspect it.

The spotlight illuminated her hiding place, but cast her position in shadows. She'd chosen the lee of the pallet, facing away from the BattleMech, but they must have gotten wise. The spotlight ceased moving in a pattern, or the *Guillotine* pilot had wised up and turned on their infrared and spotted her, a little red dot in a field of black.

The noise grew from the building as more doors opened. More guards were shouting.

But the sound of salvation grew closer as the helicopter neared. Kenja still couldn't see it, but she counted on it being the one they'd chartered for extraction and not one summoned by the ITCC.

She didn't have much of a choice. She had to move as though it was the right helicopter. If it wasn't, she was dead anyway.

At least this way, she might have a chance.

Kenja traced a path to the watchtower's ladder with her eyes, ensuring she could keep to the shadows the rest of the way there.

"That way!" she heard a voice say.

"No, over here!" another said.

At least she had confusion on her side.

Sprinting to the ladder, she began climbing, hoping she wouldn't be spotted. Her bare feet hurt with every step, but she pushed herself up despite the pain.

Such was the life of a Watch agent. Pushing through despite the pain. No matter where it came from.

She was halfway up before the spotlight tagged her. The *Guillotine* must have refrained from firing, because even its smallest weapons would have taken the entire watchtower down with her. She'd take the advantage, small as it might be, wherever she could get them.

But the forces on the ground scrambled to get into a position where they could shoot at her. Fortunately, they were firing from extreme long range and were all out of breath from running into position. Their aim was terrible, and their lasers carved chunks from the tower, but—so far—not her.

The guards *in* the watchtower hadn't shown their faces yet, and Kenja's mind shuffled through possibilities. She would just have to get to the top and figure out why they weren't leaning over the edge and firing right at her—hopefully before they started doing that.

"Thresher, this is Echo One, do you copy?" came a voice in Kenja's ear. The VTOL *was* the extraction team.

"Echo One, this is Kitefin. I read you."

"Where is Thresher?"

"He didn't make it."

"What is your location? We are heading for extraction zone three, as planned."

"No good. We have to improvise." Kenja flinched as a laser cut through the ladder right above her. The shots were getting closer.

"Improvise?"

"You read a *Guillotine* in zone four?"

"*Aff.*"

"And the watchtower?"

"*Aff.*"

She heard the helicopter coming in faster, looking for the right place to land. But they weren't going to get the chance, which was probably safer for all of them.

If she could make it work.

Ten rungs from the top of the watchtower, the tower guards decided to show their faces.

She raised her arm and fired her needler with careful aim.

One guard ducked back into the tower, the other took the flechettes to the face and slumped forward, falling from their high perch.

Kenja dropped the empty needler and held onto one side of the ladder with both hands and spun out of the way of the falling body.

Then she scrambled up the last few rungs and got a look at the situation. The remaining tower guard had pulled back to the corner of the room and aimed their laser rifle right at her. They fired, searing a deep burn into Kenja's arm. Behind him, the "face" of the *Guillotine*, the 'Mech with a medieval-looking helmet for a head and massive shoulder pauldrons, loomed as a not-so-gentle giant.

The 'Mech's overbearing appearance did nothing to assure Kenja of her survival.

But the guard's non-lethal shot allowed her to ignore the pain and charge her enemy. The guard fired once more as she closed the distance—but missed!—and Kenja grabbed the rifle when she reached them. They fought over it, but she used it as a leverage point. By shifting direction, speed, and angle, she turned the momentum against the guard and dropped them to the ground.

Wrenching the rifle from them, she aimed it at their chest and fired. The crimson laser took a millisecond to cut through the armor, pierce their flesh, and boil their insides.

"Extract One, this is Kitefin, do you copy?"

Looking around the watchtower, she saw the Anhur VTOL edging in close. "I have infiltrated the watchtower. I am going to have to jump."

"Into the VTOL, *quiaff*?" the pilot said, incredulous.

"*Aff.*"

"And what about that *Guillotine*?"

"You are just going to have to be faster than it."

"I do not like this."

"Neither do I, but we don't have a choice, *quineg*?"

"*Neg*, Kitefin. We will come around on the far side. Be ready."

Kenja watched the altitude and trajectory of the VTOL. It circled around so it was heading toward the watchtower and facing the *Guillotine* head on. She started counting the time, watching it dodge and weave through laser fire and around missiles. It deployed inferno payloads towards the soldiers on the ground, drawing the heat-seeking missiles down toward the ITCC reinforcements.

She backed up, all the way to the back wall of the watchtower, counted to three, and bolted forward. Jumping to the top of the watchtower's safety rail in a crouch so she didn't hit her head on the roof, Kenja planted a foot atop the bar and kicked off, sailing through the air.

The VTOL was right where it had to be.

They had their doors open, ready for her. She landed hard, sliding into the open door like a runner coming home. The Sea Fox crewman inside gripped her arm and held her steady as they closed the door behind her.

The crewman helped her to a seat as the the pilot pulled up hard, avoiding the wildly firing *Guillotine*. Miraculously, they took only superficial damage. Soon they left it behind, heading to their next mission waypoint.

Strapping into a seat and watching the chaotic rainbow of lasers firing impotently in their direction, Kenja wanted to feel a smug satisfaction for a job well done.

But all she could think about was Seth.

CHAPTER 5: NEW DIRECTIONS

SPINA KHANATE SAFE HOUSE
KENTWOOD
IRIAN
FREE WORLDS LEAGUE
30 APRIL 3151

More than a week of waiting in the safe house felt like a prison sentence to Kenja Rodriguez, waiting for the heat on Irian to die down and the laser burn on her arm to heal up. She hated the feeling of inertia.

Especially when the complicated feelings of grief melted her insides like a large laser to the gut.

She tried to soothe the feelings by staying busy, but there wasn't much to do in the apartment. She set up the last chess game she and Seth had been playing, remembering exactly where the pieces had been, and contemplated her next move.

It was a good distraction until she realized he had her in check in three moves and there wasn't a whole lot she could do about it. Even from the grave he was beating her.

Sitting still, waiting for her body to mend and the next mission to come in, she wasn't out there thinking about her next life-or-death challenge. She was coping with things she didn't want to. The Spina Khanate medtech who had been stationed on the planet with them had checked her out mentally and physically. She'd stated Kenja was still fit for duty—the wound to her arm was more superficial than anything, and she had learned to keep the wounds on her heart and in her head wrapped up tight enough to pass muster from the medtech's review.

The merchant-dominated Sea Fox Watch seemed to be more demanding when it came to rigorous mental and physical requirements. When she was a MechWarrior, as long as she could pilot a 'Mech and head toward the enemy, she was fit for duty. The merchant caste of Clan Sea Fox, especially those Bloodnamed retirees that both fought in 'Mechs and oversaw negotiations with other powerbrokers in the Inner Sphere, had to have their heads screwed on straight, at least for a Clan member, and check out a little bit better physically and mentally. Kenja expected she'd eventually make the transition from warrior caste to merchant, switching from Star Colonel to Merchant Colonel, when she felt the years creeping up on her.

The Watch was the branch of the Clan that purported to have the sanest and most stringently disciplined personnel, but it was all a ruse, and Kenja never felt that more acutely than when she was stuck in a safe house or some other hideaway, waiting to find out where she would be best utilized by her Clan next.

Staring at the pawns and pieces scattered across the board in front of her, she imagined her next move, and the move after that, but her concentration was broken when a warning trilled at the door.

Someone was there.

She hoped they had her new orders.

Kenja rose from the chair, whose view overlooked the gardened courtyard at the back of the building, and walked to the door.

It slid open to reveal a young woman with the bearing of a Clan warrior, but without the uniform. Instead, she wore a baggy coat and leggings, with a massive scarf wrapped around her neck in the local style. "Delivery for you, ma'am."

When she realized the woman held no obvious delivery, Kenja's mind shuffled through the various passcodes and key phrases until she realized how she should respond. "I haven't ordered anything."

"Oh, I think this one has your name on it, ma'am."

"So it does," Kenja said, trying not to make it sound rote. "Why don't you come in?"

"Of course."

The young woman stepped into Kenja's little sanctum. Her quiet cave of grief and stagnation.

Kenja hit the button to close the door behind them, and then went to the shelf to turn on the scrambling device. The scientist caste had explained it was essentially a white noise machine, but it scrambled across a much broader frequency, reducing the ability of any potential listening equipment to broadcast or record anything but static. It looked like an average noteputer, and was just one of the gadgets Kenja relied upon every day in her line of duty.

"Please," Kenja said to the young Watch agent, "take a seat."

The young woman did as she was bidden. Kenja didn't think she looked more than twenty years from her time birthed in an iron womb. Perhaps twenty-two, tops. She had a hint of the dark skin and darker hair and eyes that made Kenja think she might have been part of a post-Blackout Russo-Borghev *sibko*. Clan Trueborn weren't born to parents bound in love and relationships. They were genetically created from the DNA of their Clan's greatest warriors and born in artificial wombs, raised from birth to be the best. Kenja came from the Rodriguez bloodline, and had won the right to use her Bloodname in a long Trial many years ago.

The other thing she noticed about the woman was that she had a hard time repressing her smile, as though she were somehow taken with Kenja; either her reputation or her looks. Kenja would need to talk to her more to figure that one out.

Kenja took a seat herself and bade the young woman to get to the point.

"Pardon my intrusion, Star Colonel," the woman said, addressing Kenja by the correct rank. If she was a plant or an enemy, she had certainly done her homework. "I am Star Commander Petrichor of the Tiburon Khanate, Beta Aimag."

"Star Commander?" Kenja said surprised. She would have assumed she would be dealing with a merchant caste Watch agent. The crossover between MechWarriors and Watch agents wasn't terribly high.

"Indeed, I have been assigned to your detail by my Aimag's field commander. With the loss of Star Colonel Seth, I was the only other Tiburon field asset on Irian with clearance to deliver this message."

"Message?"

"I will play it for you, but I warn, Star Colonel, that since you have been on assignment, the Inner Sphere has changed. Quickly and drastically."

"I see."

"You will." Petrichor produced a noteputer and a silver puck that served as a holoprojector. Kenja keyed the lights in the room to dim and activated the shade on the window.

The hologram's blue light emanated from the puck on the coffee table and filled the space, but the details of the figure it showed were hazy. And their voice was masked. Kenja recognized it as the Tiburon Khanate handler she most often dealt with. She called him No-Face behind his back, because he had only given her assignments through the haze of holographs, and she didn't know his real name—for purposes of operational security. But his codename was Carcharodon.

"Thresher, Kitefin," their handler began. The message must have been old—at least by a few days—because he hadn't taken into account the loss of Seth yet. But that's what happened in a galaxy without rapid mass communication.

"I trust you have already accomplished your last mission, so I have a new task for you. This is top priority. If you have not yet completed the previous mission, it must be abandoned. This new mission takes precedence, and what I am about to tell you is strictly on a need to know basis."

Anticipation and dread swirled in the pit of Kenja's stomach—a vortex of instinct and a lifetime of proven hunches—told her she might be right about what he was about to say. The message was going to be about Terra. What the mission would be she had no idea, but if the Inner Sphere was going to change, nothing would change it more than the fall of the Republic of the Sphere to a Clan.

"Terra has fallen," he said solemnly. Carcharodon paused for a moment, letting the gravity of his statement sink in. Terra had long been the goal of the Clans, and if the Republic of the Sphere—the government who controlled it—was gone, which would change everything in the Inner Sphere and beyond.

"Both Clan Wolf and Jade Falcon found a method to bypass the Fortress Wall earlier this year. They emptied their respective occupation zones and set out to conquer the cradle of civilization and fulfill the destiny of the Clans. The Republic crumbled and the Wolves and the Falcons fought a Trial to the brink of annihilation for the right to declare themselves the ilClan."

Conflicted feelings swirled inside her. On one hand, she was excited to see how the new order of things would shake out. On the other, there was some resentment that Clan Sea Fox wouldn't be the ilClan, but would serve it instead. Kenja wondered which Clan—Wolf or Falcon—*had* come out on top, but more than that, she wondered why she was getting so much preamble before the mission. She rarely needed this much context.

"Clan Wolf was the victor. This works well for our Clan, as we have a good relationship with the soon-to-be-ilKhan Alaric Ward. We have helped in the efforts of his causes, and believe the Sea Foxes are well positioned in the new order, and what he seems bent on fashioning into the new Star League. All of this is to say that you are dealing with a very different Inner Sphere."

To Kenja, that sounded like an understatement. She glanced at Petrichor, who remained stonefaced, her eyes were fixed on the digitally glitching image of Carcharodon.

"The Khans of Clan Sea Fox have been invited to Terra to entreat with Ward and pay their respects to the ilClan. They have also been invited to a ceremony to see him installed as the First Lord of a new Star League. We are able to get you through the Fortress Wall. To that end, we give you these orders: make your way to Terra. Your assignment to locate and acquire a man named Tucker Harwell, if he is still alive. Having gone through the information received from Clan Goliath Scorpion, our scientists believe the mind of Tucker Harwell is vital to the effort to end the communications blackout and allow Clan Sea Fox to bring the HPG network back online. With our top two Watch agents

working together, I can think of no better team to take on what might be the most vital mission the Star Colonels of the Tiburon Watch will embark upon."

A pang of hurt swelled deep inside Kenja. She would have to do this alone, and wouldn't have Seth along to help.

Glancing at Petrichor again, Kenja wondered if she realized how right she'd been when she said the Inner Sphere had changed irrevocably. It would never be the same again.

"Make all possible speed to Terra. Harwell may not come willingly. Negotiate or bargain with him if you can. Take him by force if you must. What is important is that you get him to the Tiburon enclave on Hean, at the edge of the Federated Suns territory. There, Tiburon has built a facility to put him to work to fix the hyperpulse generators. There will be more instructions on Hean if all proceeds according to plan. Knowing the value of his knowledge of the HPGs, Tucker Harwell is likely a high profile target for many factions across the Inner Sphere, Clan and Spheroid alike. You will be in extreme danger the moment you embark on this mission. For now, I leave only with the words of Karen Nagasawa when she turned on the Sea Fox Chatterweb for the first time. 'The Clans have been created to end all wars and protect all of humanity. They cannot do that if they cannot speak with one another. So, let there be connections among us.' It is her work we are continuing, and you are the standard bearers Tiburon Khanate has chosen for this assignment. Such is your oath. This is our rede. May it stand until we all shall fall. Seyla, my warriors. Seyla."

Kenja sat back in her chair, falling deep inside of it, whispering *"Seyla"* to herself. Her mind reeled.

"You saw this message before reporting it to me?" she asked the Star Commander.

"Neg. I received a briefing about the Trial of the ilClan, but not the specifics of the mission."

Kenja nodded. She ran through all the different ways things could go wrong on a planet like Terra. Infiltrating the cradle of humankind seemed like a good way to die. It would be crawling with malcontents and rebels angry about the Clans taking over and the destruction they had wrought. It would be crawling with the armed entourages of every Khan come to pay their respects to the new ilKhan. It would be crawling with Wolves out to prove themselves and whatever Jade Falcons were left with their feathers between their legs.

And in the middle of it all, Kenja would have to find one man and pull him out. A needle in a haystack.

Seth was gone, but this was what she needed to pull her head back from her grief. An assignment to distract her.

She took a breath and looked back up at the Star Commander. "Transfer all the files we received on Tucker Harwell to my noteputer."

"*Aff*, Star Colonel."

"And I take it you're coming with me?"

"*Aff*, Star Colonel. I am assigned to provide whatever resources you might need."

The longer it took them to get to Terra to find Harwell, the further away he could get, so speed was of the essence. "Right now, we need a way off Irian and back to our JumpShip. And we need to get to Terra immediately."

"The JumpShip *Bull Shark* is charged and ready to go. We have a DropShip at our disposal to take us there."

"What is its cover?"

"It is traveling under a Free Worlds League IFF, and is associated with IrTech, with cosmetic panels altering its hull profile to resemble a *Leopard*-class. I figured the last ship they would harass or shoot down would be one of their own."

Kenja stood up. "Exactly what I like to hear. Let's get out of here. We don't have a second to lose."

CHAPTER 6:
RACE THROUGH THE STARS

BROADSWORD-CLASS DROPSHIP *ZEPHYR*
ZENITH RECHARGE STATION (TWO JUMPS FROM TERRA)
CARVER
CAPELLAN CONFEDERATION
20 MAY 3151

Almost a month had gone by since the beginning of her assignment, and Kenja couldn't keep from getting antsy. She'd been through the dossiers and reports a dozen times. At least twice a day. During meals—usually a patented Sea Fox nutrient paste designed by the scientist caste to keep their bone density high for their low-to-no-gravity lives—Kenja went over the available information again. Normally, she disliked the paste after spending so much time undercover on missions, enjoying local delicacies, but something about its aftertaste—vaguely like seafood she'd had on some planets—made her feel like a kid again. Plus, it provided all necessary nutrients at a fraction of the cost of regular food, a trait her Clan prized. Add in the gravity and ultra-clean air, and floating through space for a month wasn't so bad.

As for her target, Tucker Harwell, she had learned a lot about him. It always paid to have too much information rather than not enough, and she had started to feel like she knew him personally, that's how much she'd been through his files. He was brilliant, by all accounts, and seemed like a person far ahead of his time. By the age of 21, he had received his doctorate in HPG technologies and engineering, and went to work for ComStar almost immediately. At 30 years old—the time of the most recent photos in the file—he had no visible scars, but who knows what the last ten years might have done to him?

Kenja had smirked reading that part. He was brilliant like she had been. Like Seth had been. Maybe they would have gotten along if they were all working for the same team.

The notes about ComStar itself and the historical context added to the stories Kenja had heard and researched filled out the story. ComStar was an allegedly pacifist organization that had claimed neutrality in interstellar communications, but actually played all Inner Sphere Great Houses against each other *and* the Clans, helped instigate wars, and tried to impose their will on others, carefully placing their thumb on the scales of neutrality to maintain their own definition of "balance" in the Inner Sphere. They had shattered the Sea Fox—then called Diamond Shark—Clusters sent to fight them a century ago at Tukayyid, and their extremist offshoot, the Word of Blake, had unleashed devastation across the Inner Sphere sixteen years later. Even the non-extremists were also said to be quasi-religious, which seemed odd to Kenja. Why would an organization devoted to technology adopt the trappings of a religion, fraught with prayers and magic, like the long-lost Clan Cloud Cobra?

Harwell's family had been in ComStar for seven generations, though Tucker himself had officially served with them for only three months before Gray Monday and the Blackout. Kenja wondered if that was suspicious. Something in her gut said he probably didn't have anything to do with it, but seeing it written down in the dossier sure made it feel like he could have had a hand in it. Gray Monday was a hard time for everyone. She remembered it well. She had just been recruited into the Watch and assigned to Seth for mentoring, and he told her it was going to change the Inner Sphere. Irrevocably.

After Gray Monday, ComStar had tasked him with trying to figure out why the HPGs went down and how to get them fully operational again. He wasn't the only one; they'd dedicated their most brilliant minds to the challenge. And it made sense why he was of so much interest to all the parties still working on the HPG problem: he would give whoever had him a twenty-year head start on research and institutional knowledge. No doubt the torture he had endured at the hands of the Order—a militant ComStar element that had been officially disbanded by the Republic, but secretly reconstituted as the Com Guards—set him back quite a bit.

As for his personality—his desires and passions, his likes and dislikes—the dossiers made little mention of his personal habits and tastes, which frustrated Kenja. The Watch agents who wrote the dossiers never delved deeply enough into the psychology of a person to satisfy her. What did it matter which important events and battles a particular target of interest had been present for? That information was only mildly useful, more a matter of happenstance and geography than of character. She wanted to know more about the things that drove a target's passions, what made them tick.

There were still clues in the dossier for that, though. Kenja just had to read between the lines and draw her own conclusions. Harwell was clearly driven by a love of technology and a thirst for the knowledge behind the HPGs. She doubted he would have dedicated his life to it from such a young age without that drive.

For a moment, Kenja wondered how they would write up a dossier about her. Would they say she was competent and devoted to her work? Or just list the skills she had acquired and operations she had completed? Would it say she liked frivolities like playing chess or taking bubble-baths to wind down while reading romance novels set during the Succession Wars? Would there be a footnote that she spoke in un-Clan-like ways and idioms, due to a life constantly undercover?

She knew one thing for sure: it wouldn't include her deepest feelings of regret and sorrow every time she lost someone or failed a mission. They would just have to hope her list of accomplishments told that story.

Harwell's dossier made no mention of any romantic relationships, and that could have been for two reasons: one, he was a scientist, too focused on his work to care about pursuing a relationship, or, two, they simply didn't know what his proclivities were. Knowing either aspect could have been beneficial. There were plenty of situations where Kenja could use the subterfuge of romance to make missions easier. Those Succession Era bodice-rippers came in handy for that sort of research. But the dossier writers couldn't tell if Tucker Harwell was interested in men, women, both, another gender entirely, or none at all.

Given the significance of having any Clan representative set foot on Terra without a negotiated agreement, there had been no Sea Fox Watch agents stationed there when the Fortress Wall went up, so the data was stale and outdated. The solid information ended in about 3135, and the rest was supposition based on what the Watch had gleaned after the Wall to protect Terra had been activated. There was no actionable intelligence about his favorite haunts and hangouts. It was one thing to be told to extract a person from a world as large as Terra if you knew where their favorite bar was, or even what city they lived in. But with absolutely nothing to go on? Kenja would have to pull off a miracle.

Too bad ComStar's saints had no real power, or she would have prayed to them for help.

Between her dossier studying, briefings on the available information, and making inquiries to obtain more information, she whiled away the recharge time in the DropShip's zero-gee environs, doing her best to stay fit. As a Watch agent, she never knew when she would have to race to the surface of some planet or another and operate at peak efficiency. After eating, Kenja would head to the JumpShip's small gym on one of its grav decks. The amount of time it took to stay fit in zero-gee—at least a few hours a day—meant there were always a few other Sea Foxes working out as well. For them, the ability to maintain combat readiness in any gravitational environment was drilled in from birth.

Strapped into her treadmill by tight bungee cords to simulate heavier force and gravity than the grav deck alone provided, Kenja closed her eyes and started running away from anything that would hurt her—even the last memories of Seth, burned into her mind's eye.

"Star Colonel," Star Commander Petrichor said, snapping her out of the trance of her run. The young woman stepped onto the treadmill next to Kenja's, clipping its straps onto her harness.

"Star Commander," she replied, wiping the sweat from her brow. Checking the clock, she discovered she'd already been running for a half an hour, keeping her heart rate up and working to keep her legs and shoulders strong. Treadmill running was an ancient technique for keeping fit in zero-gee, and they hadn't done a whole lot to improve it over the centuries.

"We still have over a hundred hours to finish charging before we head to our last step before Terra," Petrichor said, activating her treadmill and starting to run.

"Keid, right? We aren't making bad time," Kenja said. Though secretly she was still annoyed she didn't have a command circuit of charged JumpShips at her disposal. If the mission was so important and there was an opportunity to pass through the Fortress Wall, it would have been expedient to move her through more quickly. They were tethered to the *Bull Shark*, an *Odyssey*-class Sea Fox courier JumpShip with a lithium-fusion battery that would allow two jumps on one charge, but they'd already spent the charge to get to this point as speedily as possible. Risking a second jump to get from Hamilton to Berenson could leave them without the ability to jump away if threatened during the recharge cycle.

"I expect we will be receiving information from Terra soon," Petrichor said.

"The closer we get, the more likely the possibility." Kenja noticed Petrichor sneaking glances at her when she thought she wasn't looking, and filed that information away for later.

Petrichor looked back up into Kenja's eyes and smiled warmly. "I think getting the HPG network back up and running is going to make our jobs a lot easier in the long run."

"I don't disagree," Kenja said, understating the flutter in her chest at the idea. Getting the HPG network up would be worth a line in *The Remembrance*. "But I wouldn't count on it being an easy fix. The man we're extracting has been trying to fix it for twenty years. So I'm not holding my breath."

The Star Commander left the conversation there, focusing on her run, but still thieving the occasional glance now and then.

Kenja set her mind to the workout, too. Maybe if she kept running, that image of Seth getting shot in the head wouldn't follow.

BROADSWORD-CLASS DROPSHIP *ZEPHYR*
KEID RECHARGE STATION
ZENITH JUMP POINT
KEID
CAPELLAN CONFEDERATION
31 MAY 3151

"Star Colonel," Star Commander Petrichor said through the comm, interrupting the blissful, only partially-nightmare-filled sleep of Kenja Rodriguez.

"What is it, Star Commander?" she didn't even open her eyes.

"Incoming message. It was relayed by another JumpShip at the recharge station."

Kenja wondered if this was how the ancient people of Terra had felt before they had instant communication in the infancy of humanity. Having to wait days or weeks for information to trickle in because they didn't have the technology to beam it to each other instantaneously. It was like trying to imagine life before indoor plumbing or space travel. It all seemed so impossible, backward, and ancient. It was all just humanity hitting each other with stone tools and slug-throwers.

Forget Clan Wolf taking Terra, the Sea Foxes would be the ones to bring humanity into its next golden age... "Have it sent to the ready room."

"*Aff*, Star Colonel."

Kenja hurried to put on her single-suit, a standard uniform for Sea Foxes traveling on long journeys. It was Sea Fox warrior caste blue, and bore the Clan emblem: a three-quarter view of an angular sea fox head, with its tail rendered in curling waves. She felt pride in wearing that patch, knowing how they were going to shape the future of humanity. It suited her, though that might have just been her upbringing and the genetic legacy of a few hundred years of Sea Fox DNA propagating itself with each generation improving upon the last.

Dressed and with her hair pulled into a tight knot at the back of her head, Kenja entered the ready room to find the Star Commander waiting for her there, as well as Star Captain Meridian Yung, the DropShip captain. Both were dressed in similar single-suits, but their rank pips were different. And the captain had a white stripe across her shoulders to denote she was in command of the naval vessel.

Since they were already strapped into their chairs to counter the lack of gravity, neither stood when they saluted, but both greeted Kenja with a crisp, *"Star Colonel."*

Kenja didn't like being addressed by her title as much as other Sea Foxes she knew. It made her feel exposed. She spent too much time lying to people to feel comfortable divulging that much truth. A contradiction to be sure, taking pride in being a Sea Fox, but with an overwhelming desire to hide it. Such was the life of an agent of the Watch.

"Where is the incoming message from?" she asked as she kicked off the back wall and somersaulted into the chair at the table opposite Petrichor and Meridian.

Petrichor answered as Kenja belted herself in, "This communique comes from Terra, and bears the standard Tiburon Khanate Watch codes for our current threat level."

Kenja nodded. It would be more information, and more information was always a good thing. "Play it."

Petrichor hit a few buttons on her noteputer, and the DropShip captain looked up from her screen to watch the message unfold.

"We have tracked the target asset to Puget Sound, on the western edge of the North American continent," a low-ranking Tiburon Watch agent said.

The details of their voice and image were digitally blurred, which made sense. If the message were to fall into the wrong hands and get decrypted, there was every chance they would identify the Watch agent and burn a valuable asset.

"We arrived with the Alpha Khanate, and are pulling together all the information we can for you. We will track the target's whereabouts to the best of our abilities and allow you time to create the extraction plan."

The fuzzy visage turned back to look at something, and then the image fizzled into static.

That was it.

Kenja sighed. "At least we have a general area. But that doesn't make our job any easier. Puget Sound is the home of the Court of the Star League, and if the ilKhan is really fashioning himself as the new First Lord, it's likely going to be crawling with Clan Wolf agents."

"Agreed," Petrichor said.

Yung confidently folded her hands in front of her. "Once we get through the Fortress Wall, I might be able to shave time off the burn in if getting there faster can help."

"I appreciate that, Star Captain."

"There were some other files sent as well," Petrichor said. "More background information on Terra, the target, and the happenings with Clan Wolf."

"Send it all to my noteputer," Kenja said with a smile. "And keep me updated on any other incoming messages. It won't be long now."

CHAPTER 7:
FAR BEYOND THE CASTLE WALL

BROADSWORD-CLASS DROPSHIP *ZEPHYR*
KEID RECHARGE STATION (ONE JUMP TO TERRA)
ZENITH JUMP POINT
KEID
CAPELLAN CONFEDERATION
1 JUNE 3151

There remained at least a full day before they could make the final jump from Keid to Terra. And the information trickling in from the Watch and various outbound Alpha and Skate Khanate courier ships had been only marginally helpful. Rumors in public forums were flying about everything from the nefarious conspiracies of Devlin Stone and Alaric Ward to doomsday scenarios written by people who had more time than sense. So instead of focusing on the grist in the rumor mill, Kenja spent her time between workouts and hearty meals of nutrient paste learning more about her target, Tucker Harwell.

The reports from Terra were dedicated to the actual Trial itself—not the sanitized versions the Wolf put out, but on-the-ground accounts. What had happened was shocking, and Kenja felt neither Clan Wolf nor Clan Jade Falcon had comported themselves in a way that befit the honor of a Clan Trial, especially with so much on the line as the ilClanship. Malvina Hazen had perished under suspicious circumstances more than a month ago, leaving whatever was left of Clan Jade Falcon in shambles.

It made sense why the aftermath of the battle and all the political maneuvering would take place in and around Puget Sound, where the Court of the Star League had been centered. The place was dripping with history and symbolism. It was where Stefan Amaris had killed Richard Cameron, the last First Lord of the Star League of the Cameron bloodline, and kicked off the wars across the Inner Sphere that eventually led to the Exodus, and then the formation of the Clans. For those vying for the ilClanship and hoping to become the ilKhan, it was natural for Ward and Hazen to have met there. All of the pomp and circumstance of that bloody history would be vital to them.

Kenja floated to the bridge, hoping a message would arrive. She spent the time looking out through the glass and monitors of the DropShip up at the JumpShip and space in all its glory. *It really is amazing what humanity can engineer to travel through the stars...*

And staring at the long cylinder of the *Odyssey*-class JumpShip, with exterior bulges indicating rotating grav decks within and unfurled solar collectors, was easier than getting lost in her memories. But even then, the sight of the JumpShip brought memories of a mission gone bad, stuck in one, air dwindling, death nearing. It was a good thing she hadn't been there alone...

A tone sounded, the soft trill of an alarm. It sounded harsh in Kenja's ear, and beat in time with the countdown clocks on the explosives she used on Irian—

And then Seth was there, kneeling on the ground.

He was the one who had taught her the finer ins and outs of the Watch game. As he told it, he'd picked her file after witnessing her outthink her opponents in her Trial of Bloodright. She was an accomplished MechWarrior, but he had seen additional secret skills in her, apparently, reading between the lines. Ones that told him she was smart enough for advancing the needs of the Clan through espionage. She wondered if all of that had been just a lie to gain her confidence. Nevertheless, he had brought her in and taught her how to act undercover, use contractions, and collect information for the Watch. It wasn't unlike being a 'Mech pilot. You had to be incredibly observant of your enemies on the battlefield, and you had to know which of your weapons and assets could be pitted against theirs to exploit their weaknesses.

Seth had always likened their work to a chess match. And although he always beat her, they played a lot of chess. *"When you can beat me here, you'll be able to beat anyone out there,"* he had always told her.

"Star Colonel?" Star Captain Meridian Yung said from her console on the bridge.

"What?" Kenja said, snapping from her memories and back to the *Zephyr.*

"We have an incoming data stream." The captain looked down at her console. "There is a lot coming in."

Looking at the data stream, nothing Kenja saw filled her with confidence. She looked up at the captain. "The Fortress Wall is still active, Star Captain. Unless we want to spend two jump cycles using the Wolf bypass method, the ilClan opens and closes regular access on a strictly guarded schedule."

"What?" Yung said, incredulous at the possibility.

Clan Sea Fox had dedicated resources to discover how the Wall functioned, but had not been successful as of yet. Ships that had made the attempt to pass through it bounced off and reappeared who knew where. Some disappeared completely. Many that tried to make the jump were left twisted and mangled, nothing more than destroyed wreckage, with all of the occupants dead. Others left ghost ships, sailing through the stars for all eternity. Anyone who attempted to cross the threshold to Terra without an invitation died. Horribly. It was the latest reason the Clans had been stopped in their push for the homeworld of humanity...until Clans Wolf and Jade Falcon had somehow found a way through the Wall.

Kenja read the relevant section aloud. "'...we have determined the Fortress Wall is intact and active, and the ilClan remains in complete control of its use. Do not attempt an unauthorized jump to Terra without further instructions...' and goes on from there."

"So all we do is wait?"

"For the moment," Kenja said, spotting a second urgent message. This one was labeled SECRET, and she would have to go back to her quarters to access it. "And they received my report as well?"

"*Aff*, Star Colonel. It was set to beam as soon as a Sea Fox courier JumpShip arrived to carry the message."

Kenja transferred the second urgent message to her personal noteputer. "Excellent. I will be in my quarters reviewing the new information should you need me."

"Of course, Star Colonel."

Kenja navigated through the narrow corridors of the DropShip heading to her bunk, confident her report included everything they needed to know. Not being able to cross beyond the Fortress Wall at will complicated things, but she was the closest asset they had capable of completing the task at hand.

Settled into her room, floating over her bunk, Kenja pulled up the urgent message on her noteputer and input the passcodes to unscramble it.

It started with the same warnings and oaths all the secret communiques contained, then cut right to the devastating heart of the matter. The anonymous Sea Fox handler on the other side of the communication looked solemn, and she could tell even through the distortion that they weren't happy about what they had to report.

"Tucker Harwell is missing."

Kenja's brow furrowed. The Watch agent in the message cleared their throat and continued their report.

"He was last seen on 25 May at a hospital in Seattle. Rumors abound that he murdered Devlin Stone, or at least witnessed his murder. Pirate broadcasts are spreading these rumors, along with claims that ilKhan Alaric Ward or his saKhan, Chance Vickers, were the murderers. No one has seen him since that visit to the hospital. Included in this data packet are rumors filtering out through the local news and communications outlets that our assets in the Wolf Watch tell us are being blamed on Tucker Harwell since his mysterious absence. We have not been able to confirm any of these, and believe they could be potential propaganda. We are looking into that as well, but our resources are stretched thin. We believe it is unlikely Harwell is able to leave the Sol System, as passing through the Fortress

Wall remains as difficult and lethal as getting in unless you have ilClan clearance, so once we have a time window for you to get through the Wall, we will let you know."

Kenja took in a deep breath and tried not to let her frustration get the better of her.

"More importantly, we have discovered the Wolf Watch Commander, Spurlock Conners, is personally leading the ilClan's attempts to find Harwell and bring him into their custody. You will not be able to use the services of a Wolf navigator to secure an official entry window, as other Sea Fox ships have done, or Conners could be alerted to our interest in Harwell. Random Wolf spot checks of incoming ships are using Bertillon skeletal structure measurements to verify identities, making it risky to transfer you to an inbound courier ship. It is vital that you do not let Harwell fall into Wolf hands. He is the key to the future of the Sea Foxes. We will bring in others as we can, but your skill and proximity to Terra makes you our best bet in finding him and putting him to work for the good of the Inner Sphere. The future of Clan Sea Fox is in your capable hands, Kitefin. Seyla."

The communication ended and Kenja blinked. Stunned.

Things had just gotten a whole lot more complicated. Especially if the Wolf Watch was involved. She had tangled with Spurlock Conners once, years ago on Galatea. Perhaps a decade? Seth had been with her then, and it had been cordial until they'd discovered they were after the same asset.

She didn't want to tangle with him again. He had at least a decade of experience on her, and now he worked for the ilClan to boot. And his involvement almost guaranteed that Clan Wolf believed Tucker Harwell likely had the means to fix an HPG beyond the one he fixed on Wyatt a dozen years prior and they wanted him for it.

Kenja commed the bridge. "Star Captain Yung, do you copy?"

"*Aff,* Star Colonel."

"The situation has changed. Remain charging in hopes of regaining our second jump, in case we need to use the micro-jump maneuver. Until then, do not initiate a jump to Terra except on my command."

CHAPTER 8:
BETWEEN THE DEVIL
AND THE DEEP BLACK VOID

BROADSWORD-CLASS DROPSHIP *ZEPHYR*
KEID RECHARGE STATION
ZENITH JUMP POINT (ONE JUMP TO TERRA)
KEID
CAPELLAN CONFEDERATION
3 JUNE 3151

"We have our window to Terra," Star Captain Yung said over the comm, waking Kenja from troubled dreams of her dead mentor chiding her that she would never find Tucker Harwell.

She blinked, rubbing the sleep from her eyes. "Explain, Star Captain."

"In approximately four hours, a window will open for a Sea Fox courier to transit the Wall. Thanks to some quick work by Alpha Khanate, we are now registered as the expected courier vessel."

"Was there any more information about Tucker Harwell?"

"Unknown, Star Colonel. There is a lot of news and many reports that came through with the jump window message, and I have not had time to collate it. I thought it prudent to wake you first and let you know of our potential opportunity."

"I will be on the bridge ASAP."

The news from Terra included suspected problems at the Titan shipyards, Martian unrest, and other matters, but the biggest news came in the form of an after-action report from a battle on Ceres. Ceres was the dwarf planet in the asteroid belt between Mars and Jupiter. "Belt" was a misnomer as well. Everyone imagined an asteroid belt as just teeming with asteroids, thick as a heavy snowfall, but that wasn't really the case. There was so much space between each asteroid and dwarf planet it was like being in any other sector of space. Empty and vast.

Ceres was a Belter colony and, apparently, a Wolf DropShip attacked them. The Belters and the Terrans always had a tentative or shaky truce, and it surprised Kenja that the ilClan would be so immediately hostile to them. There seemed to be a naval element to the battle, as well as a rumored incursion into the habitat Proserpina. And there were reports that several JumpShips had departed from Ceres, meaning if he'd been on Ceres, Tucker Harwell could be anywhere in the Inner Sphere now.

The second biggest might have been the fact that the Jade Falcons had been absorbed into a unit being referred to as "the tip of the ilKhan's spear," whatever that meant. That told Kenja at least enough Falcons had survived to form a unit, but they were so beaten and battered they were prostrating themselves at Alaric Ward's feet. More than anything, that made her curious about what might be happening in the former Jade Falcon Occupation Zone. With the Hell's Horses, the Lyran Commonwealth, and the Rasalhague Dominion surrounding it, there would likely be a mad rush for power and planets.

There were more rumors, too. One, supposedly attributed to Tucker Harwell, that even accused Devlin Stone of being the mind and power behind Gray Monday. According to the story, Stone had wanted to sow chaos in the Inner Sphere, and saw the Blackout as the way to achieve this.

Standing on the bridge with less than twenty minutes to the jump window, Kenja had a decision to make: whether or not to make the jump through the Fortress Wall.

There was every chance Tucker Harwell had fled Terra and their information about the jump window was a counter-op. She had to filter all the information she'd been through and make a decision. Now.

Everyone on the ship and the mission depended on it.

As she agonized over her choice, a story spun out in Kenja's head. Allies of the Republic of the Sphere would be looking for ways out from behind the Fortress Wall, but they wouldn't have their own means to do it. And there was no love for Terra from the Belters. They might be in a position to be guilted, bribed, or convinced to help get out one person just to spite the ilKhan.

So Tucker gets to the Belters. But where does he go if he gets out? The Clans, with the exception of the Hell's Horses, were under Alaric's control, nominally or otherwise. Tucker wouldn't head anywhere the Clans might be. The Lyran Commonwealth felt unlikely, as they would have to cross the Wolf Empire or the Jade Falcon Occupation Zone to get there. The Free Worlds League was a grab bag of disorganization and disparate feelings. Julian Davion had showed up with new and highly advanced Republic equipment in 3149, which meant the Republic was helping the FedSuns. If Harwell was escaping with Republic agents, they would most likely head to FedSuns territory.

"One minute to our window, Star Colonel," the Star Captain.

Kenja's stomach twisted into a knot.

All she had were bad choices and incomplete information.

Nonetheless, a choice had to be made.

She could be wrong in either case. But which made more sense with the available information?

"Thirty seconds, Star Colonel."

Kenja exhaled.

What would Seth do?

"Cancel the order," she said firmly. "Our target isn't on Terra. Set a course toward FedSuns space. Send a message to Skate, Alpha, Fox, and Tiburon Khanate vessels to give us any information about strange or unusual JumpShips that could have originated from the Terran system."

"*Aff*, Star Colonel," the Star Captain said.

And Kenja felt relief lift like a weight from everyone on the bridge, despite the lack of gravity.

BROADSWORD-CLASS DROPSHIP *ZEPHYR*
ZENITH RECHARGE STATION
EPSILON INDI
CAPELLAN CONFEDERATION
  (EN ROUTE TO FEDERATED SUNS SPACE)
10 JUNE 3151

They spent seven tense days waiting as they recharged.

Seven long, tense days whiling the time away doing nothing but running on a treadmill aboard the *Bull Shark*. Literally. Figuratively. Even in her dreams, Kenja ran on the treadmill, trying to get away from danger. Away from the problems she faced. Away from that one single laser blast to *his* face.

Star Captain Meridian Yung, Star Commander Petrichor, and Kenja met each day on the bridge to pore over the new transmissions from passing Sea Fox couriers. Traffic volume in the region had escalated massively since Khan Hawker's Alpha Khanate had begun the process of relocating from Tukayyid to the Terran system, making humanity's point of origin its new hub for message traffic. "Day" on the ship was simulated with bright lights and UV in the beams. "Night" was simulated with red lights and the UV turned off. More often than not, the day/night cycle of any DropShip was kept in tandem with their target drop zone, but with no intended destination, the rhythm of their lights kept with the day/night cycle of Unity City. A subconscious reminder of where they were supposed to be and where, maybe, they should have been.

They would surely begin adjusting their cycle if they ever figured out where it was they were heading.

Their most promising lead came while they pored over the comings and goings of JumpShips with every scrap of information they received from every passing Sea Fox vessel over the last week.

"What about this?" Captain Yung said. "I have a *Merchant*-class JumpShip designated *Estrela Cadente* that arrived in the Towne system, a holding of the Draconis Combine."

"Significance?" Kenja asked.

"Significance is two-fold," Yung replied. "First, I ran a translation of the name on my noteputer and it is Portuguese for 'falling star.' One of the major Belter sects on Ceres spoke Portuguese when they first arrived, and the language survived there. The second is that it was in system for less than thirty minutes and jumped out immediately."

"So our Foxes no longer have eyes on it?"

"Correct."

"I think that may be the ship we're looking for. Send out a message to reach anything one jump away from Towne and let any Sea Fox assets keep an eye out for it. A recharging *Merchant*-class traveling under a Portuguese name, fitted with an L-F battery. At that point, it's no longer a merchant ship and more like a courier vessel designed for rapid transits. And detail the DropShip."

"I will see if I can get the DropShip details. 'Common' was the only description in the report, and even that seems odd, since it would have been close enough to see."

"Understood."

Kenja was grateful that all of this was happening in the direction of Hean, which was the Tiburon Khanate stronghold and her intended destination, leaving the surrounding areas thick with Sea Fox merchant traffic. Having that many eyes in space made all of this even remotely possible.

It wasn't another hour before Captain Yung informed them of another incoming transmission.

"Pass it along," Kenja ordered.

But before she did, Yung's eyes widened. "Oh, you are going to want to see this, Star Colonel."

Kenja waited anxiously for the packet to hit her noteputer screen and when it did, her eyes widened, too.

Their blink-and-you'll-miss-it-*Estrela Cadente* from Towne had showed up at Ankaa and stopped to recharge there. Ankaa was the closest Federated Suns planet to Terra, and in absolutely the right direction, if her hypothesis was correct. "If that really is our ship," she said, "our time to catch them is now. They're recharging. They'll have to spend the time to replenish their batteries there, no matter what. Unless they risk using their fusion engines to recharge their KF drive, which is dangerous and risky. And if they do that, we'll know they're in a large enough hurry that we can be reasonably certain it *could* be Tucker Harwell."

Petrichor cleared her throat. "They clearly have a lithium-fusion battery in that JumpShip, which is rare. Knowing that, we can trace them back to Terra with two double jumps, easy with a lithium-fusion battery. Or they could stick to dead systems, and it's still only four jumps. Do the math. That would mean they could have left Ceres fourteen days or so ago. That's only five days after Harwell's alleged disappearance."

Kenja liked the way that worked out. It felt very possible. "Six days is plenty of time to get from the Puget Sound to Ceres. But how do they escape the Fortress Wall? Did they have information on schedules? A secret way through?"

"Do we stay here then, Star Colonel? We have twenty hours until we have a full charge of our lithium-fusion battery. Say the word and we can be at Ankaa tomorrow."

Kenja chewed her bottom lip. "Give the order, Star Captain. If there is one thing we know for sure about where we are is that it's one place we know Tucker Harwell isn't. It costs us nothing to head to Ankaa. Unless we find information to convince us otherwise, give the order. We leave for Ankaa as soon as the batteries are charged."

"*Aff*, Star Colonel."

"We are going to have some questions for everyone on that JumpShip, whether they like it or not."

CHAPTER 9: FALLING STARS

BROADSWORD-CLASS DROPSHIP ZEPHYR
ZENITH RECHARGE STATION
ANKAA
FEDERATED SUNS
13 JUNE 3151

Kenja, dressed in her black tactical suit weighed down by heavy armor inserts and the gravity of the ship's thrust, stood alongside the insertion team at the *Zephyr*'s airlock, waiting for their strike against the *Estrela Cadente*.

She turned to those assembled near her. Petrichor stood to her right. Kenja had studied Petrichor's file, and knew the Star Commander was adept at unaugmented combat. She had won more than a few Trials of Grievance or Possession where she had been underestimated for her waifish build, but was able to subdue foes twice her size. It made her an asset here—especially since they weren't sure they might encounter on the other side of the door.

"We could be facing anything on that JumpShip," Kenja told the two dozen Sea Foxes assembled before her, drawn from the crews of both the *Zephyr* and the *Bull Shark*, all capable in zero-gee combat, according to their Star Captains. They would be formidable no matter what they might face. "We have tried to hail them and get what we need, but they have ignored our hails. Once we gain access, you are to create a path for Star Commander Petrichor and I to get to a terminal where we can extract the information we need. That is the highest priority. Our secondary objective is to subdue any member of the JumpShip's crew. If you are able to subdue someone for a brief interrogation, alert me immediately. Sonic stunners and needlers only, no lasers. This is one of the most important operations being undertaken by Clan Sea Fox. Our success or failure could determine the fate of our Clan for generations. This is our duty. This is our *rede*. I know you will all do your best. Now, into the breach we go."

The screeching metal sounds of docking shuddered through the deck plates. As the *Zephyr* cut thrust for the docking procedure, the gravity vanished quickly, and the insertion team began to float. Everyone got into formation along the walls, their feet aimed down toward the door that would take them into battle.

The muscles in Kenja's stomach tightened as she listened to the pressurization rings and connection tube hissing and clamping together. No one ever liked that unknown enemy on the other side of the gate, and all Kenja could think was she wasn't ready.

Last time she had faced the unknown, her partner and mentor died.

Was she ready?

She didn't know.

But ready or not, her piece was getting pushed onto the board, and she was going to capture that rook of information if it was the last thing she did.

"All right everyone," Kenja called out. "Feet toward the door, stunners aimed. Hands on the holds."

Petrichor pushed off and easily floated to the terminal next to the door. She would be opening it on Kenja's command. Everyone else held the bars at the edge of the room and held their stunners and needlers down toward the door.

"Ready, Star Colonel," Petrichor said after tapping at the screen.

Kenja inhaled deeply and held the breath at the top of her chest.

"Open the door."

When the door opened, she wasn't sure if she should be happy or alarmed that the sounds of instant battle did not fill her ears.

No one waited for them on the other side.

Merely silence.

The docking tube between the DropShip and the JumpShip ended with a closed door on the other end. Either Petrichor had been unable to open it, or it had been jammed closed.

A closed door was better than flechettes flying through the air. But it could be a gambit from the enemy ship to funnel them all into one spot before springing a trap.

"Get it open, Star Commander."

"Aff."

Petrichor descended into the docking tube by herself. Brave of her; she did it without complaint or concern. She went to work on the controls of the inner door that would grant them access to the ship.

Another minute ticked by—a minute they didn't have to spend. Every second they took here was another second Tucker Harwell would get further away. She knew she wouldn't find him on the JumpShip itself, but she would find out where they had come from and which DropShip he was on if they'd come from Terra. That was her best hope.

And if she didn't, she would just have to try something else. But this was the most promising lead they had.

"On your command, Star Colonel," Petrichor said, her voice reverberating through the access tube.

Kenja glanced down through her feet and saw Petrichor oriented flat against the closed door. It looked as though she were laying down, ten meters below her.

She nodded. "Do it."

The door below opened. Petrichor sliding to the side and waiting at the opening while the Clan troops pushed off one at a time, sailing through the connection tunnel and landing on the enemy ship. Kenja hovered at the top, waiting to go last. These Sea Foxes had obviously drilled on boarding actions recently. It was something the Clan trained for extensively— when you're primarily space-bound, you tend to train for any likely situation. It could mean life or death when the only thing separating you from survival was a few millimeters of super-metallic alloys on ships sometimes centuries old, held together with nothing more than spit and bailing wire.

Finally, Kenja pushed off and descended through the docking tube, joining Petrichor through the passage. She still hadn't heard any of the tell-tale signs of a battle. There were no shrieks of stunners going off, there were no shouts or screams of alarm. No sounds of wounded warriors. No nothing.

The Sea Foxes ahead of her had formed up in the corridor of the JumpShip. There was no opposition at all, so she and Petrichor floated toward the front of the docking collar.

To Kenja, the JumpShip was like stepping into a different world. This *Merchant*-class was older than anything she'd ever set foot on, but somehow more pristine. It looked brand new. Granted, she hadn't been on a whole lot of JumpShips in her life, but the ones she had been on were updated with Sea Fox technology and flourishes, each one personalized in decor and color by its Aimag.

She always felt a strange vertigo when walking into a new place she shouldn't be. It swirled inside her as she led the contingent of Sea Foxes through the strange, clean, and archaic JumpShip.

There were no telltale signs that could speak to her, no clues as to who its owners were. Not definitively, anyway. The guess they had come up with—that this was likely a Belter vessel—still held sway in her mind. Though she found no evidence to support it, she found no evidence to contradict her assertion either. And that meant the mission had yet to fail.

She led the Sea Foxes into a manual access shaft running up through the JumpShip, allowing her team access to the ship's decks en route to the bridge. The interior wall was polished metal, and cut the tube so it was more of a semicircle, leaving enough room below the plates for storage. Every few meters was a bulkhead seal and a door that could slide down from above. The walls were bare, except for metal rungs for crew to pull themselves along, leaving exposed wire and the inner-workings of the ship out for all to see. Although it might look like a mess to an untrained eye, closer inspection revealed an organization to all of it. A method that showed great care and advanced techniques.

"I do not like this," one of the Sea Foxes behind her murmured. Elroy. His voice was full of all the trepidation Kenja felt.

It was too quiet.

She had never heard of someone boarding a ship like this—at a recharge station, in deep space—and not having to fight off defenders. JumpShips were far too valuable to leave unattended, so Kenja doubted the ship was without a crew. But where were they?

"Stay alert," she said to the boarding party, as though they needed a reminder. "We need to find the computer terminal as fast as we can and get out of here."

She reached the end of the corridor and a faint hiss sounded; some sort of decompression. Kenja spun around fast enough to see the interior wall section near Elroy explosively break away , smashing him into the shaft's wall with a horrendous *crack*. His head split open, and blood globules floated from his face.

From behind the bulkhead, Kenja caught a glimpse of someone emerging dressed in black and blue-toned fabrics, with an ugly mechanical arm wielding a glimmering blade.

The blade rose into the air, ready to strike the Sea Fox that was in front of Elroy, but Kenja saw no more. The bulkhead door slammed shut between her and the fight.

Her eyes widened.

It *was* a trap.

She was isolated at the top of the corridor with Petrichor and a Sea Fox with a lantern jaw whose name patch declared him *Dragan*. He and Petrichor looked at her, expecting orders. And, with no one attacking them and no other apparent trap beneath the floor in their section of the corridor, Kenja had no other choice.

"They will have to fend for themselves. We proceed with the mission."

CHAPTER 10: STARFALL

MERCHANT-CLASS JUMPSHIP *ESTRELLA CADENTE*
ZENITH RECHARGE STATION
ANKAA
FEDERATED SUNS
13 JUNE 3151

Kenja, Petrichor, and Dragan hurried up along the access shaft, looking for other signs of additional traps and a terminal they could use to complete their mission. It was outside the bulkhead leading to the bridge that they found both.

With the door sealed ahead of them, it was a dead end.

Through her earpiece, Kenja heard battles raging on in the initial entry corridor and other parts of the JumpShip. At least a few of the Sea Foxes had been killed, though it sounded as though they had also killed at least some of their enemy. Based on the enemy's garb and their ability to fight in zero-gee, she was certain they were Belters—humans living in the asteroid belts of the Sol system. They all wore midnight blue pressure suits bordered in green piping, and most had signs of cyberwear, including bionic ear implants that could make them immune to stunners, and wielded nasty, personalized weapons. Some bore furred ears like animals. One had the prehensile tail of a cybernetic spider monkey. No two were alike. Kenja recalled the Belter market report had warned Sea Fox traders that Belter spacers on the fringes of their society had a penchant for extreme body modifications.

Even though they had walked into a boobytrap of a boarding action, Kenja felt some vindication that the working theory of where they'd come from and why was bearing out. Now all they needed were confirmations of their previous destinations and DropShip manifests, and Tucker Harwell would be closer to her grasp.

Two Belters cornered them against the pressurized door that led to the bridge and Kenja didn't like what that said for the potential of a pincer trap. One, a bald woman with elaborate designs tattooed across her scalp, aimed a low-g slugthrower at them. That made sense. Belters weren't afraid of the vacuum—they usually had modifications to survive it for brief periods. The other Belter, a burly man with blond-dyed boxer braids, cat ears, and a face criss-crossed with minute scars, sliced a vibroaxe through the air, intent on carving up Dragan.

"Petrichor," Kenja said between aiming her needler at their attackers and checking the door behind them. "Get to work on the console. We'll cover you."

Kenja positioned herself between the Belters and Petrichor working at the terminal while Dragan rotated in the air, grappling the Belter with the vibroaxe. Dragan reached out with both hands, interlocking fingers with one and gripping the Belter's wrist with the other to keep the vibroaxe away from his shoulder as it buzzed like an angry hornet ready to take a pound of flesh.

The Belter aiming at Kenja fired her slugthrower, and the bullet smashed into her tactical suit's armored plating. Her wind was taken, but she also felt a sting at her neck. She assumed she'd been tagged by a shard of something, but she couldn't react to the blossom of pain. It wasn't debilitating, and that's all that mattered.

Kenja fired back, but by then, the Belter had somersaulted to the left, kicked off the side wall and zoomed to the other side of the corridor. Kenja fired again, but missed when the Belter repeated the same move. Belters were reportedly deadly in zero-gee, and Kenja vowed not to underestimate them.

"You better hurry, Star Commander."

"I am going as fast as I can."

There was no telling how many more crew they could throw against the Foxes. They could have had as many as thirty Belters on board, each one armed with a knife, a gun, and a death wish. And there was no telling how many were stationed on the bridge. They could open that door behind her at any time and just cut their throats if they felt like it.

With a shout, Kenja kicked against the side of the corridor and launched herself to the side, then picked up speed by kicking the other wall and shot forward, intercepting the female Belter. They wrapped their arms around each other and spun, their momentum shifting as they smashed into one another. Kenja reached around the Belter's waist and withdrew her enemy's knife, then, as they spun together, tried to get a better grip on its hilt so she could end the fight quickly.

The Belter punched Kenja in the face, but loosened her firm grip to do so. The knuckles smashing across Kenja's brow stung, but she shrugged off the pain, intent on capitalizing on the Belter's mistake. She had eased up just enough for Kenja to not only get a better grip on the knife, but to get enough leverage to raise it. Her enemy's eyes widened when she realized her mistake, and Kenja plunged the tip of Belter's own blade into her back. The breath left the Belter's body with a desperate gasp, and it was over.

Wrenching herself free from the Belter, Kenja kicked the body toward the back wall. The woman's limp form hit the end of the corridor and bounced forward, the wall absorbing most of her momentum. Globules of blood dripped from the wound, spurting out around the knife's blade and hanging in the air like liquid red raindrops.

With that done, Kenja wiped her brow with her forearm and spun around to see if she could help Dragan. The fight between the remaining Belter and Dragan was brutal. Their hands were interlocked in a deadly game of mercy and they both tried to jockey into a position to kick the other. The vibroaxe had been discarded, spinning end over end from the velocity it had when it was lost. Each of them tried to spin the other into the direction of the vibrating axe blade.

Finding a purchase against the bulkhead, Kenja kicked off and shot like an arrow into the fray. The Belter had his back to her, and that was exactly what she wanted.

He gagged as Kenja wrapped an arm around his neck, then applied all the pressure she could leverage. He fought like an angry ghost bear, bucking back and forth, trying to free himself from her grip. It would have likely been easier for him if he were in a gravity environment, but in zero-gee, all he did was change the direction of their spin.

He bucked harder, desperate. She could only imagine what was running through his mind as his oxygen ran out and his lungs burned to taste the scrubbed air of the ship once more.

He bucked again and his body went slack in the air. Kenja waited a moment to ensure it wasn't a ruse before letting him go. Dragan pushed him away and Kenja rolled to let the Belter's limp body go sailing back toward his compatriot.

"Leave my ship," a voice said, tinny through the speakers of the old vessel. Their accent was thick, Portuguese-tinged Star League Standard English from one of the disparate groups of old Terra that had first colonized the belt, the Brazilians most likely, based on the study Kenja had done. "Or we'll vent the lot of you. I don't care if I lose my cargo, getting rid of you would be worth it."

That wasn't an idle threat. If all the captain's people were behind bulkheads and pressure seals, it would be easy to open an airlock and jettison the Sea Foxes. And it would be more effective than engaging the DropShip, given its lack of effective anti-ship weaponry.

"To whom am I speaking?" Kenja said, panting from the fights and zero-gee acrobatics.

"I'm the *capitão*," the woman said. "Radka Macedo of the *Estrella Cadente*, though you'll know that if you're poking around our systems. But I'm not here to parlay, I'm telling you to leave. Now. You've got to the count of ten to start debarking. I give you my name so on the off chance you've heard of me, you'll know I mean business."

"Petrichor?" Kenja said quietly.

"Still working on it."

"Get it done."

"Aff."

Kenja projected loudly again, knowing full well the captain would have been able to hear their every utterance anyway. They were likely speaking from behind the safety of the blast door separating them from the bridge. Right there. Just a few meters away, separated only by the thick ferro-steel door. "Can we not make a deal, Captain?"

"No."

"I will remind you that we offered terms of a fair Trial for the information we seek."

"And we ignored you, a Trial is beneath us. You're being ignored because we owe you nothing. Ten."

Kenja's heart pounded a little harder in her chest. "All we want to know is where you are from and what your cargo to Ankaa was."

"Nine," was the only response. The captain's voice was firm.

"It would be so much easier for all of us if you just talked to us."

"You kill members of my crew and you think I want to make it easy on you? Eight."

Kenja floated a little closer to the bulkhead, imagining what the Belter captain might look like on the other side of the pressurized door. And she committed the name Radka Macedo to memory, both so she could look this woman up later, but also to ensure that she included her in her reports.

"And you killed members of my crew. We could have done this peacefully," Kenja said, and meant it. They could have answered. They could have just said what they were doing.

"Oh, you Clanners just think you own the entire Inner Sphere now that you own Terra? Four. Don't test me."

Four? So much for a fair countdown. Radka knew she was the one in the power position.

"Petrichor?"

"Almost there, Star Colonel."

"Star Colonel?" Dragan said nervously, wanting to leave.

"Three," the captain said, their voice echoing through the corridors of the Zephyr.

"Get the information," Kenja chided Petrichor. Then, she pressed a finger to her ear to speak to any of the other members of the boarding party that were still alive. "Everyone, get back to the ship."

"Two."

"We need to leave, Star Commander." Kenja turned to Dragan and nodded to him. Reluctantly, he began the journey back to the *Zephyr.*

Petrichor's fingers flew over the controls. "Just one more second..."

"That's all we have."

"One," the captain said, her voice rattling through the whole of the ship.

"*Now,* Star Commander."

But Petrichor kept at it. Kenja grabbed her firmly by the shoulders and yanked her from the console and dragged her away, kicking off toward the T-junction and the Belter corpses they'd left there.

"We are leaving," Kenja said loudly. Both to Petrichor and the captain of the JumpShip.

As they kicked their way back to the connection tube as fast as they could, Kenja glowered at Petrichor, who could have killed them all. And until they reached the *Zephyr,* Kenja couldn't be sure she hadn't.

Petrichor's demeanor wasn't that of a failure, though. She was determined and her movements lithe in her silence.

Entering the last long hallway, the blast doors were wide open and the carnage was terrible. Half a dozen corpses floated freely. All Belters. One had its face bashed in. Another had its throat cut with its own vibroblade. One boasted an arm broken at an unnatural angle. Another had shrapnel sticking out of her face in a bloody mess.

Discarded plates of the flooring floated between them, creating an obstacle course for Kenja and Petrichor to get through. How many of their own dead would she find dragged back to their DropShip?

Kenja and Petrichor navigated through the labyrinth of death and metal, doing their best to avoid the floating pockets of blood and meat leftover from the battle. Once they entered the docking tube, the JumpShip's hatch shut behind them, but just barely, giving them something to kick off against so they could speed through the tube and find themselves in the remnants of what was left of the boarding party.

There were ten left alive of the two dozen that had accompanied them. The others were dead and had been dragged back aboard the *Zephyr*. They would require a burial ritual before they could proceed with the next phase of their mission.

Petrichor, seeing all the death, actually cried. Her tears floated away, but her eyes were still wet. Kenja reached out to the Star Commander and embraced her, knowing how hard these missions could be. Especially for those unaccustomed to them.

Petrichor held Kenja tightly and they both drew a deep breath.

And over the woman's shoulder, Kenja looked at those who had perished, and all she could see of them were the same faces of those she'd lost before.

All of their eyes were Seth's, and they all glowered at her for her failure so far.

CHAPTER 11:
ANSWERS THAT RAISE
MORE QUESTIONS

BROADSWORD-CLASS DROPSHIP ZEPHYR
ZENITH RECHARGE STATION
ANKAA
FEDERATED SUNS
14 JUNE 3151

The Burial-at-Sea Ritual had to be performed quickly. The Sea Foxes and Diamond Sharks—the two namesakes of their Clan, present and past—were both from the sea, and they used space as a proxy to remit the bodies of their fallen after they died in honorable combat. The genetic material of the deceased warriors was harvested as best as they could be in the field. Their codexes received a final update. In case the operation went well, their deeds could earn a line in *The Remembrance*, and their genetics could contribute to future generations. Perhaps they had not died in vain, and their sacrifice was vital in ushering in a new era of instant, neutral communication controlled by Clan Sea Fox.

It was a somber occasion, as funeral rites always were.

After everyone left, Kenja remained there, grateful she no longer had to look at the accusing faces of those she'd lost in the boarding action. "I promise," she told the lingering ghosts of those Sea Foxes, "I will see this through for you."

They would be more tally marks in the ledger she kept in her heart.

More losses.

But there was little she could do from there.

The Ritual felt awkward as well, knowing that those who had killed them were nearby, out there in their own JumpShip, within spitting distance—at least in astronomical terms—recharging their batteries, just like Kenja and the Sea Foxes were with their JumpShip. The temptation to use the *Zephyr's* guns to obliterate the Belter vessel was strong, but with the object of the boarding action in her possession, such an act of petty vengeance would be in line with Malvina Hazen's discredited Mongol doctrine, and unworthy of a Sea Fox warrior. She took some solace in the fact that the *Zephyr* had shot out the Belters' communications array, preventing them from transmitting any warnings.

After the ceremony was handled, the lower ranked crew hands began cleaning up the bloody mess that had been made in the docking corridor and airlock.

There was always someone else to clean up.

Kenja and Petrichor dove into the information gained at the terminal aboard the Belter's ship. It was fortunate Petrichor had managed to yank out her data stick as Kenja had yanked her away.

"According to this," she said, "the *Estrella Cadente* was definitely on Towne. And, with what I have been able to unscramble, they recharged at Lockdale, one of the likely previous arrival points we had deduced. I was able to trace them back to New Stevens. They have a lithium-fusion battery, which means they pulled that same blink-and-you-miss-it routine on New Stevens."

"So where did they originate?" Kenja said, wanting to cut to the chase.

Petrichor looked up, her mouth a grim line and her eyes sparkling with confidence. "According to this, they left the Terran system."

"When?"

"The second of June. Twelve days ago."

Kenja started doing the math in her head, adding in the time for a recharge. That was four jumps and a recharge, and now they were recharging again. All that math made perfect sense. They recharged at the spot that would keep them the most well-hidden and allow them to double-jump straight into FedSuns territory. And that actually gave them a little over a full week between Harwell getting nabbed and getting out of the Terran system. Completely possible. If Tucker Harwell had been whisked from Terra, the Belters could have done it.

"Any mention of passengers?"

Petrichor shook her head. "*Neg.* There is no manifest at all. There is evidence of a DropShip, the *Darin*, making for Ankaa, however."

"And do we know who is on that DropShip?"

"*Neg.*"

"When did it leave?"

"Four days ago. As soon as they arrived in-system. They still have twenty-one days until planetfall."

Kenja hated that they were so far behind. So much could happen in four days. A head start that long meant they could get to anywhere on the planet.

"And you're sure they went for Ankaa, and didn't hop onto another JumpShip to take them deeper into FedSuns territory?"

Petrichor shrugged. "This said they were heading to Ankaa, and Fox Khanate elements there are currently tracking them burning toward the planet."

Kenja chewed her lower lip.

They still had one thing working in their favor: the time to get from the zenith recharge station in the Ankaa system to the planet's surface on a 1G burn was just over twenty-five days. It was a long way away traveling by DropShip. Inordinately long. And when you look at a four-day head start compared to a twenty-five day voyage, it seemed like catching up to them could be possible, but would it be worth the physical punishment and the potential to lose more people? Kenja could conceivably push the DropShip to at least 1.5 gees and make up some of that time. They could land on the planet at roughly the same time.

But the biggest risk was all the lost time if Harwell *wasn't* on that DropShip. Even if they shaved the travel time down a few days in each direction, Kenja would lose a month and a half if this was nothing more than a snipe hunt. At this point, she felt like she was hot on Harwell's heels, but how cold would the trail go if she went all the way down there and was wrong?

All the evidence pointed to it being Harwell. Or at least it being a strong possibility.

But there was nothing definite. Nothing concrete. And she couldn't make any more big and conspicuous moves without being sure. Otherwise she'd jeopardize the whole mission.

Still, she had to make a choice.

Kenja was sick of making choices with incomplete information.

She wanted Tucker Harwell in her possession immediately. Without any more fuss. And she didn't want to take any more risks for him.

But, as much as she had a choice, she didn't feel like she did.

Kenja sighed. "I'll let the Star Captain know we will begin our burn to the surface. We'll split the difference here so we don't lose as much time. We will burn in at 1 gee and let them have their head start if it really is them, but we will alert the Sea Foxes on Ankaa to look out for the arrival of this DropShip. If they see anything suspicious or confirm the identity of Tucker Harwell, we continue to the planet. If they come up with nothing, we turn around and burn back to the JumpShip and look for our next lead."

"A well-conceived plan, Star Colonel."

Kenja forced a smile, doing her best to seem confident. But that wasn't how she felt at all. "Let's make it happen."

CHAPTER 12: HOT PURSUIT

BROADSWORD-CLASS DROPSHIP *ZEPHYR*
ANKAA SYSTEM (FIVE DAYS TO PLANETFALL AT 1G)
FEDERATED SUNS
5 JULY 3151

The Sea Foxes on Ankaa had been nothing but helpful, and Kenja was grateful the time delay in their communications was measured in hours rather than days or months. Between the JumpShip feeding them information from the recharge station and the Sea Foxes on the ground, Kenja felt like she now had a pretty complete idea of what she would find on the planet.

Other Sea Fox and independent JumpShips continued their usual arrivals and departures. The Belter JumpShip had departed as soon as its batteries were charged.

As far as Ankaa, Kenja took all the information the local Fox Khanate trading outpost could provide. For the most part, it was a small desert planet. Even as far away from their sun as they were, it was hammered on the inside edge of the habitable zone. Water was rare, sand was plentiful, and those who had colonized it were a hardy people.

The planet had been colonized some four hundred years after the first JumpShips had left Terra by Muslim pilgrims. They were looking for a refuge similar to their homes to find a place to live free from persecution. But the Star League—back in the times of antiquity—found precious metals they needed for the advancement of humanity. This was both a blessing and a curse for the people of Ankaa. Suddenly their quiet and sleepy religious oasis was a booming mining center, but their fortunes also changed. Here, the original colonists had worked out a profit sharing scheme for their planet's bounty. If it was a natural resource, and the world sold it, everyone on the planet received a share of whatever profits the goods sold for.

Because of this, Ankaa flourished, despite its deficiency of water. But that kept the population small. It wasn't as though people were eager to have too many kids if they couldn't afford to keep them from being thirsty.

There were other challenges to daily life on Ankaa as well. Toxic dust contaminating the atmosphere ensured that gill masks and goggles were common accessories whenever they ventured out of their sealed habitats, which would make finding Tucker Harwell even more difficult if he was, indeed, here. It would be difficult enough to ascertain his identity as it was. Kenja had been given biometric information and pictures of Harwell's appearance the last time he was seen and photographed, but with a disguise including a mask and goggles, finding him in the desert oasis of the capital city of Anqabad would prove difficult. It would prove even *more* difficult if he went to one of the more remote, outlying communities in the lee of the mountains, under the shadow of the blistering sun.

Despite the excitement of feeling like she was closer to her target, Kenja's routine only changed enough to account for the gravity provided by their thrust and the new adjustments to getting about the ship, since they were no longer in zero-gee.

If nothing else, it made her workout routine a lot more interesting.

7 JULY 3151
(THREE DAYS TO PLANETFALL AT 1G)

"Star Colonel, I have an incoming comm signal for you," Star Captain Yung's voice said through the speaker in Kenja's quarters.

"Patch it through."

"Aff."

It took a few seconds for the connection to be made, and then there was the distance delay, but finally, after almost ten minutes, the signal squelched and hissed and a voice could be heard. Diana, they said their name was, a Fox Khanate Star Commander and merchant stationed at the trading post in Ankaa's capital, Anqabad, where the Khanate had upgraded the primitive local airport into a full-service DropPort following the world's secession from the Republic. As a frontier planet at the edge of four different great powers, it made sense that it would be a hotbed of trade. Exactly the sort of place someone like Tucker Harwell would try to get lost in. "You requested that we monitor all interesting arrivals and anything out of the ordinary, and I think we have something along those lines."

"Proceed," Kenja said.

The twenty-minute delay left nothing but static for a while. And then her voice returned. "We have three individuals who arrived late last night at the spaceport via DropShip. We have not been able to make positive IDs of them, but they could be traveling under pseudonyms. Once we identified the DropShip, we tracked it all the way to the Anqabad spaceport. It is an *Aurora*-class DropShip traveling under the name *Darin*. There seems to be a crew, as usual, but these three individuals have left the ship."

"Have you put them under observation?"

Waiting for an answer was excruciating, but Kenja reminded herself that this was still preferable to months-long exchanges with no response from her handler. In fact, it had seemed odd that Carcharodon had not gotten a message to her since they'd reached Ankaa. For her part, she had been sure to keep updating them regularly. A skittish void swirled at the bottom of her stomach, wondering if she was merely sending those dispatches out into the aether.

"*Aff*, Star Colonel. We have been doing our best to keep up with them, but they have slipped our gaze twice at least in the last fifteen hours."

"Keep an eye on them and report anything else suspicious."

"*Aff*, Star Colonel," came her answer after a time. "But there is one more thing. We have a local broker who brings deals to us. He met with one of these three, a Reus Tremor, and then contacted us about brokering a barter trade, offering a shipment full of high quality industrial diamonds in exchange for other goods."

Kenja focused in on the ship's panel in front of her, the patterns of blinking lights helping her think. Why would they be bartering if it was Tucker Harwell? He was a scientist, not a merchant or trader. Then a possibility spun through her mind. If they were looking to book passage off Ankaa, they could be laundering their cargo for something a little bit more valuable to ensure their passage off-planet. Industrial diamonds wouldn't be of much value on Ankaa, but in the hands of the Sea Foxes, they could turn that into a princely sum.

"Delay the negotiations. I want to know more about them."

"*Aff*, Star Colonel," came her response after an interminable time.

"Send any other information that comes in about them," Kenja said, "And keep me updated on any other likely candidates."

"*Aff*, Star Colonel, over and out."

Kenja pressed the button on the comm system and brought up the captain. "Star Captain, I think our quarry may well be on Anjaa. Get us on-planet as fast as you can."

"*Aff*, Star Colonel," she replied.

A thrill coursed through Kenja's body. The hunt was on.

ANQABAD
ANKAA
FEDERATED SUNS
10 JULY 3151

Ankaa's lighter-than-Terra gravity was a welcome respite for Kenja's legs and muscles, but she had to adjust her movements to account for it as well. Being on a planet—any planet—after what felt like eons cooped up in the cramped *Broadsword*-class DropShip felt like heaven. To be honest, Kenja had felt helpless in the DropShip, unable to take any sort of action. Unable to affect any change. Unable to make her own luck.

But planet-side, things could now start happening.

The first place she went was to the Grand Bazaar, a massive marketplace and home to her Clan's bartering outpost and warehouses. Though the Anqabad elites preferred life in the filtered air of their underground climate dome, deep beneath the mountain, space constraints forced large numbers to live in individualized sealed structures on the surface, wearing filter masks whenever they went out into the streets. Kenja had wondered why the entire bazaar wasn't enclosed in a tent and pressurized with filtered air, but had been informed that the highly individualistic surface-dwelling Ankaai preferred to build and maintain their own habitat seals, rather than relying on communal infrastructure.

She left Star Commander Petrichor to collate more data about the planet and what the local Fox Khanate outpost had put together on the potential targets. Star Captain Meridian Yung stayed behind to resupply the DropShip with the Sea Foxes who greeted them at the spaceport. They were happy to help Tiburon Khanate with such a vital mission, and had received word to give Kenja and her cadre anything they might need to fulfill their mission. To that end, everyone was extra-crisp and careful in their salutes, speech, and actions.

The makeshift headquarters of Clan Sea Fox stood in a massive adobe structure at the edge of the marketplace. There were many local buildings in the same style lined up and down the bazaar's main avenue, but there were as many sealed tents and street merchants peddling their wares as well. She made only one detour on the way to the Sea Fox merchant headquarters in the marketplace, to one of the hermetically sealed food stalls amid the labyrinth.

Entering the protected eatery and removing her gill mask, the smell of local foods wafting through the air—blistering even in the low sun of morning—reminded Kenja how good life planet-side could be. The cost-effective nutrient paste reminded her of training and being a young shiv in a *sibko*, full of nostalgia, but that didn't mean it didn't have significant room for improvement.

Dressed in a white sarong with a red criss-cross pattern, as well as a keffiyeh fashioned to cover her gill mask, Kenja also wore round driving goggles with dark lenses to shade her eyes from the sun and keep the breeze from blowing dirt into them. As far as anyone could tell, she was completely local and anonymous, blending easily with the swaths of locals crowding the eatery and bazaar.

It felt refreshing to once again be dressed as a local, anonymous, and able to operate without everyone knowing who she was and what she stood for.

With a pocket full of local scrip supplied by the Foxes at the spaceport, she bought a dish the locals called tabbouleh. Wrapped in a leaf of lettuce, a rich and aromatic mix of vegetables, both locally hydroponically grown and imported, were chopped and mixed into a seasoning of oil, citrus, and salt. Pulling down her mask, she took a bite, and tried not to gasp as the tangy flavor exploded in her mouth, so much more savory and acidic than anything she'd eaten in months.

This was always the best part of planetside missions: the variety of food and the wonder of a new place. She yearned to see as many planets as she could and taste as much of their local cuisine as possible.

"Live it up while you can," Seth had told her on her first training mission. "You never know when your next good meal is going to come from, then before you know it, you're back to the paste."

She wished he could have been there to taste the tabbouleh.

He would have loved it.

Wolfing down the rest of the lettuce wrap, Kenja wiped her hands on the sanitowels they'd handed her and luxuriated in the scent and lingering tastes of the tabbouleh's seasonings before reaffixing her mask. Then she exited the stall and headed for the Sea Fox headquarters.

From the her vantage point in the market, it appeared deceptively small. A holographic sign flashed a blue Sea Fox logo, telling everyone the Clan was operating there. She couldn't see the sides up so close, so the building looked like nothing more than an adobe wall with a door in the middle of it, the airlock opening shaded by a cloth awning.

Stepping inside, Kenja realized it was much more luxuious than it appeared. Instantly, the cool air refreshed her, its smell was clean and comfortable, scrubbed and re-scrubbed to keep out the toxic dust and mollify the delicate sensitivities of the Sea Foxes, who were accustomed to pure air on their ships.

The building sprawled high and wide as it went back. Warehouses around and behind the marketplace allowed access to all the goods and storage space they could need to make large trades, but also hid a contingent of BattleMechs in case anything untoward happened.

They played up their reputation on planets like this that they were more merchants than warriors, but the other Clans and anyone with half a brain in their head realized that you could never separate the warrior from the Sea Fox.

The receiving room at the front of the building didn't match the sand-brick exterior. It was sleek and polished metal. The Clan logo hung over the reception table, just as it did on the outside, but this one was a physical cloth banner rather than a hologram. The rest of the room was fashionably appointed as a waiting area, filled with plush couches and chairs. An impressive rug with Sea Fox flourishes woven in the corners covered the floor. It was varying shades of blue, and Kenja felt like she was about to step onto the sea.

As soon as she walked in, the Sea Fox behind the reception desk without a rank pip—a member of the merchant civilian caste, according to their suit's violet shoulder color—directed Kenja to a meeting room deeper in the building.

Only a few minutes passed before Diana arrived to greet her. It was interesting to note how Diana's voice didn't matched her physical appearance. Diana had obsidian skin and her hair was cut into a short pixie bob, shaved on one side. Likely where, as some MechWarriors swore, the leads on her neurohelmet needed more contact. Somehow, her voice made her sound smaller than her frame, but she was a full foot taller than Kenja.

"Star Colonel," Diana said as soon as they entered the room. "It is a pleasure to receive you."

Kenja nodded. "Thank you, Star Commander. Your help has been most welcome. I trust you have an update?"

Diana offered a hand, directing Kenja to the soft couch behind her. "Please, take a seat."

Kenja did so, and Diana sat opposite her. "We've observed the *Darin* since it landed, and have been keeping eyes on it and its disembarking passengers. Per your request, we have delayed the negotiations, but also inquired about more information from them. They are negotiating with us through a local dealer named Amir Ibrahim. Ibrahim is well-known to us, and has been forthright in his dealings with us in the past, despite a history of anti-Clan sentiment."

"People always seem to hate the Clans until it is time to deal with them," Kenja said, smoothing the cloth of her sarong.

"*Aff,*" Diana said. "It is regrettable, but we find ways to make it work to our advantage. Ibrahim indicated that this mysterious trio of yours wished to remain anonymous, but they were interested in trading their diamonds for concentrated liquid fertilizer."

"Fertilizer?" Kenja's nose scrunched. That seemed an odd trade for something like industrial-grade precious gems.

"*Aff.* Concentrated liquid fertilizer has a significant market share in sectors such as Ankaa, where the hydroponic farms depend on it, and across many of the frontier planets with smaller populations on both sides of the Draconis Combine and Federated Suns border. Because it is politically agnostic, it is easy to trade to any of these worlds regardless of who their current House government may be."

"It can also be used as an explosive, yes?" Not being in her uniform, it made it a lot easier for Kenja to slip into using contractions and avoiding the standard Clanspeak, like the "*quiaff*" and "*quineg*" sentence-enders.

"*Aff,* a potent explosive component."

"What's the exchange rate on the trade? Is it a one-to-one situation?"

"Not normally on Ankaa," Diana said, confirming Kenja's suspicions. "It seems as though the Sea Foxes were chosen to be the benefactors of this deal because we see the value in the diamonds, and can export them to markets where they will fetch a much higher price than they would on the planet here. The fertilizer is an expensive commodity, and they will likely try to leverage a favorable term for it. The fertilizer would be much more valuable here than the diamonds to other parties."

"When is the negotiation going to take place?"

"It has been arranged to take place in just two days time. Stalled long enough to ensure you were able to make it planet-side and acclimate to Ankaa's gravity."

Kenja smiled. "I will say, after months in zero-gee, it's nice to put firm ground beneath my feet again."

Diana smiled. "We Foxes love the weightless life, but I think those of us who chose to be downsiders have all known that particular ache at one time or another."

They both nodded, understanding the shared feeling. "My biggest question is do you know where they are now?"

"*Aff,*" Diana said, raising Kenja's hopes. "They are holing up on their DropShip, which I have more information on as well. They registered with the port authority as the *Darin* out of Delavan, but our people embedded in the ground service crews pulled some serial numbers from landing gear repairs they identified as having been recently done."

"And?"

"We ran the numbers through our yard databases, and they matched fabrication serials from Titan or Furillo."

The news all hit Kenja at once. It added a complication to her guesses, but if there was anything easily fabricated, it would be registry numbers. And if she was dealing with professionals of the Republic, they would absolutely obscure themselves in this way to hide a target as high-profile as Tucker Harwell.

"Keep an eye on them at all times. Report their every movement. Allow the meeting to happen."

"I would ask if we should we complete the deal, but would also say we would prefer if we could. The contact bringing them to us is a valuable and powerful one here on Ankaa, and has so far been reluctant to deal with us at scale. Having this go through would be a boon to the Khanate as long as it does not interfere with your mission."

Kenja nodded. "Do what you must. Give them whatever terms they want. If my target is with them, the deal is the least of my worries."

She smiled. If all went well and she hadn't missed her guesses, Tucker Harwell would be in her grasp sooner than later.

CHAPTER 13: THE SET UP

GRAND BAZAAR
ANQABAD
ANKAA
FEDERATED SUNS
12 JULY 3151

Kenja waited in the early morning light, gold and bright, for the mysterious trio to arrive at Sea Fox Central at the back edge of Anqabad's Grand Bazaar. Already the marketplace was bustling, with people coming and going in every direction, all in similarly cut capes and robes, hidden behind gill masks and goggles, streaming through the market and making purchases.

The din of chattering customers filled Kenja's ears and she picked out whatever wisps of conversation she could discern. That was the best way to learn about a place. She learned about the big 'Mech race coming up in a few days, and that two young women named Farah and Yasmin had run off together against the wishes of their fathers, and it was quite the scandal. She also heard it was going to be a real scorcher today, if she hadn't already gotten that impression.

Kenja loved wearing her dark goggles, because she could look around at things and people that needed to be examined without drawing unnecessary attention to herself. And without seeming rude. In undercover situations, seeming rude when you hadn't intended to be was a cardinal sin in espionage because it made you stand out. Standing out made you memorable and memorable was the opposite of discreet.

To stay discreet, she picked a quiet corner to stand and watch from, a makeshift alley between two market stalls. She chose this spot for two reasons. The first was that it had a perfect view of the door to the Sea Fox office. The second was that the stall to her right overflowed with bits and bobs of recycled tech. Everything from old noteputers, circuit boards, and chips with wires dangling from them to large hunks of technological detritus Kenja couldn't even begin to recognize covered every surface. From Tucker Harwell's profile, it seemed like tables full of old junk would be too enticing to keep him away. If there was a stall in the entire market that would draw his eye and distract him enough for Kenja to try to confirm his identity, it'd be this one.

Sipping black tea from a sealed container via a tube-port in her gill mask, Kenja scanned the marketplace and the steps leading to the Sea Fox entrance, looking for any trace of those she sought.

"I don't see anything yet," Star Commander Petrichor said through the earpiece. She was on the other side of the marketplace. She had never done an operation like this, but Kenja didn't have any trouble explaining how to tail a mark. It would be easy for Petrichor, she had plenty of experience in a recon 'Mech. The principle was the same, and it would be easier to blend in on foot than it was to do so in a BattleMech, especially given how the locals were dressed.

"They're meeting the broker at 1030." Kenja looked down at her chronometer. "It's only 1020. It's early yet. Have you tried the tea?"

"*Neg,*" Petrichor said.

"Try it. And the tabbouleh. It'll help you blend in, too," she said. "Like my mentor always said, live it up while you can. You never know when the next good meal is coming before it's back to nutrient paste and recycled water."

Across the way, Kenja watched Petrichor struggle with the idea of leaving her vantage point, shuffling back and forth, but eventually she stepped into the next sealed stall for tea and tabbouleh while Kenja remained alert.

The average person would never understand how exhausting it was to remain vigilant for that long, keeping watch for one particular person. Kenja was good at it, but the prolonged heightened awareness tired her out after a while. The human brain, even ones created through Clan genetic programs, was programmed, and had evolved to skip over extra information. It's why holovids worked so well. When you pass your gaze from one spot to another, you blink and don't even realize it, skipping all the extraneous data in between, the same as a cut in one of the stories. To keep a continuous look out for targets, you had to fight actively to suppress that urge, you had to open your senses and force yourself to take in and catalog every detail.

She caught sight of a trio moving through the marketplace together, all dressed in the local style, careful to have their rebreathers covered with their keffiyehs. She was not convinced they were her trio, but kept an eye on them as they stopped at a market stall selling locally-made leather bags. The trio examined the bags, turned their noses up at them, then wandered deeper into the bazaar. Probably not the right targets.

Starting over again at the Sea Fox door on the far right side and pulling her view back toward the rest of the market, Kenja spotted another group of people, walking with purpose on her left. They were in the same aisle of stalls as her, and if they continued toward the Sea Fox door, would walk right past her.

It was a group of four people, not three, though. They were led by a tall, round man with tanned deeply tanned skin, dressed in fine garments—fine enough Kenja could tell that from several meters away. Behind him walked three people. Two looked very comfortable, even under their masks, and carried themselves as though they had combat training, but the third looked as though they'd never worn an outfit like this their entire life. They kept pulling at their garment, trying to settle it, and kept adjusting the mask.

They were nothing if not a sore thumb.

Kenja wondered if the fourth person might be their contact brokering the deal. Ibrahim, who didn't care for Clans but was happy to do business with them.

"I think I have them," Kenja said to Petrichor.

They stopped for a moment, glancing at something in a stall, then talking to one another. One of them, not the local, but the one Kenja had decided was probably the leader, stopped to check their chronometer. She did the same.

1026.

They still had time.

As they chatted, the uncomfortable one in the back kept going. Was he walking with purpose? Or simply oblivious?

Kenja hated how much of a target's body language was opaque when they were wearing dark masks and goggles.

Sizing up the stray mark, Kenja decided it was a man underneath the robes, based on his gait and bearing, a wiry and thin man. The robes added more bulk than he seemed used to and he kept shifting them from one side to another, clearly not comfortable at all. He stopped in front of the recycletech stall and stepped in, going through tubs of parts and fiddling with them. Kenja looked him up and down, wondering if she'd made the right educated guess, then looked back to the rest of the party. The other three were so deep in their conversation they hadn't noticed their companion had left.

He wasn't wearing gloves, so Kenja could see his hands weren't working hands. They didn't have the calluses that defined the life of a MechWarrior gripping control sticks, and they certainly didn't have the calluses of someone from the laborer caste. They moved in the most operatic way, precise and elegant as he picked through the cast-off technology and found one circuit board that interested him. He raised it to his face, rubbed the serial number with his thumb, then held it up in the sunlight to better examine it.

Kenja glanced at the rest of them. They were still talking intensely about something.

"Petrichor," she said quietly, "can you hear the others?"

"*Neg*, trying to get in closer."

"Good."

She glanced back at her chronometer. They had only three minutes left before they were late.

That is, if it was actually them.

Stepping through the side door of the translucent stall, she figured it was time to make her move.

The man had taken the circuit board and another piece of tech was connecting them together by wires.

"What ya have there?" Kenja said in a passable replication of the local accent.

"This is really interesting," he replied, not looking up at her. Maybe he thought she was working the stall itself? Kenja was standing off to the side, rather than right behind the register, but the proprietor was out of sight, ducked down behind the counter stocking something. "It looks like old ComStar components."

Grateful her goggles hid her widening eyes, Kenja's heart beat faster. *Is* this *Tucker Harwell?* "Ah," she said, focusing on his hands again. He added another component to the bit of tech he was cobbling together. She imagined one of the components was a battery because as soon as he connected it to the circuit board and the cylindrical piece, red LEDs lit up across the board.

Even through the mask, she could see him smiling.

As she coughed, ready to ask him something else, a rough hand grabbed him by the arm. The leader. They were slightly shorter than the others and leaned in close to the guy's ear and said something Kenja didn't catch.

He turned to them and said, "I need this, though. It'll be helpful."

"Later," they responded, and pushed him forward beyond the stall.

Reluctantly, he dropped the components back on the table, letting them whirr and blink now they'd been activated.

Kenja watched all four of them walk to the front door of Sea Fox central together.

"They are definitely our marks," she told Petrichor.

"I got close enough to hear and they spoke of the negotiations, but they did not mention names. Was yours Harwell?"

"Still unsure. If it is, we might have a problem."

"What's that?"

"The leader is combat trained. You can tell by how she moves. She might be an obstacle."

"And the others?"

"One was the local contact. The fourth one had a military gait, too. Which would track if they're with Harwell, they'd be bodyguards who have gotten him this far. Who they are aligned with, though, is still a mystery."

"Next move?"

"The Sea Foxes here do not want to blow their relationship with Ibrahim, so we let them negotiate the deal as planned. The Star Commander brokering the deal for the Sea Foxes will give them what they want and set the time for the actual exchange. If it is them, we make our move at the hand-off to give them plausible deniability. Now we just need to make the positive ID." Kenja looked back down at the lit up tech he'd said was from ComStar and smiled. "I have an idea for that, but I'm going to need some help."

CHAPTER 14: THE BAIT

GRAND BAZAAR
ANQABAD
ANKAA
FEDERATED SUNS
12 JULY 3151

Kenja watched the deal meeting from a hidden security room inside the Sea Fox headquarters. Ibrahim had no problem taking the lead in the negotiations, or taking his mask and goggles off, making it easy for her to size them all up. He had a broad, easy smile and wore his facial hair in a pointed Van Dyke.

The woman—who she'd pegged as the leader of the other two—wore her auburn hair short, coiffed to one side. The name she gave was Genevie Wyatt, and the more Kenja watched her, the more she thought the woman carried herself not like infantry, but like a MechWarrior.

The other man had scruff on his face, tan skin, and a smug smile. He was the one who'd contacted Ibrahim to set up the deal, and went by Reus Tremor.

The one she assumed to be Tucker Harwell was the tech nerd. His name was given as Drake DeBurke, and he looked as vanilla and nondescript as could be. "DeBurke" rang a bell, and sitting there watching the meeting, it raised a red flag for Kenja, but she didn't quite know for what. He had black hair, dark circles under his eyes, and stubble. He didn't quite match any of the holophotos they had of Harwell, but they were all also a decade out of date.

She needed to talk to him.

See if she could coax it out of him.

While they made the final arrangements, Kenja retreated quickly back to the junktech shop. There, she paid the proprietor handsomely to take a long break, leaving the shop in her care, and picked up the bit of tech Harwell had gotten working and examined it. There was a circuit board and a rectangular power control circuit box he'd clipped on top of it. The wires leading out of it were twisted into the other wires at the edge of the board. Attached to the bottom was a battery housing the size of her thumb clipped on the back, powering the whole thing.

She marveled that anyone could stand at a junk stall in a market on one of the most backwater planets in FedSuns territory and cobble together something that worked in a minute or two. She didn't know what it was, or what it was supposed to do, so she couldn't quite tell if it would work, but it lit up, so it was doing *something*.

He wasn't lying about it being ComStar tech, either. The copper-colored circuit board was stamped with the double-oval-and-tail logo of ComStar. And when she examined it carefully, the circuit box was etched with the same logo. This one was more subtle, forcing her to feel its minute contours with her fingertips to even tell it was there. The battery clip was the only thing that didn't appear to be ComStar tech; he had apparently cobbled it together out of other scraps.

It was astounding to her. Even if this man *wasn't* Tucker Harwell—and she was growing more certain that he was by the minute—there might be every reason to take him along, regardless.

"They are leaving now," Star Commander Diana said, her voice piping through Kenja's earpiece.

"Copy that," she replied. "Eyes open, Suckerfish."

"Eyes are open, Kitefin." That was Petrichor responding. Kenja needed to give her a codename in case their comms were monitored, and Suckerfish felt appropriate. The Watch used breeds of sharks for codenames, and a suckerfish was a ray-finned fish from Terra that looked a lot like a shark, even though it wasn't one. Seemed to fit Petrichor to perfection. Maybe one day she'd swim with the sea foxes.

"Ibrahim is heading your way," Kenja told Suckerfish.

"Got him. Orders?"

"Follow them. I think DeBurke will head to me, and I have one more thing to try to confirm his identity as Harwell. Get here and I'll give you a signal if I need a distraction."

"Aff."

The whole group masked up and set out into the market place, but the tech enthusiast grabbed the handler's sleeve and pulled her back in Kenja's direction. There was some a brief discussion among them, and then they all followed him.

They all started heading to Kenja.

She smiled.

He really *was* dragging them back to the junk dealer.

Kenja glanced down at the bits and bobs "Drake" had cobbled together before the meeting, and wondered if they held some secret to fixing the HPG network, as much as Tucker Harwell did. She doubted it, though. How could a few random bits of ancient tech in a junk shop on Ankaa be the key to fixing something so intricate as the HPG network?

"Drake DeBurke" came in through the seal, pulled up his goggles, and walked to the front table, where he lifted up a cracked noteputer and looked under it. Then lifted a different component and looked under there, too. "It was here before we went in," he said, looking around.

Wyatt had come in behind him, her voice sharp and low. "If it's not here, it's not here."

As the other two came in behind them, Kenja's mind raced through possibilities of who this woman really was and what she was doing, but she couldn't spend her time worrying about it. She had to make this happen or it was never going to.

"Suckerfish," Kenja said quietly enough for the microphone to pick up. "Now."

"Aff," Petrichor said and went into action.

Tremor and Ibrahim made small talk at the back while DeBurke and Wyatt picked through the bin at the front as Petrichor came into now-crowded the stall and approached the woman. When Wyatt glanced toward Kenja, Petrichor tapped her on the shoulder. In a local accent, the Star Commander tried enticing her with some bit of information, even going so far as to call her Genevie Wyatt.

With Wyatt distracted, Kenja had a little more wiggle room, since Ibrahim and Tremor were deep in a conversation about BattleMechs.

She stepped forward as DeBurke continued his search, adopting that same local accent. "Lookin' for this?"

She presented the scrap of circuit board and technology to him from behind her back and his eyes lit up as he saw it, still blinking, just as he'd left it. His eyes were a deep, dark brown.

"Yes," he replied.

"I have to admit, I'm not sure what it does. I saw you working on it and thought it was interesting."

"It's not much...but it is definitely interesting."

"Old ComStar, you said?"

"Yeah." He reached out for the piece, and Kenja handed it to him. "You see, this is a really old controller board for a mobile comms unit. This is a circuit box and inside is a piece of a hard drive, probably a hundred years old, at least, and I wonder what might be on it...if it hasn't been wiped a dozen times."

"Is this your specialty?"

DeBurke froze. As though his mind were processing ways to not give away any more information. He *had* to be Harwell.

Kenja's eyes flicked over to Petrichor and Genevie the MechWarrior acting as gadfly and bodyguard to the tech nerd and found them still preoccupied with each other. Petrichor had pulled her away slowly so maybe she didn't even realize how far away they had gotten from the junk stand.

The tech nerd coughed nervously. "I mean, it's really just a hobby of mine."

"Does it pay well? Your hobby?" Kenja asked.

"It can."

"Where are you from?"

"All over," the man said. "I was born on Terra and spent some time there, but I've been all over the Inner Sphere."

"I see." Nothing he said contradicted anything in Harwell's file. "And you have an interest in ComStar tech?"

"Like I said, it's a hobby."

"I ask because I might be able to procure some more ComStar tech for you to play around with. Just for your hobby, you know."

His eyes brightened. "I would like that, actually."

"Are you from an old ComStar family, then? No one really talks about ComStar anymore, aside from how they failed, letting the Word of Blake take over and then there was Gray Monday... So many people died because of that..."

The man's eyes grew distant, as though he were lost in a faraway memory.

Kenja pushed harder, hoping to draw him out more. "It would be difficult watching families torn up on different sides of that conflict."

His eyes darted back and forth, and then he looked back up to Kenja. "What do you want for this?"

"What do you think is fair?"

"How about three hundred?"

"I can't go lower than four."

"Three-twenty-five?"

Kenja pretended to think for a moment. "It's a deal, Tucker."

"Great." He didn't even bat an eye. Did he not notice? He just went for the leather pouch strapped to his belt.

The mask kept her shocked expression hidden. *Are we wrong?* And a good thing, too.

The handler stepped over to Tucker, Petrichor had finally lost her attention. "We need to be going now, Drake."

"Just a second, I'm buying this." Tucker turned back to Kenja. "Are D-Bills all right?"

"Of course." Kenja nodded and exchanged the tech for the money and counted it as part of the ruse. "And come back if you want me to dig up any more."

"I will. Thank you," Tucker said, lifting the circuit board and hard drive up a little, almost as if he was saluting her.

"Trust it's my pleasure," Kenja said, not liking the feel of the local accent on her tongue.

And like that, Tucker Harwell and the rest of them walked out through the protective seal and away from the stall with his protector.

Petrichor stepped up to the spot where Tucker was standing and leaned in toward Kenja to whisper, even though she kept her eyes on the woman and Tucker. "Did you do it?"

"The tracking device is secure. And we know where they're going to be."

"And you are sure it's him?"

Kenja smiled. "Oh, it's him alright. We need to get everything ready for the extraction. I would have taken him right now if there hadn't been four of them in broad daylight."

"And if they take off before then?"

"That's what the tracking device is for."

CHAPTER 15: STORM'S EYE VIEW

The brilliant white sun brightened as it hung high in the east, reaching its apex before beginning its slow its descent for the day. After a few more hours, the sky would transform from pale blues and whites to golden hues, then fade into the darkened gray of dusk. Not long after that, night would fall completely, and the day of Kenja's victory would pass into days of her working to maintain it.

She was feeling overconfident—and she needed to temper that impulse.

Keeping an eye on "DeBurke"—thanks to the device she'd installed on the ComStar board—Kenja was surprised to see he had stayed on the *Aurora*-class DropShip, the *Darin*, the last ten hours. It seemed they were keeping him locked up and out of sight as much as they could. Or at least the woman called Genevie Wyatt was.

As she monitored his activity, she realized why the name he was using had set off her hackles. A young protege of Kearny and Fuchida named *Cassie* DeBurke had invented the hyperpulse generator in the 27th century.

Kenja felt confident that *this* DeBurke *was* her target, despite her gut telling her she wouldn't have been able to find Tucker in the first place. The odds were too great. Finding one missing person on one planet was hard enough—but one missing person in the vast space of the Inner Sphere? It felt impossible. She heard Seth's voice coming from the small place at the back of her head. "The difficult thing will be holding on to it. The thing you have to remember in this line of work is that if we've been assigned to take something, you can be damn certain someone else wants it. Badly. And they'll kill you for it, sure as anything."

His voice in her mind picked at the scab of her grief, but it had been an important rule they'd learned over and over and over again through the years.

The spaceport offered plenty of opportunities for things to go wrong. She would have much preferred just nabbing him in the bazaar earlier, but there were too many of his allies around to make it discreet. His handlers were doing a good job of keeping him in public spaces. And when they went back to their DropShip, they had kept him inside the rest of the time.

The spaceport where itself was attached to the Grand Bazaar, which made it convenient for all the trading in Anqabad. It was no wonder why the Fox Khanate had chosen the planet and their headquarters here as an important post.

Glancing through a readout of ships currently docked here, Kenja scrolled through a mishmash from all over the Inner Sphere. There were Sea Fox DropShips, all much larger than the one Kenja and her small cadre were using. They were a lot more interested in advertising their Clan, too, with Fox Khanate logos emblazoned across the hulls and the paint matching their Aimag's color scheme. Some of the older DropShips littering the port were also colored in the schemes of their units or homelands. There were quite a few ships from the Federated Suns, too, which was natural, since this was their territory. Their sword-and-starburst logo felt more fitting on a sun-kissed desert planet like Ankaa than it did on some other FedSun planets Kenja had visited in the line of duty.

The DropShip Harwell and his cadre traveled in was nondescript, in keeping with the low profile they meant to keep. It was painted a flat black and flecked with white splotches. In space, it would look just like a blob on naked visual. On the ground, it was just one of dozens of DropShips at the spaceport.

The cargo transfer would take place at the *Darin*'s docking berth. The Sea Foxes would use WorkMechs to make the switch, and that would be that. There was no money changing hands according to Diana, who was working with Ibrahim on the deal. How he would get his cut, Kenja didn't know, but she also didn't care.

Other BattleMechs littered the landscape of the spaceport, too, even more than the DropShips. Most were light and medium-sized 'Mechs, and they marched along to the beats of a dozen different drums, each with their own task.

Kenja and Petrichor watched the elaborate dance below from the roof of the spaceport's main building, using binocs to watch the deal going down. There were other Sea Fox units keeping tabs on everything, both in 'Mechs and on foot. A few *Tiburon*s and *Hammerhead*s in Fox Khanate colors patrolled the spaceport, sending telemetry to each other and the other Sea Foxes, including to Kenja's noteputer.

She planned on watching as the trade began, ensuring there were no traps or angles she missed, and then she and Petrichor would sneak down while everyone else was occupied with the trade. Then they would approach silently, stun and grab the man she believed to be Harwell and he would simply disappear as mysteriously from Ankaa as he had on Terra.

She hoped it would be easy enough.

WorkMechs arrived to cart out cargo containers from the *Darin*'s bay while other WorkMechs arrived with containers full of liquid fertilizer.

Just as Kenja felt comfortable enough to nod, ready to give the order to begin their rendition of Tucker Harwell, a fiery explosion rocked the trading zone. It was the sound she heard first ringing in her ears, missiles crashing into a target, exploding into heat close enough for her to feel.

Seth's words echoed in her head; they really were going to try to take this from her.

Instinctively, she looked toward the explosion to find a 65-ton *Scourge*, an ugly green-and-copper 'Mech with weapons for arms, firing its Gauss rifle at the WorkMechs unloading crates full of diamonds from the *Darin*. It was flanked by a trio of light 'Mechs—two *Locust*s and a *Fire Moth*—all painted similarly, all pouring missiles and flashing lasers into any passing 'Mech."

"Is this part of the plan?" Petrichor asked.

"Of course not!"

"Who else could have tracked them here and gotten here this fast?"

"No one should be this close on our heels and know about the exchange." Furious, Kenja looked back down to the site of the exchange with her binocs. The woman Kenja pegged as Tucker's handler had stripped off her robe to reveal a cooling suit beneath her clothes. She was shouting orders and pointing to the ramp of the *Darin*. She and the other bodyguard, along with the most important target, Tucker Harwell, ran for the DropShip. They were going to secure him on their DropShip, which would make their extraction all the more difficult. And a DropShip loaded with concentrated fertilizer to boot.

That was all she needed.

Her mark would be incinerated before she could take possession of him and save the Inner Sphere from itself.

"We need support now," Kenja said into her wrist comm. "Star Commander Diana, have your 'Mechs engage and have your infantry, move in. Extract Tucker Harwell by any means necessary and take him alive. Do not allow that DropShip leave until you have him."

"*Aff*," Diana replied.

The Sea Foxes turned their *Tiburon*s and *Hammerhead*s to attack the invaders. Other elements followed, igniting a conflagration of war at the once peaceful spaceport of Anqabad.

There was a scramble of warriors beneath Kenja, all in dark blue Sea Fox infantry fatigues, running for the DropShip, but as she glanced up, a team of infantry dressed in colors to match the attacking 'Mechs raced for the same target.

Another interested party, indeed.

Kenja looked over the horizon of the spaceport and saw another Inner Sphere lance of 'Mechs, tearing up everything in its path on the other side, led by an *Exhumer*—a wide, bulky

'Mech for only being 55-tons, with claws for hands and a broad, angular torso.

Before the invading infantry could storm the DropShip, two 'Mechs burst out from behind the *Darin*. Painted matte black and bearing no insignia, a *Grand Summoner* and a *Black Knight* marched forward from the DropShip's shadow, guns blazing at the infantry.

"We need to get down there. Now," Kenja told Petrichor.

"*Aff.*"

But as they rose to leave, Kenja felt the concussive force of a blast behind her, stray missiles from the fight impacting the roof and exploding.

She spun on her heels to see a trio of soldiers in fatigues the same as the invading force climbing up the side of the roof coming their way. The soldier in front hadn't noticed them yet, giving them a split second to make a decision before she and Petrichor had three laser rifles pointed at them, all aimed to kill.

CHAPTER 16: MAELSTROM

ANQABAD SPACEPORT
ANQABAD
ANKAA
FEDERATED SUNS
12 JULY 3151

Kenja hurled herself at the soldier up front, just getting her feet on the roof. The woman reacted faster than she expected, grabbing her wrist and twisting it around. Kenja's momentum brought them forward, however, and the two women grappled each other to the ground.

As sure as Kerensky founded the Clans, she was going to leave Ankaa with Tucker Harwell in her possession, even if it cost her everything.

Kenja rolled with the fall, using their combined momentum to throw her to the ground and lock the enemy in a tight hold with her legs. The other two soldiers scrambled to reach the top of the roof. Petrichor, to her credit, lunged at the next one to make it up to the ladder, pulling him down to the ground and grabbing for his laser rifle.

"We need one alive for questioning!" Kenja said, as much to remind herself as to let Petrichor know what the stakes were. And, to be honest, it was a cold thing to say about three work-a-day soldiers who were just doing their job. That level of confidence was just going to burrow into their darkest fears and, with any luck, get them to make mistakes.

Kenja twisted her grip, cracking the soldier's wrist, then took her sidearm and raised it to the third soldier, just scrambling to crest the top of the roof, firing the laser pistol. The laser burned into the man's face, melting the gill mask into his skin and charring the flesh between his eyes as it cooked his brain.

As he fell from the ladder, Kenja turned her attention back to the soldier she had gripped in her legs and put the laser pistol to her head.

Petrichor struggled with the other soldier, they kicked and swatted at each other over the laser rifle, but lost it in the fight. It clattered to the roof as the two continued wrestling with each other.

"Tell your man to stand down or we are going to have a problem," Kenja said through gritted teeth. The unit patch on the woman's uniform wasn't one she recognized. It looked like a data stick with the covering missing so as to expose the circuit.

"Go to hell," the woman said.

Kenja sighed. Pain and torture didn't work when it came to interrogations. But she *wanted* to threaten this woman and hurt her. She was standing in the way.

"We can make a deal," she said. "I'll let you go if you tell me who you're working for."

"I can't trust that. Besides, mercs don't welch on contracts."

"Your other option is I kill you."

"You'll kill me anyway."

"I'm Clan. I will happily count this scuffle as a Trial of Possession for the information on your employer. You yield, you give it to me, and you walk away from here alive, which is more than I can say for most of your comrades."

The soldier looked toward the barrel of the gun aimed right at her, ready to kill her. Kenja doubted she could feel it through the heavy infantry helmet she wore, but she knew it was there. And that was enough. Kenja had already killed one of their number and Petrichor had the other locked tight in a leg grip, his pained grimace telling just how effective the submissive hold was. There was no chance.

"I don't know who hired us. I'm just a grunt."

"Why don't we start with more simplicity? *Who* are you?"

"We're the Circuit Breakers. We've been on Ankaa looking for a contract. Got one. Came in from space. A JumpShip. I don't know more than that. I swear."

"What's your objective?"

"My team was assigned to handle lookouts. The job was to disrupt the marketplace and snatch a DropShip full of folks. I don't know who they are, that wasn't our part of the assignment, just take the DropShip."

Rage filled Kenja, overflowing like a magma river, and she wanted to just pull the trigger, but a deal was a deal. "Okay, I'll let you go. Go get your wrist looked at and stay out of the rest of the fight."

"Fine," she said, pissed. She didn't like it any better than Kenja would have, but it was either this or death, and no one wanted to die for no reason. Kenja couldn't imagine ever being a lucrewarrior, either, just fighting for a paycheck. Were things really that bad in the Inner Sphere?

Glancing over, she saw Petrichor had choked her opponent out completely. Effective and usually non-lethal. Loosening the grip of her own legs, Kenja released the woman's broken wrist and backed up, rising to her feet again. The merc lay there for a moment, catching her breath.

There was a door that led to a stairway, the same one Kenja and Petrichor had taken to get on the roof. It flew open wide, and more Circuit Breaker infantry charged through it, blocking off that avenue of escape.

"Damn it," Kenja growled. There were at least four of them, laser rifles at the ready. She'd made a deal to let this one go, but there was no way she could fight the rest of them.

"Suckerfish, we're out!" she called, then bolted into action. Firing at the oncoming infantry with the stolen laser pistol, joined by Petrichor with her stolen laser rifle, they forced them to pull back and duck for cover, giving them enough time to sprint in the other direction. Laser blasts fired wildly from behind the door flew by them, coming dangerously close to ending her.

Kenja had plotted a potential escape route hoping she wouldn't have to use it, but here she was, pumping her legs as fast as she could. Kenja ran for the back end of the building, opposite the stairs and the Circuit Breakers she kept exchanging laser fire with from behind their cover.

Petrichor arrived at her side just as she leaped over the lip of the roof and onto the first layer of cloth awnings where the building abutted the marketplace. She bounced on the fabric and rolled quickly, both to hit the next level down and another awning, but also to get out of Petrichor's way.

The clever Star Commander followed, mimicking Kenja's fall and landing position perfectly. When jumping onto an awning, one never wanted to land head or feet first, they wanted to land with as much of their body as possible lying flat. Heading down with a pointy end, head or feet, was a good way to rip right through the fabric and plummet to an ignominious death.

Two more bouncing awnings later and Kenja dropped down into the marketplace, landing on a crate of local fruit, hard like coconuts, hardy enough to grow in the desert. It felt like landing in a bed of bowling balls.

Kenja groaned and got to her feet, finding Petrichor just a few seconds behind. Finding cover behind an awning, hoping to avoid being spotted by the infantry they just left, she raised her wrist comm to her mask. "This is Kitefin, we had to vacate our lookout in the attack and are in the bazaar. There are at least two lances tearing up the spaceport. I cannot make it to my DropShip on foot. Where can I get a 'Mech?"

Diana responded with a shout, as though she were already commanding others and in the middle of a fight for her own life. "We are defending the spaceport, but get to our trading post. There are spare 'Mechs in the bay you can use. We would not turn down the help."

"*Aff,*" Kenja said and started running as soon as Petrichor was firmly planted on the ground behind her.

"We need to get to the trading post," Kenja told Petrichor.

"I...heard," she replied, out of breath and trying to keep up.

And as if things couldn't get worse, more Circuit Breakers' infantry started pouring into the Bazaar's grand entrance, likely looking for Kenja and Petrichor. The infantry were at a full run, making Kenja suspect it was part of the same group trying to capture them on the roof.

"Nope," she said, shifting direction. "Not that way."

But between them and the trading post, spare 'Mechs, and salvation, was a single Circuit Breaker 'Mech. A 20-ton *Wasp* in Circuit Breaker colors stood between them and the door to the Sea Fox warehouse.

"Damn it!" she said again.

No time to think.

She just had to act.

"We are not seriously..." Petrichor trailed off and shook her head.

"Yes. Follow me."

This *Wasp* had a laser and some SRMs, it wasn't equipped with machine guns or flamethrowers or other anti-personnel weapons. It was designed to fight other light 'Mechs and that was about it. Maybe the pilot fire at them, and maybe they wouldn't. It all depended on what it was there for.

But it stood in her way and that was all she needed to know before she formulated her plan. She didn't have a whole lot on her that could help, but she had one thing that might.

"What are you doing?" Petrichor shouted ahead in the dwindling light.

Kenja took it with her as a matter of being prepared, but a magnetic explosive—much like the one that had signed Seth's death warrant—was the perfect size to keep in a pouch on her belt. Withdrawing it and setting it to detonate on impact, she looked up at the *Wasp* and started running. Getting closer, just a few meters away from the 'Mech, they gained its attention, and it tried sighting at them, but Kenja threw the explosive as hard and fast at the face of the human-shaped 'Mech as she could.

Before the 'Mech could shoot, fire enveloped the 'Mech's head, and Kenja put on another burst of speed while it was distracted. Weaving between the 'Mech's massive legs, she ran to the Sea Fox door, Petrichor following behind her.

All those hours on the treadmill together had finally paid off.

Relishing the cooler temperature and scrubbed air, Kenja raced through the hallways of the Sea Fox headquarters, following the signs to the 'Mech bay.

"Which 'Mech am I taking?" she said into her wrist unit, waiting for the rolling door to open, hoping the Circuit Breakers hadn't caught up to them in the time it took to get there.

Diana answered after a moment, the sounds of the battle faded into the ringing in Kenja's ears. "There's a heavy 'Mech I've ordered assigned to your codename. You'll see it, it's the only heavy there."

"And what of Star Commander Petrichor?" Kenja asked.

"Working on it. Diana, out."

The door finished opening, and Kenja caught sight of the most beautiful 'Mech she'd ever seen.

Standing there, warmed, prepped, and ready, painted with the exaggerated face of a diamond shark on its pronounced, predator-like-snout, with the rest in the watery camouflage of Sea Fox colors, was a 75-ton *Maelstrom*. A Spheroid 'Mech, no doubt acquired through trade between Fox Khanate and the Federated Suns, it nonetheless radiated gorgeous lethality.

"I see it," Kenja said. "I'll be there shortly."

After quickly suiting up in a borrowed cooling suit, Kenja climbed up into the *Maelstrom*. Running through the start-up procedures more quickly than she ever had in her life, she marched the 'Mech to the back of the Grand Bazaar, hoping to demolish the *Wasp* and get the spaceport quickly.

Unfortunately, in the time it took her to get ready, the *Wasp* had been joined by friends.

Four 'Mechs stood there now, an entire light lance of Circuit Breakers. All facing her, their various weapons raised.

"Damn it..." she said, punching her control console while her gut did a somersault.

Her 'Mech's WarBook identified the new foes as a *Hermit Crab*, a *Havoc*, and a *Battle Hawk*. Altogether, they outweighed and outclassed her *Maelstrom* by almost double.

"Petrichor," she said, "you better get here quick. Things just got a whole lot worse."

CHAPTER 17: INTO THE FIRE

GRAND BAZAAR
ANQABAD
ANKAA
FEDERATED SUNS
12 JULY 3151

Just because Kenja was outclassed and outnumbered didn't mean she didn't have tricks up her sleeve. She needed to get to the spaceport immediately, and promised herself they weren't going to slow her down.

I hope Petrichor gets out here soon—I'm going to need the help.

Flames licked the darkening sky and great columns of black smoke curled up into the distance. Kenja wasted no time lining up her first shot at the *Wasp*, the closest 'Mech to her, right up against the Sea Fox warehouse. She had a lot of experience piloting 'Mechs she'd never seen before, and was fairly adept at quickly understanding how each one operated best.

She fired everything she had: an extended-range PPC and a large laser, two medium pulse lasers, and a small laser. The lightning *crack* of the PPC and the large laser bathed the ruined bazaar in hot, blue light, the medium lasers added hints of green, and the small laser lashed out with its flare of red. The large and medium lasers all found their mark, boring through the *Wasp*'s side.

The *Wasp* was a 20-ton "Mech, and on foot it seemed a lot more imposing, but looking at it from the controls of a massive 75-ton 'Mech made it seem like nothing more than a toy.

Kenja's attack snuffed it out like a candle. Its legs and arms collapsed into a pile of molten limbs. The pilot most likely got vaporized, not even knowing what had hit them.

Taking the *Wasp* down certainly helped, but it didn't completely even the odds. Kenja was still facing almost a hundred tons of 'Mech.

"Suckerfish," she called on her comm, "Sitrep."

As she waited for an answer, Kenja marched through the wreckage of the bazaar and found the *Hermit Crab* next, a few dozen meters away. It was hunched over like its namesake, and walked slowly forward, coming straight toward Kenja and her *Maelstrom.* They both took aim at each other.

Petrichor's voice came through the speakers. "The techs are coding a *Hammerhead* for me."

"Hurry," Kenja said, as her targeting reticle burned gold and she fired on the *Hermit Crab.* She skipped her short range weapons this time—she couldn't afford the heat-build up. Even after a single alpha strike, she was feeling the warmth building up from the command couch, sweating easily in the borrowed cooling suit. That was the problem with 'Mechs that were all energy weapons: you were always playing the odds between staying in the fight and a catastrophic heat shutdown.

The PPC shot went wide, arcing into the night beyond the *Hermit Crab*, but the large laser slashed across its arm, liquifying all the armor in its deadly path. It wasn't enough to take the 'Mech down, but it was definitely enough to remind it how much of a threat she could be.

Having another 45 tons of 'Mech on her side was only going to help—if she could last that long.

The *Hermit Crab* pilot had to know they were in for a hard time. There was no situation where a light 'Mech could go up against a heavy 'Mech and last long. Its pair of ER medium lasers glittered green as they covered the distance between them. They sliced into Kenja's front side armor and her 'Mech's status display went from a solid green to flashing yellow, letting her know she'd been hit, but not enough to be concerned with.

Yet.

The *Havoc* and the *Battle Hawk* opened fire, but were further away. The *Havoc*'s battery of medium lasers lit up the bazaar, but missed Kenja's *Maelstrom,* carving scars into the Sea Fox facade and exploding the holoprojector of their sign in a hail of sparks. The *Battle Hawk*'s pulse lasers, however, blistered the armor across the snout of the *Maelstrom.*

Kenja growled as she pulled the triggers, aiming at the *Hermit Crab* again. The longer she fought this lance in the Bazaar, the better chance everyone—*anyone*—else had to snatch up Tucker Harwell and whisk him away to who knew where. The medium lasers seared chunks of armor from the top of the enemy 'Mech, then the flash of azure PPC light shimmered through the distance, blasting one of the *Hermit Crab*'s arms right off.

Heat rising with every laser shot, Kenja ran for the *Hermit Crab,* knowing she was making herself an easier target, but every step she took was one closer to the spaceport.

The *Hermit Crab* jumped into the air, leaving a smoking trail of plasma behind it, igniting a trio of shopping stalls. Kenja wagered the pilot was going to try to get behind her. Her first instinct was to stop short and turn around, capturing it in an en passant maneuver, but she didn't have time to stop. If they shot her in the back, so be it. She would get to the spaceport one way or the other.

She aimed her *Maelstrom* at the next 'Mech, charging straight at the *Battle Hawk*. From the vantage of a large enough 'Mech, Kenja could have seen where someone might mistake it for Elemental armor. It moved like a human did, too, which was a disadvantage as far as she was concerned. That made its moves predictable and easy to read.

Instead of firing at it, Kenja opted to shunt her extra heat and punch the damn thing with both arms, The end of her left arm glanced off the side of the humanoid 'Mech, but her right one cracked the cockpit right open. Even through the gyros and actuators of her own 'Mech, she felt the *Battle Hawk* shatter.

The barrel of her PPC cracked right through the ferroglass and ferrofibrous armor.

The 'Mech convulsed under her blow, but that didn't stop it from returning fire. Its lasers, at point-blank range, melted through armor on Kenja's legs. Her damage indicators flashed from green to yellow, but the *Battle Hawk* had no moves left to make.

Kenja stepped forward, using her 'Mech's weight to increase the damage of the blow to the *Battle Hawk*'s cockpit and bulled it around her, getting it out of the way. It slid off her arm and crashed to the ground, and she was free to work on the last two 'Mechs in the lance.

Suddenly, her viewscreen was awash in a cascade of exploding missiles and green laser light.

The *Havoc* had flanked her on the right side, while the *Hermit Crab* kept firing from behind her.

"Petrichor?" Kenja asked again.

"Almost there, Star Colonel."

"Faster."

"Yes, Star Colonel."

Kenja turned to the *Havoc*, showing her profile to the more distant *Hermit Crab*. With her heat back down to a reasonable range, she leaped the *Maelstrom* forward and fired everything she had at the *Havoc*. It had a broadly humanoid shape, but its boxy, fin-topped head made it a weird-looking 'Mech, with weapons mounted to its wrists.

Her small laser traced a blackened outline of the *Havoc*'s right side, but the mediums scored the front of the 'Mech's torso. The PPC flayed molten armor from its left leg, and the large laser flensed armor on its right arm down to its myomers.

Kenja hit a lot harder than these guys could; all they were really costing her was time. And she didn't want to waste any more of it. She had to end this and get to Tucker Harwell fast, otherwise she was never going to find him again. His bodyguards could see how clever she had been at finding them the first time. If she let them go, they'd cover their tracks even better. She worried they'd find the tracker. They'd blend in. Disappear. They'd never be seen by anyone in the Inner Sphere again.

The *Maelstrom* shuddered as the *Hermit Crab* maneuvered around her and fired everything it had into her back. Its lasers sliced across the rear of her legs, melting off more armor. Taking another step toward the *Havoc*, Kenja put her faith in Petrichor. "I need you to handle that *Hermit Crab*, Suckerfish."

"*Aff*, Star Colonel," Petrichor shot back, the glorious bright blue blip of her *Hammerhead* 'Mech twinkling to life on the mini map on Kenja's HUD. It was a welcome sight.

Now, maybe, she could take down the *Havoc*. "I'm done playing," she said as she lined up her next shot. Though the heat gauge on her HUD spiked higher, flirting with a shutdown, Kenja fired everything she had at it. Her small laser sliced a piece of torso off like carving up a holiday bird, but her larger weapons missed.

They exchanged fire twice more with mixed results, but the real damage kept coming from the *Hermit Crab*. Even though Petrichor had finally arrived in her *Hammerhead* and opened fire, it remained single-mindedly focused on Kenja's rear quarter.

Kenja moved into point-blank range with the *Havoc* to slug it out. The mercenary 'Mech shuddered with every awkward move, a good sign that at least some of Kenja's hits were effective and had damaged its gyro. That would make their aim more difficult and her job easier.

The armor on her rear-torso screamed and screeched with every bit of new damage, and the indicators on the console flashed red. She wouldn't be able to show her back to an enemy again after the fight was over—assuming she still had a back left to protect.

"Get between us," Kenja ordered. Maybe the Hammerhead could screen some of the damage and allow her to finish her work.

"*Aff*," Petrichor said.

Kenja dragged her targeting reticle across the smoking *Havoc* again and pulled her triggers and pushed the firing studs on her control sticks, hoping this would be it. The barrage of lasers in three distinct colors formed a rainbow of damage that lanced from her 'Mech to the *Havoc*, hitting it all across the front. Liquified armor splashed to the ground as the PPC smashed through the final layer of armor. The laser volley consumed the myomer musculature beneath that and snapped the frame. The *Havoc* leaned to one side, as though it had been untethered at its center, but the 'Mech wasn't able to right itself. It toppled over, unbalanced, slamming to the ground.

Kenja's happiness was tempered by another forceful crash at her rear quarter. The *Hermit Crab* just wasn't going to let up. But she couldn't worry about that.

She'd have to leave it with Petrichor.

"Suckerfish, you need to mop it up as fast as you can. I am heading to the starport through the grand archway."

"*Aff,* Star Colonel, this won't take long." As Petrichor said that, she launched a sextet of missiles and a vibrant, violet burst of pulse laser fire at the *Hermit Crab.* Her laser cut across its front, leaving a sweltering red scar across its nose that glowed in the dwindling heat of Ankaa's day.

Then the rest of her lasers slashed right through the 'Mech's cockpit, dropping it to the ground in one brutal volley.

"That was easier than I expected," Petrichor said.

"That's just the beginning," Kenja replied, watching Petrichor run to catch up at the edge of her viewscreen. "Come on. We need to get to the spaceport before they nab our target."

As she urged her punished 'Mech into a run, Kenja hoped they hadn't already.

CHAPTER 18:
THE TRIAL OF TUCKER HARWELL

ANQABAD SPACEPORT
ANQABAD
ANKAA
FEDERATED SUNS
12 JULY 3151

In their 'Mechs, Kenja and Petrichor came through the grand archway that separated the bazaar from the spaceport proper and looked out over the battlefield.

Columns of smoke curled up into the twilight sky. DropShips were left in ruined shambles where the Circuit Breakers had gotten close enough. In the distance, the *Zephyr* bled its own trail of smoke. Sea Fox 'Mechs and others battled a few Circuit Breakers in the distance, but for the most part the battle was over.

The most devastating aspect of the tableau before Kenja was the grouping of 'Mechs surrounding the *Darian* and Tucker's bodyguards, the mysterious *Black Knight* and *Grand Summoner* D. It was as though the Circuit Breakers had just walked up to die in a semi-circle around the two heavy 'Mechs. Green and copper colored infantry had added scorching black, molten steel, and blood to their colors, littered in broken positions around the bodyguards in every direction.

Their black 'Mechs were pressed up against the *Darin* in a defensive position, protecting it from all comers. The DropShip dripped chunks of armor and to Kenja's eye was not taking off any time soon. The 'Mechs both had spots of exposed myomer and their weapons were smoking. Heat made wavy lines above them, distorting the image of the DropShip behind them, they were running in the red.

It was as though everything were about to be undone.

Standing between Kenja and the *Darian* was a lone *Scourge* in Circuit Breaker colors. The only one left who hadn't died or retreated in the distance.

"Circuit Breaker Leader," a voice said on a wide-band comm channel, "Surrender now or be destroyed."

It was a woman's voice. With her targeting computer, Kenja tagged her 'Mech as Yojimbo and the other black-colored 'Mech as Ronin. Yojimbo was likely piloted by the female bodyguard she saw in the market. Kenja could only assume that *Scourge* was the Circuit Breaker leader, taking the rear position.

"This is Henry Every of the Circuit Breakers," answered the merc captain. "We don't surrender. Give us what we came for or we die fighting."

"Have it your way," Yojimbo said.

"Aim for the *Scourge*," Kenja told Petrichor. "I think that's the ringleader."

Petrichor complied and they both charged it, attacking the heavy 'Mech from the rear while Yojimbo and Ronin fired at its front. The *Scourge* nailed Yojimbo's *Black Knight* with a well-placed Gauss rifle shot, hitting her 'Mech so hard Kenja imagined she could feel it herself. But that wasn't going to stop any of them. He was grossly outnumbered. Laser after laser stabbed at the Circuit Breaker 'Mech until it was nothing but a pile of molten rubble, true to his word, he was defeated and destroyed rather than surrender.

Looking down at her command console and damage readout, Kenja saw her 'Mech was in a precarious position. Her legs flashed red. Her entire back quarter did as well. The only place she had a solid green indicator was the cockpit zone, with the rest of her 'Mech flashing yellow. She wasn't *completely* stripped of armor, but she was in a very dire way.

Her heat levels needed attention. It had risen to dangerous levels as she and Petrichor helped to take down the *Scourge*. It would continue to run high while she pivoted.

Far in the distance, the few remaining Circuit Breakers were scattered through the spaceport; those precious few who hadn't perished in the Bazaar or Yojimbo's circle of destruction fled. Maybe they would be smarter than their captain in their next lives.

Kenja had a choice to make. On any other day, she would have chased down the Circuit Breakers to discover the identity of their employer. But she needed to acquire Tucker Harwell and she needed to do it now.

"Captain Yung," Kenja called out. "Ship's status, please."

Star Captain Meridian Yung's voice rang loud and clear through the comm. "We have sustained minor damages to weapons and armor systems, but thankfully no hull breach. We were targeted in the initial attack, but they were drawn to the *Aurora*. My crew is doing a complete sweep of damage now."

"Understood," Kenja said, cursing under her breath. Even if she made her play for Harwell, she wouldn't be able to leave immediately. "ETA on repairs?"

"Depends on parts and level of damage. Few days at best. Two weeks with no help. I would guess a week as an average, if we have help from the local Fox Khanate technicians."

Kenja knew the locals would help. They would be honor-bound to. The trick was still nabbing Harwell and holding him during that time.

"Get to work. All possible speed," Kenja told the Star Captain.

"*Aff*, Star Colonel."

And after a breath of silence, the radio filled with the voice of Yojimbo. "Thank you for your assistance, *Maelstrom*. I'm not sure how this would have ended for us if the Sea Foxes hadn't helped."

Kenja's face split into a grin she was glad Yojimbo couldn't see as she saw her opening. "Trust that it was our pleasure, but there is one last bit of business for both of us."

"What is that?"

"Protector of Tucker Harwell," Kenja said formally, hoping to shock Yojimbo with the knowledge of what she assumed was her charge's true identity, "I am Star Colonel Kenja Rodriguez of Clan Sea Fox, and I challenge you to a Trial of Possession."

"Possession of what?" Yojimbo said coldly.

"Possession of Tucker Harwell, your DropShip, its crew, and both you and your bodyguard compatriot. You would all become Sea Foxes."

The line remained quiet for a moment. Not long enough for Yojimbo to confer with anyone, but long enough for Kenja to know she was considering her options. Maybe she was doing the math. A damaged *Black Knight* versus a damaged *Maelstrom* was probably an even fight, more of less. Now it would come down to the individual pilots. Kenja was confident in her own abilities. And this was her chance to do things as easy as possible.

"And what do I win if I defeat you?" Yojimbo said. There was confidence in her voice.

Kenja had done a fair amount of guesswork about their intentions and intended destination, which now served her well. "*If* you win, the Sea Foxes will repair your ship and escort you to whatever final destination you wish, under a veil of total secrecy and anonymity."

Yojimbo fired back almost instantly, "May I have a few moments to consider your offer?"

"Of course, talk it over with Tucker." Kenja cut the line and waited. There was no escape, so it cost her nothing to give them a minute to consider her offer. She didn't like her options if they refused—all of them seemed like they would be short on honor—but she was placing odds on the fact that they felt like they had the upper hand in the duel and would accept.

After a few minutes, her comm crackled to life. "Bargained well and done, Star Colonel Rodriguez. I accept your Trial. I assume you wish to fight augmented in our 'Mechs?"

"*Aff.* Just so, but first to whom do I have the honor to face in combat," Kenja said.

Yojimbo's voice came through strong and confident, "I am Alexi Holt, former Knight of the Republic."

"It is an honor, Knight Holt, we will fight our Trial right here and now. In the spaceport. Your partner, Reus Tremor, in the *Grand Summoner* and the rest of the Sea Foxes will serve for our Circle of Equals."

"Very well," Holt said.

As the 'Mechs gathered into place, Petrichor's voice got on the line. "Are you sure about this, Star Colonel?"

"It's going to be a fight one way or the other. At least this way it's on our terms. Sometimes," Kenja said, regurgitating old advice, "we have to risk our powerful pieces to lure out the queen."

"Of course, Star Colonel."

It took a few minutes, but eventually everyone got into position. Kenja felt the tension from all sides. From the Sea Foxes, her cards were face-up on the table, and her objective had been broadcast on an open channel. It wasn't ideal, but Kenja had done what she thought was right under the circumstance. And she doubted many outside of a precious few had even heard the name Tucker Harwell, and if they didn't, it would take a fair bit of digging to find out who or what he was.

All that mattered was getting him.

The open landing pad of reinforced ferrocrete was one of the few that had been spared from the Circuit Breakers' rampage. Finding out where they came from and who had hired them was at the top of Kenja's list of things to do as soon as she had Harwell in her possession.

But right now she had to focus on the fight instead.

Holt's battered *Black Knight* stood at one end and Kenja's thrashed *Maelstrom* stood at the other. She saw the pockmarks and laser scars across Holt's 'Mech. She also noted the exposed myomer and actuators on the *Black Knight*'s hips. That would be the weak spot she would aim for. Anything she could do to render it inoperable as fast as she could was her goal.

She couldn't afford to screw this up.

Despite the damage each 'Mech had taken, Kenja's WarBook let her know both were fairly evenly matched. Comparing a standard, pristine version of each, Kenja had about a ton and a half more armor than the *Black Knight*, and she could outrun it by about twenty kilometers an hour. They were both laser boats though, prone to overheating, though the *Black Knight* had more lasers, that gave it more of a chance to overheat, too.

In such a small circle, her speed advantage wasn't going to help Kenja. Since they had both been brutalized in the conflict with the Circuit Breakers, the armor advantage was of little use. Plenty of Kenja's armor had been smashed off in the fight, and the *Black Knight* didn't look much better.

It could easily be a short fight, but Kenja didn't know if she would come out victorious. She imagined they were both eager horses waiting at a starting gate, trembling and ready to start their race. For the combatants, it had the chance to be much more lethal than a horse race. Standing at each end of the landing pad, the furthest they could get from each other was the very edge of a medium range weapon. Long-range weapons would confer no real advantage, but short-range weapons would be worth firing because they were at their upper limits of being effective. Sure, it was harder to get a good hit in, but they were in a race and Kenja doubted they would be fighting long enough to have to worry about managing heat. She'd be dead or victorious by the time she'd fired enough to force a catastrophic heat shutdown.

"Let the Trial begin!" Diana announced over the comm.

Kenja immediately put the speed of her 'Mech to good use. Running around the outside edge of the circle, she kept her backside out of the fight. One good hit from behind and she'd be finished, so that had to be her first priority. Her second priority was taking the best shots possible.

Holt was clearly dangerous and a skilled MechWarrior. As though they were doing an elegant dance, Holt predicted the path of Kenja's travel and circled in the opposite direction. They both raced around the edge of the circle, each trying to catch the other in hopes of getting that coveted rear-shot.

Kenja twisted to her left, lining up a shot against the *Black Knight*. Her targeting reticle shifted color and the tone of a good lock sounded. She committed to an alpha strike, ignoring her heat gauge completely. The lasers burned off more of the flat black paint from the side of Holt's 'Mech, but nothing connected enough to make a killing blow.

Bracing for return fire, she was not disappointed when a volley of lasers sliced into the side of her *Maelstrom*, searing her arms and burning off more armor than she could afford to lose.

She needed to make an unexpected move and gain the upper hand, but hadn't figured out how to do that yet. They mirrored each other's movements again, and continued boiling off small bits of armor every time they shot at each other. One of them was going to lose an arm soon if this kept up much longer.

The *Maelstrom* groaned when Kenja decided she couldn't keep circling any more. She moved around just enough to try and lull Holt into thinking they were continuing their dance, but then wrenched her 'Mech back and ran straight for the *Black Knight*.

"Show me that opening," Kenja muttered, sighting the hole in the armor's on the 'Mech's hip that left its inner structure and myomer muscles exposed. That was the spot where she could press the advantage. That was how things were going to come to a swift and decisive conclusion.

She fired and missed the opening as Alexi put on an unexpected burst of speed.

Alexi returned fire, but Kenja slowed to the same effect.

In this way, they traded volleys firing back and forth, shooting their weapons conservatively and dodging liberally. Kenja kept her eyes wide open for that weak spot, and when she glimpsed it again, she unloaded. Heat spiked and sweat poured from her brow. The heat alarm screamed at her like a boiling tea kettle. She must have lost a heat sink at some point, because the scorching temps weren't dissipating as fast as they had been. Or maybe all of her heat sinks were malfunctioning.

Anything could have been the matter after so much fighting.

The lasers glinted bright and true in the space between them, connecting with the *Black Knight*. The jade beams cut into its arm, but as it moved, its gait allowed the PPC's lightning bolt to score a direct hit on the vulnerable point.

That rocked the 'Mech and it slowed. Its actuators couldn't help it turn fast enough to get a shot off at Kenja.

So Kenja stood pat, taking the risk to take her shot again. It was as though the shrieking heat alarms were silent now, she ignored them so effectively.

Sweat streaked everywhere, she felt it slicking her entire body. Even with the cooling suit pressed against her skin, the heat was unbearable. She leaned over to the bite valve next to her mouth and took a sip of water, hoping to put off the risk of heat stroke.

Standing still, lining up her shot, Kenja watched the *Black Knight* make its feeble turn to get her in its sights. Alexi Holt was probably sweating just as much as Kenja was, especially since her mobility had been reduced drastically.

But Kenja knew she could end it soon.

Alexi Holt fired back as soon as she was in an acceptable firing arc. Another hit to Kenja's leg and her mobility would be cut in half, but fortune favored her. All of the damage lit up across her wireframe's torso, flensing armor she couldn't afford to lose.

The hit took another heat sink with it, too.

She was going to suffocate in the sweltering sauna and burn to death if she wasn't killed by a headshot to her 'Mech first.

The heat rose even further; it wasn't dissipating. Just operating the 'Mech was causing a heat deficit. But the aiming reticle was right over that hole at the *Black Knight*'s hip. It had been blown open larger and wider with the last attack. And now the Republic Knight was showing it to her openly, coming at her straight on.

Kenja pulled her triggers and mashed her firing studs.

She had enough time to watch the bolt of lightning of her PPCs crackle into the weak spot, but that's when her viewscreen shorted out and blackness enveloped her. It lasted only a split second, but enough to worry her that it was the start of a catastrophe. Then it came back. Only temporary.

Reassessing the situation, she was pleased to see she'd done enough damage around the weak spot that the left arm of the *Black Knight* hung limp and useless, and the left leg was getting dragged behind it as it took a step forward. Holt opened fire with her remaining arm and torso weapons, but half missed. The other half immolated what was left of Kenja's armor and caused the short in the viewscreen to return, the heat rising to even more dangerous levels.

It was clear they were both going to fight to the death, neither willing to give, neither willing to stop until they had exhausted every last measure of their bravery.

Tucker Harwell was that important to both of them.

Kenja limped her *Maelstrom* forward, bringing her enemy even closer than she had before. Then, she flipped the switch on her console for the heat override, took aim at the *Black Knight*'s exposed inner structure once more, and fired with everything she had left.

Then, her viewscreen went dark.

Her BattleMech powered down and hung there in the air for what felt like a long minute. In that minute she could not hear or see anything. The windows to the outside world had b had fogged over completely, letting in nothing but the intense but diffused Ankaa sunlight. Her 'Mech couldn't keep its balance and toppled over, pressing the ferroglass cockpit against the ground and leaving her cut off in the dark.

"Welp..." In the dark she boiled alive and blew out a hot, held breath, hoping she'd done enough damage to stop the *Black Knight* and win Tucker Harwell for the good of the Sea Foxes.

CHAPTER 19: SPOILS OF WAR

ANQABAD SPACEPORT
ANQABAD
ANKAA
FEDERATED SUNS
12 JULY 3151

Everything was quiet for a long minute.

No light penetrated Kenja's compartment. Very little sound did, too. Her radio wasn't working, so if anyone was speaking to her, they were just screaming into the void.

Baking in the blackness, Kenja found a strange sense of peace in the experience. Like a trip to the sauna after a long workout or training session. Or a hyperbaric chamber, allowing her to meditate freely, cut off the sights and sounds of the rest of the world.

And it would have felt exactly like that, if it weren't for the utter terror in her heart.

The idea that she could still have lost the trial, and Tucker Harwell with it, swelled inside her, a hot, swirling vortex of failure that hit the cold front of grief still swirling in her middle. When they collided, they combined to create a hurricane in her gut.

Kenja couldn't sit idly any longer.

She couldn't stand to not know the outcome.

She had to know.

Taking a deep breath and closing her eyes, Kenja tried regaining her center, looking for the eye of her internal storm so she could get back to clear-headed thinking and the peace she needed. She needed that quiet calm to perform her job at the professional level of excellence it demanded.

The glow of lights returning to the cockpit faded red behind her eyelids, and she took a tentative peek through cracked lids. Her 'Mech had come back online, and the viewscreen flickered back to life.

The systems came back online one at a time, ending with the comm system.

"—do you copy?" she heard a voice say.

"This is Kenja, I copy," she said, looking out at the scene beyond her, the swirling hurricane inside her subsiding immediately as she pulled her 'Mech back to its feet, ready to take another shot.

But that's when she saw it.

There, on the ferrocrete landing pad, emergency teams crawled all over Alexi Holt's *Black Knight*, working to extricate her. An ambulance was on the tarmac. Had she been wounded or killed?

Regardless, the *Black Knight* was flat on its back.

And Kenja had stood her *Maelstrom* back up under its own power.

Kenja tentatively stepped forward. Her heat levels had definitely cooled some, but the *Maelstrom* was still running hot. If she had fired at the *Black Knight* again, she'd have risked another shutdown.

"You did it, Star Colonel," came Petrichor's voice finally. "She went down first. Tucker Harwell is ours."

Kenja's posture slackened and she let out a deep sigh of relief.

Now, they just had to work out the details and get Tucker to Hean with all possible speed.

SEA FOX HEADQUARTERS
ANQABAD
ANKAA
FEDERATED SUNS
13 JULY 3151

The Fox Khanate outpost had graciously hosted Kenja and her cadre, as well as their new additions, in their headquarters off the Grand Bazaar. They put Alexi Holt, Reus Tremor, and Tucker Harwell in a locked room and posted guards outside it, just in case the local Federated Suns planetary guards attempted to challenge the sovereignty of the Sea Fox outpost when investigating the spaceport and market fights. Kenja told them they could take no chances. Before that, Holt and Tremor were given a chance and space to clean up. Holt had suffered only minor injuries, but Tremor needed his arm set, so the EMTs saw to them first.

They had been waiting for her for an hour or so, just long enough for Kenja to take a shower, change back into her Sea Fox jumpsuit, and read up on the long history of Alexi Holt, Knight of the Republic.

Then, she steeled herself for what came next. She could only imagine the uneasy trepidation they felt as they waited for Kenja to arrive and hold them to the Trial. But she made it as quickly as she could.

Walking past the Sea Fox guards on post duty, the door slid open, and Kenja walked inside. Alexi Holt and Reus Tremor, both looking exhausted, sat comfortably on a couch the Sea Foxes had provided. Kenja noted she had met with Diana in this same room.

Tucker Harwell, however, paced back and forth behind the couch, wearing his anxiety on both his sleeve and his face.

According to Petrichor, there had been an intense conversation in the room just a few minutes ago. Harwell was the one doing a lot of the talking And it made sense. He had just been promised to Clan Sea Fox, and probably knew what they were going to be asking of him. Of course he would be a little uneasy.

Kenja decided Alexi Holt looked better without the spiked hair, prevalent in her pictures in the old records. She liked the former Knight's auburn hair draped to one side much better. It made her look more modern. If she was going to be a Sea Fox, it was good to know she could change, even in small ways.

"Thank you all for your patience," she said, wanting to welcome them with polite kindness. She had known too many fellow Clan members, both Sea Foxes and others, who preferred to intimidate and pressure others with overbearing statures, aggressive postures, and hostile words. Kenja had found that, especially in the Watch game, she attracted more prey with bait than traps. Using carrots and honey, like the old sayings went. "I understand this has been a trying time for you all over the last few months, and the last twenty-four hours in particular."

"Understatement of the century," The man with a few days of stubble, mischievous eyes, and a faux-hawk of brown hair—Reus Tremor—said with a grimace. Likely due to the painkillers and his recently slung arm. And being taken as a bondsman.

"See, Alexi?" Tucker said, raising his hands to his head as though he couldn't contain himself. But he was speaking as much to himself as anyone. He glanced at Alexi and Reus, then nodded in resignation. "I told you it's not paranoid if everyone really *is* after you."

Kenja opted to ignore him for now and stayed focused on Alexi Holt. "If you haven't guessed by now, I'm Star Colonel Kenja Rodriguez, and I was the one who challenged you to the trial."

Alexi snapped into a military bearing. Respectful but not warm. "Star Colonel Kenja Rodriguez, I am Alexi Holt." She reached out to shake Kenja's hand. "Our trial was well fought. I can see how you earned the Rodriguez Bloodname."

Kenja cataloged the fact that as a Knight, Holt had knowledge of the Clans and how they worked. She'd file that away for later in case she needed it. "It was a hard-fought trial, and you should be proud. If my last strike had not downed your *Black Knight*, I would have lost." *If flattery—nearer to the truth than I'd like to admit—makes this easier,* Kenja thought, *I'll continue with the pleasantries.*

Reus nodded, but said nothing.

Tucker turned to Kenja and stabbed an accusing finger at her; a marked change from the nerdy tech in the bazaar. "What do you want? Why did you do this? You should have just let us go."

Kenja gave him the honest answer. "Clan Sea Fox is determined to rebuild the Inner Sphere's HPG network, and you could be the key to making it a reality. If I'd had a chance to speak with you honestly, Tucker, I would have been able to make our intentions known. But your friends here," Kenja waved a hand at Reus and Alexi, "did too good a job obscuring your movements."

"How did you find us here?" Alexi asked. No doubt she was still stinging from the double defeat. The first was that Kenja had seen through her ruse, the second was that she had so quickly capitalized on it. That, and the whole defeating her in an honorable Trial thing. "Ankaa isn't the most hospitable world, and it's as far out of the way as anything. But you knew exactly where we were."

"Let's just say there was a lot of informed guesswork involved, and I took some risks that happened to pay off," Kenja replied.

"So your lucky guesses paid off." Reus Tremor interjected before yawning. Where Alexi's posture had straightened and come to more attention, Reus's had slackened. He was tired, sure, but to Kenja's reckoning it was clear he didn't care for the authority of the Sea Foxes. He would need to develop that trust.

Kenja was willing to put in the work to do it, but they needed time. Time they probably didn't have. "Not exactly. I was sent in to extract Tucker from Terra, and was outside the Fortress Wall when we received word he had disappeared. All of our suppositions cascaded from there, leading us here. But that's beside the point, it's all in the past. You're all Sea Foxes now."

"I'm not a Sea Fox," Tucker said. "I'm not anything. I don't know why you think you need me."

"Tucker," Kenja said, looking him straight in the eye and pleased to see he met her gaze squarely. "The Sea Fox scientist caste has been working on HPG technology for years, trying to discover the source of the Blackout, what caused Gray Monday, and how to mitigate it. They've made some strides, steady progress, but you're the only person in the Inner Sphere who has gotten an HPG back up and running since the galaxy went silent. We have the resources, the equipment, and new information you might need, all to give you the best possible chance for figuring out this communications problem once and for all. Help us solve this, and you can go free."

"Over the last decade—maybe more—I've been the 'guest' of everyone from ComStar to the Republic of the Sphere, and they all wanted the same thing from me. Some offered me the illusion of freedom, others a prison cell." Kenja noticed a deep pain in both his eyes and his voice. He almost choked on some of his words. "But there's no freedom in any of it."

Alexi snapped her head up to Tucker, a soft look of genuine concern and care on her face. That was also information Kenja tucked away, both to explore further—and to exploit if necessary. The Knight's face bore as much pain as Tucker's did.

Tucker gulped hard. "So where's my prison cell going to be?"

Kenja shook he head. "There won't be a prison cell."

His laugh was tinged with sarcasm and a distinct lack of trust. "I've heard that before."

"Tucker," Kenja said, "My goal is to get the HPG network up and running. I think humanity is better served by being able to communicate openly and freely—"

"I've heard this speech before, too," he said, cutting her off. "Everyone wants free and open communication for the benefit of humanity. And I used to believe that, too. But whose jackboots will be on my neck this time? Clan Sea Fox? If this helps Alaric and the Clans conquer more of the Inner Sphere, you can count me right out."

"Obviously rebuilding and maintaining the HPG network will cost something. I don't think any of us have any illusions about that. And yes, Clan Sea Fox would profit from it, as we do in every deal we make. But we would profit more if we did not interfere with communication than we would using it for nefarious purposes as any of the more crusading clans might."

"Right." Tucker nodded sarcastically. "Sure."

Kenja furrowed her brow. "You would prefer it—and you—in the hands of Clan Wolf?"

That stopped Tucker for a moment, but he knew something about Clan Wolf. "Clan Wolf is the ilClan now. Right? Aren't you all one big happy family? It's all the same, Sea Fox and Wolf. Isn't that how it works? They have Terra."

"Yes and no."

"What's that supposed to mean?" Tucker said.

Kenja felt the hostility and incredulity radiating off him. She let it guide her answer because she understood she could use it to benefit her mission.

"Yes, Clan Wolf is the ilClan. And yes, Clan Sea Fox has pledged our loyalty and honor to the agreement that they are the Clan of Clans. But that does not mean Clan Sea Fox is merely a vassal of Clan Wolf, merely propped up to do their bidding. For a hundred years, our Clan has brokered alliances with every major player and House in the Inner Sphere to maintain a neutrality of trade. Yes, to profit. Yes, to show our superiority in such matters. It's the right thing to do for Clan Sea Fox. It will ensure we have a powerful position in the new Star League regime. But also because it is the right thing to do. Thanks to Khans like Malvina Hazen and Alaric Ward, there is a misconception in the Inner Sphere about the entire point of the Clans."

"Misconception? Please." Tucker's sarcasm returned. "Then enlighten us."

"What would the Federated Suns or the Free Worlds League do with the ability to repair HPG technology?"

Tucker Harwell's mouth turned into a thin, grim line as he clenched his jaw at her question.

"Do you think they would share that technology if you helped them with that breakthrough? What would communication look like on planets controlled by the Capellan Confederation with the FedSuns in charge of it? What about the Draconis Combine? Can you really see the First Prince or Captain-General waving an HPG-shaped olive branch to Yori Kurita or Trillian Steiner?" If that didn't make him think twice, she didn't know what would. "ComStar is dead, Tucker."

"Don't remind me."

"Who else *but* Clan Sea Fox has the reach, the freedom of movement, and the resources to create a communications network for the people of the Inner Sphere?"

"Compared to the House Lords, the Sea Foxes are remarkably neutral," he said, relenting some. "But you have an army of 'Mechs, just like ComStar did. What happens when some splinter faction of Sea Foxes decides to go rogue and declare a Trial of Possession for some backwater planet? And they interdict all the communications? And put their thumbs on the scale of justice and intercept messages, just like ComStar did? I don't have some rosy view of what ComStar was. I know what they were. More than ever, I know what they did, what they hid and harbored, and what they were capable of."

Kenja nodded. "Aleksandr Kerensky left the Inner Sphere to create a force that would return and save humanity from its petty squabbles. From the very first days of the Clans, our *rede*, our charge—our *sacred* charge—is to protect humanity and end the suffering of war for all inhabitants of the Inner Sphere. Clan Wolf and Clan Jade Falcon twisted our doctrines into something that revered conquest more than anything in their quest for power. We are not supposed to be in power as much as we are supposed to be the safeguards of humanity. What better way to safeguard humanity than to ensure that they can all communicate with each other? Silence breeds fear, fear breeds war, and we want to end that silence. Since our ships are everywhere, and commerce flows through our vessels across every border, who better to ensure that aid and supplies reach even the most far flung territories? No, Tucker Harwell, the Sea Foxes are the *only* choice for the Inner Sphere when it comes to control of the HPG network."

She waited for him to take that in. It was a convincing argument, and the truth she believed in.

"I can't speak for anyone else, Tucker," she said after a few moments, "but I truly believe that Clan Sea Fox is the only chance humanity has to have the Sphere-wide ability to communicate like it *needs* to. To end that silence. I've spent so much time on planets, major and backwater alike, and the thing I've seen is that connected people are happy people.

Connected, transparent governments are safer for those happy people. Clan Sea Fox has the resources, the knowledge, the parts, the ownership of the ComStar assets and HPGs, and the cooperation across the Sphere to make all of that happen."

"And now you have me," he said quietly.

"Yes," Kenja said in a tone to match Tucker's, "and now we have you."

"You said he's not a prisoner," Alexi said. "What is he then?"

"Technically?" Kenja said, folding her hands behind her back. "According to the dictates of the Trial and the ways of the Clans, you are all bondspeople. You would wear bondcords and become something akin to provisional members of Clan Sea Fox, bound to me specifically. When I believe your duty has been done, and that you are loyal and honor-bound to our way of doing things, when I believe you have earned the right, I would cut your bondcords. At that point, you would be considered a full Sea Fox, with all the rights and privileges that position affords. You would also then be bound to provide service to the best of your ability to your adopted Clan. How you serve would be your prerogative."

"So it's just a prison by another name until then," Tucker said. Then he whispered the word "bondcord," trying it out with a sarcastic raise of his eyebrows.

"Yes and no," Kenja said carefully.

Reus Tremor chuckled. "You keep saying that."

"Well, it's true," she replied. "Everything depends. Nothing is black and white, *quiaff*?"

"That is definitely *aff*," he replied. "Nothing is as it seems. And I think there's more to you than you're letting on, too, Star Colonel."

Kenja shrugged with a knowing smile. "Come with me and find out."

"What's the alternative?" Alexi asked.

"There really isn't an alternative. Had you won the Trial, I would have honored my word and escorted you anywhere you wanted to go, even if it meant I would be stripped of rank and station for failing my mission. I do not want to make you prisoners, but that is really the only other option. And, as Tucker said, he's been a prisoner for this purpose before, and although I do not consider him to be one one now, I would also rather not allow this situation to be an unpleasant one for any of you."

The three of them remained silent. Each chewing on the alternatives. Each of them rifling through possibilities. Kenja really had given them the best deal she could. And this was their best outcome.

She did have one other card to play. And she waited for a long moment to play it. Watching Tucker Harwell's face, she saw the surrender there. But doubt remained. The key to intriguing him wasn't in pressing him into service. And it wasn't in showing him her honest vulnerability. It would be in stimulating his mind and his passion. "There is one other thing, Tucker, that I haven't mentioned."

"And what is that?" He stood straighter and folded his arms.

"Recently we received a transmission of information from the Scorpion Empire. It contained a cache of research materials about the functionality of HPGs."

"So?"

"Among the notes was a trove of information from the Terran Hegemony. It's highly theoretical material on the nature of hyperspace through which HPG transmissions travel. The cache also included many, many detailed schematics for HPG equipment. The information isn't just about *how* HPGs work, but *why* they work, and more. And it would all be yours. In fact, I have all of it on my DropShip. Come with us willingly, adhere to the results of our Trial with honor, and it's all yours."

Tucker narrowed his eyes. Then he shook his head in defeat. Finally, with a sigh, he said, "Well, it's like you said. It doesn't look like we have much of a choice, does it?"

Kenja smiled.

The hard work was about to begin.

CHAPTER 20:
CODENAME: VOIDBREAKER

VOIDBREAKER STATION
PAUPER
HEAN
TIBURON KHANATE TERRITORY
18 AUGUST 3151

The long trip back to the JumpShip, then to the Hean system, then the burn to the top secret VoidBreaker station on-planet, where the hard work of solving the HPG problem would begin, gave Kenja Rodriguez plenty of time to work with Alexi Holt and Reus Tremor.

One of the first things she wanted to do was find out who had hired the Circuit Breakers to launch their attacks. "Know thine enemy" was an important commandment in her line of work. In the week it took to repair their respective DropShips and get underway, Kenja, Reus, and Alexi had all made inquiries to find out who instigated the attack.

Unfortunately, the Circuit Breaker mercenaries who survived had escaped for the most part, getting to their DropShip and taking off, or going to ground. The two they had pulled from the wreckage of the battle were in no shape to talk. One was on life-support, with a tube doing all her breathing for her. The meds weren't sure if she was even going to be able to talk once she was out of her medically induced coma; there was a significant amount of brain damage. The other had died by the time he made it to the hospital.

There were no easy answers, and no intercepted communications for them to study for leads. The Circuit Breaker DropShip had made for a pirate point as soon as it was loaded, and what was left of the mercenary unit had left quick and quiet, with their tail between their legs.

The Sea Foxes in the region had been notified to be on the lookout for the Circuit Breakers, and would report to Kenja if anything came up. With the Fox Khanate getting into the business of brokering mercenary contracts, it was only a matter of time before the Circuit Breakers would need to find a Sea Fox to handle a deal for them, and then Kenja would get her answers.

She only hoped she wouldn't get those answers too late.

Kenja found the working relationship between herself and Alexi and Reus to be professional, but distant. She still needed to build trust between them and her, and to let them know neither she nor the Sea Foxes truly meant them any harm. They bristled at the bondcords on their wrists, but if they hadn't wanted to wear them, Alexi shouldn't have agreed to the trial.

Not that she had much of a choice.

To Kenja's surprise and delight, Tucker Harwell wasn't the only prize she had bagged in the Trial. Tucker came with the Republic's complete research program. And while she, Alexi and Reus worked on the pressing issue of their mysterious interlopers on Ankaa, Tucker Harwell dove into the long, arduous task of studying the trove of HPG research. Kenja gave him more data cubes, disks, and crystals full of HPG information than he would be able to read in a year, let alone in the month it had taken them to get to Hean. And he threw himself into it as though there was nothing else in the Inner Sphere to worry about.

Kenja felt it was better to let Tucker have his space and lose himself in his work. It would make it easier to build a relationship with him later, when it was much more vital. He would get lost in the details, and value being left to his own devices.

Though naturally, she had to spy on him.

She was a spy, after all.

It was like the old adage of a cat left to watch a mouse. Obviously the cat was going to hunt the mouse.

Of *course* Kenja had to keep tabs on what he was doing. Not because she *wanted* to spy on him, she didn't think she would be able to learn anything specific from him. But because she needed to make sure he wasn't planning to send a distress signal through some back door in the system. Or alert people to his presence. As much as she didn't want to believe it was a possibility, until she knew for certain where the request for the Circuit Breakers mercenaries had come from, she couldn't rule anything out.

And Tucker was still wary. He could have easily arranged it. Just hired whatever merc group was on the planet in some vain bid to end the stress of his flight. Their objective was to rescue him, why not make another bid to escape by having someone else bust you out?

It would have offered him cover and plausible deniability. And they could have dropped him off wherever he wanted to go. It didn't quite fit, but she couldn't rule it out entirely.

He seemed to have a much better relationship with Alexi than Kenja would have guessed, though, so maybe that idea didn't make the most sense. They were a full-blown couple, and spent many nights visiting each other's bunks. Maybe it was a plan for the two of them to get out from the thumb of Reus Tremor?

VoidBreaker Station—the name Kenja had given to the station and this phase of the operation to repair the HPG network—was in a remote area on Hean, and a legacy of the Federated Commonwealth's civil war. Archon-Princess Katherine Steiner-Davion had paid ComStar exorbitant sums to create a chain of worlds between New Avalon and Tharkad with two HPG stations each to facilitate real-time communications between her capitals. Many of the secondary HPG stations had been located far from civilization for technical reasons, and had been abandoned once the system had gone silent. There had once been a town there, but like its name, Pauper, suggested, they grew poor, shriveled in the cold silence, and died. The HPG station failed shortly before the mines dried up, and when both sources of income for the town evaporated, so did the population. Those who managed to survive the financial collapse moved to places where they could get jobs, either on Hean's other continent, or off-planet entirely.

Its remote location and the sparse population made it the perfect working station for their mission. The planet varied in climate, but VoidBreaker was located in an arid desert, snowy in the Hean winters and blisteringly hot in the summers, which made it even less appealing for lookie-loos to randomly pass by. From orbit, it looked serene, but when they disembarked from the DropShip they found themselves in a winter squall, with sharp winds and frigid temperatures.

The structure itself was utilitarian and square, resembling Clan architecture, and would make a warm home. There were Sea Fox scientists inside, already working on the Goliath Scorpion data cache.

The fact that there was a fully-loaded Tiburon Khanate complex within an hour's flight and could arrive with reinforcements sooner than any DropShip—even from any of the likely pirate points—could get to them, made it the perfect spot for the work ahead.

With the only on base personnel the DropShip crew and a few extra guards from the Sea Fox base, the atmosphere felt absolutely cavernous and empty. They had all been in such close quarters for so long that it was a nice change to actually have space to spread out in. Occasionally, Kenja imagined, they would eat together, probably by happenstance, and it would be the same as when they recreated and exercised.

"This is your new home for the time being," she said as she showed Tucker Harwell the lab they had assembled for him.

"Sure," he said. Quietly. Angry about something. There were a hundred reasons for him to be angry.

Which is why she made sure to equip his work lab with anything she thought he might need. Noteputers, delicate instruments, all the scrap HPG material they could find, conference rooms, holoprojectors, old fashioned whiteboards, anything he might need to spur his brilliant mind. And she told him so.

"Or what's left of it," he muttered.

"What?" she asked him.

"Nothing. I'll need some more things. I'll need material to manufacture circuit boards. Digital machining tools, fine machining tools if I need to manufacture parts from scratch. Fine-tuned calipers, wrenches, and the like. A metal printer and modeling software..." He made a long list, too long for Kenja to remember, but Star Commander Petrichor was on hand, writing all of it down.

"We will do everything we can to fulfill your needs, and get it to you as soon as we are able."

"Thank you," he said. His voice was calm and quiet, and the aura of his personal energy gave Kenja the impression he was expecting a fight. Or to have to justify his requests. He could be asking for parts to build a homemade DropShip for all she cared, as long as he didn't use it. But he seemed to calm when he talked about the work, so Kenja decided to do her best to keep him focused on that.

He scratched his wrist where the bondcords encircled it.

"It is no problem," Kenja told him. "We are here to get you anything you need. Your problem is our problem."

Tucker shook his head. "Do you even know the breadth of the problem?"

Kenja shook her head. She knew quite a bit, but the finer details of hyperpulse generator science was not one of them.

"Hyperpulse generators are incredibly complex machines based on the physics technology in a Kearny-Fuchida drive that can send a pulse fifty light years across space. They're burned out. Almost all of them. They're effectively *lostech* now."

"And you think fixing the HPG network is actually possible?"

Tucker shrugged. "Possible? Yes. With the information you gave me, I think it's more possible than ever. But at this point, I don't even know where to start. I guess I need to figure out how to get the HPG station here working without burning out its core. And then, once we get it working, we need to send a message using hyperspace and make sure it gets received without either station blowing up on all of us. And then we need to make sure it's repeatable."

"What do you need now?"

"Other than the list I gave you, nothing at the moment. Let me just get to it, and we'll see," he said and walked deeper into the massive laboratory, leaving Kenja and Petrichor at his back. Although Kenja had felt capturing Tucker would be the end of this grand mission, she realized this was just the beginning.

Kenja and Petrichor walked out together, heading for the comms room so they could relay Tucker's requests to Sea Fox Central on Hean. Tracking down each individual bit of equipment would be their job.

"Make sure they get everything he needs or its equivalent. And ask them to send an additional Star of folks from the technician caste with the equipment, in case he can use the help or assistance installing it," Kenja told Petrichor as they headed down a sterile corridor.

"Do technicians come in Stars?" she asked.

Kenja shrugged. "Doesn't everything?"

"I will have to ask."

"Then don't say Star, just ask for five technicians. Leave it up to the Star Colonel there to vet them and choose who they think would be well-suited and has the proper clearance, but have them send their files ahead so we can go through them, too. I don't want to introduce any potential leaks into the system. He is going to need help, though. No one person could do this alone."

"*Aff*, Star Colonel."

They reached the communications suite, but Petrichor seemed reluctant to go in. She held her noteputer to her chest with both arms and chewed her lower lip. Lingering like she had something else to do or say.

"Is there something else, Star Commander?"

"Permission to make a personal request, Star Colonel?"

Kenja's brow furrowed. What sort of personal request would the young Star Commander want to make? "*Aff*, Petrichor."

"I-I was," the Star Commander stuttered, a sharp departure from her usually capable demeanor. "Well...I was wondering, if you had time...or, rather, during your down time...i-if you would be interested in coupling... With me. That is..."

Kenja felt a flush hit her face and a smile broadened, but she had to chuckle—tenderly, so as not to hurt the girl. "Star

Commander, I am flattered that you have asked me. But how old are you?"

"I am twenty, ma'am."

"So, you were born in what, 3131?"

"*Aff.*"

"I was your age then. I had made my Trial of Position just a year or two before. And I had been drafted into the Watch. 3131, I think I might have been on my first real mission after an extra year of training."

Petrichor's face tightened, still clinging to hope, not knowing where the answer was heading. "That sounds amazing, ma'am."

"You're in that same situation now." Kenja put a caring hand on Petrichor's shoulder. "Maybe I've spent too much time in the Inner Sphere, but something makes me feel it would not be right to couple with you. Even taking our age difference out of it, I am your superior—"

"—in the case of coupling with superior officers, it is often the duty of a *coregn* to provide such service as required," Petrichor said as though she'd been rehearsing.

Kenja felt a little blindsided. The Clans looked at coupling as nothing more than recreation. She had been in situations in the line of duty in the Inner Sphere where she had to couple with Spheroids, and according to their customs, they had much more emotion and feeling tied up into it, but Kenja had never quite looked at it that way.

It wasn't like she didn't find young Petrichor attractive. It was that she was young. So young. *Too* young.

"Why don't we get through this mission first? We'll talk about it again once the HPG network has a fix."

"Of course."

Petrichor looked down to the ground. Almost as though she were feeling embarrassment, something not as common among the Clans, either. What was there be to be embarrassed of?

Kenja thought it through, and realized that Petrichor must have been harboring what the Spheroids would call a "crush" for quite some time. She hated disappointing the young woman, but that was the way of it.

And maybe it would be months or years or decades before the HPG network was back up. So maybe it would be quite a long while before they would have to revisit the conversation. And who knows? Maybe Kenja would feel differently by the time their assignment was complete.

"Just be sure to get the orders in, *quiaff?*" she asked, changing the subject back to business.

"*Aff,* Star Colonel."

Kenja smiled at Petrichor, who tried to smile back weakly, but it was clear her heart wasn't in it. Instead, she nodded and proceeded to the communications suite.

Alone in the corridor, Kenja tried to put the thoughts of the young Star Commander out of her head, and focus on the monumental task ahead. She'd only completed phase one. Phase two was getting the HPG working. Phase three, well that was spreading the HPGs across the Inner Sphere. Before they could get there, there were still a hundred more steps to take and problems to solve.

She hoped she'd simply solved the hardest one, and it was all downhill from that point.

But, she thought of the old Terran proverb about the best laid plans of mice and men.

They often went awry.

CHAPTER 21: LIVING OFF THE GRID

VOIDBREAKER STATION
PAUPER
HEAN
TIBURON KHANATE TERRITORY
22 SEPTEMBER 3151

Kenja pushed her hulking, 100-ton *Mackie* forward across the savannah, looking for enemy 'Mechs on the horizon. She didn't want to be caught off guard again, especially in so slow a 'Mech, but this was agreed-upon the weapon of choice, and she had to deal with it.

The last time she went out on the field, she'd gone down in literal flames, and she couldn't afford to lose any more face.

"I'm coming for you," Alexi Holt's voice, confident and focused, came through the comm. "You can't escape."

Kenja grinned at the other woman's bravado. "Watch me." She looked down to her mini-map, looking for any sign of the enemies through her radar systems, but still didn't find a single blip.

Searching for the other 'Mech with half her mind, she realized the other half was on Tucker Harwell, still working on the HPG puzzle.

Naturally, with him busy, that meant she had time to train and build a rapport with her bondsmen. That meant 'Mech simulators with Alexi Holt and Reus Tremor—occasionally Star Commander Petrichor would join them to make an even foursome. It allowed them something to talk about and bond over, without needing to talk about personal things.

For this latest challenge, Reus had suggested they go back to the very beginning, and that's how Kenja found herself sitting in the simulated cockpit of a *Mackie*, facing off against two other similar crude brutes, each piloted by Reus and Alexi.

The *Mackie* was the first real BattleMech, designed three quarters of a millennium prior by the Terran Hegemony. The early Terrans were convinced they were going to end war as they knew it. They were only half-right.

"These things are slow as hell," Reus said over the comm, his preference for a faster ride showing.

Finally, Kenja sighted Alexi's *Mackie* far off on the digital horizon. She always chose flat black for her 'Mech's color, giving her the appearance of a silhouetted outline instead of a detailed 'Mech. Kenja hadn't spotted Reus, who picked wildly different colors every match. Sometimes it was camouflage to blend into the environment, sometimes it was the most offensive, contrasting colors one could imagine. Kenja wondered if he was doing it to get a rise out of her, but she remembered it was freeing to pick whatever paint scheme you wanted, and have it bear no stakes whatsoever. *And if it makes him easier to find and shoot, who am I to argue?*

"I don't know how they ever got along with these," Alexi agreed.

"It was this or a tank," Kenja reminded them. "And I'd take this over a tank any day."

They both agreed with her.

It was easy to forget that the Clans and the Inner Sphere had had thousands of years of shared culture and history before their split, and getting to duke it out in *Mackie*s reminded them all of that common past.

The Clans and the Inner Sphere weren't always as different as they made themselves out to be.

Kenja marched her 100-tons of 'Mech toward Alexi, the only target she could see. The thing about *Mackie*s was that they were basically just sluggers. Their armor alone weighed more than some 'Mechs. And they had all gone with the most primitive load out of the venerable war machine, armed with nothing more than a prototype PPC in one arm, an autocannon-5 in the other, and a large laser mounted in their viscera. To fight in a *Mackie* was a test of endurance because battles were measured in hours, or sometimes days. With the heaters turned up on the simulators and the simul-gyro bouncing them around authentically, six hours in a simulator slugging it out with *Mackie*s was almost as good as a workout, and worked up just as much sweat.

Alexi came straight at Kenja.

It felt like a comedy routine, where they just kept running and running and running, but never seemed to get any closer to each other. And it wasn't even as though the terrain was difficult. They were fighting on a randomized rendering of the African veldt, with no elevation changes and only the occasional gnarled tree rising from the tall grass like a leafy question mark. It was easy terrain to traverse, but the *Mackie* tapped out at about fifty kilometers an hour. Which was painfully slow. The *Tiburon* Kenja favored could run at more than twice that speed, and was better equipped than the MSK-5H *Mackie* at only a third as many tons.

Battle technology had come so far in 700 years, and it was nice to get the occasional reminder that things were a lot better now. But if there was one thing humanity could count on, Inner Sphere, Clan, or otherwise, it was that humankind would always develop more efficient ways of killing each other.

Plodding out to meet Alexi's *Mackie* gave Kenja plenty of time to think, and she pondered how many advances and new 'Mech designs there had been since Gray Monday, but there hadn't been any comparable advances in communications technology.

Humanity chose its priorities.

She was just glad to be working on the more ethical priority.

"Are you running away?" Alexi asked Kenja over the comm.

"*Neg.* Are you?"

"These things are painful."

"*Aff.*"

Reus' disembodied voice added, "I'm amazed you two can even see each other. The computer put my drop zone at the ass end of nowhere."

Kenja stifled a laugh as her rangefinder told her Alexi would be within firing distance of her laser and PPC soon. She hated the torso-mounted laser, because it meant she really had to be looking at what she was aiming at dead on, which always meant her opponent likely had a straight shot back at her. When fighting *Mackie* versus *Mackie*, you'd constantly find yourself facing front against each other to do the most damage. Kenja knew there were people out there who preferred the slower pace and the older weapons, but for the life of her, she couldn't figure out why.

Her targeting reticle turned gold, and she fired her PPC and laser at Alexi. They carved deep scars into the armor, leaving globs of molten steel to drip hot from the frame, but that did nothing to disrupt its oncoming assault. Alexi fired back at about the same time and got the same result, mildly charring Kenja's *Mackie*.

"That I saw," Reus said, confusing Kenja, and forcing her to look at her HUD and mini-map to find him. If he saw that and announced himself, he was ready to pounce, but she still had no visual on him.

The glimmer of another laser firing at Alexi tipped Kenja to Reus' position, and she kept barreling forward, hoping to catch sight of him.

Soon enough, there he was on Alexi's eight. His *Mackie* was a full-blown rainbow of color, ostentatious and proclaiming loudly, "Here I am, die mad about it!"

"Damn it, Reus!" Alexi called out. As the simulation had dropped her between the other two 'Mechs, it was almost certain she'd be knocked out of their little contest first.

Reus hooted victoriously. "Ha ha!"

Kenja marked every laugh from the pair of them as a step to winning them over to her side and toward their loyalty to the Sea Foxes.

They exchanged fire once more before a voice crackled in on the comm. "Star Colonel, do you copy?"

It was Petrichor. She sometimes fought as Kenja's partner in the scrimmages against Reus and Alexi and always knew where to find her.

"*Aff*, Star Commander."

"Your presence is requested for a briefing."

Kenja's heart leaped. "Has there been a breakthrough?"

"Tucker Harwell made it sound urgent."

"Understood." Kenja switched her comm line back to the simulation. "Alexi, Reus, it looks like we're going to have to take a raincheck on this *Mackie* fight."

As if to contrast her words, Reus's *Mackie* committed to an alpha strike against Alexi's. He shrieked giddily as he did so.

"Damn it, Reus!" Alexi called again, the cockpit of her *Mackie* getting battered in.

Kenja didn't let them continue, shutting down the simulation. "Tucker has news. It's time to get back to work."

CHAPTER 22:
BREAKTHROUGHS AND SETBACKS

**VOIDBREAKER STATION
22 SEPTEMBER 3151**

Tucker Harwell's lab had become a messy nest of papers, parts, and noteputers. The Clan Sea Fox scientists assigned to work with him had lodged one formal complaint about the mess and Tucker's eccentricities at the beginning of their assignment. Kenja had had a chat with them, Clan warrior to scientist caste member, explained the importance of the work, and aggressively intimated there would be no more complaints lodged whatsoever. And if they wanted a reassignment, she would assign them to a new team to find aliens in uncharted space in a broken DropShip.

She had assured them they would not like it.

But as she walked into the lab, she understood their complaints. Sea Foxes, for the most part, were raised in JumpShips and DropShips, mostly in zero-gee, where everything has its proper place. It was an environment where anything out of order could cause a catastrophe, and Tucker Harwell's shambolic methods of research were enough to cause anxiety in even the most ardent Clan Sea Fox warriors.

He'd cleared just enough space and had enough chairs brought in to offer a briefing for Kenja, Petrichor, Alexi, and Reus. It was need-to-know, and aside from Star Captain Yung, there was no one else on the base with clearance to receive his briefing. The scientists stood at the back of the room in Sea

Fox blue lab coats, arms folded and toeing the ground, waiting for Tucker's urgent briefing to begin.

Kenja took her seat and watched the scientist manipulate his noteputer at the back of the room. She hadn't talked to him a whole lot in the last couple of months, preferring instead to get occasional check-ins and leave him to his work.

He looked better than she'd seen him. The stability and consistent gravity had done him well. He had the run of the place, he had no real guardrails, and he could associate with anyone at the station he wanted, though he spent a lot of time with Alexi, taking long walks through the corridors. Kenja hoped it felt like some sort of home to him. Or at least somewhere safe.

Without fanfare, the lights in the room dimmed and the holoprojector whirred to life, bathing the room in the pale blue light.

"Thank you all for coming on such short notice," Tucker said, walking toward the image he projected. It looked like a lot of technical elements Kenja didn't understand, nor did she feel like she needed to. "I'm sorry I haven't made a more substantial briefing to this point, but I think we're close to ready for our next phase."

Kenja took a deep breath as though she was buckling into her *Tiburon*'s command couch. Ready for the ride.

"As a refresher," Tucker said, switching the image on the holoprojector to a schematic of an HPG station, but it looked bigger than Kenja had ever seen. It was labeled *"Super Hyper Pulse Generator."*

"In researching and developing a Super-HPG, the Word of Blake discovered it had the uncanny ability to create standing interference patterns that hinder any translations through hyperspace. Called the Clarion Protocol, the method was unstable, a Pandora's box of problems that even the Blakists decided wasn't worth pushing the theory or technology any further, so the idea of a Super-HPG was dead on arrival.

"When the Republic of the Sphere found the Blakist research, they refined that theory into something more practical. Theoretically, a Super-HPG could only disrupt a patch of space, but the Republic had larger aims. The Republic scientists came up with a system for rigging the entire HPG network together to disrupt an incredibly *wide* area of space. When whoever pulled the trigger on the Blackout decided to do so, they sent a cascade download through the network with the Clarion firing instructions and an insidious secondary method to control targeting protocols. That cascade fried some of the old HPGs outright. We theorized then that there was a virus at work, but couldn't identify one—until much later.

"What the Blackout cascade did was disrupt the 'band' of hyperspace HPGs operate in, while the embedded virus up kept any replacement cores from functioning by smartly offsetting a targeting event into dangerous locations—like the core of a nearby star—often with disastrous results. With new code, new components, and new calculations, we can remap these intersections of the hyperspace topography and their flux rates, to account for the variables and bypass the virus."

"In English maybe this time?" Reus said.

Tucker shook his head and adopted a tone much like an adult lecturing a small child. "Let's say the HPG system operates on calm waters that make it easy for boats to navigate. They found a way to make tidal waves on that calm water, making it so choppy no one could really cross it, and then messed up the boats for good measure. Well, I think I can build a better boat, regardless of the water's chop."

Reus harrumphed, but didn't say anything else.

"If the water was that choppy and the boats were messed up," Kenja asked, "why did some stations stay online?"

"Good question. It seems that by sheer happenstance, some of those stations didn't receive the virus packet in the cascade update, and the topographical distortions canceled each other out, creating eddies of calm where HPG messages would work. That's probably why some stations were physically attacked and destroyed when the architects of this calamity realized there were holes in their work. All in all, even today, only a small fraction of regular HPG stations still work correctly, let alone the handful of mobile HPGs floating about. With the limitations of distance standard HPGs can transmit, the remaining working ones are of limited strategic use because there aren't enough to send a message to another HPG that could reply or relay it onward. At least, not an encrypted message."

"Tucker, you mentioned mobile HPGs. Our Khanate has a few that work," Kenja asked, "but my understanding is they are not a fix for the Blackout?"

"Another good question. Mobile HPGs work differently than ground stations so they can send messages, but they suffer from an enormous error ratio. According to the data provided by your Sea Fox scientists and our own findings, on average a mobile HPG sends the same message twelve times before it's received, with an eighty-percent chance of significant data loss. Any transmission that makes it to its destination arrives solely thanks to stubborn repetition." Harwell shook his head. "I'm sorry Star Colonel, but mobile HPGs won't rebuild the network."

Petrichor raised a hand, as though they were back in their Shiver asking a question of her Shiv-trainer.

Harwell pointed at her. "Yes. You. What?"

"Who caused the Blackout then? ComStar, or the Word of Blake? Or someone else?"

Tucker's shoulders fell. "Frankly, I doubt we'll ever know for sure. I have enough evidence to believe Devlin Stone himself, Exarch of the Republic of the Sphere, may have put the plan together as a contingency in case the Republic fell. Whether he put those plans into motion before his cryo-sleep, or some still-unknown entity stumbled upon his plans and enacted it for other reasons altogether, is still a big question mark. At the end of the day, my guess is we'll really never know who did it. And more to the point, it almost doesn't matter *why* anyone did it, we've been living in a dark age for nearly twenty years because of it, and we need to fix it. Most important, I think we might have found a way out of it once and for all."

"Might?" Kenja asked.

"Might." Harwell nodded and switched the projection hovering in the room between them.

It was a map of systems centered on the Hean system. Ankaa was there to its coreward— "north" if reading it as a two-dimensional planetary map—and Tybalt to its eastern spinward, both colored yellow to mark them as controlled by the Federated Suns. To the rimward—which appeared south to them—were half a dozen systems, all colored green to mark them as controlled by the Capellan Confederation. Basalt and Tigress were the closest ones in that region. Then, to the coreward, northern, and western anti-spinward side were another half a dozen systems in red, owned by the Draconis Combine, with Deneb Kaitos and Addicks the closest to Hean there.

"All of our work has been theoretical so far. I think the reason we couldn't figure this problem out is twofold. First, we didn't know what caused the Blackout in the first place, and second, we didn't understand how it works. Now that we understand how hyperspace distortions affect HPG translations thanks to that old Terran research information gleaned from the Scorpion Empire, we know how to develop the fix.

"The VoidBreaker protocol is a two-part solution. First is the physical targeting modulator, a component taken from the same research and studied by the Foxes. We've modified the design in the lab, and it must be physically installed on each individual HPG. This targeting modulator will circumvent the HPG's original targeting hardware and mechanics, and bypass the embedded virus, but otherwise doesn't affect any other HPG use.

"The second part is the new software we'll need to hardcode into the HPG stations. In combination with the research from Project Sunlight, the Scorpion files, the data from ComStar's efforts, and my own work, we've created a software package that makes the modulator adaptable to changing topographical conditions without micro-second-by-second turning. Once the modulator and software is installed, it will adapt the transmissions to the topographical conditions, and it contains an algorithm I designed to automatically tune to the local area. Essentially, it'll allow the HPG targeting to ride the hyperspace distortions as they change, like a wave. If we were to remove either one of these advances, the HPG in question would cease to work immediately. Think of it as a really complicated boat and its highly competent navigator to forge ahead on the sea."

Kenja felt a wave of excitement, but also like the legs were about to drop out from the bottom of her 'Mech. That *might* was killing her.

Then, as if to validate her feelings, Alexi leaned over to Reus and whispered, "This is usually where the bottom falls out." Reus nodded in vigorous agreement.

"What do you need from us?" Kenja asked, hoping to get straight to the point.

"We have re-coded the software for the prototype targeting array and installed the modifications on the HPG station here. We've thoroughly documented the VoidBreaker protocol, but it is subject to testing. If it works, we're in good shape for replicating it wherever we go. We have created a number of prototypes, ready to go."

"This all seems like good news," Kenja said. "Your summons for this briefing implied a problem."

"As I said, we aren't sure any of this works."

"Why not? Haven't you tested it?" Kenja asked. That seemed like a silly thing to skip.

"We've tested it by sending pulses to the main HPG station on Hean in Cadaceus, into the outer solar system, to the mobile HPG on loan here, and to the *Bull Shark*. The modulator works locally and bypasses the original targeting apparatus perfectly. We don't know if we can get clear signals to other HPGs' transceiver chambers across multiple light years, in systems with a different interference topography than Hean's. Being able to maintain two artificial jump points between two modulators needs a second HPG in range of the first. Our test data packets failed an acceptable margin of error, except for the pulse we sent to Cadaceus' HPG. The modulator worked sending a transmission to its receiver room."

Tucker paced back and forth as he spoke, lost in his head. "The Cadaceus receiver room is a static location that gives the modulator's algorithm the lowest error probability with minimal diffusion of the transmitted information packet. The test pulses sent in the clear or to the mobile HPG all suffered from varying degrees of degradation during translation. We even tried to install a modulator on the mobile HPG, but the targeting bypass wouldn't work with its system architecture. We have to send a targeted signal to a distant HPG's receiver room to see if it has the same success rate as our Cadaceus test. While pre-Blackout HPGs could send radio pulses anywhere they liked, within range, our test data suggests the modulator requires a shielded transceiver to be on the receiving end. If VoidBreaker works, HPGs may be effectively limited to transmitting to other HPG receiver rooms, since nobody has been building stand-alone EMP-buffered transceiver units outside of HPG compounds."

The map suddenly made sense. A number of the planets darkened and more brightened as Tucker pointed up at the floating systems. "This is a map of all the nearby systems within one jump of Hean that have an HPG system that could potentially receive a message. I need a couple of my scientists here," He waved a hand at them in the back, "to get to one of these planets, get inside the HPG station, and, hopefully, receive a message from here. Naturally, I have to stay here so I can monitor the progress and ensure we don't have another burnout and don't have to start over, but that's where we're at. I feel confident. We *think* we've got a solution, we've got a working hypothesis based on all the available data, and we think it's likely to work. But we need you to get us to a non-Hean receiver we can transmit to."

Kenja looked up at the worlds, split evenly between the Capellan Confederation and the Draconis Combine, making an incursion of any sort a dangerous risk. It would be a gamble for an iteration of the VoidBreaker protocol whose success they couldn't guarantee.

Reus raised his hand, taking his lead from Petrichor.

Tucker pointed at him. "Tremor."

"What makes this time different?"

"What do you mean?"

Reus looked around as though his meaning was obvious. He had a direct manner Kenja found refreshing. Maybe she'd been spending too much time around Clan-folk after too much time in the Inner Sphere.

"I mean, you've been working on this for twenty years."

"Close to," Tucker said. "Off and on."

"And what makes you think suddenly, in the last two months, you've actually made the breakthrough that's going to make it work? You haven't been able to scrub the virus from infected HPG targeting systems? I don't mean to be a downer, but it seems a little too easy, right?"

"You're not wrong," Tucker told him. "The virus has resisted every removal attempt. I know how to bypass it, but it could take another twenty years to find a permanent fix. Its creators knew what they were doing when they wrote it." He shrugged, a look of disappointment flashing across his face. "And that's why we need to test it. But the point is you're right. I *have* been working on this for a long time, but I've never had all these pieces together at once. The data dump taken from Clan Goliath Scorpion included some ancient Terran Hegemony hyperspace research the Sea Foxes pulled the schematics from for their original targeting modulator and the underlying physics behind it. Coupled with my Sunlight research, I was able to account for variables I simply couldn't have before. With the schematics themselves, we were able to engineer the right hardware and add the correct software to install within an HPG's physical core. We've spent years replacing burned out cores and scrubbing code, only to have it burn out with a single transmission attempt because of an impossible to cure software virus creating interactions with some really terrible gravitational variables, like a star's interior."

"So?" Tremor said.

"So, the biggest difference is this hardware mod and auto-resolving gravitational targeting algorithms. They address the hyperspace distortion and the virus problem, and should work after installation and local tuning. Who knows? Maybe it doesn't work. But I think we've got it. But it's going to make repairing the HPG network tedious as all hell, because we're going to have to go station by station to make the repairs with this protocol, and we'll still lose significant functionality, compared to pre-Blackout, since we won't be able to send to standard radio receivers any longer with any degree of success—just HPG transceivers. We'll have to replace cores entirely in places where they're burned out, but—" he glanced at Kenja, "—based on what you've told me about Sea Fox production capabilities, they should manage to keep pace with our implementation teams."

Kenja looked back at the Sea Fox scientists assembled at the back of the room and called out Pernilla, a woman with dark black skin and a pulled back tangle of graying dreadlocks in a Sea Fox lab coat. "You think this is going to work?"

Pernilla stood forward, ahead of the rest of the scientists, and nodded. "The science is sound, but just a working theory at this point. Tucker is correct, we will not know if it works for sure until we test it. But it is all theoretically possible, given what we know. He is not the only one who has spent many years working on the problem, the Sea Fox scientist caste has never stopped trying to solve it, but I think his solution—the VoidbBreaker protocol—will be our best chance of meeting this challenge."

That was enough for Kenja. Members of the Sea Fox scientist caste knew they had to have their facts fully straight prior to committing to a field test that could cause catastrophic failure. She had heard of several scientists who had been sloppy in their calculations being challenged to a Trial of Grievance by their peers, and demoted to a lesser caste if their calculations proved flawed. Scientists were unafraid to test, but had to be sure their work would stand up to rigorous scrutiny before committing to implementation.

Kenja knew this was going to come down to her, but she couldn't leave Tucker Harwell alone on Hean. She would have to stay. Not to babysit, per se, but to ensure he didn't escape. She could very easily see him trying to use the excitement and possibility of a test to try and head out to parts unknown. No, she would definitely have to stay behind. Both she and Tucker would need to work by proxy on their destination planet to make the test work. She doubted Alexi Holt would leave his side, so Reus Tremor would likely need to go on the mission as well.

And suddenly, a plan came into focus.

"Star Commander Petrichor," Kenja said.

"Yes, Star Colonel?" Petrichor answered, all traces of the twenty-something with a crush replaced by a very Sea Fox-like all-business attitude.

Kenja tightened her jaw. It was an awful risk, but she didn't have another choice. "I have an assignment for you."

PART 2
INTERLUDE

"The distance between insanity
and genius is measured only by success."

—Ancient Terran Proverb

CHAPTER 23: INCURSION

FORTRESS-CLASS DROPSHIP _FILIBUSTERO_
PIRATE POINT
ERRAI
DIERON MILITARY DISTRICT
DRACONIS COMBINE
20 OCTOBER 3151

Star Commander Petrichor didn't like wearing the uniform of a mercenary. Nor did she like having to bear one of their names either, in this case "Ruby Havelock." It felt wrong to use a last name she had not earned. But this was what the mission required, and it was what the Sea Foxes needed of her.

After the last year, she had grown accustomed to burns to a planet, and heading into Errai at almost one-and-a-quarter-gees to cut the insertion time to a few hours was a necessity.

"Nothing quite like it, eh, Havelock?" Aura Patel, the major in charge of the mercenary unit, asked Petrichor, watching her like a jade falcon.

"No. Nothing like it," she replied, assuming she meant the heavy pull of the gees. They were all strapped down inside the briefing room that let out into the 'Mech bays of the ship, all hands awaiting landing, ready to fulfill their part of the mission.

Sea Fox Watch reports revealed the Filibuster Brigade was a relatively new unit, formed in the last decade in the wake of the Kell Hounds scattering after the fall of Arc-Royal. Their leader, Aura Patel, had been a Kell Hound for a decade prior to that, but had not joined them in exile in the Periphery. There were reports that the Kell Hounds, a legendary mercenary unit now based in what was being referred to as the Hinterlands and led by Callandre Kell, the great-granddaughter of the man who founded the unit, had begun to reform, but the Petrichor didn't have the most up to date information about that.

Through a series of intermediaries, Star Colonel Kenja Rodriguez had hired the Filibuster Brigade to take Petrichor, Reus Tremor, and Pernilla among their numbers, escort them to Errai in the Draconis Combine, and break into a derelict HPG station in a deserted area of the planet. Constructed by ComStar in the 3060s as part of the chain enabling real-time communications between New Avalon and Tharkad, it was located in the equatorial deserts of the Carrigan continent, on the opposite side of the planet from the bustling capital of Errai Prime, and had been abandoned after Gray Monday. If all went well, the plan would be a success, and everyone would go home rich. Or something like that.

Unfortunately, the Third Dieron Regulars—known as the Ever-Vigilant of Kessel—were stationed on Errai, and the chances for trouble were high.

Reus Tremor was traveling under the name of Smith. John Smith. The most generic name Kenja could have assigned to him. Pernilla was traveling under the name Caitlin Thunderbolt.

The only thing more unusual than traveling under a pseudonym, Petrichor thought, *is wearing a Filibuster Brigade coverall rather than my Sea Fox uniform.* The Filibuster Brigade wore gray mechanic's coveralls on the DropShip.

Patel, a beautiful woman—not quite as beautiful as the Star Colonel, but no one was—with dark brown skin and a larger frame, looked at the noteputer on the table and checked the readings. "One hour left," she said. "And the plan remains unchanged. You ride along with the hovertanks, and they'll get you and your team to your target. We'll keep the Third Dieron off your back for as long as you need. If anything goes south, we claim you as ours."

"How you doing?" Reus asked Pernilla, who looked ready to throw up.

"Not well," she replied.

"I hope you're well enough to get this job done," he said. "No pressure, but you know everything's riding on it."

"I'll be fine," Pernilla said, lurching forward and raising her hand to cover her mouth.

"We'll be okay," Petrichor said, practicing a contraction, just as Pernilla had, even in the middle of their grav-sickness.

They'd do fine once they landed.

To make sure the incoming HPG signal's potential EMP blast did not cripple the vessel if Tucker's experimental targeting workaround ended up missing the shielded transceiver chamber, the closest the DropShip could safely get to the HPG station was a flat stretch of wasteland on the equator, about ten klicks away. The Star Colonel had chosen the site because of its speedy distance from surface to pirate point and back, and because it would take at least a few hours for the Third Dieron to mobilize and oppose them. Hopefully, their mission would be complete and they would be long gone by then.

Petrichor had read about the exploits of the Third Dieron and their presence concerned her, but the Star Colonel's insertion plan was sound. Kenja had assured her that the careful timing gave them the best chance of success. They would go into the abandoned HPG facility, make it ready, receive the message in the carefully synchronized mission window, and leave like a crack of lightning, as fast as they had come.

Petrichor marveled at the logistics planning that had gone into such a mission, and her admiration for the Star Colonel doubled. Perhaps even tripled. She found every detail about the Star Colonel so incredibly compelling she couldn't decide if she would rather be *with* her or just *be* her.

The major had the comm piped into the conference room so they could hear the local authorities complain as they raced toward their entry zone. "Unidentified vessel, broadcast your IFFs and immediately alter course to New Atlanta Spaceport. Repeat..."

Soon, the pleas for identification became threats when their cover identity was not believed. "Unidentified vessel," the comm squelched again, "identify yourself immediately or we will blow you out of the sky. You have ten seconds to reply, or you will be destroyed."

Patel looked over to Petrichor with a wry smirk. "They can't shoot us down. They don't have anything big enough to scramble from the far side of the planet in time to deal with us, so don't worry about that at all."

Petrichor nodded, placing her faith in the major, but more importantly the Star Colonel.

To the credit of Kenja and the mercenary commander, they were right about the defensive capabilities and timing for the operation. The Draconis Combine forces were unable to scramble anything to oppose them by the time the DropShip landed. Then, with the force of normal gravity under their legs, they unbuckled and scrambled.

Major Patel stood first, reiterating her orders through the comm and offering a cool and calming sense of assurance to everyone. Even Petrichor felt safe in this woman's hands. Capable and confident. *She would make a good Clan warrior, too.*

"Let's do this," Tremor as Smith said, leading Pernilla and Petrichor through the corridors to the cargo bay holding the tanks. There, they met Ivar Fenrir, the androgynous tank commander who would whisk them from the drop zone to the HPG Station.

They welcomed everyone, and offered a salute Petrichor couldn't decide if it was mocking or not. "Hello, everyone. I'm Ivar Fenrir and it's my job to get you to the conflict zone in record time. We're in a little rush, so if you'll all just get on board, we'll get out of here."

Fenrir offered them seats on a Falcon hovertank in a back compartment. Cramped, for sure, but it was likely the best and fastest vehicle they had to offer. It also had offensive capabilities in case they were harried by the unfriendlies— namely a medium laser and two short range missile launchers. There was always a danger the Third Dieron Regulars would show up, but the intelligence suggested their foes would attack the DropShip rather than the station. That was part of the Star Colonel's reasoning as well. There was no compelling reason for the Erraians to believe the HPG station was the target of an incursion. It had been dead for two decades, and attached to an abandoned city. Unless they had a deep knowledge of the current state of the HPG network, Sea Fox plans, and the knowledge of Tucker Harwell's whereabouts, they weren't going to be doing much but scratching their heads in confusion at the DropShip setting down in the middle of nowhere.

Truly, the HPG station was abandoned because it was useless to everyone—except the Sea Foxes.

Riding in a hovertank was a drastically different experience than a 'Mech, or even a DropShip for Petrichor. For one, they moved *fast*. Much faster than the vast majority of 'Mechs. And they were *so* low to the ground. It was like being in a small, well-armored troop transport. They zipped along through the equatorial desert on a cloud of air. Supported by the powerful fans that held them aloft and carried them, frictionless, across the sand, they listened to updates about the incoming 'Mechs and aerospace support the entire way. Petrichor worried about the dusty signal they left behind for all to see, but Ivar assured her it wouldn't be an issue.

Besides, 10 klicks at 150 kph wasn't all that long, and the Erraians couldn't scramble anything in time to intercept them from New Atlanta, the closest major city.

"We've got aerospace fighters en route," Fenrir called out. "Probably reconnoitering."

Petrichor felt dizzy, both from the motion and speed of the hovertank, and from that fear of discovery she hadn't yet learned to quash.

The tank's engineer held her fingers to her earpiece, then looked up to Ivar Fenrir, concerned. "Sounds like a DropShip's been scrambled. Some 'Mechs, too."

Of *course* the Draconis Combine wouldn't want to have an unknown enemy force wandering around one of their planets.

"Seems like things are getting real." Reus smiled as though he enjoyed it, forcing Petrichor to wonder about herself and the sort of person who relished these jobs. And whether or not she was in the right place.

The HPG station was an oasis in the vast desert, far away from foothills and populated cities. A ribbon of ferrocrete road led to the impressive structure and stretched far from it, but that wasn't the course they had taken with the hover tank. The building itself was decorated in solar panels that reflected the hot sun overhead like mirrors. All of it topped by the massive parabolic dish.

"Here you go," Fenrir said. "We'll be waiting for you to finish. There's only a couple hours until the mission window opens, and then we're getting the hell out of here as soon as we can. Hopefully before their cavalry arrives, *quiaff*?"

"*Aff*," Petrichor said automatically, and Fenrir and Reus both laughed.

Reus leaned close to her ear as they crouched to get out of the hatch of the hover tank. "Might want to drop the '*affs*' and '*negs*' for a bit, friend."

Petrichor nodded. He was right. She needed to watch it. She was, for all intents and purposes, not Clan in that moment and couldn't act like it. And her respect for the Star Colonel unexpectedly swelled even more inside her. Her job was even harder than Petrichor imagined. Getting out of the hovertank, Petrichor saw five other Falcon tanks flanking them.

Reus nudged her with his elbow. "They're taking this pretty seriously."

But Petrichor would have expected nothing less from the Star Colonel and her arrangements. If she was going to do something as distasteful as hire mercenaries, she was going to ensure they were the best she could find. So far, the Filibuster Brigade had been everything they needed them to be. Professional, skilled, and discreet.

With Pernilla in tow, Petrichor and Reus were ready. Tremor raised a laser pistol and led the way. Petrichor wielded a needler; a suggestion at Kenja's behest. "They're quieter for one. They're more discreet, for two. And, frankly, I just prefer them." Kenja had handed one to Petrichor that was the same model as the one she took into the field.

Pernilla, a scientist rather than a warrior, remained unarmed and would be forced to rely on the other two for protection.

Tremor led them to a massive roll top door at the side of the HPG facility, caked in fine orange dust from the desert. No one had been out here in a decade or more. For a moment, Petrichor wondered how they would power up the station to receive the potential message, but she remembered from her briefing that most HPG network stations were independent of any planetary energy grids. ComStar preferred to have control of their own power generation. That meant there was an auxiliary fusion plant in there somewhere, and they would have to stoke its flame.

After Tremor bypassed the security pad outside the door with an old Republic code, it rolled up with a cough and a rattle, shaking the dust from its gears as though it had been asleep for a hundred years.

Petrichor and Tremor pointed their weapons at the technocomplex, but there was no sign of human activity inside. The massive warehouse space looked completely desolate, with the only lights flooding through coming from the hovertanks. An indigenous desert toad scurried to the corner, right through the largest spider-like web Petrichor had ever seen. The flesh crawled up her back, but not enough to get her to fire her needler.

"Easy there," Tremor told her, sensing her bristling. "No need to waste ammo."

Petrichor distracted herself by looking at the chrono on her wrist, another gift from the Star Colonel before the mission. She liked the way it looked on her arm, a bold black line on her wrist. "We have two hours before our reception window opens. We are going to have to get the power on and change the settings in time to receive the message."

"If it even works," Tremor said with an uncharacteristic hint of pessimism.

"Which direction, Pernilla?" Petrichor asked.

"This way. Follow me."

Together, they trudged deeper into the bowels of the abandoned temple of communication.

CHAPTER 24: POWER TRIP

TYBEE HPG STATION
SHERMAN DESERT
CARRIGAN
ERRAI
DIERON MILITARY DISTRICT
DRACONIS COMBINE
18 OCTOBER 3151
    (T-MINUS 1:34:00 BEFORE RECEPTION WINDOW OPENS)

The fusion generator was completely missing, and Petrichor couldn't describe how furious that made her with the scouts who'd reported the HPG intact.

She understood that not everything would be working, but to have their power station just gone, that was nothing short of a punch to the gut and she wanted to punch someone else for it. She needed to learn better how to keep her cool otherwise she wouldn't be assigned to her post for very long, if she even lived.

"I bet the locals took it when they realized no one would need it here," Reus Tremor said. " I would have. And the informants must not have checked inside the structure, taking Fox credits without doing the work."

"It matters not *why* it is not here," Pernilla said, "only that it is gone. And we still need to power the building."

"Options?" Tremor asked.

Petrichor thought frantically for options and remembered one possibility. "Those were solar panels on the roof."

Pernilla sighed. "Those are backups for nominal systems. They power the lights, HVAC, and secondary systems most likely. They will not be powerful enough to do what we need them to do."

Petrichor raised a crooked finger. "Even if the HPG isn't beaming a transmission, but just receiving? I thought it only needed the fusion core to transmit."

"Who knows in this old station?" Pernilla shrugged. "We can try it."

And they scrambled, pulling up schematics and wiring plans on their noteputers, downloading them from the nominal systems in the building. They found the solar panels, but they wouldn't work on their own. The wiring systems they were hooked up to couldn't carry the necessary voltage required by the HPG. It might have worked if it had a different output module and battery system, but as it was, they would need parts they simply didn't have.

"We have forty minutes left," Petrichor said, trying to control her desperation.

The three of them stood outside the utility closet, unwilling to disconnect the lights that were working just fine.

Petrichor felt a growing tinge of annoyance. "They have nothing but sunlight in this desert, why wouldn't they run everything with it? It doesn't make sense."

"They would likely not assume someone would just steal the fusion generator from the facility," Pernilla said. "Especially if they saw the lights on and the secondary systems functional."

"Next option then?" Petrichor said, reminding them of the urgency they faced.

"I have an idea," Pernilla said. "But I doubt Fenrir is going to like it."

And when it was explained to them, Ivar Fenrir did not, in fact, like it. "You want to do *what*?"

"We don't have power to rig up the HPG station," Reus said to them. "We need one of your tanks and use its engine and batteries to connect the solar panels to power the command console and receiver room pickups."

"You realize these Falcon tanks are running ICEs, right?"

Though she'd had experience with them, Petrichor was always shocked to discover *anything* still ran on internal combustion anymore. From a logistics standpoint, they made no sense. With fusion you had almost unlimited power, but with an ICE, you had a finite amount of fuel. Sounded like a nightmare for any military operation. And it made sense why Ivar Fenrir would be reticent to just idle their engines for three hours to help power a station that, by all appearance, was abandoned.

"Yeah, we realize that," Reus said.

"We really don't have any other options," Pernilla continued. "The solar array is not adequate, but there are cables enough to run from your hover tank to the systems we need to operate. Essentially, your Falcons would be a very mobile bypass."

"What happens when we're under attack and beatin' feet to get out of here and I run out of gas?"

Petrichor stepped in, showing Fenrir the terms of the contract on her noteputer screen. "You can radio Major Patel if you need authorization, but the terms of the contract with the employer state clearly that our objective is highest priority, and any consumables—including fuel costs—will be completely reimbursed."

Fenrir's eyes narrowed as they looked at the clause on the screen, then growled harshly, "Fine. You got it. Anything you need. Just not my tank." They poked their head into the hover tank, shouted some orders, and pulled their head back. "Fitzgerald's gonna take care of you. Tell him where to park his tank and what you need to do."

They looked over to see one of the other hovertanks in a defensive posture in a circle around the station coming right in their direction.

Fitzgerald—who insisted they call him Fitz—was as congenial as he was pissed. It was the accent. His thick accent made him sound as delightful as he was angry, shouting curse words at them. "You wanna do *what* to my tank?"

"We want to—"

"I heard ya the first time. I don't think it's possible, and I certainly don't like it."

Petrichor readied the contract clause on her noteputer again, but Fitz—an older man with short curls of gray-white hair and a ruddy complexion—raised a hand to stop her. "I know what the contract says. No need to quote chapter and verse. I'll do it, I'm just registerin' my disgust and displeasure. Don't like anyone in the guts of my Bessie, and certainly not the likes of you."

Pernilla understood and said so. "I can handle all of it."

"Nay," Fitz said. "My tank crew will handle the modifications. You just tell me what needs to be done."

As Pernilla explained hooking the power couplings and cables up to the ICE power amplifier unit on the Falcons, Petrichor kept checking her chronometer and the dwindling minutes before the opening of their reception window. They had a scant twenty left to get the HPG station ready to receive a message.

After giving all the instructions to the increasingly vexed Fitzgerald, Pernilla turned back to Reus Tremor and Petrichor. "You two help Fitzgerald get this rigged, and I'll get to work on the receiver."

Petrichor raised a hand in protest. "You are not going anywhere with at least one of us to escort you."

The scientist's eyes darted between Petrichor and Tremor. Tremor spoke first. "You go with Thunderbolt, Havelock. I'll take care of things here and make sure no one gets inside further than this. I'll be on the radio if you need me."

Petrichor almost said *"Aff,"* but stopped herself. "Will do." She looked to Pernilla and cocked her head at the HPG receiver. "Let's go."

Petrichor and Pernilla broke into a sprint, winding through the dimly lit hallways until they emerged in the heart of the facility: the actual hyperpulse generator control station. Petrichor hadn't quite seen anything like it before, and didn't know what to expect. It looked old, ancient even, despite being constructed less than a century ago. Technology from well over half a millennium earlier, preserved but not improved by ComStar, boxy and out of date by Clan standards. Lights and dials, switches and keyboards, monitors and display screens, they all littered the machine that took up half the space of the cavernous room.

But it was dead. An inert dragon, sleeping and still.

They had to rouse it to obtain the gold it slept on.

Out of breath and panting, Pernilla trotted to the consoles and started toggling switches. "They're mechanical switches," she said. "I can change these settings before we get power."

"What can I do?" Petrichor asked.

"I need you to stay out of the way and make sure no one disturbs me."

Petrichor nodded, then glanced at her chronometer. Six minutes before their receiving window opened. If they missed the message being sent on its first go, there likely would be no second chance with the Draconis Combine closing in on them. Anything could go wrong. *Everything* could go wrong.

All the possibilities spun webs of doubt throughout Petrichor's middle, tightening her guts.

Dutifully, she raised her needler and checked the entrances and exits of the room while Pernilla kept pushing buttons and doing her thing. Petrichor checked behind the machine and in front of it, looking for anything out of the ordinary. Not just an intruder, but a bomb or anything else that could blow up in her face.

The one thing she wasn't looking for was a desert toad. Let alone a mischief of them nestled between the wall and the side of the HPG. The biggest one hissed at her, its evil eyes glowing red.

Petrichor didn't realize she'd pulled the needler's trigger. With its own quiet hiss, the weapon discharged and the desert toad was nothing more than a shredded lump of meat staining the ground.

Immediately, guilt and regret set in. There was nothing about Petrichor that wanted to murder small animals, no matter how annoying. But she'd been startled.

Maybe I am not cut out for this type of work...

She couldn't focus on that, though. She had to complete the mission.

Three minutes.

"Smith," she called through her comm. "Where are you with the power?"

Tremor practically yelled back, trying to be heard over the roar of the combustion engines in the background. "We're doing the best we can. We're pumping energy out. It's all hooked up. I don't know what's wrong."

"We have three minutes." Petrichor looked back down at her chronometer and corrected herself. "Two minutes."

"Everything's all right here, we're doing great," Tremor said, but Petrichor didn't believe his sincerity.

"I hate to break it to you," Major Patel's voice crackled in on Petrichor's earpiece, "but we've got problems. Third Dieron incoming."

"For the DropShip?" Petrichor asked. "Or Tybee Station?"

Patel's voice got serious, low. "Both."

"Are you hearing this?" Petrichor asked Pernilla.

Pernilla nodded, doubling her efforts. "Are the leads on the right nodes?"

"Come again?" Tremor shouted over the din.

"Switch. The. Leads." Pernilla said, loud and slow, for them. "I am not getting power, you probably have the ground on the wrong lead."

"Wrong lead?" Tremor shouted, but Petrichor couldn't tell if he was shouting at them or at Fitz and his crew.

One minute left.

"It's now or never," Petrichor said.

With the clock ready to click over to their operational window, the HPG station whirred to life. The lights of the machine brightened the room and added a mosaic of a hundred colors across its front. The monitors boasted boot up sequences and Pernilla dashed to a keyboard below one of the monitors, doing her best to finish the sequences she needed to complete to receive the message at the correct frequency wave.

The power cycled and stuttered. The lights and monitors dimmed for a heart-stopping moment, then roared back to life and remained consistent.

Pernilla looked back to Petrichor and nodded. "We should be receiving any minute now. As soon as they send the transmission."

"*If* they were able to send a transmission."

"It will work," Pernilla said with hopeful confidence.

Petrichor clenched her jaw. "It better."

CHAPTER 25: ENEMY ACTION

TYBEE HPG STATION
18 OCTOBER 3151 (T-MINUS 24:00 BEFORE RECEPTION WINDOW OPENS)

"They're getting closer!" Tremor shouted over the sound of incoming missiles and laser fire.

But there was nothing Petrichor could do except brace for an invasion of the HPG station. Or death, if the Third Dieron decided to level it entirely. Her crew had to keep the station running for as long as it took to receive a message or their three-hour window closed. Then they had to make it back with the reports on the machinery. Failure wasn't an option. The last thing Star Commander Petrichor wanted to do was travel all the way back to Hean, look the Star Colonel in her chestnut eyes, clever like a raven's, and tell her the mission had been a failure—and it was all her fault.

"We have at least two lances of Third Dieron Regulars 'Mechs incoming," Tremor told Petrichor. "They've got a *Marauder II* on point, likely a nasty sniper configuration, heading right for us. Looks like the second lance has a *Warhammer* fronting it."

Petrichor rolled her eyes. "That is exactly what we needed."

"Is that sarcasm I hear in your voice, dear Ruby? I like this new you."

"Stow it, Smith. We need a way out of this."

"Oh, wait. Looks like they've got some tanks incoming, too. Faster. Harder to see over the dust they're kicking up."

"See what Fenrir can do about it. I'll contact Major Patel and see what defense she's got planned. We *must* defend this station until the mission is complete."

"I know," he said. "I'll talk to Fenrir."

"Acknowledged." Petrichor touched the button on her earpiece to change the comm channel. "Major Patel, this is Havelock."

"Go for Patel."

"I take it you see the issue before us."

"Indeed. We'll screen you as best we can. We don't want to throw 'Mechs out as far as your position, because that would mean loading you up and leaving them behind. But we have an artillery and air-strike option that could work. Fenrir is equipped with targeting equipment and if they can paint 'em, we can hit them from here."

"Smith and Thunderbolt will be thrilled to hear it."

"One more thing, Havelock: you let me know the second your objective is completed or our window closes. The Third Dieron has a nasty reputation. *Tai-sa* Lynwood Rich isn't one to fool around. Imagine all the stories about competence and effectiveness rolled into one commander and that's her. The sooner we have the Combine in our rearview, the better."

"Acknowledged, Major. I want to leave ASAP, too."

"Good. As long as we're all on the same page."

"Aff...irmative," Petrichor replied, then turned to Pernilla. "You heard all that?"

The scientist nodded grimly. "I heard it. But there's nothing I can do. All we do is wait and see if things worked out on their end."

"I hate waiting."

Twenty minutes passed in agonizing slowness, and Petrichor and Pernilla listened on the comm as the carnage began. The Filibuster Brigade sent their tanks out to meet the oncoming assault, painting targets for artillery and air support. Fitz was left behind to continue feeding power to the HPG station, which earned Petrichor several strings of curse words loud and in her ear. She heard somewhere in her studies that no one could swear like the Irish except for, perhaps, a Scot. She didn't have a Scot to compare against, but the Irish was sufficient for her to know that Scots must curse a lot.

The *Filibustero* had enough aerospace fighters configured as bombers to mount a decent offensive against the Regulars coming for the HPG station. And, by the sounds of it, Ivar Fenrir and their lance of tanks were doing their best to stay in the fight, dodging blasts of weapons, missiles, and the hot carving knives of enemy lasers.

Escaping would be a challenge if they couldn't leave soon.

"What's that?" Petrichor asked as the sounds in the room changed. The sedate beeps and whirrs from the HPG's control panels transformed into a rough clacking. Half the lights grew brighter and the other half grew dim.

"I think this is it," Pernilla said, inserting a data drive into the slot next to her monitor, then typing on the old-fashioned keyboard.

Terror clutched Petrichor's middle, wondering if they were actually en route to success, or if these were the sounds of an HPG on its deathbed.

When Pernilla's eyes widened, Petrichor could only imagine the worst.

"It failed, didn't it?" Petrichor's heart thumped in her chest, the steady bass drum of death.

They were going to die, and it would all be for nothing. *No, she told herself, that isn't true.* They were dying for a chance. Not just for the Sea Foxes, but for the good of every single person in the entire Inner Sphere. And that was worth it, even if their mission wasn't a success. More importantly, she was doing it to win the approval of the person she admired most. And she was *not* going to lose it.

"Not yet," Pernilla said. "The transmission window opened. We are ready to go. It is all on them now."

Petrichor held a breath at the top of her chest and started counting down from sixty, hoping that would distract her enough.

Otherwise, the suspense might kill her.

"Hold on a second," Pernilla said.

Petrichor let go of her breath and looked to the scientist. "We have it?"

"I'm receiving an incoming transmission."

"What's it say?"

"It says, 'To my delight, he came and declared that he had heard and understood what I said.'"

"What is that supposed to mean?"

Pernilla's eyes moistened. "It's what Alexander Graham Bell wrote in his diary about the first successful telephone transmission. When Cassie DeBurke sent the first HPG transmission, the first words she beamed into the stars were the same as Bell's first words on the telephone, ordering Watson to come see him. Tucker has a sense of history."

"It worked then?"

Pernilla nodded her head gratefully. "It worked."

"Praise Kerensky," Petrichor said. The hard part was just about to begin. "Gather all the data you need. We have to get out of here. Now."

Pernilla's gaze snapped from the screen to Petrichor, as though things were finally becoming real. She nodded and got to work at the keyboard, gathering all the data.

Petrichor didn't like it, but she finally understood the Star Colonel's annoyance with her on the JumpShip. Finally, she grabbed Pernilla by her shoulders and dragged her away from the console.

Pernilla bucked out of her grip, stepped back to the HPG, and withdrew the data crystal from its slot on the front of the machine. "We are leaving, I swear..."

"Good." Petrichor activated her radio again. "Smith. Havelock and Thunderbolt are on our way back. Be ready to go."

Reus' reply was exuberant, "Boy, are we ever!"

CHAPTER 26: BEATIN' FEET

SHERMAN DESERT
CARRIGAN
ERRAI
DIERON MILITARY DISTRICT
DRACONIS COMBINE
18 OCTOBER 3151

Strapped into Fitz's Falcon rather than Ivar Fenrir's was an odd experience for Petrichor. The hovertank was more beat up than the one they'd come to the station in, and Fitz stood on no ceremony. He had no respect for them. In fact, he only seemed angry, grumbling through the comm about how little fuel they had. "It'll be a miracle if we make it back at all."

The other thing Petrichor discovered about Fitz was that his piloting was nothing short of reckless. She held on tight, unaccustomed to the speed and the immediate direction changes of the hover tank. Fitz's crew—a gunner named Grace and a Sikh driver named Bheesham with a grizzled beard and a turban—were a competent team. They worked in tandem, steering and firing at each passing 'Mech. The highly customizable Falcon was armed with target acquisition gear and two short-range missile systems, so it was Bheesham's job to weave in and out of the 'Mechs, between their legs if necessary, and Grace's to blast them every chance they got. Fitz's job was to call out targets and paths.

"*Marauder II* coming up," Fitz called out.

"Got it." Grace wheeled around in her chair and aimed. "Target locked."

"Goin' for a forty-four," Fitz said. Petrichor had no idea what he was talking about.

"Acknowledged," Grace said.

"Now!" Bheesham tweaked the steering yoke, sending them careening in a completely different direction, right past the legs of the *Marauder II*.

For Petrichor, it was terrifying to see a 'Mech battle from this vantage point. She piloted 'Mechs, and was usually looking another 'Mech in the eye. Staring up at them looming over her like ferrosteel and ceramiplast giants, she had a new respect for tank crews. Their job was much more harrowing than she wanted to admit.

Looking up at the viewscreen and matching that with her view out the ferroglass windows, Petrichor watched the puff of smoke and heard the launch of the missiles from the tank. She tried to watch to see if the missiles hit the *Marauder II*, but they whizzed by too fast.

"Direct hit," Grace said, satisfaction in her voice. "Coming around?"

"Nay," Fitz said. "We dinna have the fuel, and the recall order is absolute."

"So we just hit what we can as we go?"

"Aye." Fitz pulled the yoke back and sent them racing toward the DropShip, but Petrichor knew the Third Dieron Regulars weren't going to let them escape without a scratch.

As if they read her mind, something smashed into the top of the hovertank. The vehicle shuddered, the impact hitting it with enough force to bottom it out.

Fitz wiped his brow and expertly read out the damage report instruments and snarled. "They missed the skirt, but we're down one launcher. Gauss hit took it right off. One more like that an' we're done for."

Petrichor wondered if the shot had come from the *Marauder II*, turning back in revenge for what the Filibuster Brigade had done to it. Helplessness enveloped her. Her lack of control untethered her heart like a balloon ready to float away.

"You think we should have blown the station?" Tremor asked. "Leave no trace?"

But Pernilla shook her head. "No. If we get this working, we'll need all stations operable. The Combine won't know it's us, but they'll be grateful for it nonetheless. After they forget this mess, of course."

Before Petrichor could offer her opinion on the matter, she was compelled to grip what Fitz had told her were the "Oh Shit!" handles on the sides of her seats to compete with the gees they were pulling with their maneuvers.

"We got more incoming," Fitz said.

"Looks like two *Bishamon*s," Bheesham said.

Grace looked over to him, incredulous. "I thought Fenrir painted these targets and they all got waxed by fire support."

"Obviously a SNAFU," Fitz told her. "We'll raise hell when we get to the DropShip, but not before."

Petrichor had heard of a *Bishamon*, but had never seen one until now. They were quadrupedal 'Mechs, rare in the 'Mechs world, and mediums, rarer still in the world of quads. Renderings made them look like crawling spiders, and seeing them in person didn't dampen that impression. They were well armored, and boasted a stout array of medium lasers and missiles. Fast, deadly, and low to the ground, they were the perfect 'Mech to fight a lance of hovertanks. Unlike the massive, 100-ton *Marauder II*s, *Warhammer*s, and other bipedal 'Mechs, there was no maneuvering beneath them and hitting them with turreted weapons.

"We're going evasive," Fitz said. "I'll call in a fire support request. Grace, be ready to fire whatever missiles we got left, and paint 'em with the TAG, just in case we can get the fighters in for another run."

"Got it."

"I'll get 'em on the horn."

There was a flurry of activity in the crew compartment of the Falcon while Fitz, remaining cool and furious as ever, juked the hovertank back and forth as though he were approaching a defensive line on a handegg field.

The Brigade's aerospace fighters arrived and started their bombing run, bathing the hilly desert under them in fire and destruction. But no artillery fire came from either the DropShip or its general vicinity.

Petrichor wondered where they could be. Were they too busy with their own problems? That seemed silly, since her crew's safety was the entire point of the objective.

On the other hand, they could have been defending themselves. Made sense. If Petrichor didn't have a DropShip to board, it would all be a moot point anyway. They would fall into the hands of the Draconis Combine, the secret of the operable HPG would be known to their enemies, and Petrichor would have let down the Star Colonel in her vital mission to get the network back up and running.

"Let's try this again then, shall we?" Fitz said as he spun the hovertank around the *Bishamon*s.

"You're going back for more?" Tremor asked. "You said the recall was absolute. We need to get out of here, not fight them!"

"We should leave," Petrichor said. "Our mission is vital, and has nothing to do with bagging enemy 'Mechs."

"Not much of a choice," Fitz said, aiming a thumb the other way.

Petrichor and Reus glanced back to see more 'Mechs barring their way to the DropShip. A pair of *Warhammer*s. The other lance?

"That's just terrific," Reus said. "That doesn't change the fact that we have to get back, and we're already taking hits that would flatten lesser tanks."

"And lesser crews," Fitz said. "Don't worry, yer in good hands."

"I'm not worried," Tremor said flatly.

Petrichor put a hand on his arm and shook her head at him. She couldn't change the battle, but perhaps she could keep Tremor from distracting them. "Let them do their job. That's what they're here for."

Tremor grumbled, but stayed out of it. Seemed like he wanted to do the fighting himself.

And then the gee-forces of a tight turn sent them all spinning in the opposite direction, pressing hard into each other.

Fitz spun the tank around again and aimed it right at the *Warhammer*s. "Well," he said, "It's time to see what the Third Dieron Regulars are really made of."

"You're playing chicken with them now?" Tremor said.

Pernilla just kept her eyes shut. Muttering something. A prayer? Petrichor doubted it. She was too science-minded for that sort of hokum.

Petrichor wobbled as the Falcon fishtailed across the sand, hovering just above the next rising hill, pointing its nose right in the direction of the *Warhammer*s, painted in the distinct light gray and dark gray trim of the Third Dieron, ghosts against the clear blue sky. Both aimed their devastating PPCs at the speeding hovertank and fired.

Lightning crackled around them, turning sand to glass on either side of the Falcon.

"Goin' too fast for 'em to get a clean shot," Fitz said, hooting and hollering as he sped right for them.

"We're doing it, I guess," Reus said.

But his words were accompanied by a drastic rise in heat and the wash of a laser carving into them.

"Or not," Petrichor said.

"We're gonna make it!" Fitz said.

"They took our TAG," Bheesham said. "And a *lot* of armor."

"They bent the turret," Grace said. "Our field of fire is a sliver of what it was."

The engine shuddered, but kept going. Why did they use internal combustion again?

"We got this," Fitz said confidently.

All Star Commander Petrichor could do was hold on tight to hope.

And the "Oh Shit" handles.

PART 3

"The great dilemma everyone faces—Inner Sphere, Clan, or otherwise—is what to do with the time they are given, and how to best act in a way that is both authentic to the individual and beneficial to the overall society. It's not always clear or easy. It's not a binary choice. We all face dilemmas that create the illusion of two opposing sides when the only fight is against ourselves."

—Xopher J. Dalton
Neo-Philosophical Musings in a Post-Clan Inner Sphere
Commonwealth Historical Press, 3148

CHAPTER 27: "COLD WISDOM WAITING ON SUPERFLUOUS FOLLY"

VOIDBREAKER STATION
PAUPER
HEAN
TIBURON KHANATE TERRITORY
21 OCTOBER 3151

Star Colonel Kenja Rodriguez knew she would be unable to sleep until Petrichor and her team arrived at the Hean recharge station with word on whether the message had been received. It shouldn't have taken longer than a day for them to get back, but that didn't mean she wasn't worried. Kenja waited in Tucker Harwell's laboratory with Tucker and the other scientists. They were just as nervous about the results as she was.

She tried to keep up on her reading, hoping that she could distract herself from worrying about the fate of the rest.

Alexi Holt sat on the other side of the table from Kenja, trying to do the same.

Tucker Harwell lay on a table at the back corner of the room, tossing a red rubber ball into the air and catching it.

Up and down.

Up and down.

The other scientists paced back and forth.

As far as things at VoidBreaker station went, yesterday's test had gone well. They transmitted *something* to another system, and the core of the HPG transmitter hadn't burned out. That in itself was a major victory.

For an hour after the transmission, Harwell led the scientists in poring over the code and checking and double-checking the integrity of the transmission information, especially the bypass of the original targeting system. Then they double-checked the core itself to make sure it hadn't overheated, and that nothing had gone wrong there. The machine had drawn an enormous amount of power, but Tucker had explained it was an HPG station sending a signal twenty-eight light years away. Of course it was going to draw a lot of power. Then they checked the circuits. And the casings and housings. And everything else. Twice.

The HPG station Kenja and Tucker had chosen to receive the message was located on Errai and wouldn't be able to send a message back. That's why they had planned an elaborate operation to send Star Commander Petrichor, Bondsman Reus Tremor, and scientist Pernilla to a Draconis Combine world, break into the HPG station, receive the message (hopefully), and come back.

But with no word from the strike team, Kenja couldn't contain her dread.

She didn't want to think she'd sent them all on a suicide mission. It was a calculated risk that sent them to a world where a unit as storied as the Third Dieron Regulars were stationed, but the burn time from the pirate point to the surface would give them the advantage. She was sure *Tai-sa* Lynnwood Rich of the Third Dieron Regulars was talented, but not invincible.

But had they been lost?

That risk was part of why she'd hired mercenaries to escort the team. First, they were expendable. Second, they created a layer of plausible deniability between the incursion onto sovereign territory and Clan Sea Fox.

More than anything, Kenja didn't want to lose Petrichor. For better or worse, she had adopted the young Sea Fox as her mentee, in much the same way she'd been adopted. Kenja didn't want her career cut short because of a preventable mistake.

"Any word?" Tucker asked, his voice monotone, as if he hadn't asked every ten minutes since he had finished his work.

"Neg," Kenja said, glancing back at the noteputer.

Every minute that ticked by was a minute more likely that they were gone. Perhaps they had been bombed inside the HPG station. Perhaps they had been killed escaping from it. Perhaps they had been ambushed, and their DropShip was destroyed on departure. Perhaps their JumpShip had been ambushed by the Third Dieron Regular space forces. Perhaps they got all the way to the DropShip, made the burn back to the JumpShip, and just misjumped.

Though her heart beat thunderously in anticipation for word from the advance team, Kenja had other things to worry about, too. Her most important mission during the test was to make sure Tucker Harwell didn't take that as an opportunity to try and vanish again. To his credit, he seemed invested enough that he didn't bother trying to escape, which meant he didn't notice the leash she had around him, and if he did, he was content enough to ignore it and work on the problem at hand anyway.

Not that he had much of anywhere to go as it stood.

While Tucker made sure their HPG wasn't about to self-destruct, Kenja had to oversee the logistics for a sudden and abrupt departure of all base personnel in case they were successful. Upon the completion of a successful test, their orders, straight from Carcharodon, were to make the long voyage to the coreward edge of the Inner Sphere and begin repairing stations—starting with the Tiburon Khanate's capital world, a far-flung planet in the Hinterlands called Twycross.

Though the Sea Foxes had controlled vital enclaves on Twycross for decades, with Tiburon assuming control after Skate Khanate relocated to the Capellan market, sharing the system with the Jade Falcons, there was no recent information about who controlled the former Falcon holdings on-planet, if anyone. It was part of a hotly contested region in the center of a power vacuum. As the Falcons had emptied their territory in their foolish, fatal march to Terra, the eyes of the surrounding factions grew large as dinner plates. As it was on the border of Clan Hell's Horses territory, Kenja figured they were the most likely current co-occupant, but anything was possible, and incoming information was scant. She'd learn more the closer she got to Twycross.

So, everyone waited in the laboratory, knowing that if, by some miracle, the *Filibustero* arrived via JumpShip and had nothing but good news for them, they were all spending their last minutes on solid ground for months, as the voyage to Twycross was no less than 18 jumps.

Kenja sighed.

Such was the life of a Sea Fox Watch agent.

Her noteputer trilled, startling her. The alerts began firing off, one after the other.

"What's that?" Tucker asked.

"It's a JumpShip," she told him, scanning the data.

"Is it them?" Alexi asked.

The weight Kenja felt at her shoulders and the tightness in her neck melted. "It's them."

Tucker bolted upright and the rubber ball rolled to the floor, forgotten in his excitement.

"I'm trying to get them. Hold on."

Tucker bit the already-denuded nail on his right thumb, spitting a sliver of it from the side of his mouth. "They got the message, right? They received it?"

Kenja's eyes widened. "I'm still trying to get them. You know there's a delay, right? They're here, we just need to be patient."

Tucker took a deep breath. Obviously, he knew there was a delay. He knew more about the physics of communication through the stars than anyone in the entire Inner Sphere. He'd apparently just forgotten it all at the sound of the incoming JumpShip.

"*Filibustero*, this is Vee Bee One. Do you copy?"

Another painful hour passed before the response came. "Vee Bee One, this is Suckerfish, do you copy?"

Kenja's heart leapt. Petrichor was alive.

They had jumped in at a pirate point to reduce the delay, but it was still a hefty delay. It would take a while to have the conversation, but it was worth having.

"We copy, Suckerfish. Please report."

The delay caused a palpable stress for everyone who gathered around the table. Kenja felt it in the way they held their breath, huddled around her when the reports started to stream in, and hunched closer to her noteputer where the microphone for the communication was located.

Kenja looked up and saw Alexi's face, worry still writ large upon it, in every laugh line that had turned to stress.

"This is the *Filibustero*," Petrichor said. "Suckerfish reporting. I am delighted to report that the message was received, and we are glad that you are delighted. We are sending a download of the information Pernilla collected on mission and remain on standby for new orders."

"Excellent news, Suckerfish. That changes things. If the captain has prepared to deploy the DropShip, please ask them to hold. I would like to renegotiate their contract."

There came a long pause.

"Acknowledged," Petrichor finally said. "Awaiting new orders. Captain Ryback is holding on the landing procedure, and Major Patel is awaiting renegotiation terms."

"I will send a message with new terms. Proceed with the download and standby." Kenja put the noteputer down and stood. The gathered assembly pulled back, giving her room to address them all. "I need you all to finish packing up. We are departing aboard the *Zephyr* in exactly thirty minutes. Do not worry about going over the data now, you will have time to do so on the DropShip."

Then Kenja turned to Tucker. She expected him to be elated, but his face had soured and his eyes were wet, threatening tears.

"Tucker?" Kenja put a hand on his shoulder, but he couldn't meet her gaze. "I know this is overwhelming, but you did it. It worked. And we are going to celebrate this win. But not here. Not now. There is too much work to do. So pack your things and let's go."

Alexi stood and wrapped an arm around Tucker. "Come on, Tucker," she whispered.

But Tucker merely collapsed into Alexi's embrace, burying his head into the crook of her neck and sobbing.

This was his life's work. And he'd done it.

It wasn't her fault they didn't have time to revel in it. Maybe they could have some sort of party on the DropShip when they were safe and on their way.

CHAPTER 28: "WITH HAWK AND HORSE AND HUNTING-SPEAR"

BROADSWORD-CLASS DROPSHIP ZEPHYR
HEAN
TIBURON KHANATE TERRITORY
22 OCTOBER 3151

Like a good Sea Fox warrior, Kenja fell easily back into the routine aboard the DropShip. Yes, they were still in the thrall of gravity, the last she would likely feel for weeks, but that was fine, too. What need did a Sea Fox have of gravity?

It would take take days to get to the jump point, and they were heading to where their JumpShip awaited at the nadir jump point, many astronomical units from the pirate point where Petrichor and the Filibuster Brigade were recharging. The next time she would see them in the flesh would be when they arrived at Twycross. It was going to take two months, which made Kenja question the wisdom of Tiburon saKhan Andreas Sutherland, but she felt she was in no position to argue. Sutherland's orders, relayed to her on Hean, were that Twycross must be the site of the first formal HPG reactivation so that the credit could properly accrue to his Tiburon Khanate. A high priority command circuit would await them once they reached Tiburon territory, so the *Bull Shark* needed only to traverse the Draconis Combine the slow way.

All she wanted was to get some rest while there was relative safety. Unfortunately, it seemed the night cycle of the ship was when all the bad news came.

"Star Colonel," Star Captain Yung reported from the bridge. "I hate to wake you."

"Then don't," Kenja said, still half-asleep.

"You will want to hear about this."

"I'm sure. What is it?"

"A JumpShip has just arrived."

Kenja's eyes widened with the jolt of adrenaline at the captain's words.

Before she even had a chance to ask, Meridian answered the question for her. "It is a heavily armored *Odyssey*-class JumpShip with three attached DropShips. It is not returning hails, but its IFF gives its name as the *Third Son*, which is not found in our database."

"Any markings?"

"None. It's gunmetal gray. Primed but no paint. No logos. No letters. No registry numbers. Nothing."

"It's an insertion ship. A burner. Where did they arrive? Are they heading in our direction? Or did they hit the zenith?"

"They are at a pirate point."

"How close are they to the Filibuster Brigade?"

"Close enough to worry."

Kenja chewed her bottom lip. The *Filibustero* and the rest of the Filibuster Brigade were recharging at the pirate point they'd jumped in at, leaving them exposed to whatever predations this mysterious JumpShip had in store.

"I'll be up in five. In the meantime, raise Major Patel of the Filibuster Brigade."

"*Aff.*"

As she dressed, Kenja's mind spun with theories. Ships that flew no flags nor bore logos or identification were considered suspicious, so Clan Watches usually used false registries that looked innocuous. The Clans liked to pretend they didn't use subterfuge and deceit, dismissing them as *dezgra* and the sneaky ways of the Inner Sphere, but they *all* did it, and always had. Humans were hypocrites at their base, Clan or otherwise. Remembering that the *Odyssey* was a Clan designed JumpShip class, like the *Bull Shark* that had carried the *Zephyr* in pursuit of Harwell, she wondered if it could be a Snow Raven vessel of some sort. Their schemes were convoluted enough to involve intentionally arousing suspicion to serve an ulterior motive.

It would make sense. The Snow Ravens were a constant thorn in the side of Clan Sea Fox, and had been for centuries. Could they have been the ones who hired the Circuit Breakers on Ankaa? Or was this someone else entirely? It felt like too late in the game for the Snow Ravens to have caught wind of things, but they had an excellent Watch network, and they could not be counted out. Kenja struggled with the biggest fact of all: she simply didn't have enough information.

Maybe the JumpShip's appearance was an accident. Or maybe it could have been a miscalculation on their part. Kenja had chosen to base the operation from the nadir jump point because it was the busier of the two points over Hean, and she was a big believer in hiding in plain sight when possible. But when things were serious, she would switch to the opposite theory. And then she would try to double-blind what she was doing and pick the point opposite of what she thought would be expected. It just added a layer of protection and strategy to what would ordinarily be a simple decision. She second, third, and fourth-guessed herself often.

The other thing to consider was that the Filibuster Brigade could have been witnessed and approximated. That was just a matter of the timing of their jump from Errai and back.

What if they were being followed...? It was considered impossible to track a ship jumping out of a system, but she had heard rumors of it happening.

Dressed in her Sea Fox blues, Kenja headed to the bridge. "Any new information on our friend the *Third Son*?"

"*Neg*," the captain said. "But I do have Major Patel on comms."

"What's the delay?"

"We are looking at ten minutes or so."

Meridian pointed to the duty station Kenja had adopted as her own, and Kenja went for it immediately. "Major?"

"Go for Filibuster One."

"I see you have company. If I wanted to add some clauses to the contract, would that be something we could arrange at our intended destination? Retroactively?"

The lag was killing Kenja. Slowly and surely. Not a day went by where she didn't absolutely hate the comm lag. It made it so hard to have an oblique conversation.

"I definitely think the rates would increase significantly," Patel said. "But it is something we are amenable to. I imagine I can already guess what it is."

"Screen our departure and follow behind us once your recharge is complete. I am transmitting a letter of credit you can use with any Sea Fox courier ship. You will be able to utilize the express courier circuits once you reach Tiburon territory. Send reports if there are further complications. The conditions of our original contract will remain in effect, and I will add an additional bonus if things go well. We can discuss exact terms at our next meeting, fully understanding that I am at your mercy here."

Patel must have known how dire the situation was, even without a complete understanding of what was going on. For a Sea Fox to cede so much, even in the most basic of negotiations, meant things were both important and dangerous. They knew what they were getting into.

After another few minutes, Major Patel's voice came back. "I think the terms will be easy to work out. Is this a defensive contract? Offensive? Offensive if provoked?"

Kenja had to think about that. She wanted to say defensive, but no matter who was out there in that JumpShip, the Filibuster Brigade could handle themselves. She had read the reports of what happened on Errai, and Patel was a cunning strategist and shrewd with her forces. And her people were top notch. It was odd thinking something so complimentary about a mercenary group, but they were the shield to her deceptions, and they were a good one. "Offensive if provoked."

Eventually, the response came back. "Understood. We will be following you as soon as our drive is charged."

"Stay safe, Major."

"You, too," came the late reply.

Nervous, Kenja hoped the Filibuster Brigade made it out of this engagement in one piece. Deep down, she hoped this JumpShip was nothing more than some drifter passing through. It had a lithium-fusion drive, and it may well have been out of energy after a double jump. Maybe it was just recharging and leaving. Like the Belters she'd encountered, maybe they just wanted to keep to themselves.

But there had been too many issues. Too many problems. Too many complications.

Someone was dogging their steps. But who? And why?

Those questions were much harder to answer.

BROADSWORD-CLASS DROPSHIP _ZEPHYR_
NADIR JUMP POINT
HEAN
TIBURON KHANATE TERRITORY
23 OCTOBER 3151

Zephyr neared its JumpShip, and all had remained quiet.

The _Third Son_, at a pirate point on the other side of Hean, had made no aggressive moves against the Filibuster Brigade, but neither did it answer any hails. Kenja was afraid of sending any other messages or beaming any further data out to the _Filibustero_ for fear of it getting intercepted. Yes, the Sea Foxes had good encryption protocols, but they were not infallible, though she was sure she could find any number of warriors or scientist caste folks who would fight her to the death in a Trial of Grievance for even thinking such a thing.

"We've begun our docking collar procedure," Star Captain Yung informed everyone on the ship.

As the deceleration burn ended, the gravity dwindled and left them floating, as though the air were being slowly let out of a balloon. It was important to keep everyone updated on changes in gravity, lest they find new and interesting ways to hurt themselves.

Kenja bristled with tension. They were ready to leave.

Finally.

It would be another ten minutes before they were securely docked on the collar of the JumpShip and they would be departing directly, which would take another twenty to thirty minutes.

Her worst fears about the strange JumpShip were probably unfounded. Too much time working in espionage, *quiaff*?

"Four minutes until the docking procedure is completed," the captain reported. Then she started calling it all out one minute at a time.

"Two left."

"I'm not convinced the other JumpShip isn't going to be a problem," Alexi said, floating beside Kenja on the bridge, staring out at the stars, knowing one of those pinpricks of light was their dogged pursuer.

"What makes you say that?" Kenja asked.

"If it were in distress, it would have activated a beacon to ask for help. Or even used Morse code or something. It would have found a way to communicate. If it was just passing through, it would have nothing to hide and just say so."

Kenja nodded. "Sounds like we've been having many of the same thoughts. But we can't just attack it."

"Can we risk not giving the order to attack it?" Alexi asked.

"One minute left," the captain said.

And that's when the comm squelched back to life. "*Zephyr*, this is *Filibustero*, do you read? We are under attack! The *Third Son* has launched fighters."

"I told you," Alexi said. "They were waiting for us to dock and get ready to leave. They might have jumped the gun."

Kenja shook her head. "It's a feint. They're trying to get us to stay."

"How do you know that?"

"Because that's what I would do. They're probably waiting for reinforcements that could be here by the time we made it to the other jump point."

"I would do the same. Which means we need to get the hell out of here," Alexi said. "Let's not give them a chance to corner us. We'll let the *Filibustero* deal with them and leave ASAP."

"That's my thinking, too."

"The docking is complete," the captain said, then turned to Kenja, looking for orders.

Kenja's head swirled with possibility. She didn't want to leave the Filibuster Brigade, Petrichor, Reus Tremor, and Pernilla to the aggressive mercies of this mystery ship, but she had the most important components on the *Zephyr* with her. She had Tucker Harwell, the newly manufactured parts he'd created for the VoidBreaker Protocol, and all the data.

The Filibuster Brigade wasn't helpless. They could still find their way to Twycross.

"Orders, Star Colonel?"

"How long until the *Filibuster Brigade* is charged enough to jump?"

The captain looked down at her console. "Two hours. Fortunately, they're using their fusion reactor to recharge, so the raiders can't just shoot out their jump sail."

Two hours was an eternity in battle. It could be long over by then.

Kenja exhaled deeply, wondering what Seth would have advised her to do, wishing she still had his counsel in her ear. But she couldn't spend more time worrying about what he would say. She had to make her own decision. And she did.

"Tell the Filibuster Brigade to hurry if they can, but they know how to handle themselves. Make the jump, Star Captain."

"*Aff*, Star Colonel."

And within a minute, it was as though they were twisted inside out and stretched into a trillion particles, jumping up to 30 light years across the Inner Sphere in nothing more than one miraculous instant.

CHAPTER 29: DRIVE

BROADSWORD-CLASS DROPSHIP ZEPHYR
NADIR JUMP POINT
NASHIRA
DRACONIS COMBINE
23 OCTOBER 3151

In an instant, it felt as though the entirety of the *Zephyr*, the attached JumpShip, and all souls aboard were transformed into atoms that traveled faster than light, moving thirty light years to an uninhabited system in the blink of an eye. Then, the JumpShip captain repeated the process a scant twenty-two minutes later, readjusting their target coordinates and jumping again using the charge from the lithium-fusion battery.

But now they floated in space, waiting for the JumpShip batteries to recharge. To Kenja, it felt as though they were making the slowest escape in history, despite just traveling fifty-five light years in roughly half an hour.

Kenja didn't like being remanded to Draconis space, especially so soon after their incursion, but she didn't have a choice. There were only so many expedient paths to Twycross.

"Star Captain," she said, floating on the bridge. "Anything to report?"

"*Neg.*"

"Good."

Alexi Holt spun around to face Kenja. "Is the *Filibustero* taking the same route we are?"

"*Neg*," Kenja told her. "I gave them a different jump route. If we are being pursued, it will force our pursuers to split their forces. That's not to say there's no overlap in the routes, but there is more than one safe way to get to Twycross."

"This route takes us through Clan space?"

"After the Combine, yes. Which means I can offer Fox Credits or hold Trials if necessary to get priority time at recharge stations, or even switch JumpShips to get us there faster, until we hook up with a Tiburon courier route. Everything depends on our haste."

"Hean was a good idea, being the closest Tiburon possession to Ankaa, but you probably should have taken us to Twycross or your Aimag first." Alexi brushed auburn hair from her face and pulled it back, tying it up into a single knot with a band she pulled from her pocket. "Why risk sending us all the way out here now and on our own?"

Kenja had thought about that same point. "For Clan Sea Fox, space is home. And this particular area is where my Tiburon Khanate has decided to begin the relaunch, from their primary hub on Twycross. It makes sense in a way. I can only speculate, but I would guess the idea is twofold. First, Hean is far too close to at least three Great Houses that could try to take Tucker's solution by force, whereas the region that used to be controlled by the Jade Falcons people are now calling the Hinterlands is like the wild west."

"The wild west?" Alexi asked.

"You know... In the holovids? The ancient Terrans on the lawless frontier with the slugthrowers, the hats, and the horses? Like some parts of the Periphery."

Alexi just nodded slowly.

Kenja didn't know if she understood or just wanted her to continue, so she kept going. "There is no law or order out there minding the store, and the 'store' in this case is most often provided by the Tiburon Khanate, which services both the Lyran Commonwealth and the Clan territories. It's barely-controlled chaos. Secrets thrive in chaos, and until we have this ready to launch, secrecy is our friend. Every power in the Inner Sphere will be after us if they think they can take it from us before we're ready to announce ourselves."

"What's the other reason?" Alexi asked.

"Profit thrives in chaos, too. If there is any place where no single power could oppose the Sea Foxes *and* pay to use a new HPG network, it's there, in a place where *everyone* is jockeying for power. It's a lot easier to make deals with that small handful of lesser powers than it is a Great House. Not to mention, it'll be a way for Tiburon to gain singular glory among the Khanates—we are still Clan enough to value recognition for our deeds."

"Makes sense," Alexi said. "So that's it, then? We just wait?"

Kenja smiled and nodded. "It's going to be a long trip."

Kenja remained on the bridge long enough to ensure nothing was going wrong and that no one at the jump point treated them with any hostility. Then she sought out Tucker Harwell.

Since they'd been in space, he hadn't reported for a meal, nor had he been exercising, which concerned Kenja. He had to stay fit. The last thing she needed was for him to be an atrophied noodle as soon as they hit gravity again. And, for the most part, Alexi said he wasn't sleeping at night, spending the small hours going over the research instead.

So Kenja paid him a visit, knocking on the door to his quarters.

"Enter," he said faintly through the door.

It slid open on his command and Kenja floated inside with ease.

Tucker was strapped to the bed, reading on his noteputer. Of course he was. What else would he be doing? "Can we talk?"

Tucker waved a hand to the scant empty space in the room, not looking up from his reading. "Sure."

After Kenja's feet slid past the plane of the door, it whipped shut behind her. "Alexi said you've been a little withdrawn."

Tucker put the noteputer away, magnetizing its back to the bulkhead on the side of his bed. Then he looked at Kenja sternly. "I don't like being an asset."

He meant it.

"I don't like you being an asset either," she said. "I wish there were other ways we could do this. But there are a lot of people after you, many who would kill to get the information in your head."

"And the parts we carry on this ship."

She understood his implication. He thought he was nothing more than a cog in the machine. A part to be protected and used. "I understand where you're coming from. I'm a Clan warrior. I know what it's like to feel like a disposable cog in a machine."

"But isn't that how you were raised? That should be completely normal for you."

"You know, by now I've spent more time among Spheroids than I have in my own Clan. Seeing what we left behind and having to live it changes your perspective. Makes other things come into focus. Makes a person—even a Clan warrior—think maybe there can be some rest and peace to be had after all of this."

"Sure," Tucker said, obviously unconvinced.

She wasn't lying to him, but maybe there was no use trying to convince him she was genuine. It would only come off as more subterfuge. "I hope you'll find time to make it to the gym and get your exercise in."

Tucker shrugged and unbelted himself from the bed he shared with Alexi. Untethered, he hovered over the mattress. "What's the use?"

"Have you ever hit gravity with all that muscle and bone loss from zero-gee? It's not fun, and it's a lot harder to recover from than just hitting your daily routine like you're supposed to."

Tucker just shrugged.

"I'm sure Alexi would prefer you stay up on it."

"She's mentioned it. A few times."

"And, you know, exercise will keep your mind sharp. All this paste isn't everything."

"Frankly, it all feels a little pointless."

"What makes you say that?"

"Because you need my mind, not my body. I'm just a really expensive data card. One that talks back. I'm not convenient at all. The Inner Sphere's most troublesome meat data stick. If it's not ComStar, it's Blakists. If it's not them, it's the Republic. Or the Federated Suns. Or the Sea Foxes. No one except Alexi and Reus actually cares about *me*. You all just want what's in my head."

"I don't think it's—"

"Did you know my sister was part of a counter-reformist ComStar splinter sect known as the Blessed Order—practically a Blakist?"

Kenja's eyes narrowed. "That was in your file."

Tucker scoffed. "Did your file tell you she tortured me? All for the little bits of data she could remove from my brain? She forcefully installed a neural interface in my head and tried to extract the information that way. I never thought I'd be able to work again. Did your file say anything about *that*?"

Kenja swallowed heavily. "No."

"Well, it's true. You can put it in there now. Alexi can help you fill in the details."

"Tucker, I came here not just to talk, but to...congratulate you."

He laughed.

"I'm serious. You did something amazing. Something no one else was able to do. You're going to change the Inner Sphere."

Sighing, Tucker put a hand on the ceiling and nudged himself downward, back toward his bunk. "I want to revel in my achievement. But it was just math. Plain and simple. And the data. I think anyone with enough time, the Sunlight data, and the files and schematics you provided could have done it."

"Maybe. But I doubt it. And if they did, their time would be measured in years or decades. You did it in a matter of months. And I truly believe this is what the Inner Sphere needs. We just need to talk to each other and *hear* each other. And you're going to enable that."

"I bet the merchant warriors of Clan Sea Fox are super proud of me." The sarcasm in his voice dripped like ichor from a xenobug's teeth.

"I'm not your enemy, Tucker."

"Are you trying to convince me, Star Colonel?" Tucker asked, twisting the bondcord around on his wrist. "Or yourself?"

"Tucker, I need you to know that whatever happens, it is my *rede*, my oath to my Clan, and more importantly my oath to myself, to keep you safe no matter what happens. You have done a great service to the Inner Sphere, even if they don't realize it yet, and you deserve your well-earned peace."

"Who gets peace in a universe that knows nothing but war?"

To that, she had no answer.

Tucker activated the door and it slid open with a *whoosh*. "I appreciate you stopping by, Star Colonel. I promise I'll get to the gym. I'll just bring my noteputer and keep my mind sharp at the same time."

"I appreciate that." Taking the hint, Kenja kicked off the back wall toward the door, floating back into the corridor. She made eye-contact with Tucker on her way out, and his expression made her catch the door jamb and turn to face him.

"For what it's worth, Star Colonel," he said quietly, "I'm grateful to get the chance to do this. And I know you're doing your best. This has all just been...felt really complicated. I should be happy, but I can't figure out why all I feel is despair."

"It's the emptiness," she said, waiting for him to close the door in her face, but he lingered there for a moment.

"The emptiness?"

Kenja nodded. "After a mission is complete and we've wrought all the dopamine we can from a job well done, we look for the next challenge. The longer the mission, the more hollow the emptiness, right? You don't know what to do with yourself. And you're convinced that the results you achieved are so easily replicated that even a meat-headed Clan warrior could figure them out. So, you look for the next challenge. But this particular problem has been your life's work. And now it's solved, right?"

Tucker sighed. His eyes, dark windows peering out at her, told a story Kenja couldn't quite read. They were almost wet again, and reflected back in Kenja one thing she *did* understand and recognize.

Drive.

He was driven.

"Alexi said much the same thing," he said.

"I imagine you're still too close to it to believe it. I had a hard time figuring it out for myself. But we're going to get through this, Tucker. I promise." She let go of the door jamb and drifted out into the hallway.

He nodded hesitantly. Then pushed the button that closed the door.

Leaving Kenja alone in the corridor to do the calculations and math on the costs of the things she did. Whether for herself, Clan Sea Fox, or the Inner Sphere as a whole.

Everything had a price.

CHAPTER 30:
A QUANDARY OF CONDUCT

BROADSWORD-CLASS DROPSHIP ZEPHYR
NADIR JUMP POINT
NASHIRA
DRACONIS COMBINE
5 NOVEMBER 3151

Strapped to her chair on the bridge, Kenja awaited the last hours of the recharge and the next jump. This time, they'd skip to Pike IV and then Moore, escaping the Draconis Combine and heading to the Rasalhague Dominion. The Ghost Bears were, according to recent reports, in some manner of disarray, but whether Kenja had to deal with hardliners on either side of their political issues, the Dominion had been Tiburon's well-traveled trading territory for decades, and they wouldn't refuse a Trial against a Sea Fox for something as inconsequential as recharge time or a ride on a JumpShip. Hell, they might even let her pay for it and skip the Trial altogether.

Alexi Holt was ever present at the station to her left. She had been nervous about the lack of word from the Filibuster Brigade and, in turn, Reus Tremor. They were confederates and thick as thieves, so her worry was understood. Kenja worried about Petrichor in the same way, though she worried there might be even more to it. Alexi and Reus were just friends. Kenja felt responsible for Petrichor.

There were as many plausible, good, or even reasonable scenarios as there were catastrophic ones to explain the lack of word from the Filibuster Brigade, and Kenja and Alexi reminded each other of that often.

It was nice to have someone like Alexi around, to be honest—a competent colleague who understood the nuances of the work. They couldn't be equals in the strictest sense while Holt, Tremor, and Harwell all wore bondcords, but they were all adjusting.

"How is Tucker doing?" Kenja asked. After their last conversation, she thought it better to give him a wide berth. He was working through a lot of conflicting feelings. More than anything, according to Alexi, he was struggling with whether he'd done the right thing in fixing the network and handing it to anyone, let alone the Sea Foxes. And with all that swirling around inside him, the last thing he needed was a Sea Fox hovering around him, reminding him he was technically a prisoner by her very presence. He wasn't really a prisoner. He had the run of the entire ship. He could do what he wanted. Within reason. But it wasn't like she was going to let him just pack up and leave.

She couldn't argue with his feeling of being captured.

It made sense, as loathe as she was to admit it.

Alexi adjusted the strap around her waist, keeping her attached to her duty station. "He'll be fine. He's Tucker. He's lost in his own head. You gave him reams of data to trawl through. He's going to go through that rather than his feelings. And when he gets to his feelings again, I'll be there to help him through that, too."

"I didn't know how much he'd been through," Kenja said. "I'm grateful he's on the team."

"He *is* the team."

Kenja grinned at that. "True enough." She took a moment to take in the beauty of the starfield visible through the viewport, then turned back to Alexi. "What exactly happened with his sister?"

"He mentioned that, did he?"

Kenja nodded.

"Patricia was a ComStar extremist. I don't think she looked at her brother as human, let alone a blood relation. I think she was jealous of him. And she wasn't above torturing him for what she saw as the greater good."

"I have never understood torturing a person," Kenja said. "You see it in the holovids all the time, but the way to get actionable intelligence and cooperation is the exact opposite of torture. They have to believe you have something to offer them."

Alexi's expression grew distant. "You've worked undercover before. You know sometimes you have to do things to keep from blowing it."

"As a reason for torturing someone?" Kenja asked. Not because she disagreed, per se, but just wanted to clarify.

"It can be difficult. Put you in impossible situations," Alexi said, shaking her head. "And yeah, you might do something you're ashamed of."

Kenja readjusted the braid floating at the side of her head, keeping her hair out of her face. "I understand that. Far too well." She looked up at the stars on the outside of the ferroglass, the thick layer of material keeping them safe from the vacuum and the stars safely on the other side of their ship.

Suddenly, alarms keened on the bridge.

"What is that?" Kenja asked the Star Captain.

Meridian Yung turned to her from the captain's chair, pulling information from her noteputer. "JumpShip emergence nearby. One-hundred-thousand kilometers, give or take. Sea Fox make. Not answering hails, but I'm getting a distress signal from the DropShip."

"Who is it? Do you know?"

Star Captain Yung went to work getting information, collecting it all. "It's the Fox Khanate DropShip *Polyphemus.*"

Kenja nodded. "Do the honor, Star Captain."

Technically, the honor should have been hers, as the highest ranking Clan member and the leader of the mission, but Star Captain Yung was the second in line, and also the captain of the DropShip. Kenja really just hoped to keep her own involvement a secret.

Meridian nodded and spoke into the comm. "DropShip *Polyphemus*, this is Star Captain Meridian Yung of the DropShip *Zephyr.* What is your distress?"

The signal from the *Polyphemus* crackled with static, as though their transmitter was broken. Every fifth word or so dissipated in the space between them. "...*Zephyr*...meteor strike at the...misjumped and damaged...JumpShip. No responses aboard we think...dead." There was a long pause, and then they came back. "Five aboard...need rescue."

Meridian looked back to Kenja, awaiting her answer to the question.

Kenja nodded. "Make way and prepare to board."

"You don't think that's risky?" Alexi said.

Kenja raised a hand to the Star Captain, belaying the order. Then she turned her attention to Alexi. "They are in trouble, and we are nearby to help them, why wouldn't I?"

"I'm not saying we don't help them, or help them get help. But we don't know anything about them. We can let them get in their escape pod and have the nearby locals from Nashira scoop them up." Alexi's voice was plaintive. "I want to help them as much as the next person, but we can't jeopardize the operation."

"Star Captain," Kenja directed her voice to the other side of the room. "How long until our recharge is complete?"

"We have just over fourteen hours until the JumpShip completes its charge."

"And those in distress are Sea Foxes, *quiaff*?"

"*Aff.*"

"And how long would it take to effect a rescue?"

"With no complications? Three hours."

Kenja turned to Alexi, as though that answered everything. "So?" Alexi said.

"They are not going to interfere with our operation. We can offer them quicker assistance than Nashira. And Nashira is Draconis Combine territory."

"How do you know they are Sea Foxes?" Alexi asked. "How do you know they aren't some enemy agents in disguise?"

Kenja sighed. "It's a Sea Fox ship. With Fox Khanate IFFs. We have the ships in our database, do we not, Star Captain?"

Meridian tapped at her noteputer. "*Aff*, Star Colonel."

"More than that," Kenja continued, "we can't just leave people to die in space."

Alexi's face tightened. Confused. "No one is suggesting we leave them to die. We just leave someone else the job of rescuing them."

Kenja raised the fingers of her right hand to her temple and closed her eyes, frustrated by the pushback from Alexi Holt, of all people. She never wanted to command a bondsperson in the first place.

"Kenja," Alexi said, returning her own first name, which she surely knew was disrespectful, at least to her ears and culture, "we have a high value target on board this ship. This DropShip and this DropShip alone carries the knowledge of fixing the HPG network across the Inner Sphere. Is it wise to introduce *any* unknown element to it? Or would it be better to minimize the risk and leave it as a closed system? If this were a virus we were talking about, you wouldn't hesitate to enact quarantine protocols. It's better to just leave them for the Combine."

Kenja wanted to groan, but merely set her jaw. Yes. It was good to have Alexi Holt advising and bouncing ideas off. She was technically right, and Kenja should definitely consider that option. "You are right. I would quarantine the ship. Tucker is too valuable."

"Then tell them we're under quarantine, and cannot take them on. They can't argue with that. They should just get picked up in the escape pod."

But something nagged at Kenja. They would likely be left out there to die. To suffocate in their damaged ship, unless they were rescued. There were five Sea Foxes in there. "And what if the Combine can't pick them up in time?"

"I don't see how that would be our fault."

Alexi wasn't making the decision any easier.

But Kenja had been left in a DropShip to die before. Air running out. Cold creeping in. Floating there in the dark, waiting to freeze to death or suffocate. It was not her favorite memory. Granted, the situation had been different. And the way she had gotten out of it was different, but she wouldn't wish that fate on anyone.

"How about this? We pick up the escape pod quickly. Then we can keep them under house arrest until we get to Twycross," Kenja said.

Kenja turned to Alexi, hoping the worry in her chest wasn't apparent on her face. All she wanted to radiate was cool confidence. The sangfroid of a spy and the calmness of a warrior in control.

But to be honest, she wasn't sure what the right choice was.

But Alexi said nothing. It was Kenja's choice.

"We can't let them die," she said. Half trying to convince herself. "Not like that. We'll keep them on the JumpShip."

"I'm not saying it's a setup, Kenja, maybe it's not. It's probably not. Maybe the extra time to deal with the survivors is worth the risk, same as the rescue, but it's up to you to decide if that risk is worth what the Sea Foxes—the Inner Sphere will gain."

Kenja bit her inside lower lip. Almost hard enough to draw blood.

She was torn.

But she was also capable.

She knew how to mitigate risks. And they could drop the rescued Sea Foxes off sooner than later. They didn't need to go all the way to Twycross with them. And what damage could they do? It's not like they'd have access to a DropShip. And if the captain kept strict security protocols for bridge and airlock access, there wouldn't be an issue.

"I acknowledge the risk until we can vet them," Kenja told Alexi. Then she looked at the displays showing the battered DropShip and the JumpShip in even worse shape, floating out there, more lights winking out every second they left them to the mercy of the great black void. "But we owe it to them to try."

Alexi's face flushed, but she kept her composure otherwise. "I hope you're right."

Kenja looked to Meridian. "Proceed, Captain. Tell them to hit the escape pod, we'll scoop them up."

"*Aff*, Star Colonel."

CHAPTER 31: THE ROAD TO HELL

BROADSWORD-CLASS DROPSHIP ZEPHYR
ZENITH JUMP POINT
MOORE
RASALHAGUE DOMINION
5 NOVEMBER 3151

The five Sea Foxes rescued from the *Polyphemus* waited in the secure conference room of the *Zephyr*. Locked up and waiting for a debriefing and a final decision about what would happen to them.

Ultimately, Kenja and Alexi had agreed to debrief them, keep Tucker hidden—which wouldn't be a problem, he'd be elated to be told to stay in his room—then ship them up to the JumpShip. That way, they'd be kept separate from everything, and minimize the risk. Kenja didn't like leaning into Tucker's melancholy, but they agreed to keep him separate for his safety. Tucker was fine with that, because it meant everyone would just leave him alone.

Alexi was right that they shouldn't have taken the risk, but Kenja decided she couldn't leave her fellow Clan members to die. Losing five Sea Foxes to the Combine or the void of space wasn't a price she wanted to pay, especially since they weren't even going to lose any time by doing so, since they were still charging.

There was a sixth sense growing inside Kenja, and she couldn't figure out where it was coming from. But the disagreement with Alexi felt like the source of it. She'd suspected repeatedly that The ex-Paladin would steal off with Tucker in the night and change directions. What better way to lose yourself than get to caught, head in a completely different direction than anyone expected, and disappear from there? Maybe they'd find a planet with some nice beaches and just retire from the woes and worries of the Inner Sphere.

Kenja couldn't blame them for trying that.

Maybe one day she would just disappear on a beach somewhere, too.

But they'd given her no indication whatsoever that they would just take off, so Kenja was left to wonder where those bad vibrations were coming from.

"According to their story," Star Captain Yung told Kenja, Alexi, and the senior crew of the ship aboard the bridge, since their conference room was currently in lockdown, "and as confirmed by their logs, they suffered a misjump departing a pirate point. At some point immediately before or after the jump, there was a catastrophic collision with something, we think a meteoroid, aboard the JumpShip. It vented the crew at their previous location *after* they had begun the jump sequence."

"Were they under attack?" Alexi asked.

"There is scoring and blast marks and scorches on their hull, but that's to be expected in these old DropShips. There's no evidence any are recent. It seems like they got caught in a freak meteoroid storm."

"The odds for that seem low," Kenja said.

"Agreed," Meridian said. "However, they did jump in from the Miyazaki system."

"Miyazaki?" Alexi asked. "I've never heard of it."

That wasn't much of a surprise to Kenja. There were thousands of planets, it was impossible for anyone to have heard of every one.

Meridian elaborated as she brought up a picture of the desolate planet on the side viewscreen. "Miyazaki is a small world. Our market assessment maps stopped including it for a while since nothing was there. But our last entry included information about substantial meteoric activity."

"Why would they be in a system that's not even really on the map anymore?"

Meridian shrugged. "They didn't seem to know. They say they were just hitching a ride. People stop at dead planets all the time, for a number of reasons, only some of them nefarious."

Kenja stroked her chin. "Hmm..."

"As far as I can tell," Meridian said. "It all checks out."

"Contact the *Bull Shark*. Tell them to expect five new passengers."

"*Aff,*" Meridian said.

Then Kenja directed her attention to Alexi. "Satisfied?"

Alexi shrugged. "We haven't exploded, and we're playing it as safe as we can, Star Colonel. I'm as satisfied as I can get, and just want to keep moving."

"All right then. We all have work to do. It's only another week before we're recharged, and leaving and I want to be ready for anything."

"Aff!" everyone barked back at Kenja.

BROADSWORD-CLASS DROPSHIP *ZEPHYR*
ZENITH JUMP POINT
MOORE
RASALHAGUE DOMINION
9 NOVEMBER 3151

The ship's red running lights flashed and alarms howled into the DropShip's night.

Kenja preferred her sleep uninterrupted by security alarms, but lately this seemed to be her lot in life. Wearing nothing but her skivvies, she didn't bother dressing. That was an intruder alarm. Clothes wouldn't help as much as weapons. She grabbed her belt and wrapped it around her. It held her needler, a pair of knives, and a pouch with other instruments she might find useful.

Installing her comm earpiece, Kenja activated her door, which slid open quickly. She grabbed the frame of the door and pulled herself through the passage to see more movement in the corridor. Alexi was in a similar state of armed undress, wielding a needler.

"What the hell's going on?" There was venom in Alexi's voice, and there was nothing Kenja could do about that.

All she could do know was figure out what the hell was actually going on.

"Star Captain Meridian," she said, touching her ear, floating in the hallway waiting to discover which direction to head. "Sitrep."

But when no response from the Star Captain came, Kenja worried.

Then the explosion sounded, shaking the *Zephyr*. Not decompression, but something bad nonetheless.

"Where is that?" Kenja asked. "The gym?"

"Tucker," Alexi said urgently.

"Where is he?"

"He said he couldn't sleep. May as well get on the treadmill."

Alexi kicked past Kenja, sailing like a missile to the end of the corridor and turned, Kenja struggling to keep up.

There was no way they were here for him.

They were *Sea Foxes*.

They couldn't be.

And how would they have gotten aboard from the JumpShip without setting off the alarms? As Kenja turned the corner, the air left her like it had been sucked from the airlock as she realized exactly how wrong she'd been.

Tucker screamed, a black bag over his head and three "Sea Foxes" dragging him from the gym. "Alexi!" he shouted. "Help!"

One of the faux Foxes wrapped a length of tape over the hood right where his mouth would be, silencing him for the most part. He gagged, but that was about all Kenja could hear.

At least until Alexi screamed. "Tucker!"

Alexi and Kenja moved like an old, practiced team, jetting through the hallway like sea foxes on the hunt. But the enemies didn't stop to fight, they merely went about their kidnapping. Two of their number stopped to screen the escape of the others.

Kenja fired at the closest one, right at her legs, hoping to keep her alive. She wore a Sea Fox coverall like her confederates, but the way she moved made Kenja wonder if she had ever really fought in zero-gee. She kicked her legs like a frog, rather than a fox, trying to get out of the way. It was enough for Kenja's flechettes to fly wide.

Alexi fired, and her flechettes blasted the other one in the face, halting his forward momentum and spraying droplets of blood into the air, leaving the globules to float.

"Non-lethal," Kenja growled at Alexi.

"I'm not letting him go."

"Non. Lethal." Kenja repeated.

Alexi *had* to see the wisdom in taking a prisoner.

Kenja fired at the woman's legs again, scoring a hit, but not enough to stop her, only filling their view with more hovering blood droplets.

"Star Captain," Kenja tried hailing help. "This is the Star Colonel. Do you read?"

But only silence came from the other end.

The faux-Foxes carrying Tucker had turned the corner of the corridor, taking him out of sight. "They're getting away!" Alexi said.

The remaining "Fox" used her good leg to kick forward at them, leading with the point of a knife and aiming straight for Alexi. Alexi would kill her, and Kenja was trying to keep her alive. It made sense to go for the more lethal aggressor.

Alexi caught the woman's hand and shot her needler in her general direction, but the woman pushed herself out of the way. Struggling with the bleeding woman, Alexi turned her head to Kenja and screamed, "I'll deal with her! Get Tucker!"

Kenja launched herself down the tube, following Tucker's muffled shouts. She knew exactly where they were going to take him. But she took the sparest moment to shout behind her. "We need her alive!" to Alexi.

Kenja could only hope the enemy agent didn't hurt or kill Alexi in the meantime.

She turned the corridor, needler raised, and took in the scene before her.

They were facing up, in the airlock breezeway standing at the wide-open docking corridor to the JumpShip. They must have overpowered the JumpShip crew up there and then broken into the *Zephyr*. Kenja wondered who had hit the alarm that had woken them, but also wondered why no one had hit the alarm sooner. The *Zephyr* was supposed to be on high alert.

The four remaining enemy spies were hiding behind Tucker's form. He was the easiest target she could see, and she wouldn't risk shooting him, which they must have known. Lowering her pistol, she bounced from one wall to the other, gaining momentum as she torpedoed toward them, hoping to get her hands on Tucker before they made it through the blast door and sealed it.

One peeked his head out from behind Tucker and threw a knife in her direction. Kenja saw it coming and instinctively used her needler to bat it out of the way, keeping her safe from its razored edge. That killed her momentum, however, so she had to try again. By that time, they'd pulled in further toward the docking tube and the door began closing.

One chance left, she kicked against the back door with all the might in her legs and flew toward the door.

But it was too late.

The door sealed shut with a final *hiss*.

"Star Captain," Kenja shouted again. "I need this door open. I need to be on that JumpShip *now!*"

But the Star Captain still did not respond.

Kenja went to the controls at the side of the door in a vain attempt to override the lock, but it was no good. Everything she tried was shut down. If only Petrichor was around to help...

"Kenja," Alexi said, floating into the breezeway, blood smeared across her face and soaked into her clothes. "Where is he?"

Instead of answering, Kenja merely pointed to the closed door aggressively, and went back to the console trying to get the door open. There was no breath to waste.

Alexi screamed at the top of her lungs.

An angry, brutal scream. Fury dragged across broken nails of vocal cords.

And Kenja couldn't blame her. She'd been right the whole time.

CHAPTER 32: CROSS EXAMINATION

BROADSWORD-CLASS DROPSHIP *ZEPHYR*
ZENITH JUMP POINT
MOORE
RASALHAGUE DOMINION
9 NOVEMBER 3151

"Where are they going?" Kenja demanded of the woman they had captured.

She was tied to a chair in the conference room, bleeding from her legs and her face. Alexi had worked her over pretty good while capturing her, bruising her face and swelling an eye, but kept her alive.

According to the patch on her uniform, her name was Ariana. But her codex said her name was Vera of the Kalasa Bloodhouse. Kenja assumed neither were correct. Both stolen.

There was no way to tell.

It didn't matter.

What mattered was finding out what her and her little band had done with Tucker Harwell.

But Ariana or Vera or whatever her name was wasn't talking.

"I don't know," she said.

Kenja wasn't convinced. "Why don't we start further back?" she said. "Why don't we start with your name and what outfit you're with?"

"My name's Ariana. I'm a warrior of the Fox Khanate."

"I know that's not true. Not just with the contractions you're using, but the fact that your name and codex don't match. Also, the fact that if you wanted Tucker Harwell, you would have come and offered a Trial of Possession."

"It's not like you'd've accepted a Trial with him at stake."

She had a fair point.

"This was *dezgra*," Kenja said. "If you were really Clan, you wouldn't have done it this way. If you were Sea Foxes, you would have known we shouldn't have been bothered. Our orders come from the highest echelons."

Ariana merely shrugged.

"What do you want?"

"I'm not saying anything."

"I'll bring in my bondsperson. Would you prefer that?" Kenja wondered if the threat of Alexi coming back in the room would help.

Alexi was angry. Naturally. And things were bordering on catastrophic. Not only had they taken Tucker, but they'd taken most of the parts they needed to affect the VoidBreaker protocol. They'd raided the project data, too.

Kenja wouldn't tell Ariana or whatever her name was how bad they were. But if she was in on the plan, she likely knew exactly how bad things were because she helped enact it.

The entire bridge crew had been murdered. The bodies of Star Captain Meridian Yung and her crew were currently decorating the DropShip control room in various shades of floating red blood. And instead of taking off in a DropShip, Tucker's captors had left in the *Bull Shark* after detaching the *Zephyr*. They effectively left the *Zephyr* in a worse situation than the one they had pretended to be in when they arrived.

There was lightning precision in the math for the ruse. Whoever planned the operation was a genius. Knowing what their approximate route would be. Knowing where they would likely be recharging and what their recharge time would be. They must have had a file on Kenja, too. Or maybe they didn't. But pulling on her experience in a DropShip like that was a low move, if not brilliant if it was intentional.

But she couldn't think of any players that would have that information outside of her own Clan. Which also didn't make sense. Would another Khanate risk the entire mission just to steal the glory from Tiburon?

So there they floated.

Kenja worked on getting the necessary information while Alexi worked on getting the ship back together. There were less than a dozen people left on board. What remained of the crew—those who had been off shift—had been forced to start cleaning up the mess of their *trothkin*.

Kenja had no idea where they would go. At this point, she wasn't sure how they'd get there.

Ariana seemed unconcerned that Kenja was implying threats. She seemed unconcerned that she had been captured. There was no concern in her at all. And that frustrated Kenja, too.

She had no leverage. And it seemed she couldn't offer Ariana anything.

All she had to do was wait.

"What can I do for you? What would mean something to you? How do we come to an agreement?"

"You don't have anything I want."

"You're a mercenary, right?"

Ariana didn't respond.

Kenja wanted to scream.

She floated around the mercenary, tapping her hands continually on the bulkheads to reorient. Circling. Kenja tried imagining herself as a shark in the water. An actual kitefin trying to find the right opening. It was a dance. A zero-gee ballet.

She'd had to attend a ballet once. Undercover. It was a dance reinterpretation of the Amaris Civil War. The dancer who had portrayed Amaris was as big as an Elemental, with a bulging body sock, but they moved with such grace she couldn't tear her eyes from them. She wondered why so much grace and beauty could be assigned to the person who had quantifiably damaged the Inner Sphere in such long lasting ways.

She wondered if anyone had ever had a dance for a Trial.

"What if we were to Trial for the information I need? You say you're not a mercenary, that you're Clan. If you're so confident, we'll fight. If I win, you tell me where they took Harwell and who hired you. If you win, I'll let you go. No questions asked. Honorable. Strict *zellbrigen*."

The mercenary laughed, exactly as Kenja expected she might.

"Fine," she said. "If that's the way you want to play it. We'll see if there's someone else here that can be more persuasive."

Kenja left her behind, seeking out Alexi.

Speaking with Alexi came with its own dread. The double cross implied so much more than just a conspiracy against them. Alexi had been separated from Reus Tremor, who had functioned as her partner, and Tucker Harwell, who she loved with everything she had. She had counseled Kenja, wisely, about the follies of bringing the wayward "Foxes" aboard.

And she had been right. Kenja should have listened and just surrendered them to the Combine.

Alexi was on the bridge. She had no rank or reason to be in charge, but it seemed like the other Sea Foxes naturally fell into step behind her. Kenja worried that might mean she might have a mutiny on her hands—a Trial of Grievance for how she had handled the situation. For losing Tucker. She hoped she didn't, but she wouldn't blame them if they did. She just had to assert herself and be clear headed and come up with a plan to get them out of the mess they were in.

But Kenja still didn't see a way forward.

And even if they could move forward, where would they move forward *to*?

Their JumpShip was gone. Their asset was missing. Their lead wouldn't talk.

"Star Colonel," Alexi said coldly.

"Alexi," Kenja replied.

Alexi glared at her for a long moment. "Well, you're in charge. You knew the risks and still took them. Against my advice. Now tell me you've got a plan to get these bastards and get Tucker back? Or do you?"

The shame Kenja felt blossomed into fury. She knew she wasn't a normal Clan warrior. She had been bred into something else, and had spent more time blending into the Inner Sphere than climbing into a 'Mech.

But she was still Clan. And she was not going to tolerate that disrespect.

"Clear the bridge," she said to the others cleaning the blood. They looked around, wondering about whether or not they should listen. "Now," Kenja added icily.

Everyone who wasn't Alexi found a hand or foothold and left, taking their cleaning tools, sponges mostly, with them and zooming away.

The mess was horrific, but they had gotten the bridge into some semblance of cleanliness.

After the last one left, the door closed behind them.

Alexi and Kenja locked eyes.

Silence permeated their war of wills. Kenja needed to make this right, but she wouldn't be able to do it if Alexi stood against her.

She had to fix that now.

And to do it, she needed to bury her fury and rely on her sense of sangfroid.

"Like I said. What are you going to do, Star Colonel?" Alexi said.

"We are going to deal with this. One thing at a time. But I can't do that if you're running around like a live wire, angering everyone else left on this ship."

"I have every reason to be angry."

"I know. I was wrong. I made the wrong call. But that doesn't mean we're no longer working together. You are my bondsman."

"Bondswoman," Alexi said.

"If you prefer. Bondsman is what they usually call it. I've never heard anyone use Bondswoman. I don't know why."

"That's as ridiculous as this entire situation. They should start."

"I don't disagree."

Alexi floated closer to Kenja, and Kenja floated to her.

Tension rose. Almost drawing them toward each other, an elastic band tightening around the both of them.

If they nudged closer to each other, Kenja didn't know if they would start trading blows or just scream at each other. In either case, Kenja couldn't see how it would help.

"We need to get on the same team here, Alexi. And I am not going to say that again."

"We *were* on the same team. You fumbled the ball away."

They were even closer now. Almost nose to nose. Alexi's face was tightened into a scowl. Kenja felt her own features radiate angry heat.

"I made a call. It was the wrong one. Now how do we move on? Do I need to beat you again to get you to help? Or are you just going to hold this against me for the rest of the mission?"

"There's no mission, Kenja. We lost Tucker. They took half the parts. They raided the data. They took our goddamned JumpShip."

"There's a mission if we find out where they're taking Tucker. But our captive has no incentive to talk."

"Of course she doesn't. She won."

"You think you can do better? You're welcome to it. I can get the Ghost Bears to get us a ride if I know where we're going. But it's all a moot point if we can't catch them."

"Fine."

"Fine?" Kenja wasn't expecting that. She thought they were going to have to trade blows. She really did.

"We need to get Tucker. You're right. We can't if we don't know where we're going. You get us a ride and we'll figure it out from there."

"You're not going to try to hit me?"

"You're not going to try to hit *me*? I thought that was the Clan way."

"We work better together than fighting each other."

"Perfect. Now let's work together. I actually have an idea," Alexi's fierce grimace turned into a sly grin, and Kenja couldn't wait to see what she had planned.

Alexi tore into the conference room like a bat screeching for its prey. Kenja followed close behind her, much more restrained.

"Oh," Ariana said. "This is how you're gonna try it, huh?"

Kenja shut the door behind them and stayed close to the wall. "I'm sure you got all kinds of mission briefings for the incursion onto our ship," she said. "And I'm sure you know exactly who this is."

The merc shrugged. "It doesn't matter who you bring in here."

"Sure. It doesn't. But let me tell you a little bit about Alexi Holt. She's my bondswoman. I won her in a Trial she fought over the possession of Tucker Harwell. If you hadn't noticed, she's a bit upset about what happened to him and what your friends did to him. Or might be doing to him. And I will tell you she will stop at nothing to get him back."

Alexi circled around one of the chairs. Grabbing it with one hand and crouching low, she aimed her body in the general direction of their prisoner. In her free hand she held a knife. The same blade she'd already worked Ariana over with when she fought and captured her the first time. Ariana knew what she could do with the blade.

But still, the merc was unmoved by the sight. She simply shrugged again. "Do your worst."

"Hold on a second now," Kenja said. "I'm not in the business of torturing people. It's messy, it doesn't work. There's no reason for it."

"So why are you trying to threaten me with her?" Ariana said, cocking a head toward Alexi.

But Alexi answered, her voice low and slithering. "Because I'm not going to torture you. I'm going to kill you. I'm not going to make it fast or anything. I'm just going to kill you for what you did. For the people you killed. For making Tucker's life worse. And I won't feel a drop of remorse from it."

"That's fine," Ariana said. "You still won't know where they're taking him, and you'll still be stuck here. Killing me doesn't buy you anything. So you're not going to do it. I'm no fool."

Kenja nudged off the wall and hovered in the spot between Alexi and the mercenary, halting her momentum by grabbing a bulkhead. "I know you think that. But if you won't cooperate and we can't learn anything from you, and we're floating out here in space and our resources dwindle every second while we wait for rescue or a new JumpShip, we have to take care of you. That's work we'll have to do. Labor. Labor I don't want to do. I'm a Star Colonel. I'm a MechWarrior. You think I'm going to take care of you? You think I want to? No. It's easier for me to just let Alexi kill you and be done with it."

"They said you'd stoop to this."

"Who?" Kenja's eyes widened as she felt the sting of the other woman's words. Who could have been behind their operation that knew anything about her?

"Go to hell."

"Fine." Kenja calmed her momentary panic and slid out of the way. "If we don't have anything to offer each other, I can't be held responsible for what Alexi will do. I don't want to do this. But this is all you've left me with."

Ariana eyed the blade in Alexi's hand. Then her eyes darted back to Kenja. For the first time, her eyebrows turned up at the center in concern. Her eyes screamed with pleading. And then she took in a deep breath.

Alexi rocketed forward, blade first, ready to cut Ariana's throat.

Ariana flinched. "Fine. I tell you everything I know, and you cut me loose and take her out of here."

Alexi stopped short and looked to Kenja, who had raised a hand. "Don't, Star Colonel. Let me dance with her first."

"Alexi, stand down. We'll keep her. If she tells the truth, we'll let her go once we confirm it. If we find out she's lying, you can have her."

But Alexi didn't stand down. She launched forward, lunging for Ariana with a shrill yell.

Kenja twisted and kicked at her, sending Alexi spinning to the other side of the room.

"I'll take care of my bondswoman. And I'll take care of you," Kenja said. "Now tell me who you work for!"

Ariana, eyes wide, twisted her head as far as she could, trying to see where Alexi had gone to. But Alexi was behaving in the back of the room. "Honestly, I don't know. There were some dead drops and instructions. It was a shadowy figure in a recorded holo. Told us where you'd be and when, when to jump, and how to do it. Said you'd be all over it. Said you'd threaten me, but ultimately lose your nerve, but..."

Alexi leapt once more for Ariana, but Kenja redirected her again, gripping the back of Ariana's chair and shoving the aggressive woman back.

Hitting the back wall with a grunt, Alexi wiped her mouth and stared daggers at Ariana.

"Fine. Where were you heading?"

Ariana looked over to Alexi, genuine fright in her eyes. "You promise to keep her away from me?"

"*Aff,*" Kenja said.

The merc sighed. "Twycross. They're taking him to Twycross."

CHAPTER 33: THE COLONEL'S GAMBIT

BROADSWORD-CLASS DROPSHIP _ZEPHYR_
ZENITH JUMP POINT
MOORE
RASALHAGUE DOMINION
10 NOVEMBER 3151

"Why the hell would they take him to Twycross?" Alexi asked Kenja as they floated around the bridge.

"Perhaps they believe there is something essential to Tucker's technique on Twycross, not realizing only saKhan Sutherland's ego drove the choice of destination," Kenja said.

She couldn't be sure with one-hundred percent certainty that the merc was telling the truth. She could have been sending them on another chase in the wrong direction to keep them from their goal.

But why would she lie? Just to prolong her life by a matter of days or weeks? If Kenja managed to hitch a ride and get to Twycross, if they didn't find Tucker, she must have known her life would be forfeit.

"What if Twycross is an ambush?" Alexi asked. Her blood was still up, joined now by her suspicion.

"By whom? The ArcShip _Titanic_ and several Clusters of Tiburon forces should be there, unless they've redeployed recently. Or already been destroyed. If Twycross is an ambush, our foes must have firepower to spare. Why go through all this trouble?" Kenja glanced around at their surroundings and found them clean, but its emptiness was palpable.

There was a lack. The *Zephyr* was missing Petrichor and the Star Captain. With luck Petrichor would fill its space again, but Star Captain Meridian Yung never would.

In between the tasks of figuring out their next move, they took the time to hold another funeral, performing the *giftake* ceremony to preserve the genetic material of those they'd lost. Another ceremony Kenja wanted nothing to do with, but didn't have a choice.

She blinked and came back to the present. "If they knew we were heading to Twycross, they would have wanted to strike before we had our entire *touman* at our back. Unless they thought they were going to get away completely. Leaving behind someone who would tell us their plan wasn't a possibility."

"Wasn't it?" Alexi said. "Your friend in there sure seemed to know you were going to try to torture her, or at least threaten it."

"That's nothing. It's vague. It's something anyone could imply and try to get a rise out of me. Common tactic."

"Sure." Alexi busied herself, strapping herself into a chair in front of a console.

"But seriously," Kenja said, heading for her own preferred duty station, leaving Meridian's empty, "if they didn't expect anyone would get caught, why would they keep heading to Twycross? They think they're heading there alone."

"The Filibuster Brigade would still need to be dealt with."

"Sure, but it's easier to deal with one foe than it is two."

"So do we believe her?" Alexi asked. "Should we head to Twycross? For all we know these people could be from House Marik and taking Tucker spinward into the Free Worlds League."

"We need to go somewhere. We're in the one place we know for sure he isn't. And we know our people are heading to Twycross as well."

"Even if Tucker's captors are gone, I bet we can still learn something from the mercs and Petrichor. It's worth a shot."

"I agree," Kenja said. "So all I need to do now is find us a ride."

"This is Star Colonel Troy Hall of the 357th Assault Cluster," the deep, booming voice said over the comm line, delayed between the zenith jump point and the DropShip they found him in. A lucky break, or else the comm lag would have made their haste all for naught.

"Star Colonel, this is Star Colonel Kenja Rodriguez of Clan Sea Fox, and we are aboard a DropShip at your zenith jump point. I would challenge you to a Trial of Possession for passage aboard a Dominion courier vessel to allow us to continue our journey to our final destination."

Alexi watched as Kenja did her best to sound happy and calm, and as though this was no big deal. It would probably work, and Kenja wanted to make things as smooth as possible. More than anything, she wanted to make it look easy so that Alexi would gain some of her confidence in her plan.

Eventually, his response came. "A Trial of Possession for the use of a courier JumpShip?" He laughed. "Augmented or unaugmented?"

"Well, I had something a little different in mind, if you would indulge me. We are in a great hurry. Our mission is of vital importance. It would add more than a week to my timetable to burn to the planet, hold our Trial—augmented or otherwise—and get back to a JumpShip."

"My DropShip captain informs me that we could meet in a day and a half aboard our vessel."

"Again, that would take time we don't have."

"What then do you propose?" he asked after several minutes.

"Our battlefield becomes a chessboard, our BattleMechs pawns, rooks, and queens. If I win, you provide the JumpShip until we reach our destination. Then I will release it back to the Ghost Bears. If I lose, then we can discuss what happens then. In either case, even the possibility of rescue and escape will ensure my eternal gratitude and allow you more favorable trading terms from the next Tiburon Khanate traders coming through Moore."

It took a long time for a response to come back, but Hall did eventually respond. "If I win, I would love to take so bold a warrior as a bondsman," he said, chuckling. "But I warn you that chess is of keen interest to me."

"Likewise, Star Colonel. Bargained well and done," Kenja said easily.

Alexi's eyes widened. "Are you serious?"

Kenja knew they didn't have a choice and said so. Alexi closed her eyes meditatively and took a deep breath.

"I have contacted the planetary governor," Hall came back to say, "and we have agreed this deal would be amenable. The next Dominion courier vessel is scheduled to arrive in twelve hours. If you win, the JumpShip will be at your disposal. If I win, you burn to the planet. *Quiaff?*"

"*Aff,*" Kenja replied.

But clearly, Alexi was confused. "Why would he need to check with the planetary governor?"

"The Ghost Bears of the Rasalhague Dominion are not like other Clans. They are one and the same. Hand in glove. They are the military under a more direct democracy. He would need permission to utilize what might be a civilian JumpShip."

"Learn something new every day," Alexi said.

By that time, Hall's voice boomed back. "As the attacker, you have chosen the form of our Trial. We will set the board. As the defender, I will choose the battlefield, and I choose black as my color. Let us begin."

"*Aff,*" Kenja acknowledged.

The noteputer screen showed an overhead view of the chessboard. Nothing complicated.

Kenja, playing white, advanced her king's pawn two spaces. Hall responded by pushing forward his queen's bishop's pawn two as well. A Sicilian defense to counter her opening and exactly the same stratagem Seth had favored in their games.

She lost to Seth far too much to like the moves she'd made against him, usually pushing another pawn into the field to create a cascade of checks and balances to prevent pieces from being taken. But she needed to be bolder. Kenja brought out a knight. And another knight. She planned to push the Hall into the center of the board.

Oddly, Hall pushed forward nothing but pawns, putting them into a position across the queen side of his board.

Kenja wondered if her bullying tactics would work. His Sicilian defense was holding. But then she realized this was what the board looked like from the other side every time Seth had beat her. He was the aggressive player and she played his tune. But now she would play her own.

"I see what you are up to," Hall said as he took first blood; her queen's pawn, leaving one of her knights vulnerable to his predations.

She took his piece with her other knight before he activated his queen-side bishop.

"I see what *you* are doing, Star Colonel." Kenja brought her bishop forward, nestled behind her knights, ready to strike.

The game pushed forward slowly. Kenja knew part of it was the communications lag to the planet, but it was also due to the fact she was causing Hall to sweat. It might have seemed like she was just randomly tossing pieces out on the board, but that was her strategy. Keep him guessing about what would happen next. There was no reason to make it easy for him.

Soon enough, she castled, leaving her vulnerable king behind the protective line of her pawns on the right. Alexi had started to suggest something, but Kenja shushed her. She had already planned the move, but protocol dictated she win this Trial on her own, honorably, and in her own way.

"Smart move, but it will not avail you," Hall said as he moved his queen up a row diagonally, as though he planned to cut into the defensive wall of Kenja's pawns.

She set a trap with her own queen, hoping to keep him from edging further with his, and it worked. Instead, he activated a knight, but that threatened the center of her board, so she took it, pressing her knight right into his territory.

"Not worth the sacrifice, I think," Hall said as he took her knight with his queen.

They jockeyed for better positions in the center of the field, neither one yielding ground. Hall kept a second defensive line in front of most of his pawns consisting of his queen, a bishop and a knight, all ready to start taking her pieces and there wasn't a lot she could do, but she felt very much like she was in the stronger position still. The thing about chess, though, was that you could always underestimate your opponent.

After she positioned her castled rook into an open channel to strike at the heart of his half of the board, she sent a bishop deep into his territory to draw him out. Instead of taking the bishop with a pawn, he ignored it and castled, seeing the precarious cliff he teetered on.

Then he finally took a bishop, but not the one Kenja was expecting. It was with a pawn, and as much as she was trying to think three moves ahead, she somehow hadn't seen that particular play happening. She thought he would take the piece closer to his side of the board.

"Huh," she said.

And a few moments later, as she struggled to decide her next move, he laughed. "This is an excellent game, Star Colonel. I would have vastly preferred we do this face to face."

"Perhaps another time," Kenja replied, "and under better circumstances."

"When I win, I imagine I can arrange plenty of time for us to play."

"When I win, I would be happy to play by courier."

Kenja thought back to the games she'd played, and how Seth had always found a way to beat her, and he managed to always retreat after a strike. Hit and run. But as she looked at the board and imagined it five turns later, she found that strategy a loser. She had to play this her way.

She took the pawn that had taken her bishop. Instead of licking her wounds, it was better to clear that area of potential threats and deeper incursions.

Hall responded by threatening more valuable pieces with his queen, so Kenja moved her knight in even further, taking his second knight in the process. Kenja didn't have another move ahead of her, her front pieces were all vulnerable to his pawns, but it was exactly the position she wanted him in. People make mistakes when they are confident.

She only hoped she wasn't falling into the same trap.

The game dragged on even further.

She forced Hall to retreat behind his fortification of pawns, but Kenja was still vulnerable. She felt the upper-hand slipping, but she wondered if he felt the same way.

They picked away at each other. He took her last bishop. She ate away further at his pawns.

He moved his queen into an attack position, but that's when she realized he'd made a mistake. His queen was in play on the other end of the board, too far away to defend his king. And she had created long striking zones for her pieces at the back of the board, free of obstructions.

She moved in with her queen. "I believe that is check, Star Colonel."

"And so it is," he replied after a moment.

But still he did not move a piece.

He had a couple of different ways to fight it, but there was only one move he could make that would keep her from getting checkmate with the next move.

She held her breath.

Waiting.

Was it the damned lag?

Or was he considering?

She just wanted to end it.

When his king moved behind the protection of his last bishop, Kenja sighed in relief.

She had him.

Quickly, she moved her other rook into position, trapping the king in a move between the rook he hadn't noticed in her back corner and her queen.

He had nowhere to go, and no way to fight it.

"I believe that is checkmate, Star Colonel." Kenja looked up to Alexi with a smile on her face. Alexi beamed back at her, and that smile said everything Kenja needed to know about how things might finally be going in their favor.

"*Aff*, it is," he said after the delay. "That was an excellent game, well played, and a Trial well bargained. I salute you, Star Colonel. The courier JumpShip will arrive shortly. I hope your travels are speedy and safe."

They exchanged pleasantries for a moment, dissecting the finer points of the game, and then the line clicked off after Kenja thanked him one last time for a thrilling Trial and they exchanged information to continue playing by message services.

Then she looked at Alexi. "Now all we need to do is get to Twycross."

PART 4

"Stab the body and it heals, but injure
the heart and the wound lasts a lifetime."

—Mineko Iwasaki
Ancient Terran Philosopher

"Growth for the sake of growth
is the ideology of the cancer cell."

—Edward Abbey
Ancient Terran Philosopher

CHAPTER 34: TWYCROSS TO BEAR

BROADSWORD-CLASS DROPSHIP ZEPHYR
ZENITH RECHARGE STATION
TWYCROSS
ALYINA MERCANTILE LEAGUE
11 DECEMBER 3151

Twenty-one days later, Kenja jumped into the Twycross system.
It felt like it would never be possible.

Over the course of nearly a month, she wondered how things had changed. In all that time, they had heard nothing from the Filibuster Brigade. Nor did they hear any whispers of what happened to Tucker Harwell. Ariana—still likely not her name—remained mute for as long as she was in their custody.

They had jumped through the Rasalhague Dominion on a series of Clan Ghost Bear JumpShips until Kenja could requisition passage aboard a Tiburon Khanate express JumpShip courier route and replacement DropShip crew. She was also able to pass the care of Ariana to the Watch, allowing them to do a more formal debrief.

They assured her if they learned any more information, they would let her know.

Over time, they received more and more information about the changing nature of the Inner Sphere, and learned they were heading into a war zone that might be hotter than they would have liked. And if they did encounter Clan Hell's Horses, it might not go well, since they were on the warpath, stampeding through space and ignoring the will of the ilKhan.

After almost two months in zero-gee, Alexi Holt and Kenja whiled away hours learning everything they could about the HPG network, sticking to their workout routines, and sparring matches. They both got pretty good at throwing knives at each other in zero-gee. It had only caused two accidents, one each that sent them to the infirmary. Kenja was still adamant it was Alexi's fault for not moving her head in time. Kenja wasn't really aiming for her neck.

When Kenja went to the infirmary, she'd just been simply out-fought by Alexi, and it felt good to have a challenge.

As they jumped into the Twycross system, the first thing they did was have the new Star Captain of the *Zephyr*, a Tiburon named Dae, scan for other JumpShips and see if there were any surprises. The zenith jump point swarmed with Tiburon trading vessels, including Delta Aimag's CargoShip, the massive *Volga*-class *Liberator*, preparing for an outward jump. Many ships identified as Jade Falcon merchant caste vessels likewise were at the jump point, but bearing unfamiliar livery, broadcasting IFFs announcing themselves as something called the Alyina Mercantile League. None appeared hostile. Sensors likewise detected both AML and Tiburon vessels in orbit over Twycross, including the imposing mass of the ArcShip *Titanic*, mobile home base for Tiburon Khanate. Kenja felt a surge of relief—they had made it home, and no calamity had befallen the Khanate during her absence.

The biggest shock came when sensor readings returned from the far side of the system.

"What about the nadir?" Kenja asked the Star Captain.

"There are two unmarked JumpShips there."

"IFF tags?"

"Similar to the *Third Son*—somebody over there thinks traveling like that makes them invisible, rather than sticking out like a sore thumb."

Alexi and Kenja looked to each other, eyes wide. It looked like Tucker's captors had indeed gone to Twycross.

"Any sign of our mercenary JumpShip?" Alexi asked the Star Captain, showing him the registry codes for the Filibuster Brigade's vessel.

"*Neg.*"

"They might not have made it yet," Kenja said.

"Any read on DropShips heading planet-side?" Alexi asked.

"I have hundreds of them burning in," Dae said. "The distance to the planet is just over three weeks, though. Depending on when they arrived in-system, they may still have weeks until they land."

"We made up considerable time using express couriers. If they did the same, the earliest Tucker's captors could have arrived is a week ago." Kenja rubbed her hands together, thinking as best she could. "We can still pull this off."

Alexi's jaw fell open. "We have just over a single lance of 'Mechs onboard. How are we going to play this?"

"It's a Star."

"What?"

"We have a Star of 'Mechs."

"We're going to war against two opposing forces with five 'Mechs, and all you can do is be pedantic about what I'm calling them? I want to know your plan. And I want to know if I can help fix it."

"It's my responsibility to make sure you get it right. But you've got the long and the short of it." Kenja turned to her friend. "Alexi, this cloak-and-dagger stuff is the part I've been doing for a long time. If they're here and they have Tucker, where are they going to take him? An HPG station. We can get intel about it on the way. We can infiltrate that. That's not the difficult part."

"What's the difficult part then, Star Colonel?"

"Everything that comes after."

Alexi rolled her eyes.

"I'll need your help to figure it out," Kenja admitted. "The bigger problem is who to trust. Are our enemies aligned with this Alyina Mercantile League? I've never heard of them. Are there rival Khanates at work here? Could there be conspirators within Tiburon Khanate plotting against us, and that's why Tucker's captors felt safe coming here? Depending on who's calling the shots locally, checking in with the *Titanic* might get us a hearty 'welcome home' and an army at our disposal, or might get us exterminated. There's something more than I can see going on here, and we can't afford to act rashly."

But they had been forced to act, one way or the other. They were here. Tucker was likely here, unless they dropped him off somewhere along the way, but given the times they'd all likely arrived, she doubted it. And they still had two weeks before they got to the planet. If Star Captain Dae burned in at one-and-a-half-gees, they might be able to cut that head start significantly. Not that Kenja wanted to go straight from two months of zero-gee to a-gee-and-a-half in an instant, but what else were they going to do?

She looked out at Twycross itself, twinkling in the distance. A hot mess of a desert—Kenja had her fill of deserts, thanks to the ordeal on Ankaa—the swirling storms could be seen even from space.

And they were headed straight into those storms.

"Star Captain, take us down. I'll give you a more detailed location as we get closer and the situation becomes more apparent."

"One gee?" she asked.

"To start," Kenja said. "We'll increase speed when we have a better plan. *Quiaff*?"

"*Aff*, Star Colonel."

CHAPTER 35: CLOTURE

BROADSWORD-CLASS DROPSHIP ZEPHYR
EN ROUTE TO TWYCROSS
ALYINA MERCANTILE LEAGUE
12 DECEMBER 3151

They began their burn at one gee, and after all the time floating, the gravity was excruciating for the Spheroids. They had to make up time, but jumping right into the a-gee-and-a-half burn without easing into it was only going to make them sick. Two months in zero-gee, even with the benefit of a JumpShip's grav deck, was enough to make any freebirth brittle, no matter how many hours a day they put in on a treadmill. The Spheroids, of course, lacked the genetic traits Sea Fox scientists had added to better adapt their people to lives spent mostly in space without sacrificing their ability to function in gravity wells.

It was two days in when they decided which HPG station to focus on.

Twycross had two major facilities. One in the capital of Camora, on the Twycross South continent, and a backup transmission station on Twycross North. With the constant storm systems that interfered with communications and sensors—including the massive permanent storm the locals referred to as Diabolis—Star League engineers had determined long ago that Twycross should have a backup HPG. As part of the Sea Fox plans for restoring interstellar communications, the Tiburon Khanate had assumed control of both sites through an agreement with Malvina Hazen's Jade Falcons, whose scientists had been focused entirely on breaching the Wall rather than solving the Blackout.

Thinking logically, if Kenja had Tucker, the last place she would want to fight and defend would be the capital, where any number of potential enemies would be nearby in the crowded warren of the underground habitat. So it made sense for anyone else running a clandestine operation to head for the more discreet location on Twycross North, with no local populace and greater control over site access.

The fact that the unmarked JumpShips and their DropShips had been able to approach Twycross unchallenged told Kenja the enemies she faced were working with allies on the planet. Not that it was even easy to tell who that might have been—traitors within Tiburon, this Mercantile League, or other players.

As the time approached when the vessels would be on orbital approach, Kenja hunched over the sensors, tracking every ship's telemetry. She exulted when she saw several break away from the Big Island and Twycross South approach lanes and vector toward the largely unpopulated wastes of Twycross North. Her quarry had exposed themselves.

The hunt was on!

Kenja marveled at the idea that she had been on this particular mission for almost eight months. Granted half of it had been in transit, but life is short and time is precious. A month on one project in her line of work was a lifetime. She only hoped it was worth it. She thought it was, but she hoped Clan Sea Fox didn't abuse the power she had worked so hard and long to give them. She wanted the Inner Sphere to listen to itself and each other, and if the Sea Foxes broke that trust, she wasn't sure what she would do.

A voice came over the comm like the clap of thunder without the warning flash of lightning. "*Zephyr*, come in. Do you copy?"

"Who is that?" Kenja asked.

Dae, a severe woman with snow white skin dappled in freckles and a ponytail of red hair, turned back to Kenja, shocked.

"What is it, Star Captain?"

"It's the *Filibustero*."

Kenja's heart stopped for a moment. Then she looked down at her console station and engaged the comm. "*Filibustero*, this is *Zephyr*. We read you loud and clear. Nice of you to drop by."

"Glad to see you made it. We've had some problems." She hadn't heard the voice in half a year, but Kenja was confident she was speaking to Major Patel, especially with that level of understatement. Since the *Filibustero* had arrived at a pirate jump point formed by the gas giant, Twycross IV, the lag was negligible, measured in seconds rather than minutes or hours.

"Do they have Smith?" Alexi asked Kenja, but realized she could get louder and ask herself. "Is John Smith still with you?"

"Yeah, he's here. Ruby Havelock is still with us, too. Thunderbolt is here as well."

Kenja didn't realize she'd been holding her breath for half a year, but hearing that Petrichor was alive opened her lungs and she could feel air fill her lungs completely.

Wiping a tear from her face, she smiled. "Thank Kerensky."

Petrichor and Reus Tremor were valued assets to the team, and Pernilla was their back up plan for getting the HPG network up and running if they couldn't retrieve Tucker Harwell.

"Major," Kenja said after she had composed herself, "there is a lot to catch you up on."

"We have some updates, too."

"I'll beam you a report, please do likewise. Once I have the data, it will be easier to formulate a plan. I will warn you, though, Major, the situation has changed significantly."

"For the better? Or worse?"

"Always worse."

Patel laughed. "I assumed as much."

14 DECEMBER 3151

Kenja put together all the information the Filibuster Brigade needed to know, encrypted it, and shot it to them in a tight wave beam. When she got their report in turn, she didn't realize how rough things had been for them. With their report, she briefed Alexi.

"How did they get away from Hean?"

"They screened the *Third Son*'s fighters and made their escape, but the *Third Son* managed to catch them at the next destination, and actually tried boarding them." Kenja knew all too well how terrifying that would have been and the feeling conjured itself inside her, deep in her bones. "Naturally, they weren't successful, but they did get the idea the *Third Son* could intercept transmissions. Possibly even decode them."

"That could explain how their agents found us at Moore and were able to fool us into that ruse to nab Tucker." Alexi's voice cracked at the sound of his name. It was obvious she loved him, and the time apart had done nothing to quell that feeling.

"That could also be why they decided on Twycross. If they knew that, they could know anything."

"It seems like the "Third Son" is the person who has been dogging both of our steps since Ankaa."

"But who are they?"

Alexi shrugged. "We're going to find out who this Third Son is sooner than later. And I would very much like to put a laser through their middle."

Kenja clenched her jaw. "You'll have to get in line."

The information she *did* have helped paint a picture for Kenja that whoever was commanding the *Third Son* was brutal and demanding. There were no standard rules of war or etiquette that mattered to them to fulfill their mission objective. It had long been a courtesy to any military— both to Inner Sphere and Clan— that JumpShips were off-limits. Spheroids had adopted the unspoken rule since their technology was so rare and difficult to repair. Clan warriors, having never experienced such limitations, instead regarded the ships and their technician caste crews as non-combatants, making it *dezgra* to attack them. Since the Jihad, JumpShips had regained their place as sacrosanct and, during the Blackout, they were the primary form of communication between systems, so they were more important than ever.

But this Third Son attacked them with abandon, and used JumpShips as tools to obtain their objectives. They were brilliant and calculating, and could not be underestimated.

After all they'd put Kenja through, she wanted nothing more than to pull the curtain back on the mastermind bedeviling her days and then, very slowly and painfully, end their life. To pull the trigger on a needler and watch the flechettes make mincemeat of their face.

Maybe she was just angry.

Two months of eating nothing but nutrient paste and the occasional grav deck grub might do that to a person, she figured. But she had her reasons. This person had wronged her severely. They'd harassed her team and killed key members of it. Meridian Yung had been added to the cemetery of the dead that haunted Kenja's soul, and she didn't like it. And that death was specifically on the head of whoever was pulling the strings on the other side.

If she only knew who it was, she could at least put a face to a name and start ascribing motives. It was always easier to determine a next move when you understood the reasoning. Otherwise, there could be no telling what they did or why. That gave her foe the advantage. They knew where Kenja was going, what she was doing, and who she was doing it for.

"There are a lot more questions to answer," Alexi said. "Did this Third Son think we were going to make it here alive? Or at all? Maybe our prisoner was supposed to send us down a different rabbit hole. Or maybe she sent us down the right one?"

"I doubt they planned on her talking. Not with those *Third Son* lookalikes right there on the other side of the planet. They must have assumed there was some special aspect of Twycross' HPG that led us to deploy the repairs here first."

With the information she gathered, Kenja—in consultation with Alexi—formulated a plan. Looking at the options, few as they were, she realized this was going to be even harder than she thought. She had to find a way to take back the initiative. She'd been on her back foot since Hean, reacting instead of acting.

But at least now, with the Filibuster Brigade to back her up, Petrichor back in the mix, and a skilled fighter like Reus Tremor ready to do the Queen's bidding, Kenja had what she considered a fighting chance.

CHAPTER 36:
ASYMMETRICAL INFILTRATION

TWYCROSS NORTH
TWYCROSS
ALYINA MERCANTILE LEAGUE
15 DECEMBER 3151

"Buckle up," Hovertank Commander Fitzgerald of the Filibuster Brigade told Kenja. He pointed to a handle firmly welded to the bulkhead beside her chair. "Word ta the wise: that's the 'Oh Shit' handle. Use it."

Kenja looked over and clutched it tentatively. Dressed in her full tactical compliment, she was armed to the gills, shrouded in midnight blue that looked black in most lights. Fitting for a Sea Fox.

Fitz, as he said he liked to be called, looked back at her one more time. "You ready?"

The driver, a Sikh with a full beard and a turban, had introduced himself as Bheesham. "You're in good hands," he assured Kenja. "Never mind Fitz. He's a great commander."

From the other side of the hovertank, the gunner peeked their head from behind their station. "I'm Grace. We got this thing back in fighting shape."

As she saw the people around her, Kenja realized this was the crew that had saved Petrichor, Pernilla, and Reus Tremor from the Third Dieron Regulars. It made sense that their commander, Ivar Fenrir, would assign them the deadly task once more. They'd already proven they could do it. That was the thing about combat missions: the more missions you came back from, the more you were likely to come back from missions in the future. She only wished she could have seen Petrichor before the mission and told her how proud of her she was.

They didn't have time for such things, though. And Kenja wondered if that doggedness was a flaw rather than an asset. Didn't she deserve something of her own?

"Ready?" Fitz said in his thick accent.

Kenja nodded.

"I'll get you where you're goin', no trouble. It just might be a bumpy ride."

"I'm used to it," Kenja said. Their DropShips had made a shuddering descent toward the Twycross North continent, just ahead of a massive storm front moving in over the HPG outpost. The turbulence had nearly caused both ships to crash-land; a testament to the crews' skills that they had landed safely. Kenja's stomach still hadn't fully come down out of her throat.

Fitz hit the accelerator, and they went from zero to a hundred and fifty kph in about six seconds. It was like having all the gees of their fast burn to the surface pushed right back into her gut right after she'd just gotten used to a sensible gravity again.

The HPG station was underground, like most buildings on Twycross, but aboveground was the massive parabolic dish endemic to all HPGs. It was a dead giveaway about the building's sole function. At the back of the HPG station was a secondary entrance and a ventilation shaft she was going to come in through.

They were going to drop her off her right there.

Her job was to infiltrate the facility, disrupt and neutralize the Third Son's forces inside, and hopefully find and extract Tucker Harwell. Then they'd clear the decks and start over. She would be a one-woman army because it was easier to insert one person than smash their wave against the rocks of the defense of the station. Reus, Alexi, and Petrichor had all offered to go with her, and she had definitely considered it, but she thought a stealth mission would be the best way. It was what she'd been trained to do, and they wouldn't expect it. The Filibuster Brigade and all the Sea Fox 'Mechs they could muster would fend off any enemy 'Mech forces—whether that included more mercenaries or the Alyina Mercantile League, who apparently happened to think they owned Twycross at the moment, judging by the frenzied challenges beamed from Camora orbital control when the *Zephyr* and *Filibustero* had diverted toward Twycross North.

"We got 'Mechs," Fitz said.

Kenja watched Bheesham go to work, identifying the targets. "The WarBook is picking up their makes, but there's no IFF signals transmitting their identities or factions."

"What about paint and logos?" Kenja asked.

"I have a *Stormwolf* in standard desert camo. No logos. No identifying markings. Same for a *Mad Cat* and a *Rifleman*. Definitely not anything local."

"Must be *Third Son* 'Mechs."

Bheesham showed them on his screen, and since his station was the closest to hers, her hand still gripping the "Oh Shit" handle, Kenja squinted at it, searching for clues. Many Clans and Spheroid armies eschewed parade-best paint schemes for sensible camouflage, appropriate for the theater of battle. That wasn't surprising. Usually, they all had some sort of flourish that identified them with the Clan or House or mercenary unit they served. But these 'Mechs bore no such markings.

The camouflage was colored such that if they had flaming orange highlights, she might have taken them for 'Mechs of Clan Wolf—the choice of 'Mechs themselves were very much like the sort the ilClan would probably field. But if they were here, they wouldn't be defending or making alliances with the Alyina Mercantile League—the ilClan would be making pronouncements and demands. They certainly wouldn't begin repairing the HPG network on Twycross, of all places. They would start with Terra and branch out. No, whoever was here had no direct connection to the ilClan, otherwise they wouldn't be here in the first place.

As for the enemy's 'Mechs in the other DropShips, scout reports came in that they would make it to the field sooner than later, so their window of time was narrowing even further.

"Go evasive!" Fitz shouted as they zipped toward the front 'Mech in the formation defending the HPG station—the *Stormwolf*. "Get ready to fire!"

"Affirmative, Captain!" Grace shouted. Her chair swiveled and the viewscreen went with her. She sighted up the *Stormwolf*, and Kenja couldn't even imagine how she could aim at something when the velocity and direction were controlled by someone else entirely—and whose driving felt like being constantly yanked back and forth.

As if sensing her worry, Bheesham told her, "Makes us a harder target to hit."

"I figured."

Grace fired the missiles, Kenja heard them launch overhead. The crew compartment of a hovertank was a lot less insulated and soundproof than a BattleMech, and Kenja found it slightly unnerving. She watched the missiles pepper the *Stormwolf*, leaving divots in its armor. It was a good shot, and Kenja had to give her credit for that.

"Coming around the next one. Two klicks to the drop off."

Kenja steeled herself for what was coming next. She only had a couple minutes to prepare for her infiltration. The hovertank juked left, and she was grateful for the handle. Holding on kept her upright, though it strained muscles in her arm.

Looking out through the window slits, she saw the other hovertanks in the Star, or lance, or whatever mercs called a squad of tanks—a parliament? A murder?—race by, offering cover. There was sense in swarming the 'Mechs.

She watched the feet of a 'Mech as they sped by, and Kenja was unnerved by the difference in size between the hovertanks and the 'Mechs. They could literally squash her and the other three on board just by stepping on them. And it wouldn't even be a reach.

The rest of the hovertanks fired at the 'Mechs.

"'Mech support coming in range," Bheesham called out.

That would help cover their penetration behind the line, too. Not that any 'Mech commander liked hovertanks with SRMs buzzing around them, but they were much less important targets than opposing 'Mechs. They could be annoying. They could deliver the occasional kill shot. They could help plink off armor. But they weren't doing enough damage to be a threat on their own. And they were so damn fast, it took a miracle to hit one in the first place. Better to aim at the bigger targets.

Grace fired at the *Rifleman*, the sound of missiles ripping through the tubes echoing through the tank.

Kenja saw Fitz's screen light up. Grace hit with a full half of the missile salvo, but the *Rifleman* looked no worse for wear. Another series from a different hovertank spattered explosions across the other side of the *Rifleman*, but so did a crackling beam of PPC energy. The support 'Mechs had arrived, and Kenja breathed a little easier.

"Comin' up on it now, *cailín*. Get ready to give it a lash," Fitz said.

The hovertank executed a crash-decelerate maneuver, coming to a screeching halt right at the dropzone.

"Now!" Fitz shouted as the hatch opened.

Unbuckling from the seat and affixing her mask and goggles, Kenja leaped through the hatch, rolled in the sand onto her feet, and ran as fast as she could to the ventilation shaft.

CHAPTER 37: SANGFROID

HPG STATION
TWYCROSS NORTH
TWYCROSS
ALYINA MERCANTILE LEAGUE
15 DECEMBER 3151

The ventilation shaft offered Kenja an easy entry point, and once she was inside, she slowly checked each empty hallways for enemies. On the ground floor of the installation, which extended below her for at least five stories, there were no guards she could see, which felt unusual.

She hadn't seen any infantry guarding the doors, either.

If she didn't know better, she would have thought she was being invited in. But you don't field 'Mechs in front of a facility you *want* someone to infiltrate.

As if she'd summoned them with a thought, Kenja heard footsteps before turning the corner. Then she peeked around quickly. Two, a man and a woman. Both in military tactical gear, bereft of color and personality. No unit patches. No specific uniform style. It was as if they had gotten their gear at a surplus store. She'd only glanced for a second, but saw they were carrying laser rifles, and they were exposed at the arms, neck and legs. Tightening her grip on her needler, she waited until their patrol took them closer.

Leading with the gun, Kenja popped out and fired at each one twice, both in the face. There was no time to take anyone alive. The thugs dropped to the ground like cockpitted 'Mechs.

It was a silent kill; the only sound came from the soft hiss of the needler, the exhalation of breath when the flechettes hit their face, and the tinkle of their equipment against itself as they collapsed. After checking them for access cards and radios, which they oddly didn't have, she stepped quietly over them. The floor, covered in thick, soft carpet kept her footsteps silent as she walked through the entrance they had been guarding.

Inside, she found a staircase. Leading down. Metal stairs in an echoing well.

Enough to cause Kenja to second-guess her intention to travel that way. If the Third Son forces were herding her, it seemed like that would be the obvious way. On the other hand, if they were anticipating her to take a different route after failing to take this bait, nowhere was safe.

If they were truly smart, it wouldn't matter what route down she took. All of them would be equally guarded.

Assuming the worst, Kenja stepped into the stairwell, taking steps as softly as she could, keeping her needler in front of her and checking each corner as she came to it, descending further and further into the HPG station facility.

This one seemed more comfortable than the VoidBreaker facility. As though it had been built in a different time, with a different architectural paradigm. One that eschewed all of the angular features and stripped down design of the station on Hean in favor of the opulence of the Star League era, when everyone wore a cape and high collar, and they built ornate buildings to match their ostentatious peacock costumes.

Kenja descended four floors and encountered no one, though she fully expected to find someone on the other side of the egress door of the stairwell.

It was a gamble to open it. And she wished there was another way to get through. She placed her ear to the door, the one not blaring battle reports through her comm piece, and listened for movement on the other side. It took every ounce of her will to shut off the sounds of Alexi, Reus, Petrichor, and the rest of the Filibuster Brigade fending off the combined might of the Third Son forces and their reinforcements. There were no voices on the other side and no footsteps she could hear.

In fact, the only sound was the void of the sea, as though she'd pressed a shell from the beach to her ear.

Either the coast was clear, or the door was too thick.

Kenja holstered her needler and withdrew a small device the size of a pocket noteputer with a screen on one side and sensors on the other. Activating it, she held it up in front of her while it did its work. Passing it back and forth across the door, it scanned the area on the other side. Soon enough, images of heat signatures appeared. The rainbow of warm colors showed her exactly where the Third Son goons were throughout the hallway beyond in perfect human-shaped outlines. They each wielded a laser rifle. Kenja ran through the math of the situation.

They all faced the door. She noted the elevator on the other side of the exit she planned to use. Maybe she could use that to her advantage.

Running up one more flight of stairs, double-checking there were no guards on that floor, Kenja dashed across the hall and pressed the call button on the elevator. Then she rigged one of the small magnetic explosives from her pouch to the side of the elevator and set its timer for two minutes.

She sent the elevator down one floor and raced down the stairs to beat it.

Then, she watched events unfold through her IR device.

The elevator dinged and the doors slid open. The four guards approached it cautiously, confusion apparent in their body language and gaits. Kenja looked down to her chronometer, its stopwatch synced to the timer: forty seconds left.

Two guards approached the elevator. Inspecting it. Wondering when the disaster would strike. Confused. Curious.

Ten seconds.

Kenja took one last look at the disposition of the forces she faced, pocketed the device.

Five seconds.

She raised her needler and began.

She timed sliding the door open to the explosion and rolled in on her shoulder, just in case any of them had thought to keep covering the stairwell door.

The explosion caught the first two close enough that they were blasted in the face, their ears surely ringing, so Kenja started with the two closest to her. As she rolled into the corridor, she leaned to the right and shot the guard at her side. Then she adjusted her aim, raising her arm up shooting the other rear guard.

The screams and the explosion surely would have alerted anyone else around, so she had to work quickly. Keeping up her momentum, Kenja rose to her feet in time to see one of the guards caught in the blast turn around and watch her pounce on him. He didn't have time to aim and fire, so he brought up his rifle and tried to bat her away with it. He cracked her in the face with the stock.

Kenja spat a tooth out, but never lost her focus, bringing the needler right up the man's temple and pulling the trigger. Bloody chunks of brain and flechette sprayed across the distance between him and the fourth guard. It spattered across Kenja's face, too. She blinked as it hit her, but still kept a laser focus on the fourth guard.

She'd already readjusted her aim and fired twice at the last one, but he juked and shot. The laser tore into her middle, but the armor laced inside her tactical gear took most of the damage. At the very least, it was going to leave a nasty burn, and the searing pain traveled up her belly.

She fired twice more, this time connecting with the target. She'd felled all four of the guards in a matter of moments.

Kenja didn't bother to look around at the destruction and blood throughout the hallway. She just kept moving for the central HPG chamber, the burn from the laser shot reminding her of it with every step she took.

CHAPTER 38:
GHOSTS IN THE MACHINE

HPG STATION
TWYCROSS NORTH
TWYCROSS
ALYINA MERCANTILE LEAGUE
15 DECEMBER 3151

En route to the HPG core, the place she hoped to find Tucker if he was planetside, Kenja kept an ear on the calls of battle on the surface. They only needed to buy her more time. She was so close.

But it wasn't going well for her people.

Star Commander Petrichor and Alexi's former Republic troops were leading the assault against their mystery foes, and hadn't learned anything else about their identity. Thanks to the Filibuster Brigade's hovertanks, they'd taken down two 'Mechs and only lost one tank and one 'Mech in trade. On the other side of the battle, defending against the incoming reinforcements—a mix of Spheroid and second-line Clan equipment marked with the insignia of the Green Winds Free Guild—were two full lances of the Filibuster Brigade, led by Major Patel. She was leading a valiant defense against a single Star, but the Free Guild troops were all in assault 'Mechs, pushing the odds heavily in their favor. Kenja knew the Green Winds also ran courier networks in the Occupation Zones, which explained how Tucker's captors had both reached

Twycross so quickly and picked up reinforcements, though she had never heard of an armed Free Guild before.

Kenja wanted to reach out to her people. To tell them to just hold on. But she had to stay silent, creeping her way toward the central hub of communications that would have the power to renew near instant communication across the entire Inner Sphere. With her forearm, she wiped blood and sweat from her face and edged closer to the door she had already identified on the schematic.

The words "*GENERATOR CORE*" were stenciled on the door right above an old-fashioned ComStar logo, lined renderings of their shielded shooting starburst. The door must have been set to open on approach, because she didn't have a chance to plan her entrance or open it herself, it simply irised wide.

Inside the massive room were the exposed guts of a hyperpulse generator. The main unit was a box the size of two small 'Mechs, studded with panels and consoles. Wires dangled from it in several spots. The master control board was exposed through ripped open paneling. Kenja had learned enough to know the HPG she was looking at would take copious amounts of work to fix.

She knew exactly who could do it.

She looked down to the floor and there he was. Tucker Harwell. Lying on his back. Blood pooling around his head.

"Tucker!" Kenja dashed for him.

Glancing around the room on her way, it felt curiously empty. Ringed around the back side were a number of soundproof booths, all made of ferroglass, perhaps? They looked like the sort of place a person would record a message in before the ComStar folks would send it off, but the public would never be allowed in this part of the station. They'd record back in Camora and have it relayed here for transmission when the Diabolis was too intense over Twycross South. These must have been used for internal messaging by ComStar staff . There were switches on them that could make the glass opaque, too, and half a dozen were; just flat gray walls instead of transparent like the others. Perhaps they were confessionals for the ComStar adepts? Whether it was religious or administrative in function, she couldn't guess and didn't need to. She had more important things to worry about.

Kneeling next to Tucker, Kenja began cataloging his wounds. The laceration across his face would leave a nasty scar if it wasn't taken care of soon. Otherwise, it would leave him looking like the average Jade Falcon. They always seemed to have scars up and down their face to the point where Kenja wondered if Clan Jade Falcon medics were under orders to leave facial lacerations from healing properly, simply for the aesthetic.

"Are you all right, Tucker?" she said, trying to revive him.

But he was completely unresponsive.

"I've got the package," Kenja said into the radio. Putting her fingers to his neck, she checked for a pulse. He was definitely breathing, his heart beating. She scanned his torso for damage. He seemed to be out for reasons she couldn't see. Perhaps he had a concussion?

If they captured him and wanted him working on the HPG station, why would they just leave him unconscious in the middle of the floor?

Who was watching him?

Who was guarding him?

She needed answers, but she wasn't going to get them with Tucker in his current state.

Reaching into her bag, she found the first aid kit. She wiped the blood from his face, slathered anti-infection salve on it, then slapped a bandage patch over one side of the gash and tightened it against the other side. She fished around inside the kit again and withdrew a small pill-shaped piece of cloth. Ammonium salts. Kenja cracked it, the pungent odor widening her own eyes, and waved it beneath Tucker's nose.

He gasped violently and shot up into a sitting position. His eyes widened, and then he winced from the pain. He scrambled backward, clearly afraid, then he looked at Kenja and really saw her. Before, she must have just been a phantom, some last vestige of his torture and torment.

"...Kenja?"

She nodded. "It's me. I'm going to get you out of here."

"A rescue?"

"Yes. What did they do to you?"

He shuddered. "It's been two months."

"I know. I got here literally as fast as I could. It's a long way from Hean to Twycross."

"You're telling me." Tucker touched his face and the bandage. He flinched as he poked and prodded at himself. "Listen, we need to get out of here now. He's coming back."

"Who? Who's coming back? Who took you?"

"You should have died long ago," a voice said behind Kenja. "Or left when you realized you were going to lose. But you couldn't leave him to me, could you? It was always your empathy and belief that things could be better that got in the way."

Kenja's brow furrowed.

The voice was familiar...

Tucker's face was contorted in fear at hearing the familiar voice of the person standing behind her. This was the source of his terror.

Slowly, Kenja stood and turned to see...

"Seth?"

He grinned cruelly, arms spread wide, as though welcoming her back. "Did you miss me?"

He didn't look anything like she remembered. A metal plate had replaced a good chunk of his scalp, and the skin on the other side of his face was mottled with burn scars. He was no longer the attractive secret agent who had mentored her for all those years. His eyes—once warm and kind—now looked dead, driven by what she didn't know.

He was something else now.

And if Seth really was the Third Son—of *course* he was—and he'd betrayed her and the Sea Foxes so thoroughly, then she knew she would have to fight him to the death.

And it had to be her.

May as well get the drop on him.

Kenja reached one hand into her bag with lightning speed and unholstered her needler with the other. The explosive charge was in the air in a flash, and she brought her gun up to shoot at it.

But he was faster on the draw and fired. He knew all her tricks, and shot the explosive far too close to her.

There was a *boom* and a loud *crack*.

And the lights went out for Kenja Rodriguez.

CHAPTER 39:
INTERLUDE: THE DEAD LINE

Star Commander Petrichor rode high in a borrowed 70-ton *Warhammer* WHM-9S, painted in the same flat black as Alexi Holt and Reus Tremor's 'Mechs.

The mission had been going sideways since Ankaa, and it seemed like someone was constantly a step ahead of them. Nothing had gone right, and whoever they were fighting was dogging their every turn.

"Suckerfish," Alexi called on the comm, "focus fire on the *Third Son Jade Hawk.*"

The thought of focusing fire on a 'Mech was not normally part of Petrichor's repertoire of acceptable things, but she had no choice. It wasn't like the enemy 'Mechs were adhering to anything even close to *zellbrigen*—the honorable ways of combat the Clans employed to reduce waste. These opponents fought like Spheroids, and it didn't matter what damage they wrought in their fights. They were in it to win, and there was no telling them they should stick to a single, honorable target in a duel. They simply didn't care.

"I'm on it, Carp," Petrichor said. Carp was the codename Kenja had given Alexi. Kenja had also designated Reus as Flounder. And she reminded Petrichor not to use Clan terms like *"Aff"* over the comms. They were almost certainly being intercepted, and there was no reason to make the enemy's job any easier on them.

Petrichor pivoted her *Warhammer* and lined up a view of the *Jade Hawk*. It was a 'Mech closely associated with the Jade Falcons, designed by them as a totem 'Mech, complete with the partial wing assembly and claws. Petrichor wondered if this one had been salvaged on Twycross, a remnant of the Jade Falcon occupation.

Her extended range PPCs lanced blue lightning across the field, ablating the armor from the *Jade Hawk's* legs, boiling it off in molten sheets that scarred the desert floor. Then she fired her medium lasers. They missed their mark entirely and carved great gashes into the HPG facility.

"Damn it, Suckerfish!" Reus called out. "We need to keep that facility whole. *Everyone* is in there."

"The package is in there," Alexi reminded them with a renewed certainty since they'd heard his exchange with Kenja.

Petrichor imagined hearing Tucker was alive had bolstered Alexi's spirits. After spending so much time with Reus on the *Filibustero*, Petrichor *knew* it lifted his spirits.

"So is Kitefin," Petrichor reminded them.

"Kitefin," Alexi said, as though Petrichor had reminded her of that fact, "Sitrep, come in."

Petrichor sidestepped, trying to get a better angle on the *Jade Hawk* so that any shots that missed might not affect the HPG station. It already looked haggard; it had taken an entire bevy of missiles from the hovertanks whizzing by.

The hardest thing about fighting with the tanks underfoot was the danger that she might step on them. She'd gotten to know the crews of the tanks quite a bit, too, and found she liked them as well.

Petrichor couldn't understand why they were supposed to be so disdainful of warriors other than MechWarriors in the Clans. She'd found warriors of all stripes in the Filibuster Brigade to be honorable, resourceful, and generally good people. Was it all just a story to keep them separate?

As she fired again at the *Jade Hawk*, the enemy 'Mech took more fire from other sources: lasers slashed across it from

Alexi's *Black Knight* and Reus's *Grand Summoner*, which he'd dubbed *Tremor*.

Petrichor fired again, scoring burns along its torso and right arm. But the *Jade Hawk* didn't go down.

Nor did Kenja report from inside.

"Something's wrong," Petrichor said, wishing she'd been able to see the Star Colonel before they went on their separate missions with burning regret. She understood why she couldn't, separated by time, space, and intent, but it did nothing to assuage her fears. "Kitefin, sitrep, do you copy?"

But still no answer came.

Petrichor lined up another shot against the *Jade Hawk*, trying to ignore the deepening pit in her stomach, three full gees of pain falling into a black hole, but that's when her *Warhammer* shuddered forward. Her shots missed, and her wireframe 'Mech on the HUD display changed colors, flashing green to yellow. Then another volley hit her back, and the wireframe flared from yellow to red.

Turning her attention to her rear quarter, Petrichor saw a massive juggernaut of a *Stone Rhino* hammering the back of her 'Mech. It was all legs, cannons, and cockpit, firing rounds from a pair of Gauss rifles and coruscating violet beams of pulsing lasers. She wouldn't continue to stand up to such abuse, so she pivoted back.

"Suckerfish," Major Patel said over the comm from her *Timber Wolf*, painted up in black with gray flourishes and their logo, a hound bearing a gavel in its teeth. "That *Behemoth* broke through our line and is gunning for you. It's changed its behavior. Something must be going on, because its orders seem to have changed."

"Copy, Major." Petrichor turned her signal back over to Alexi and Reus. "You copy that, Carp?"

"Copied. Still nothing from Kitefin. Something is definitely wrong."

Petrichor continued backing up and turning, trying to keep her now-vulnerable back quarter protected from the sniping enemy commander. "We just need to protect the facility and give Kitefin more time."

"I'm going in there," Alexi said. "Someone's got to save the package."

Petrichor's face flushed with anger—already fevered from the heat in the 'Mech's cockpit—and she wanted to scream. "We need to stay here, bondsman—"

"Bondswoman," Alexi shot back.

"We *must* hold the line. If we lose and the line falls, there won't be anyone to save Kitefin *or* the package."

Alexi growled.

Petrichor fired back at the *Stone Rhino.* Her PPC's crackled across its stubby nose, leaving charred marks across it, but against the 100-ton assault 'Mech, even two blasts of man-made lightning did little to stop it.

But that was all she could do.

She just hoped Kenja's line had gone dead for a good reason.

CHAPTER 40: THRESHER

**HPG CORE
TWYCROSS NORTH
TWYCROSS
ALYINA MERCANTILE LEAGUE
15 DECEMBER 3151**

Everything hurt.

That was the first thing Kenja noticed. Even before opening her eyes, she needed to catalog the damage. Pain seared through her face. There was a gaping hole in her gums that reminded her she had a missing tooth. It stung every time she probed it with her tongue, which she couldn't help. Her muscles ached. Aside from the occasional spin in the grav deck during the breakneck transit along the express courier route, she'd really only had a few weeks to get used to gravity again. Her stomach also radiated a dull, throbbing pain, most likely from that laser rifle hit.

As alert as she was, taking note of every small ache, her head was hazy. Maybe a concussion. She wanted to let out a ragged scream, but she couldn't.

Playing possum was a sound strategy for the moment.

As she continued her inventory of agony, she realized her hands were behind her back. Bound together with ties. That would be a problem. Worse than that, her ankles were tethered to something—the legs of a chair? She was slumped over, but sitting upright.

Her awareness spread outward. She could no longer hear the battle, meaning her earpiece had been removed. Neither could she feel the weight of safety provided by her utility belt and needler at her hip.

She'd been robbed of every single one of her useful tools.

"It's no use," Seth said. "I know what you're doing. You're looking for a way out."

How did he even know she was awake?

Because he'd taught her to do exactly what she was doing. All those years ago.

Kenja forced her eyes open and took in her surroundings. She was in one of those small recording booths, perhaps three square meters, that ringed the HPG apparatus. The ferroglass was transparent, so she could see a haggard Tucker standing in the background, looking at some part of the battered HPG station under duress and threat of more torture.

In front of her, sitting in a backward chair with his forearms resting on its back, was Seth. Despite the scars and the metal plate, he looked no worse for wear. Determination was carved resolutely on his face. Kenja recognized the look. He would joke, he would act jovial, but when the prize was before him, he got very serious. "That's twice you tried to kill me."

Kenja didn't think it was worth arguing about the fact that the MaxiTech folks were the ones who tried to kill him. Not her. But he was probably counting her leaving him for dead as close enough. "And what about all the times you tried to kill me?"

"By that point, it was all part of the mission. You of all people should know that mission parameters aren't personal."

"You were supposed to be *on* this mission with me. Instead, you went rogue. Against me. Personally. How is that not personal?" She glanced out the window, wondering if Tucker could hear them. It didn't look like it, but she dragged her gaze back to Seth as he answered.

"You left me for dead, and I found a better deal."

"This is *dezgra*, and you know it! You taught me what *dezgra* meant more than anything in my training. Yeah, we were a special exception in the way Clans work, bending traditions and rules, but we're still Sea Foxes and Clan warriors, and you taught me honor. I thought you believed in the cause."

Seth laughed. "Did you know I was won by Clan Sea Fox in a Trial of Possession? Do you even know what Bloodhouse or Clan I'm from?"

"We never talked about that." Disappointment hit her in the chest like the ax from a *Hatchetman*. Why had they never talked about it? They were so close—or so she thought. Was everything she knew a lie? Or a clever lie by omission?

"We didn't have to. You just assumed, which always worked to my advantage."

"Then who are you that you'd sell out your Clan? Who did Clan Sea Fox take you from?"

Seth's smile widened. "I am Seth Wolf of the Bloodhouse Ward. And thanks to the help MaxiTech offered me, I may yet reclaim that honor and secure my genetic legacy with the ilClan."

"That's preposterous," Kenja said. "There's no way they'd let you back in. You're a Sea Fox."

"If *I* get the HPG network up and running and bring that power to the ilKhan, do you really think I would not be rewarded? And the boon I want is simple. I wish to be a Wolf once more."

Kenja sighed, searching for a way out of the mess she was in. She was bound to the chair. She ached with every fiber of her being. Her tools were gone. Her wits were all the only thing left, and she didn't know how to force him to make a mistake.

And he was the person who had trained her. Taught her everything she knew. Panic flooded inside of her, an ocean crashing down against her, but she had to keep it at bay.

"So what are you going to do to me?" she asked, hoping to draw him out further.

His smile was more sinister. More wolf-like. "You left me for dead and have gotten in my way far too many times. I'm going to torture you, of course."

"Why? You obviously know everything I do. I assume you held onto all the Sea Fox decryption codes and pass-phrases, which is how you could predict my every move. You intercepted all my courier reports using Watch protocols and decrypted them on your own." She started putting the pieces together.

"You were in orbit over Ankaa and hired the mercs to steal Tucker there, didn't you?"

"It was regrettable it didn't work out there. I underestimated you. And Tucker's caretakers. But I didn't make that mistake again. I've been three moves ahead of you from the moment I learned where you would intercept Tucker." Seth straightened his posture and stretched his neck to one side until it cracked. "I've certainly kept you on your toes though, haven't I?"

"I still don't understand why you'd torture me. You're the one who drilled into me that it didn't yield any information." She mimicked his voice, reminding him of his own words verbatim, "'No actionable intelligence would arise from torture.'"

"First off, I think it would be fun. You left me to die, and I want you to know what that feels like. You were always so eager to do what I did and concerned yourself with how I thought, well, now you can concern yourself with how it felt to be abandoned. But second, have you read his profile?" Seth cocked his head back toward Tucker, who had stopped his work to watch Kenja and Seth with wide saucer eyes. "They've tortured him off and on for the last two decades to get him to do this, but I realized that wasn't his pressure point. Maybe it might have been, but it isn't any longer. No. I torture Tucker Harwell, and he'll just crumple like a lasered Cameron."

"Why did you cut his face then? You've already tortured him."

"That was all a show for your benefit. Yes, it was a threat, but it was to force your reaction. Haven't you learned enough to know everything in our game is an emotional manipulation? That's why my mercs had such an easy time snatching him from you in the first place. I knew which decision you'd make. You're even easier to read than he is. I scared him, yes. Let him know what I was capable of. Hurt him. Knocked him out for you to find when I realized you were on your way. Now I'm going to torture you to show him what happens if he doesn't fix the HPG. And my wager—and I could still be wrong about this, anything is possible—is that watching you get tortured, screaming silently in this little sound-proof booth, will motivate him to work. Because only when this station goes live again will I stop. But if it doesn't motivate him, it won't matter; it will still have brought me a great amount of pleasure."

Seth had lost any sense he'd had. Something was broken in him, and Kenja couldn't understand what.

Tucker had planned to fix the HPG anyway. The only reason he wouldn't would be to keep the power from a person as violent and out of his mind as Seth clearly was. "It won't work," Kenja said. "He doesn't care about me. I'm just another one in a long line of his captors."

Seth laughed heartily, rising from his seat and moving the chair out from between them. "Of course it will. Everything I've planned to this point has worked exactly as it was supposed to. This will, too. I am sorry it has to be this way, but I am going to earn my reward and not get cast off as some *solahma* has-been on the *Titanic*, left to float around the ArcShip for the rest of my life and teach Sea Fox whelps the skills I fought a lifetime to earn. Whelps like you..."

Kenja tried to ignore the hurt of that statement and the anger in Seth's face as her eyes flashed to Tucker.

Tucker looked at her, annoyed and hurt. She couldn't tell what he was thinking. He was fiddling with the data transfer lines leading to a control panel, but she couldn't tell if he was fixing it, sabotaging it, or just playing with it because it was his nervous tic.

Seth flipped a switch at the side of the wall and a little light went on above it, indicating the sound was being piped out into the main room. "Mister Harwell."

Tucker's attention focused in on Seth.

"What now?" Tucker said, his voice sounding distant and far away. Like it was coming through a string and a tin can.

"I just wanted to let you know what the price is of not completing the work on my HPG station. It's going to be the Star Colonel here. I'll make a recording of all her screams and cries as I do this, and it will be your lullaby from now until this facility is completely operational."

"Don't do it, Tucker!" Kenja shouted, and caught the back of Seth's hand right in the face.

It stung worse than anything she had ever experienced; he'd slapped her right where her skin had been burned away by the explosion.

"Let's begin, Mr. Harwell. I suggest if you want this particular symphony to end, you'll get to work."

Kenja, her mouth agape in pain, looked over to Tucker, pleading with him to just ignore it using only her eyes.

Then Seth grabbed her roughly by the chin and forced her gaze up to him. "Now let's see just how well I trained you."

CHAPTER 41: REFLEX POINT

HPG CORE
TWYCROSS NORTH
TWYCROSS
ALYINA MERCANTILE LEAGUE
15 DECEMBER 3151

Kenja did her best not to scream. She didn't want Tucker to feel as though he was going to have to hand the technology over to someone who would use it for nefarious purposes and personal gain.

It wasn't easy.

Especially when Seth came in at her with the knife, making slow cuts across her legs and arms, bleeding her slowly as if to attract sharks with blood in the water.

Her head spun and she dizzied a bit, but kept her jaw set and focused on maintaining her quiet demeanor.

She wasn't going to give him the satisfaction of screaming.

In training, she had been told to find a calm, safe space and lock herself away there. To breathe through it and close her eyes to get there. Her space looked like a beach on a tropical paradise, as far away from a war and a BattleMech as could be. The water lapped up on the beach in soft, ebbing waves. The sun kept her warm and the gravity kept her grounded.

There, in that safe space in her mind, nothing could hurt her.

Not even Seth.

Seth backed away, his knife dripping with her blood. He was actually working up a sweat and panting. As soon as he stepped away, she stepped off her beach and went to work trying to escape the bonds at her wrist incognito.

"I'm impressed," he said. "You *did* take all that training to heart. I'm actually proud of you, little Kitefin."

"You don't get to call me that anymore." *Keep him talking.* That's all she had to do and she could be free.

He smirked. From his back pocket, he drew a kerchief and wiped the sweat from his scarred and mottled face. Then he used it to polish the metal plate that had replaced so much of his cranium before putting it back in his pocket. "I'll miss the work, you know? That was the worst thing about getting older, knowing that at one point, well before my prime, the Sea Foxes would bench me, stop me from reaching my true potential. I would have stuck around, though. All they had to do was treat me better." Then he made fierce and direct eye contact with her. "Or just not leave me for dead."

Kenja spat blood, a copper-tasting pool forming at the bottom of her mouth, right near Seth's feet. "What did MaxiTech offer you?"

"Other than my life and riches beyond my dreams? All the resources at their disposal. You would be shocked and amazed what an interstellar conglomerate like MaxiTech can put together when they think they can gain superiority in a field as important as interstellar communication. They're ignorant to my real plans and, I assure you, completely inconsequential."

Seth looked down at the blood at his feet and on his hands. And Kenja saw none of it mattered to him. He was completely numb to all of it.

Wholly desensitized.

"I thought we were building something for the good of everyone. That's what we'd worked toward for so long. What happens when the ilClan uses the technology to subjugate the entire Inner Sphere? What then?" She said, doing her best to wind him up. That was the only tool she had left to get him to make some mistake she could exploit.

Seth looked confused, a frown on his face and brows upturned. "I'm sorry. I thought you were Clan. Is that not the right of the Clan who reaches Terra first? To rule the Inner Sphere through the renewed Star League? To set things the way they ought to be."

Kenja shook her head. "The Clans are protectors of humanity. Its guardians. Standing sentinel to end wars. Not cause them and not to be tyrants. There are checks and balances."

Seth smirked again. "We must have had different indoctrinations."

"I spent my career trying to do what you would have done, to earn your pride. I thought we were different, that we were making the Inner Sphere and the Clan both a better place."

Seth laughed. "Clan Sea Fox is a farce, and the Inner Sphere is full of people too stupid to know what's good for them. And now the ilKhan will show them what is best for them."

Kenja knew she couldn't rely on her initial instincts. She had to stop thinking about what Seth would do and start focusing on what *she* would do. Then inspiration hit.

She flicked her gaze to Tucker once more, then back to Seth. "Do you listen to yourself? Are you hearing this? What would happen if anyone else out there heard this drivel? What would happen then?"

"But they won't," Seth said.

But Tucker's eyes went from hurt confusion to realization. And he went to work because it finally dawned on him she was talking to him and not Seth.

"Seth," Kenja said. "You can stop. Our legacy is secure. All we're trying to do is create a level playing field of communication for the Inner Sphere. Free. Fair. Open. Neutral. We were going to cut across the political borders of the Inner Sphere and make it possible for everyone to once again live in a world where we can sue for peace with our words rather than bid for battles with our 'Mechs."

He scoffed. "You're lying now, Kenja. The HPG network, no matter who controls it, isn't going to do anything to slow wars and battles across the Inner Sphere. If anything, it will hasten them along. We're humans. Inner Sphere or Clan, this is what we do. War is our way of life."

Kenja was almost out of the bonds at her wrists. Her tactic was working, and Seth kept talking. Maybe he had forgotten he'd taught her how to dislocate her thumb to push her narrow wrists through cuffs, ties, and binders. Kenja certainly hadn't. And now they were talking, and Tucker seemed to be getting a fuller picture.

"Besides, the ilKhan would only use it for the good of the Inner Sphere."

"You believe that?" Kenja asked. Hoping to buy a little more time.

"I do, Kenja. And I'll tell you why. Because the Inner Sphere and the Clans are his now. They will all come under his heel, one way or another. For the Clans, our entire way of life is predicated on the notion that might makes right. And Alaric Ward has made right by the Wolves by taking Terra. We fight wars to end wars."

Seth cleaned the blood from his blade, wiping it against his pants, then turned to look at Tucker. "You hearing all of this, Mr. Harwell?"

Tucker stopped his work and turned to regard Seth and Kenja.

As Seth's back was turned, Kenja's wrists were finally free!

"Why are you stopping?" Seth asked. "You're only going to force me to continue."

Seth cocked his head back at Kenja and pointed at her with the tip of his blade.

Kenja reached out with blinding speed, grabbing Seth's wrist. She twisted his arm until he dropped the knife into her other hand. Every muscle in her body screamed. It was all fire and she just wanted water.

Seth's eyes widened and he brought his other hand back, punching Kenja in the face as he wrenched his hand free. Stars exploded in her vision, and her head slammed against the chair, but she had what she needed.

"Kenja!" she heard Tucker call through the tin can.

"A bold move," Seth said, projecting arrogance. "But it still doesn't matter. I'm in control here."

Kenja gripped the knife she'd taken from him and stabbed at him, but he parried her strike as if she was nothing, chopping her wrist away.

Seth reached out to grapple her, but that's when she tried something he *hadn't* taught her. Kenja tipped the chair over in a roll, reaching down with the knife to cut the cord at her right ankle, and coming back up on her feet.

Brimming with confidence, Seth just scoffed. "You're only making this harder for yourself, little Kitefin."

Glad he was underestimating her, Kenja made another move for him. Standing upright with her freed right foot planted firmly on the ground, she brought her left around with the chair, smashing it into Seth's knees.

Instinctively, Seth raised a leg to deflect the blow with his shin. The chair hit him solidly, but he stood his ground while grabbing the chair, stopping it completely. With her left leg still attached to it, Kenja stood awkwardly on one foot.

"Seth, you don't need to do this."

"Don't I?"

"I know you can't trust anyone says under torture, but you can trust this," Kenja said, struggling against his grip. "I'm going to put an end to this. And I'm going to make sure your genes never find a place of honor in the Clans. Wolf. Sea Fox. It doesn't matter. This ends with you. Believe that."

Seth, leaning to counter-balance the weight of the chair, sighed. Disappointed. "Kenja, when will you ever learn? The only person you can care about is yourself."

He tossed the chair up and over, toppling Kenja to the ground. She swooned on the way, dizzy. She'd lost too much blood to keep this up.

He had every advantage, and there was nowhere to maneuver. The room was too small.

And there was no one coming to help.

Kenja scrabbled backward, the chair screeching against the floor as she pulled back, searching for a way to prevail.

Seth edged in closer. "I admire your effort. But you're alone. And if you don't inspire Tucker to finish the job, I'll just find others he cares about. And soon, there won't be anyone left for me to torture. He'll have fixed it, or they'll all be dead."

Kenja, never losing eye contact with Seth, reached down and cut the cord on her left leg, freeing herself from the chair. Then, she kicked it forward, hoping to trip him.

He didn't.

There was a *whoosh*, and Kenja wasn't quite certain what was going on, but she knew she had to press the advantage while they were both distracted. She leaped to her feet.

Seth had turned his face turned to the now-open door. The sounds of the HPG station filled the little soundproof booth like a cacophony.

And there stood Tucker.

"Leave her alone."

He laughed. "Get back to work, Harwell."

"No."

Kenja lunged for Seth, but had a fist ready to swing.

He punched her and she pinwheeled back. Then he turned to Tucker, palmed the scientist's face, and tried to shove him to the ground.

Tucker grabbed Seth and pulled him toward the door.

Kenja shook off the blow, ignoring the dancing lights at the edges of her vision.

Seth laughed.

And that's when she stabbed the knife right into the spot between his neck and his shoulder.

His laughter turned into a harsh, ragged gag. Then he collapsed.

All that was left was Tucker and Kenja, wheezing from the effort.

A tear ran down Tucker's cheek as Kenja grabbed him, embracing him in a hug. "Thank you."

"Well," Tucker said, trying not to sob. "That's what you get for treating me like a person..."

CHAPTER 42: INTERLUDE: STAMPEDE

TWYCROSS NORTH
TWYCROSS
ALYINA MERCANTILE LEAGUE
15 DECEMBER 3151

Petrichor's wireframe flashed yellow or red on every part of her 'Mech. Her armor had been blasted off by great Gauss bullets or melted away by superheated lasers. Her inner structure was showing no matter which direction she faced, and there wasn't a lot she could do about it.

It was the most desperate situation she'd ever been in, and she didn't like it one bit.

"Carp," Petrichor said on the comm, "any suggestions?"

They had already pulled back into a defensive perimeter around the DropShips, hoping their defensive lasers would keep them safe. Or safer, at least. The Filibuster Brigade's aerospace fighters were valiantly struggling in the sandy storm that had kicked up, pouring missiles and laser fire into the assault 'Mechs of the Green Winds. The Free Guild had the advantage because most were long-range snipers, with the ability to take hard hits and the armor to soak up a lot of damage. On the other side of their flank, there were the mystery forces of the Third Son, with their desert camo and deadly aim.

"There aren't a lot of options at the moment."

"Well, what else can they do?" Petrichor asked. She fired at the *Stone Rhino* that had refused to give her up as a target while Alexi took a moment. Hopefully it wasn't for anything other than thinking.

"With the DropShips, it's a stalemate," Alexi said. "The Guild can keep us hemmed in, but they could also make it really hard for us to leave."

Petrichor frowned. "They could call in reinforcements when the Diabolis clears. They have DropShips on-planet, presumably."

"They could call in an airstrike," Alexi said.

"So could we, if we could be sure which Aimags are on our side." Petrichor didn't like going through the possibilities, but it was necessary to form a cohesive counter-attack. Unfortunately, they were outnumbered. The Green Winds assault Star seemed barely damaged. Petrichor's team had worn off some armor off here and there, but overall they looked no worse for wear.

"They could starve us out," Alexi continued.

Then Reus chimed in. "They could also surrender to us, but I don't see it happening."

Petrichor looked down at her mini-map and saw the Third Son forces growing larger. Where they'd come from, she couldn't tell, but they poured out from behind the HPG station. Perhaps they had a second drop zone?

It spelled doom for her team. Her side had a numerical advantage, especially with their hovertanks and aerospace fighters, but the mystery enemies that continued pouring out of nowhere were going to turn the tide away from them at any minute.

She had to take on the very real possibility they were going to lose.

And she didn't even know what that looked like. Would she simply die? Cease to exist? Or taken as a bondsman?

A surprising voice rang in through her speakers, broadcasting on an open channel.

"Mercenaries from the *Third Son*, hear me!"

It was Kenja! Petrichor's heart skipped—this was music to her ears.

"Your leader is dead. Your contract is null. You have no one to fulfill it. But I am ready to make a deal. I will pay you to complete Seth Wolf's contract and grant you amnesty for crimes against my forces. But you must cease your attack immediately."

Petrichor wondered how much Kenja was going to reveal on an open channel, but as she checked the frequency, she realized it was tuned directly to the enemy 'Mechs of the *Third Son* and her own forces. The Green Winds stood in the dark.

"We were paid in advance," came a voice. Petrichor could only assume it was the mysterious *Third Son* commander.

"And I will pay you more," Kenja said. "The man who purchased your contract will make you enemies of the Clan Sea Fox, which will ensure that you never receive another mercenary contract, and hunt you down to the ends of the Sphere. Join us, and I will pay you twice the contract he gave you. Besides, he found you inconsequential, and planned to betray you when the time was right. Listen to this!"

Another voice came through the comm. Their employer, this Seth Wolf, presumably.

"*—other than my life and riches beyond my dreams? All the resources at their disposal. You would be shocked and amazed how much a conglomerate like MaxiTech can put together when they think they can gain superiority in a field as important as interstellar communication. They're ignorant to my real plans, and inconsequential.*"

Petrichor wondered if the lucrewarriors would take the bait. Voices could be faked. But Petrichor had learned from her time with the Filibuster Brigade that things weren't that easy. Nothing was black and white—except maybe their 'Mechs.

There was no immediate response from the enemy commander.

But, curiously, their 'Mechs stopped firing.

Petrichor had to continue juking, dodging, and firing, trying to remain a hard target at the foot of the *Filibustero*, because the Free Guild refused to cease their assault. She had the sneaking suspicion the only reason she was still alive was that the Diabolis storm was playing hell with *everyone's* instruments, making it difficult for anyone to score solid hits.

Kenja continued. "We are on the brink of a new order, with communication about to be restored throughout the Inner

Sphere. I will tell you this, even though I shouldn't, but this is how much I believe in the power of free communication: we have discovered the methods to fix the HPG network. And if you stand in our way, there will be nowhere you can hide. Clan Sea Fox has also made strides to become the premiere mercenary bond guarantor. You will need to work with us to do anything. Send messages. Work in any part of the Sphere worth working in. And if you help us, it will be the easiest thing in the world for you. Cross us and you have made your last enemy."

Petrichor fired back at the *Stone Rhino*, but a *Dire Wolf* sliced the myomer in her 'Mech's left arm with its large lasers. She heard the shearing of metal as the internal supports and skeletal structure of her *Warhammer*'s bicep snapped.

The wireframe of her arm flashed from red and just... disappeared.

"So, I say again, Mercenaries of the *Third Son*. Your contract is over. There are greener pastures ahead. That I can promise you. But if you do not take my offer now, it will catch up to you sooner or later."

Petrichor fired with her remaining PPC at the *Dire Wolf* and the crackling energy connected below the cockpit in a blow that left molten armor dribbling down its front, but still not enough to make a killing blow.

Then she took another hit from a different Green Winds 'Mech altogether.

They were focusing their fire on her.

She supposed it served her right for throwing in her lot with mercenaries like the Filibuster Brigade—dark caste guildsmen would not give her the honor her rank warranted. But the mission was the mission, and for a member of the Watch, that was the most important thing.

Limping her battered *Warhammer* away, Petrichor fired her last remaining PPC again, but couldn't connect the shot.

"If it's double the contract, Sea Fox, and favored status on jobs..." the mercenary commander said grimly over the comm, "then count us in."

Petrichor smiled, watching the IFF signals on her minimap shift the enemy mercs from red contacts to blue, and then all of them readjust their aims to the Green Winds.

They were going to pull it off!

"Maybe the Free Guild *will* surrender to us," Reus said. "I genuinely wasn't expecting that."

Petrichor just had to last through the rest of the battle in one piece. But seeing all the other forces arrayed against them, she realized she still had one card of her own left to play.

"Warren of the Green Winds," she said on the open channel, hoping the intel about the forces they faced was correct. "This is Star Commander Petrichor of Clan Sea Fox. Our forces, Inner Sphere and Clan alike, have united to common purpose. You are outnumbered and outgunned. I will offer you *hegira*. Depart the battlefield with no further loss and leave Twycross, and we will fire no more."

The *Stone Rhino* lowered its arms, no longer aiming at her.

And the fire across the battlefield ceased, leaving only the last vestiges of smoke, carried by the whipping wind as the only evidence of a fight.

"This is Warren. Bargained well and done. We accept."

And with that, the Green Winds turned to leave, and not another shot was fired in the battle to secure Twycross North and its HPG station.

CHAPTER 43: ONE LAST TRICK

**CAMORA HPG STATION
CAMORA
TWYCROSS
ALYINA MERCANTILE LEAGUE
24 DECEMBER 3151**

"Excellent work, Kitefin," Carcharodon's shadowy figure said in the holovideo message transmitted to Kenja from the orbiting ArcShip *Titanic.*

"It was unfortunate to lose Thresher as an asset and operative, but his loyalty was clearly questionable, and we will deal with the MaxiTech situation in due time. Spina Khanate has Watch agents in that area, so you will be able to take all the time you need to rest and heal. I was dismayed to learn about your condition in your report. Now that the Green Winds have been driven from Twycross, our interests have been served."

Through the bandages and the pain, Kenja focused her mind, not letting it wander to think about everything else; things ranging from the real identity of Carcharodon to the lingering questions about Seth. Why he would have felt slighted, and wanted to deliver the HPG network to the ilKhan to earn his place back in Clan Wolf seemed... Well, it made her angry.

She sipped her citrusy restorative beverage, designed to give her body all the calories it needed to knit back into shape and assist her skin grafts to heal over the burns she had suffered on her face and her stomach. Once her body's natural processes had gone as far as they could, good old-fashioned Clan medical technology would take over and make her look like herself. No scarring, nothing.

It would be akin to a miracle. Most Sea Foxes with similar injuries accepted the scars as badges of honor, or at the very least, as signs that they were unwilling to have their Clan spend its resources on something so vain as mere appearance. However, distinctive scars were a decided drawback for a top Watch infiltration specialist, so exceptions were made when the value proposition made sense.

"Before you get your rest and relaxation, though," Carcharodon added, *"we have one more mission to ask of you."*

Kenja smirked.

Of course they'd have one more thing.

"You need to make the first steps in connecting the network across the Hinterlands. If your report on the VoidBreaker Protocol is accurate, it should be no difficulty for you and your team to spread communication across that area of space and establish the first new nodes of the Sea Fox HPG network. I have already dispatched Petrichor to Almotacen to begin restoration work there. I have included an encrypted data packet with information of where we would like you to start. Seyla, Kitefin. You have done what no one else could and this will surely be added to our Remembrance. *Your Sea Fox* trothkin *will never forget your valiant actions on behalf of our Clan. To this, I say again:* seyla."

The Twycross North station was again operational, and once Tucker Harwell finished repairing the Camora station, Twycross would be completely up and running, and she'd be able to take him along for the rest of the ride.

VoidBreaker worked. And she knew it.

And it was going to make the Sea Foxes the most powerful Clan in the Inner Sphere, even if the other Clans didn't realize it.

ALYINA MERCANTILE LEAGUE HEADQUARTERS
EXCHANGE PLACE TOWER
NEW DELHI
ALYINA
28 JANUARY 3152

The journey to Alyina had treated Kenja well enough. She had forgotten what it was like to travel without urgency and allow herself time to heal. Instead of traveling on the DropShip, she spent her time in the grav deck of the JumpShip so she could recuperate, rather than stress herself with zero-gee exercises just to maintain her health.

So much in the galaxy had changed in the year since she'd gotten this mission in the first place. And the changes in the Inner Sphere she noticed most acutely started with Alyina and its new order with the Mercantile League.

It had founded by former Jade Falcon merchants who decided they no longer wanted to work for warriors and had expelled those leftovers warriors from their borders, hired mercenaries for protection in addition to their own homegrown militia, and were making a go of things on their own. Syndic Marena, the merchant in charge, was known to the Sea Foxes as a shrewd negotiator, and she would have made a brilliant Sea Fox. But the Clan way of life was behind her now. When she had traveled to Twycross in 3151 to seek accommodation with Tiburon Khanate, they had recognized each other as kindred spirits, and set terms for Twycross to join the League while the Tiburon enclaves retained full autonomy and independence.

Now, Kenja sat up straight in her Clan Sea Fox dress uniform in the Syndic's office. Star Commander Petrichor sat beside her, dressed similarly. The only difference between them were their rank pips.

They had a beautiful view of the city of New Delhi as they waited for the Syndic's arrival; her office was on the top floor of the exchange, and the glittering gems of lights at night sparkled all the way around in almost three-hundred and sixty degrees of views.

"Don't be nervous," Kenja reminded Petrichor.

"I'm not nervous," the Star Commander said.

"I almost believed you that time. You're doing better. You'll do well out here."

Petrichor smiled at Kenja. Bright and genuine. "Thank you, Star Colonel. I have learned so much in the last year from you. Your pride in me means a lot."

Kenja frowned, thinking of her own mentor and drive. "If you listen to anything else I say, make it this: don't worry about making me proud. I already am. Don't worry about what I would do. Listen to yourself. You have good instincts and a good head on your shoulders. Do it your way, and you'll do fine."

Petrichor took that in carefully. Kenja still sensed that unspoken tug of fondness from the young woman, but hoped the young Star Commander would be able to put that behind her in time.

The elevator *whooshed* as its doors slid open behind them. Kenja and Petrichor both rose to their feet to politely greet the Syndic.

Syndic Marena had dark skin and had a mane of curly black hair, old enough for white streaks to thread through it. She looked tired, but confident. Kenja hoped she looked as good in twenty years, when she reached the Syndic's age.

"Sea Foxes," Marena said. "To what do I owe the pleasure?"

"I am Star Colonel Kenja Rodriguez, this is Star Commander Petrichor. We are happy to meet with you, Syndic."

"I'm sure." She stepped around her ornate desk, positioned in the center of the room, and sat down behind it, waving them to their chairs.

Kenja cleared her throat. "I am aware of your misgivings about the traditional order of the Clans, where warriors dominate."

"I have made no secret of it."

"But I think you have found that Clan Sea Fox is a like-minded partner amenable to dealing with you."

Marena raised her eyebrows and spoke with supreme confidence. "In time, I think everyone will be amenable to dealing with me."

Petrichor squirmed in her seat just enough for Kenja to wonder if bringing her here had been the best idea. There wasn't much to be done about it now, though. Kenja wanted her to see how it was done, because Petrichor was going to be dealing with this sort of thing on her own soon enough. After this, Kenja would likely be sent elsewhere, and Petrichor would be left for a time to oversee the commerce of the HPGs in the Hinterlands . She would have to grow accustomed to the halls of power, and quickly.

"I am sure they will be," Kenja said. "But the Sea Foxes would like to hasten your ability to do so."

Marena stifled a laugh. "And why would the Sea Foxes want to do that? I'm no fool. I know you see me as a potential competitor. I'm a small merchant, and the Sea Foxes are the largest merchant fleet in the Inner Sphere, by my reckoning. What could you possibly offer me that isn't some kind of trap?"

Kenja smiled, matching Marena's fierce energy. "How would you like to have a working HPG network across your territory?"

Marena blinked. "That would be worth quite a bit to me. But the HPGs are dead. Gray Monday wiped them all out. We've been trying to fix our station on Alyina for years with no results, but I assume you already know that. I've also read intriguing reports from my people on Twycross about recent Tiburon activities at the stations there."

"If we could get the HPG station working on Alyina, would that be worth a contract to you?" From her inner jacket pocket, Kenja withdrew a noteputer containing the terms of the deal. She placed it on the desk and slid it across to the Syndic.

Marena took it and scanned the proposal. Then she slowed down, reading the details more closely.

Kenja watched the woman's eyes, brilliant sapphires, as they reviewed each and every line. Shrewd indeed. Kenja would be surprised if she'd skipped a single word.

After a few long minutes, the Syndic put the noteputer on the desk and tented her fingers over it. "If you can deliver what you promise here, I would happily pay these rates."

"Bargained well and done." Kenja's smile broadened. "And now, with your leave, we will get to work."

CHAPTER 44: EPILOGUE

ALYINA CLASS-A HPG STATION
NEW DELHI
ALYINA
ALYINA MERCANTILE LEAGUE
7 AUGUST 3152

Kenja watched through a wall of plate glass as Tucker and his team put the finishing touches on the Alyina HPG system, soldering the last bits onto the targeting bypass. Tucker had had a little problem with some of the hardware, but that was more of an issue of how Seth had damaged the prototypes they'd built than anything wrong with the VoidBreaker Protocol. He had spent all of his free time en route to Alyina documenting and developing it further so it could be more easily replicated, and the data collected on Errai reinforced what they'd already learned on Hean: VoidBreaker could overcome Clarion and break the Blackout. HPGs could communicate with each other again.

Fixing the HPG network would not be a fast process, and it would take skilled techs days or weeks to fix each one, even with Tucker's detailed instructions and replacement parts, but it could be done. It *would* be done.

And in time, the disaster of the Dark Age would be behind them once and for all.

"What's next then, Star Colonel?" Reus Tremor said as he strolled up next to Kenja, joining her as she watched Tucker, hip deep in coding the VoidBreaker box.

"You going to just keep moving us along, place to place?" Alexi asked, appearing on Kenja's other side. Her hair had grown out a little and the slightest hint of a curl was beginning to show.

"For now," she replied, "We'll go where we're ordered to keep rebuilding the network. But who knows what happens in the future? We could go anywhere."

Kenja looked left to Alexi and right to Reus and realized there was still one thing she had to do.

From her belt, she drew the knife she'd killed Seth with. She hadn't wanted to kill him. Sometimes she still wished he had simply remained her friend and mentor, who had died valiantly on Irian. Then she could have remembered him that way. Haunting, yes, but not a nightmare.

Gripping the hilt, she relived the experience of piercing his flesh as she drove it into his neck.

She blinked, and banished the memory to the deeper recesses of her mind.

"Whatever it was," Reus said, seeing the glint of light on the knife she drew, "I'm sorry."

Kenja shook her head. "Give me your hand."

"Seriously, it was Alexi. I had nothing to do with it." Despite his sarcastic protests, Reus offered her his hand.

Kenja gripped his wrist and slid the knife between his flesh and his bondcord. "You have earned this, Reus."

And then she cut the cord.

Reus's eyes widened. Maybe he hadn't been expecting it. He rubbed his wrist for a second, caught up in a moment of thought. "You know, Merchant-Colonel Kenja Rodriguez, now that I am a Sea Fox, I think it is time I properly introduced myself."

Kenja's eyes narrowed at Reus's words; the fact that he didn't use a single contraction wasn't lost on her either. Alexi seemed nothing short of surprised as well.

Reus held up a hand to forestall her questions. "I am Reo Jones, former Ghost Knight of the Republic." He gave her a smart, crisp salute.

Kenja blinked. Ghost Knights were the Republic equivalent of the Watch. He probably had as many skills and resources to help on their sojourn as she did. More probably. He could have likely escaped at his leisure. Until that moment, she had no idea how valuable a person he really was.

Alexi had no reaction either, leading Kenja to believe she was as shocked as Kenja was, though probably not for the same reasons.

"Why now?"

"I've been a Ghost for a long time. Spies often toss assets like Tucker aside the second they are no longer useful. Since Hean, I've watched you put yourself in harm's way to protect Tucker after you achieved your objective. That earned my respect, and the Sea Foxes at least a little trust. Cutting my bondcord did the rest."

Kenja eyeballed Reo with a newfound respect for the former Republic spy. There was more to this man than she had first thought, and he could be another valuable asset for the Clan. There would be time to determine that later, or she might challenge him to a Trial of Grievance over the lie—although given his background, she wasn't sure if she would push it that far. She'd figure it out some other time.

"We have much to talk about Reo Jones, former Ghost Knight, but we can save that for later," she said smiling.

Then she turned to Alexi. "Do you have any secrets to reveal, too?" Without waiting for an answer, Kenja took Alexi's hands, softer than she expected them to be, and cut her bondcord as well. Then she smiled. "Bondswoman no more."

Alexi rubbed her wrist where the cord had been. "And what does this mean?"

"That you're your own person again. That you can be a Sea Fox. Hell, you could leave now for all I care, but I would love to see you wear Sea Fox blue."

"What about Tucker?" she said, pointing to him at his console, lost in thought and focused on his code.

"I'll cut his cord, too. He's documented everything. Naturally, I'd prefer if you three stuck with me and we went from place to place doing this for now, and I can keep you all in sight. But the mission is over, and you've all earned your own path."

"You know," Reo said, "The Republic's gone, but if Tucker and Alexi decide to stay, I will too. The Sea Foxes are going to rebuild the network, and I would not mind sticking around for a while. They may need some help, and I want to see what this Clan has to offer. If it produced a warrior like Kenja Rodriguez, then it might be something pretty special."

Kenja turned to Alexi, wondering what she would say.

Alexi shrugged. "I'll leave it up to Tucker. I still feel like it's up to me to protect him and he's been a prisoner so long, for once he deserves a say in the matter. I'll go along with wherever he decides."

With twin nods, Reo and Alexi left Kenja to watch Tucker work.

He tapped keys at his console like a conductor directing a symphony, each percussive keystroke telling a story of its own in the context of the broader tune.

Kenja couldn't help wondering how the annals of history had created such a remarkable man. He was brilliant and sensitive and willing to sacrifice everything for the good of humanity, when all humanity had ever done was try to exploit his gifts and torture him. He'd been betrayed, held prisoner, and beaten down at every turn.

She hoped his life would be at least a little easier from here on out.

Kenja edged into the massive room, and Tucker must have sensed her presence. He turned to greet her, his face lighting up. "Do you want to see it boot up?"

"I'd like that very much," she said, getting closer to the console.

"Then here we go."

He flipped a breaker, and the entire system went dead. Then he flipped it back on and she watched the screen as the HPG started its boot-up sequence. The capacitor flow read steady, as did the power levels. The hyperspace coil variances, primary and secondary, hovered within normal parameters. Tucker cleared the buffer, and the status bar confirmed that all systems were nominal.

"Signal incoming," he said. "Dampening field holding... electromagnetic receivers are picking up the transmission!"

Kenja furrowed her brow. "We're getting a connection?"

Tucker nodded. "A message even. From Twycross, right on time."

The screen in front of Tucker blanked out for a moment, shifting from the boot screen to the Sea Fox logo. The message was a line of text from the Twycross station welcoming Alyina back to the network.

"We've got it down to a science," he said.

"If only people were that easy," Kenja said

Tucker turned around to her, the wide smile fading from his face, his expression tightening pensively; compassionately. Whatever he wanted to say, it looked difficult for him. "Star Colonel...Kenja, if I may..."

She nodded.

"Kenja," he continued. "You can't hold yourself accountable for the actions of others. You couldn't possibly know he had survived. And more than that, you can mourn the mentor he was, the person you loved, and still hate the person he became. I...have a lot of experience with that sort of thing."

"Your sister?"

Tucker shook his head, his eyes wet. "No, someone else. I forgave Patricia a long time ago. This was another mentor. I miss him still, even after everything he did to me. You know that?"

Kenja didn't know who Tucker was referring to, but it didn't matter.

She understood, she really did.

Because she still missed Seth.

Tucker put a hand on her shoulder. "We can still hold dear the things we love about them and discard the things we don't. It's the only sensible way."

Kenja sighed. "Tucker, thank you. Thank you for that."

"No. Thank you. Because if it weren't for you, we wouldn't even have a chance at this network being repaired. And I truly believe there can be no freedom or peace in the Inner Sphere without it. If Seth would have gotten ahold of it, or even my sister and her fellow fanatics, or any number of other bad actors, I think things would have only gotten worse."

His voice wavered, almost ready to cry. Not a sad tear, though. "For the first time in a long time, I have some hope. And that's not for nothing. I didn't for a long time, but I trust you to do the right thing with this. Maybe not the Sea Foxes, but after everything we went through, *you've* earned my trust. I really do believe you want the best for the Inner Sphere, regardless of the patch you wear or the Clan you belong to."

Kenja couldn't help but feel bolstered by his words.

They meant a lot.

She'd sold him on her, at least—if not the Sea Foxes.

But her thoughts went back to words Seth had shared with her once. The old Seth. Not the villain whose life she had ended, but the man she had trusted for years. "Love all," he had told her once. "Trust a few, do wrong to none: be able for thine enemy rather in power than use, and keep thy friend under thy own life's key: be cheque'd for silence, but never tax'd for speech."

She'd asked him what it was and what it meant, and he had smiled in the starlight of a world whose name she'd long forgotten.

"It means to be kind, but trust only a few. Harm no one and spread no hatred, even to your enemies. Keep your friends close and, even in their silence, be open to speaking with them. It's Shakespeare. An old Terran bard from a couple thousand years ago."

She marveled at him, the stars twinkling in her eyes.

And then she saw the same lights reflected in Tucker's eyes, but instead of stars, they were the colored lights and readouts of the repaired HPG station.

Kenja looked down and grabbed his hand. He didn't resist.

When she drew the blade, he didn't flinch.

She cut the bondcord with a quick flick of her wrist, as though she were cutting a flower, and it fell with a sound just as soft. "Here's to a new beginning, Tucker. For both of us."

He smiled at that. "For the Inner Sphere."

Kenja smiled back. "For the Inner Sphere."

ACKNOWLEDGEMENTS

There are a number of people key in making this book a reality. The first is Michael A. Stackpole for going to bat for me and getting me into *BattleTech* into the first place. I was already writing books and he saw that I would be a good fit for this fictional universe he spent so much time (among many others) crafting from the ground up. Naturally, John Helfers goes second, for believing all those kind words Mike had to say about me and giving me a shot... and then continuing to give me more shots to the point where I think I'm just overwhelming him with work.

Ray Arrastia deserves the next mention, if we're doing this in order. At the *BattleTech* creative summit at the beginning of 2023, Ray pulled me aside and the two of us stared at a map of the Inner Sphere tacked to the wall in that stuffy hotel conference room where we'd been cloistered for days charting the path of *BattleTech*. He proposed the initial idea for how *VoidBreaker* would go and how it would work and let me run with it and for that I am forever grateful. This really started with a need in the overall story, and we got excited for what it could really become and I'm proud of the end result.

I'd also like to call out specifically everyone in that story summit, because it was one of the most creatively exhilarating weeks of my life, and it was due to their infectious creativity and love of *BattleTech*: Loren L. Coleman, Randall N. Bills, Bryn Bills, Jason Schmetzer, Philip A. Lee, Michael J. Ciaravella, Aaron Cahall, and, of course, John, Ray, and Mike Stackpole again.

Next in line here—and perhaps the MVP of the process—is Joshua Perian. Josh is an Associate Developer at Catalyst Game Labs, and he has amazing organizational skills and a hell of a brain on him. He was with me every day as I wrote this book, calculating jump routes and solving problems in the canon before I got to them. This book would not have been such a joy to write without his work.

Jason Hansa and, again, Randall N. Bills are owed some thanks here as well for their prior work with the Sea Foxes. *Hunters of the Deep* in particular was a great help. Also, Blaine Lee Pardoe and Steven Mohan for Tucker Harwell, Alexi Holt, and Reo Jones, they were incredibly fun characters to play with. But if I have to thank them, I should also thank Ian Fleming, whose works I devoured while conceiving and executing this novel.

I'd like to take a moment to thank *BattleTech* fans in general. I know they've been waiting for hints about how this particular dangling storyline would play out, and their patience has been great. Better than their patience, though is their enthusiasm. There is a huge swath of *BattleTech* fans out there who truly love this game and all of the fiction that goes with it, and their embrace of me and my work in this universe has been palpable. From the positive interactions in the Discord servers and the trips to local hobby shops to talk to folks and play *BattleTech* with them, to all of the conventions where people come up to me and tell me how much they love the direction *BattleTech* is headed. All of you fuel this universe and without it, we wouldn't be doing this at all. Keep up the enthusiasm. Eschew the online negativity and focus on what you love. That's the best way for it.

Of course I need to thank my family for putting up with my erratic work schedule and love me anyway. Patty, Dawn, Anakin, Scout, and Kingston, you're all the best. Seriously.

My writing community is also, as ever, deserving of thanks. Especially the League of Utah Writers. Established in 1935, the League is a consortium of writers from across the state and they have offered me a brilliant community and seen fit to honor my BattleTech work with their highest award—the Diamond Quill— not once, but twice. The people of the League are there to help with my writing, offer me a community, and allow me to give back to that community through volunteer efforts in helping other writers. If you have something like the League in your area and want to be a writer, run—don't walk—to get involved.

There are dozens and dozens of others who deserve thanks, you know who you are.

Thank *all* of you for going on this journey with me.

ABOUT THE AUTHOR

Bryan Young (he/they) works across many different media. His work as a writer and producer has been called "filmmaking gold" by *The New York Times.* He's also published comic books with Slave Labor Graphics and Image Comics. He's been a regular contributor for the Huffington Post, StarWars. com, *Star Wars Insider* magazine, SYFY, /Film, and was the founder and editor-in-chief of the geek news and review site Big Shiny Robot! In 2014, he wrote the critically acclaimed history book, *A Children's Illustrated History of Presidential Assassination.* He co-authored *Robotech: The Macross Saga* RPG and has written five books in the BattleTech Universe: *Honor's Gauntlet, A Question of Survival, Fox Tales, Without Question,* and *VoidBreaker.* His latest non-fiction tie-in book, *The Big Bang Theory Book of Lists* is a #1 Bestseller on Amazon. His work has won two Diamond Quill awards and in 2023 he was named Writer of the Year by the League of Utah Writers. He teaches writing for Writer's Digest, Script Magazine, and at the University of Utah. Follow him across social media @ swankmotron or visit http://swankmotron.com/.

BATTLE HAWK
LIGHT—**30** TONS

BISHAMON
MEDIUM—**45** TONS

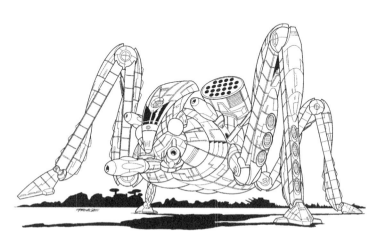

BLACK KNIGHT
HEAVY—75 TONS

GRAND SUMMONER (THOR II)
HEAVY—70 TONS

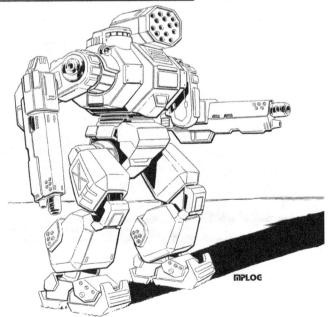

MPLOG

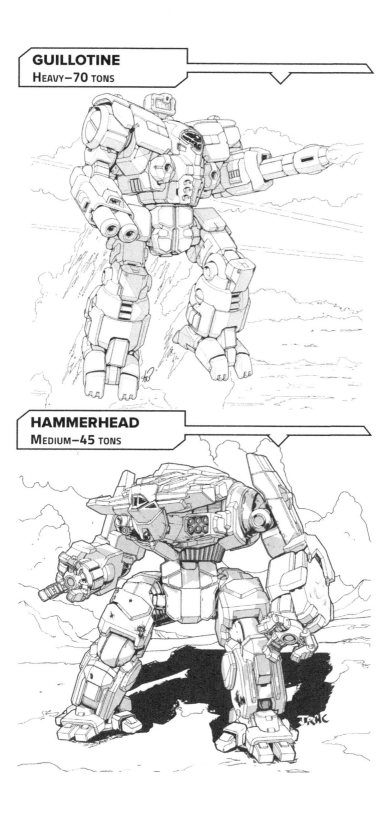

GUILLOTINE
HEAVY—70 TONS

HAMMERHEAD
MEDIUM—45 TONS

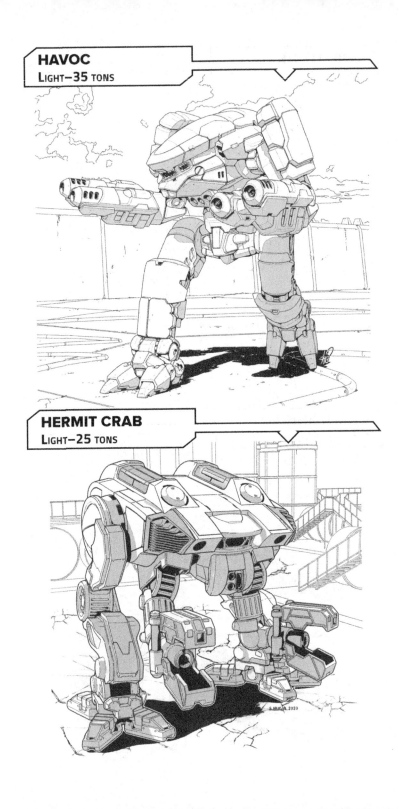

HAVOC
LIGHT—35 TONS

HERMIT CRAB
LIGHT—25 TONS

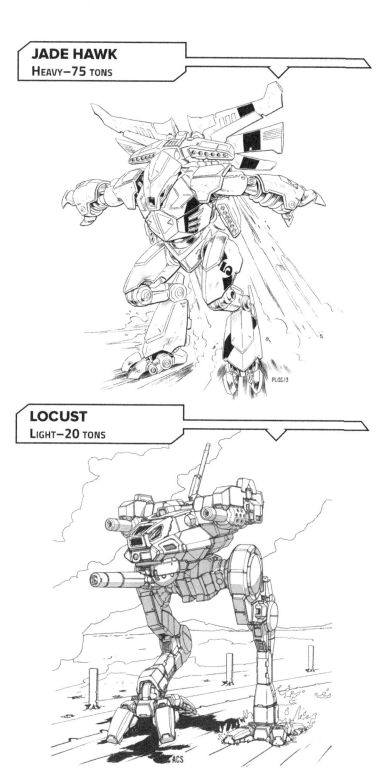

JADE HAWK
HEAVY—75 TONS

PLOG13

LOCUST
LIGHT—20 TONS

ACS

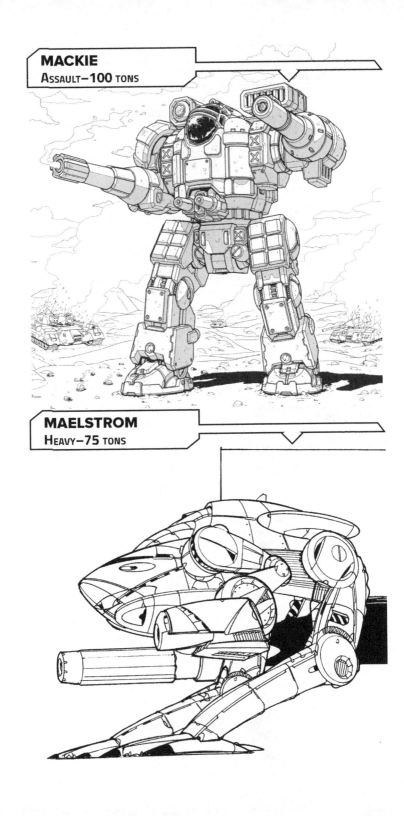

MACKIE
Assault—**100** tons

MAELSTROM
Heavy—**75** tons

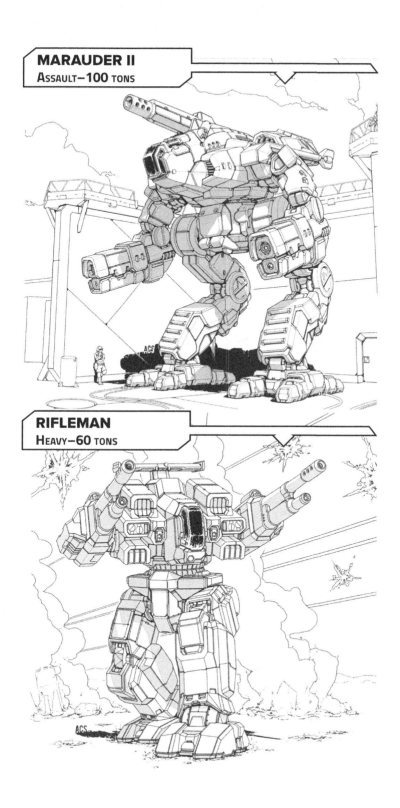

MARAUDER II
Assault—**100** tons

RIFLEMAN
Heavy—**60** tons

SCOURGE
Heavy—65 tons

STONE RHINO (BEHEMOTH)
Assault—100 tons

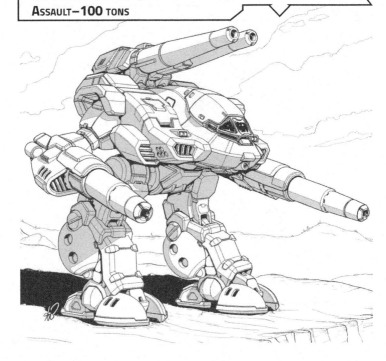

STORMWOLF
MEDIUM–50 TONS

PLOG19

TIMBER WOLF (MAD CAT)
HEAVY–75 TONS

PLOG19

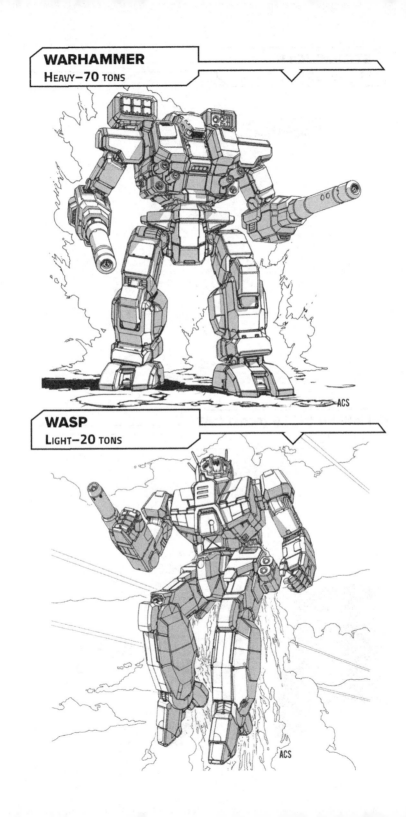

WARHAMMER
Heavy—70 tons

WASP
Light—20 tons

BATTLETECH GLOSSARY

AUTOCANNON

A rapid-fire, auto-loading weapon. Light autocannons range from 30 to 90 millimeter (mm), and heavy autocannons may be from 80 to 120mm or more. They fire high-speed streams of high-explosive, armor-piercing shells.

BATTLEMECH

BattleMechs are the most powerful war machines ever built. First developed by Terran scientists and engineers, these huge vehicles are faster, more mobile, better-armored and more heavily armed than any twentieth-century tank. Ten to twelve meters tall and equipped with particle projection cannons, lasers, rapid-fire autocannon and missiles, they pack enough firepower to flatten anything but another BattleMech. A small fusion reactor provides virtually unlimited power, and BattleMechs can be adapted to fight in environments ranging from sun-baked deserts to subzero arctic icefields.

DROPSHIPS

Because interstellar JumpShips must avoid entering the heart of a solar system, they must "dock" in space at a considerable distance from a system's inhabited worlds. DropShips were developed for interplanetary travel. As the name implies, a DropShip is attached to hardpoints on the JumpShip's drive core, later to be dropped from the parent vessel after in-system entry. Though incapable of FTL travel, DropShips are highly maneuverable, well-armed and sufficiently aerodynamic to take off from and land on a planetary surface. The journey from the jump point to the inhabited worlds of a system usually requires a normal-space journey of several days or weeks, depending on the type of star.

FLAMER

Flamethrowers are a small but time-honored anti-infantry weapon in vehicular arsenals. Whether fusion-based or fuel-based, flamers spew fire in a tight beam that "splashes" against a target, igniting almost anything it touches.

GAUSS RIFLE

This weapon uses magnetic coils to accelerate a solid nickel-ferrous slug about the size of a football at an enemy target, inflicting massive damage through sheer kinetic impact at long range and with little heat. However, the accelerator coils and the slug's supersonic speed mean that while the Gauss rifle is smokeless and lacks the flash of an autocannon, it has a much more potent report that can shatter glass.

INDUSTRIALMECH

Also known as WorkMechs or UtilityMechs, they are large, bipedal or quadrupedal machines used for industrial purposes (hence the name). They are similar in shape to BattleMechs, which they predate, and feature many of the same technologies, but are built for non-combat tasks such as construction, farming, and policing.

JUMPSHIPS

Interstellar travel is accomplished via JumpShips, first developed in the twenty-second century. These somewhat ungainly vessels consist of a long, thin drive core and a sail resembling an enormous parasol, which can extend up to a kilometer in width. The ship is named for its ability to "jump" instantaneously across vast distances of space. After making its jump, the ship cannot travel until it has recharged by gathering up more solar energy.

The JumpShip's enormous sail is constructed from a special metal that absorbs vast quantities of electromagnetic energy from the nearest star. When it has soaked up enough energy, the sail transfers it to the drive core, which converts it into a space-twisting field. An instant later, the ship arrives at the next jump point, a distance of up to thirty light-years. This field is known as hyperspace, and its discovery opened to mankind the gateway to the stars.

JumpShips never land on planets. Interplanetary travel is carried out by DropShips, vessels that are attached to the JumpShip until arrival at the jump point.

LASER

An acronym for "Light Amplification through Stimulated Emission of Radiation." When used as a weapon, the laser damages the target by concentrating extreme heat onto a small area. BattleMech lasers are designated as small, medium or large. Lasers are also available as shoulder-fired weapons operating from a portable backpack power unit. Certain range-finders and targeting equipment also employ low-level lasers.

LRM

Abbreviation for "Long-Range Missile," an indirect-fire missile with a high-explosive warhead.

MACHINE GUN

A small autocannon intended for anti-personnel assaults. Typically non-armor-penetrating, machine guns are often best used against infantry, as they can spray a large area with relatively inexpensive fire.

PARTICLE PROJECTION CANNON (PPC)

One of the most powerful and long-range energy weapons on the battlefield, a PPC fires a stream of charged particles that outwardly functions as a bright blue laser, but also throws off enough static discharge to resemble a bolt of manmade lightning. The kinetic and heat impact of a PPC is enough to cause the vaporization of armor and structure alike, and most PPCs have the power to kill a pilot in his machine through an armor-penetrating headshot.

SRM

The abbreviation for "Short-Range Missile," a direct-trajectory missile with high-explosive or armor-piercing explosive warheads. They have a range of less than one kilometer and are only reliably accurate at ranges of less than 300 meters. They are more powerful, however, than LRMs.

SUCCESSOR LORDS

After the fall of the first Star League, the remaining members of the High Council each asserted his or her right to become First Lord. Their star empires became known as the Successor States and the rulers as Successor Lords. The Clan Invasion temporarily interrupted centuries of warfare known as the Succession Wars, which first began in 2786.

BATTLETECH ERAS

The *BattleTech* universe is a living, vibrant entity that grows each year as more sourcebooks and fiction are published. A dynamic universe, its setting and characters evolve over time within a highly detailed continuity framework, bringing everything to life in a way a static game universe cannot match.

To help quickly and easily convey the timeline of the universe—and to allow a player to easily "plug in" a given novel or sourcebook—we've divided *BattleTech* into eight major eras.

STAR LEAGUE
(Present–2780)

Ian Cameron, ruler of the Terran Hegemony, concludes decades of tireless effort with the creation of the Star League, a political and military alliance between all Great Houses and the Hegemony. Star League armed forces immediately launch the Reunification War, forcing the Periphery realms to join. For the next two centuries, humanity experiences a golden age across the thousand light-years of human-occupied space known as the Inner Sphere. It also sees the creation of the most powerful military in human history.

(This era also covers the centuries before the founding of the Star League in 2571, most notably the Age of War.)

SUCCESSION WARS
(2781–3049)

Every last member of First Lord Richard Cameron's family is killed during a coup launched by Stefan Amaris. Following the thirteen-year war to unseat him, the rulers of each of the five Great Houses disband the Star League. General Aleksandr Kerensky departs with eighty percent of the Star League Defense Force beyond known space and the Inner Sphere collapses into centuries of warfare known as the Succession Wars that will eventually result in a massive loss of technology across most worlds.

CLAN INVASION
(3050–3061)

A mysterious invading force strikes the coreward region of the Inner Sphere. The invaders, called the Clans, are descendants of Kerensky's SLDF troops, forged into a society dedicated to becoming the greatest fighting force in history. With vastly superior technology and warriors, the Clans conquer world after world. Eventually this outside threat will forge a new Star League, something hundreds of years of warfare failed to accomplish. In addition, the Clans will act as a catalyst for a technological renaissance.

CIVIL WAR
(3062–3067)

The Clan threat is eventually lessened with the complete destruction of a Clan. With that massive external threat apparently neutralized, internal conflicts explode around the Inner Sphere. House Liao conquers its former Commonality, the St. Ives Compact; a rebellion of military units belonging to House Kurita sparks a war with their powerful border enemy, Clan Ghost Bear; the fabulously powerful Federated Commonwealth of House Steiner and House Davion collapses into five long years of bitter civil war.

JIHAD
(3067–3080)

Following the Federated Commonwealth Civil War, the leaders of the Great Houses meet and disband the new Star League, declaring it a sham. The pseudo-religious Word of Blake—a splinter group of ComStar, the protectors and controllers of interstellar communication—launch the Jihad: an interstellar war that pits every faction against each other and even against themselves, as weapons of mass destruction are used for the first time in centuries while new and frightening technologies are also unleashed.

DARK AGE
(3081-3150)

Under the guidance of Devlin Stone, the Republic of the Sphere is born at the heart of the Inner Sphere following the Jihad. One of the more extensive periods of peace begins to break out as the 32nd century dawns. The factions, to one degree or another, embrace disarmament, and the massive armies of the Succession Wars begin to fade. However, in 3132 eighty percent of interstellar communications collapses, throwing the universe into chaos. Wars erupt almost immediately, and the factions begin rebuilding their armies.

ILCLAN
(3151-present)

The once-invulnerable Republic of the Sphere lies in ruins, torn apart by the Great Houses and the Clans as they wage war against each other on a scale not seen in nearly a century. Mercenaries flourish once more, selling their might to the highest bidder. As Fortress Republic collapses, the Clans race toward Terra to claim their long-denied birthright and create a supreme authority that will fulfill the dream of Aleksandr Kerensky and rule the Inner Sphere by any means necessary: The ilClan.

CLAN HOMEWORLDS
(2786-present)

In 2784, General Aleksandr Kerensky launched Operation Exodus, and led most of the Star League Defense Force out of the Inner Sphere in a search for a new world, far away from the strife of the Great Houses. After more than two years and thousands of light years, they arrived at the Pentagon Worlds. Over the next two-and-a-half centuries, internal dissent and civil war led to the creation of a brutal new society—the Clans. And in 3049, they returned to the Inner Sphere with one goal—the complete conquest of the Great Houses.

LOOKING FOR MORE HARD HITTING BATTLETECH FICTION?

WE'LL GET YOU RIGHT BACK INTO THE BATTLE!

Catalyst Game Labs brings you the very best in *BattleTech* fiction, available at most ebook retailers, including Amazon, Apple Books, Kobo, Barnes & Noble, and more!

NOVELS

1. *Decision at Thunder Rift (The Gray Death Legion Saga, Book One)* by William H. Keith
2. *Mercenary's Star (The Gray Death Legion Saga, Book Two)* by William H. Keith
3. *The Price of Glory (The Gray Death Legion Saga, Book Three)* by William H. Keith
4. *Warrior: En Garde (The Warrior Trilogy, Book One)* by Michael A. Stackpole
5. *Warrior: Riposte (The Warrior Trilogy, Book Two)* by Michael A. Stackpole
6. *Warrior: Coupé (The Warrior Trilogy, Book Three)* by Michael A. Stackpole
7. *Wolves on the Border* by Robert N. Charrette
8. *Heir to the Dragon* by Robert N. Charrette
9. *Lethal Heritage (Blood of Kerensky Trilogy, Book One)* by Michael A. Stackpole
10. *Blood Legacy (Blood of Kerensky Trilogy, Book Two)* by Michael A. Stackpole
11. *Lost Destiny (Blood of Kerensky Trilogy, Book Three)* by Michael A. Stackpole
12. *Way of the Clans (Legend of the Jade Phoenix, Book One)* by Robert Thurston
13. *Bloodname (Legend of the Jade Phoenix, Book Two)* by Robert Thurston
14. *Falcon Guard (Legend of the Jade Phoenix, Book Three)* by Robert Thurston
15. *Wolf Pack* by Robert N. Charrette
16. *Natural Selection* by Michael A. Stackpole
17. *Ideal War* by Christopher Kubasik
18. *Main Event* by Jim Long
19. *Blood of Heroes* by Andrew Keith
20. *Assumption of Risk* by Michael A. Stackpole
21. *D.R.T.* by James D. Long
22. *Close Quarters* by Victor Milán
23. *Bred for War* by Michael A. Stackpole
24. *I Am Jade Falcon* by Robert Thurston
25. *Highlander Gambit* by Blaine Lee Pardoe
26. *Tactics of Duty* by William H. Keith
27. *Malicious Intent* by Michael A. Stackpole
28. *Hearts of Chaos* by Victor Milán
29. *Operation Excalibur* by William H. Keith
30. *Black Dragon* by Victor Milán
31. *Impetus of War* by Blaine Lee Pardoe
32. *Double-Blind* by Loren L. Coleman
33. *Binding Force* by Loren L. Coleman
34. *Exodus Road (Twilight of the Clans, Book One)* by Blaine Lee Pardoe
35. *Grave Covenant (Twilight of the Clans, Book Two)* by Michael A. Stackpole
36. *The Hunters (Twilight of the Clans, Book Three)* by Thomas S. Gressman
37. *Freebirth (Twilight of the Clans, Book Four)* by Robert Thurston
38. *Sword and Fire (Twilight of the Clans, Book Five)* by Thomas S. Gressman
39. *Shadows of War (Twilight of the Clans, Book Six)* by Thomas S. Gressman
40. *Prince of Havoc (Twilight of the Clans, Book Seven)* by Michael A. Stackpole
41. *Falcon Rising (Twilight of the Clans, Book Eight)* by Robert Thurston
42. *Threads of Ambition (The Capellan Solution, Book One)* by Loren L. Coleman
43. *The Killing Fields (The Capellan Solution, Book Two)* by Loren L. Coleman

98. *Honor's Gauntlet* by Bryan Young
99. *Icons of War* by Craig A. Reed, Jr.
100. *Children of Kerensky* by Blaine Lee Pardoe
101. *Hour of the Wolf* by Blaine Lee Pardoe
102. *Fall From Glory (Founding of the Clans, Book One)* by Randall N. Bills
103. *Paid in Blood (The Highlander Covenant, Book Two)* by Michael J. Ciaravella
104. *Blood Will Tell* by Jason Schmetzer
105. *Hunting Season* by Philip A. Lee
106. *A Rock and a Hard Place* by William H. Keith
107. *Visions of Rebirth (Founding of the Clans, Book Two)* by Randall N. Bills
108. *No Substitute for Victory* by Blaine Lee Pardoe
109. *Redemption Rites* by Jason Schmetzer
110. *Land of Dreams (Founding of the Clans, Book Three)* by Randall N. Bills
111. *A Question of Survival* by Bryan Young
112. *Jaguar's Leap* by Reed Bishop
113. *The Damocles Sanction* by Michael J. Ciaravella
114. *Escape from Jardine (Forgotten Worlds, Part Three)* by Herbert A. Beas II
115. *Elements of Treason: Honor* by Craig A. Reed, Jr.
116. *The Quest for Jardine (A Forgotten Worlds Collection)* by Herbert A. Beas II
117. *Without Question* by Bryan Young
118. *In the Shadow of the Dragon* by Craig A. Reed, Jr.
119. *Letter of the Law* by Philip A. Lee
120. *Trial of Birthright* by Michael J. Ciaravella

YOUNG ADULT NOVELS

1. *The Nellus Academy Incident* by Jennifer Brozek
2. *Iron Dawn (The Rogue Academy Trilogy, Book One)* by Jennifer Brozek
3. *Ghost Hour (The Rogue Academy Trilogy, Book Two)* by Jennifer Brozek
4. *Crimson Night (The Rogue Academy Trilogy, Book Three)* by Jennifer Brozek

OMNIBUSES

1. *The Gray Death Legion Trilogy* (ebook box set) by William H. Keith
2. *The Blood of Kerensky Trilogy* (ebook box set) by Michael A. Stackpole
3. *The Legend of the Jade Phoenix Trilogy* (ebook box set) by Robert Thurston
4. *The Founding of the Clans Trilogy* (ebook box set) by Randall N. Bills

NOVELLAS/SHORT NOVELS

1. *Lion's Roar* by Steven Mohan, Jr.
2. *Sniper* by Jason Schmetzer
3. *Eclipse* by Jason Schmetzer
4. *Hector* by Jason Schmetzer
5. *The Frost Advances (Operation Ice Storm, Part One)* by Jason Schmetzer
6. *The Winds of Spring (Operation Ice Storm, Part Two)* by Jason Schmetzer
7. *Instrument of Destruction (Ghost Bear's Lament, Part One)* by Steven Mohan, Jr.
8. *The Fading Call of Glory (Ghost Bear's Lament, Part Two)* by Steven Mohan, Jr.
9. *Vengeance* by Jason Schmetzer
10. *A Splinter of Hope* by Philip A. Lee
11. *The Anvil* by Blaine Lee Pardoe
12. *A Splinter of Hope/The Anvil* (omnibus)
13. *Not the Way the Smart Money Bets (Kell Hounds Ascendant #1)* by Michael A. Stackpole
14. *A Tiny Spot of Rebellion (Kell Hounds Ascendant #2)* by Michael A. Stackpole
15. *A Clever Bit of Fiction (Kell Hounds Ascendant #3)* by Michael A. Stackpole
16. *Break-Away (Proliferation Cycle #1)* by Ilsa J. Bick
17. *Prometheus Unbound (Proliferation Cycle #2)* by Herbert A. Beas II

18. *Nothing Ventured (Proliferation Cycle #3)* by Christoffer Trossen
19. *Fall Down Seven Times, Get Up Eight (Proliferation Cycle #4)* by Randall N. Bills
20. *A Dish Served Cold (Proliferation Cycle #5)* by Chris Hartford and Jason M. Hardy
21. *The Spider Dances (Proliferation Cycle #6)* by Jason Schmetzer
22. *Shell Games* by Jason Schmetzer
23. *Divided We Fall* by Blaine Lee Pardoe
24. *The Hunt for Jardine (Forgotten Worlds, Part One)* by Herbert A. Beas II
25. *Rock of the Republic* by Blaine Lee Pardoe
26. *Finding Jardine (Forgotten Worlds, Part Two)* by Herbert A. Beas II
27. *The Trickster (Proliferation Cycle #7)* by Blaine Lee Pardoe
28. *The Price of Duty* by Jason Schmetzer
29. *Elements of Treason: Duty* by Craig A. Reed, Jr.
30. *Mercenary's Honor* by Jason Schmetzer
31. *Elements of Treason: Opportunity* by Craig A. Reed, Jr.
32. *Lethal Lessons* by Daniel Isberner
33. *If Auld Acquaintance Be Forgot… (Kell Hounds Ascendant #4)* by Michael A. Stackpole
34. *Giving up the Ghost (Fortunes of War #1)* by Bryan Young
35. *Blood Rage (Fortunes of War #2)* by Craig A. Reed, Jr.
36. *A Skulk of Foxes (Fortunes of War #3)* by Jason Hansa
37. *Let Slip the Dogs of War* by Bryan Young
38. *Hounds at Bay (Fortunes of War #4)* by Geoff Swift
39. *Heavy is the Head (Fortunes of War #5)* by Philip A. Lee
40. *A Night in the Woods* by Michael A. Stackpole

ANTHOLOGIES
1. *The Corps (BattleCorps Anthology, Volume 1)*, edited by Loren. L. Coleman
2. *First Strike (BattleCorps Anthology, Volume 2)*, edited by Loren L. Coleman
3. *Weapons Free (BattleCorps Anthology, Volume 3)*, edited by Jason Schmetzer
4. *Onslaught: Tales from the Clan Invasion*, edited by Jason Schmetzer
5. *Edge of the Storm* by Jason Schmetzer
6. *Fire for Effect (BattleCorps Anthology, Volume 4)*, edited by Jason Schmetzer
7. *Chaos Born (Chaos Irregulars, Book 1)* by Kevin Killiany
8. *Chaos Formed (Chaos Irregulars, Book 2)* by Kevin Killiany
9. *Counterattack (BattleCorps Anthology, Volume 5)*, edited by Jason Schmetzer
10. *Front Lines (BattleCorps Anthology, Volume 6)*, edited by Jason Schmetzer and Philip A. Lee
11. *Legacy*, edited by John Helfers and Philip A. Lee
12. *Kill Zone (BattleCorps Anthology, Volume 7)*, edited by Philip A. Lee
13. *Gray Markets (A BattleCorps Anthology)*, edited by Jason Schmetzer and Philip A. Lee
14. *Slack Tide (A BattleCorps Anthology)*, edited by Jason Schmetzer and Philip A. Lee
15. *The Battle of Tukayyid*, edited by John Helfers
16. *The Mercenary Life* by Randall N. Bills.
17. *The Proliferation Cycle*, edited by John Helfers and Philip A. Lee
18. *No Greater Honor (The Complete Eridani Light Horse Chronicles)*,
    edited by John Helfers and Philip A. Lee
19. *Kell Hounds Ascendant* by Michael A. Stackpole
20. *Marauder* by Lance Scarinci
21. *Fox Tales* by Bryan Young
22. *Gray Death Rising* by Jason Schmetzer

MAGAZINES
1. *Shrapnel*, Issue #1–*Shrapnel*, Issue #19

Made in the USA
Las Vegas, NV
23 June 2025

23984481R00174